PURGED SOULS

PURGED SOULS

KAGAN TUMER

LUMINARE PRESS

WWW.LUMINAREPRESS.COM

Printed in the United States of America

Copy editing by Lori Stephens and Julia Houston
Cover art by Colas Gauthier
Author photograph by Kara Cooper Photography
Cover design by Claire Flint Last

Luminare Press
442 Charnelton St.
Eugene, OR 97401
www.luminarepress.com

LCCN: 2019921272
ISBN: 978-1-64388-249-9

PART I
EMBERS

CHAPTER 1

AMBUSH

"Be as hard as the world requires you to be and as soft as the world allows you to be."

−OKINAWAN PROVERB

The orange tree taunted Lori Rose, assaulting her adolescence memories of succulent oranges with sour, misshapen fruit. It teased her with its blossoms' promising scent each spring but bore fruit that ripened only when she was away on a mission. Still, with roots that sought out deep water, it survived while anything that needed care had perished. Like most of her life choices, planting that tree hadn't been right or wrong but a reminder that simple wishes turned into convoluted knots when tangled with the real world.

She crouched to pick up a yellow-green, lemon-sized fruit from the ground and tossed it into a basket, saving it for the marmalade she'd never make. Dry, cracked clay that in another lifetime might have supported a lawn separated the tree from the four steps in front of her bungalow. She ambled around the grayish weeds that occasionally interrupted the dusty brown, sipping her tepid coffee, and sat at the third step, her elbows on the rough, worn porch, feet on the first step.

A jade-eyed tabby appeared by the sidewalk and strolled toward the tuna bowl Lori had left on the porch. The tabby's left whiskers were growing back. The mishap that had deprived her of her valuable sensors had faded into the past, but the added caution she'd gained remained. She hugged the opposite side of the steps from Lori, her undulating ribs scraping the metal railing to exploit every inch of width the steps provided. Lori drained her coffee and put the cup on the steps. She stayed still, letting the tabby reach the bowl on her own terms.

The tabby sniffed the tuna, nudging her pink nose forward and back over the bowl. She licked the top, her eyes darting between the tuna and Lori. The only way the tabby ate was when Lori stayed on the steps like a living scarecrow. They'd made a silent deal years ago; she did not name the tabby or invite her in, and the tabby accepted her offerings with only mild suspicion. Though the deal kept their fragile relationship impersonal, it turned the tabby into the only living thing in the neighborhood not frightened of Lori.

Satisfied Lori wasn't going to bolt, the tabby dug into the meal, using a paw to immobilize the bowl and swallowing the tuna with quick shakes of her head. Belly full, she licked her paws and brushed them on her whiskers. She gave Lori a glance that may have been a thank you before slouching away, too cool to allow herself to be patted. They repeated this routine a few times a week, often enough for Lori to become a food source but not for the tabby to consider that source reliable.

With the tabby gone, Lori interlaced her hands and stretched her arms, palms facing out. She held the pose for three breaths and stood. She picked up the bowl and cup and rinsed them in the kitchen sink. It was a clear, sunny day, so she walked to the Marin military headquarters to clear her head. To her south, the lonely tower of the Bay Bridge's east span rose five hundred feet above the water like the spire of a long-gone cathedral, connecting nothing to nothing.

Next to it, Treasure Island shimmered like a ghost as the cool morning air hit the sun-kissed rooftops and rose in a haze. Then again, it was a ghost. She'd spent her last innocent summer on the playgrounds there while her mom had worked on the Pearl Harbor Centennial Commemoration. She never got to hear the solemn promises to not repeat the mistakes of the past. Before December rolled around, the artificial island had become a quarantine zone, absorbing the sick and dying from the rapidly spreading Purge virus. The new year took her mom and sister along with everyone she'd known. It had taken her years to stop shaking herself awake from her recurring nightmare of begging her mom to not go to work the morning they'd locked the island down.

Ten minutes after Treasure Island and its memories disappeared around the coastline, she reached her office. She tossed her jacket on the closest of the two tan leather wingback chairs that sat to her left across from her desk. She tapped the screen on her desk, and the computational glass came to life, displaying messages needing her attention on the right, news that may interest her on the left, and her schedule and to-do list scrolling in a loop in the middle. She swiped the messages clear. If they were important, they'd reappear anyway.

Her stomach growled as she sat. She'd skipped dinner because she'd worked late, and she didn't do breakfast, the appendix of meals. She was running on coffee and sugar, a combination that didn't let her overstimulated brain generate measured thoughts.

She filled her coffee mug with water from the pitcher on her desk and took a sip. The growl was only a reminder, not a warning. Certainly not a complaint. She hadn't felt hunger, real hunger, in almost two decades. Still, the stomach cramps that ruled out sleep were etched in her memory as were the taste of bile and the stench of her breath, the products of digestive fluids breaking themselves down because they didn't have anything else to break down.

Today, lunch was a few hours away, but that gave her little comfort. She dreaded her monthly lunch with Executive Ann Lester, the attorney general of Marin. They'd talk about law and order. Lester would insist that Lori keep her soldiers off the city streets, and she'd remind Lester that those soldiers were the only reason violence stayed outside the gates of Marin. They'd give each other insincere smiles and sip coffee.

A knock on the door pulled her away from the intelligence report detailing the movement of Kern officials her agents were supposed to gather and those of Marin officials they weren't. She waved to the screen to close the file.

"Colonel?"

"Come in," Lori said.

Sierra Rendon, her second-in-command, popped in. "Lieutenant Tran did not report for duty this morning," she said with the sheepishness of someone telling on a friend. Though Lori had warned her, Sierra still socialized with the officers.

That was one sin of which Lori had never been guilty. On most days, the thought of spending more time with her officers exhausted her. On rare occasions, she did wish she could leave Colonel Rose's skin for one night, go out for fun, check her expectations at the door, and slam down drinks with her officers. But that wouldn't do.

The dedication she demanded, the professionalism she cultivated wouldn't survive even one drink in such company, which made Sierra her link, liked by the troops and respected by the officers. Sierra most likely earned that respect by hiding minor infractions from her. That she was here meant it was serious this time. Not Tran's first offense then.

"Send her my way when she gets in."

Sierra's nod was noncommittal, her loyalties caught on a link in the chain of command.

Lori had given Sierra the wrong job. The woman could incapacitate most anyone in eight seconds if she was in a charitable mood. Otherwise, she needed half that to kill. These weren't skills that translated well to managing maintenance schedules and officer postings. Still, armies ran on logistics, and that was doubly true for Special Forces. Sierra was her executive officer because she needed to come to terms with that simple truth. Besides, Sierra was the only person in Marin quick-tempered enough to make Lori's responses appear measured.

"Tran was scheduled to lead the new class on their first field mission," Sierra said.

Every sixteen weeks, another twenty recruits took their first steps to join Special Forces. Perhaps five made it through the training. The first field mission meant they had reached week four. They were headed to a decrepit quarter in the Uregs to clean up a few square blocks of dirt and store enough adrenaline to tolerate more abuse on their path to earn a green beret. Best-case scenario was nothing happened on their trip. Worst case was they busted a few gangbangers too dumb to hide a block away for an afternoon and concluded they were hot shit, which created a problem week five had to fix.

Now they were down one team leader, a logistical glitch that Sierra should have handled without bothering her.

"And?"

"The convoy leaves in forty-five minutes. I request permission to take this mission."

So that was it, Sierra itching to get back to the field.

Lori stood and walked to the large window facing Declaration Square, which stretched below her and connected them to the Marin Senate two hundred feet away. A plumber in a wide-brimmed hat worked on the octagonal fountain that had once hurled water sixty feet into the air. At a time of limited resources, it was the only artifact engineered with no practical purpose. An act of defiance, spitting at the heavens.

At least it was supposed to be. With roots getting into the pipes, it mostly sputtered and occasionally compounded its sins by spraying brown water.

The plumber tipped her hat at two passing soldiers and exchanged a few words that probably didn't mean anything. As the soldiers moved away, she went back to her pipes. A major announcement was in the works, and the fountain had a duty to perform that required clear water.

The plumber, the soldiers, the fountain were all too mundane, too orderly, a sharp contrast to the chaotic tent city where Rachel Czernak had announced the birth of Marin nineteen years ago. One hundred and nine boulders, three deep, ringed the fountain to remind them of their history, one for each woman who'd died defending the nascent state that first winter.

Lori hadn't been there.

The square outside her window was the same place yet not the same place. The reality of those early battles had faded. The memories that replaced them were unfaithful beasts. They morphed, painted by the mood of the moment. They lied, tainted by emotion. Collective memories were even worse, and this square had become an altar to the collective memory that they'd triumphed over cruelty, over nature.

It was a lie she worked hard to fabricate, but she knew how fragile the illusion was. They were never more than two bad decisions away from watching it shatter.

"No, you run the office today. I'll handle the recruits," Lori said, hoping this wasn't one of those two bad decisions.

"You have lunch with Executive Lester. General Gardner will be here at two, and—"

"Just deal with it." She couldn't tell whether Sierra dreaded playing politician for a day or had set her mind on shooting up a neighborhood. It didn't matter. Everything Sierra mentioned could wait forever.

Sierra hesitated for a second, said "Yes, ma'am," and headed toward the door.

"By the way, did HR ever get back to you about those discharged veterans?"

"Yes." Sierra stopped by the door. "Two moved to a small town north, one to New Cal."

"Did you verify that?"

Sierra swallowed. "Since they were grunts who'd never dealt with intel of any kind, I took HR's word for it."

"Have a quiet look. I asked for all files on discharged soldiers but received incomplete info. You know how cranky I get when I have to ask twice for anything."

"Will do. Anything else?"

"Send me the recruits' files and the mission profile."

As Sierra left, Lori brought her fingertips to the window. Polished and cold. The reflection of Colonel Rose stared back, alone. It was the result of her choices, and she was past assessing whether it had been worth the price. She wasn't here because she liked power. She was here to ensure that no new boulder would be added to the square.

Her stomach growled again, a simple biological function, her only link to a past she'd left far behind. It had not been much, but that hunger had been her own. Now she didn't even have that, because unlike young Lori, decorated war hero and Head of Special Forces, Colonel Rose had never been hungry.

Ninety minutes later, Lori swiped her screen to the last recruit's file as she sat in the passenger seat of the Humvee that led two troop-transport trucks into the Uregs. This class was miles ahead of the last two cohorts, with smart, committed soldiers acing their way forward. They even had two pilots and a combat medic, both in short supply. The promise of specialists and a high yield allowed her to smirk with pride.

She took a bite of her mushy chicken-spread sandwich and chewed three times before swallowing. It had no taste, but it did provide the calories she needed. At least the spread had the texture of the chunky peanut butter she'd loved as a kid. Since she hadn't seen a peanut in over two decades, she pretended that was what she was chewing. She stuffed the last of her sandwich in her mouth and put the screen down just in time to catch a raccoon skitter across the street and disappear behind a collapsed wooden fence. That it was active at this hour meant it had found an unlikely food source or had been disturbed. Neither bode well.

Her eyes swept the intersection and settled on the road ahead. The light of day did not flatter the Uregs. The desolate blocks so menacing at night turned into soulless structures more sad than intimidating.

The ruins scattered across the landscape bore witness to old tragedies. In the distance, two rising columns of thick, inky smoke signaled a new one was unfolding. Wispy, gray smoke from smoldering branches always filled the Uregs. This hot-burning mess that created an impenetrable wall of fire did not belong here.

Sergeant Lise Gold eased up on the gas, keeping both hands on the wheel as they pushed up a gentle hill. The Special Forces were as much Gold's as they were Lori's, with the seasoned sergeant training, cajoling, threatening, and coaching recruits into thinking fighters without so much as raising her voice. She must have had the same reaction to the fire as Lori had, because she raised an eyebrow and shot a quick sideways glance. Lori met Gold's inquiring eye and pointed forward. Their convoy rolled on.

Halfway down the next block, three wannabe thugs stood on the sidewalk in their hand-me-down military jackets and field boots. They looked but didn't act the part, projecting excitement rather than intimidation. This was where gangs came to hire muscle for jobs they deemed too risky for their own. Considering the little regard that gangs wasted on new recruits, it said something when they shopped here. These three didn't have enough sense to scamper when a Marin unit approached. It was a miracle they were still alive, an oversight that would be corrected if they ever landed a job.

The stink of burning rubber hit her as they reached the last block. Whatever game was unfolding, it wasn't the one she'd expected. Lori took an elastic tie from her upper jacket pocket and tucked her hair into a ponytail before stepping out of the Humvee. "Proceed," she said to Gold. "Keep your eyes open."

Gold motioned the recruits out from the two trucks behind them. They disappeared into bungalows in pairs and reemerged standing guard in front of empty structures. Two recruits moved toward the five-story building perched over the previous intersection. Two others approached a van parked in the middle of the street in front of the burning tires. It was dirty with mud, not soot. Someone wanted it to look dirty, like it had been abandoned there long ago, but the mud wasn't even dry in this hot spell. The whole scene looked staged.

The recruits had shown they'd absorbed their training. She'd decided to continue the mission when gunfire erupted to her right.

A recruit stood at the entrance of the five-story building, gun pointing in.

"Report!" Gold called.

"I saw something."

"What?"

"Movement." The recruit's timid voice trailed off. "It went up."

It? After a month of training, Lori had hoped the recruits could distinguish an armed assailant from a raccoon or know raccoons had too much sense to stick around burning tires.

Gold pointed two fingers at the building's door. The recruits took their positions. Good, at least Gold was on the ball. An hour ago, she'd have admonished the recruit for her sloppiness and used this as a teaching moment, but she was all business now.

Lori took out her tida and tapped the frosted glass. The finger-sized, featureless cylinder lit up, and a bird's-eye-view map centered on their location floated in front of her. She zoomed in, spanning ten blocks, and let it synchronize with the transport providing air support. The three wannabes were gone. She zoomed out and saw a van twenty blocks out. It wasn't moving toward them, but she didn't like that it moved at all. Though she trusted her recruits' training, she didn't yet trust their judgment.

"Load back up. We're leaving."

Gold didn't hesitate to cancel a training exercise she had spent a week setting up. She barked orders, collecting recruits two by two. The recruits had disappointed, accusing looks, but disappointed was better than dead.

Lori had rarely been accused of being too cautious, because most people didn't understand the difference between danger and risk. Danger was a fact of life. Risk quantified exposure to danger. It let you prioritize actions based on possible outcomes. Right now, there was no upside to staying here.

Her tida chimed. She tapped it, and the map popped up again.

The van had changed direction. It would cross directly in front of their path of retreat in less than a minute. She swiped her tiered intelligent digital assistant to call the pilot of the light transport hovering above them. Unlike its big-bellied, four-rotor cousins that could have carried their entire contingent, the light transport was a responsive craft. It was built for urban combat, two tilt rotors protruding from its wing stumps to provide vertical thrust when needed. With the lack of urban anything these days, it had been relegated to supporting training exercises.

"Lieutenant Pen."

"Yes, Colonel." The pilot's reply came loud and clear from Lori's tida.

"Take out an intersection between us and the van."

"Arming. I need…twenty seconds to line up a clean shot."

"Do it." In the unlikely event the van was in the wrong place at the wrong time, it'd be spooked and leave.

"The van picked up speed," Pen said. "It will be past the last intersection by the time I can engage."

If not, the van would notice the transport and show its hand. The risk of staying had just been quantified. "If you can't take out the intersection, take out the van."

"Copy."

Her eyes moved from the map to the road and back to the map. "Take out anything that comes within two blocks of our retreat."

"Copy that."

With a distant explosion, the van blinked out of her map. All three vehicles had completed their three-point turns and now faced the way they'd come with the burning tires to their back. The five-story building stood like a watchtower over their retreat. Perhaps the recruit had seen something. Perhaps not.

"Lieutenant."

"Yes, Colonel."

She tapped the tall building hovering on her map. "One shot into this building. Now."

The explosion shook the trucks, but they were out of debris range. She was about to motion the trucks forward when a second blast engulfed the remnants of the building. She ducked behind a truck as desk-sized concrete blocks rained down on them. She stood as the dust cleared. The intersection was buried under rubble.

"Pen, I said one shot," she said in as even a voice as she could project.

"Not my incoming, Colonel."

She spun around to confirm every suspicion she'd harbored for the last fifteen minutes. The recruits had jumped back out and taken defensive positions. Some were behind the trucks, some in front of the cleared buildings, and some covering their backs by the burning tires near the parked van that shouldn't be there.

The out-of-place thugs, moving van, burning tires, staged van, the building rigged to detonate at one end of the street. The incongruities crystallized as she glanced at the other end of the street. They were trapped in the kill zone.

"On the dirt!" she yelled a split second before the muddy van turned into a fireball, shooting metal and glass in all directions. She dove, more instinct than conscious action, letting most of the pressure wave pass over her.

"Colonel!" Gold rushed to her.

Lori took a few seconds to gather herself and stood. "I'm fine," she said though her ears were ringing. One recruit lay crumpled, her neck hanging at a disturbing angle. Another lay eight feet away, the back of her head no longer there. Lori knelt next to a third recruit. So young, though she couldn't tell who she was with all the dirt and blood on her face. She wiped the name tag: Asher.

Fuck.

Eva Asher had been a promising one. She was smart, tough, hardworking, trying to do the right thing, not the easy thing.

Though Lori erected barriers at every step, Asher had moved through them, getting past Lori's defenses. She'd never admit it, but she felt a kinship with Asher and even liked her as a soldier, as a mirror, but only if she flattered herself. Even at her best, she'd never been a natural like Asher. But none of that mattered when your luck ran out.

The blood Asher coughed up dripped down her cheek and chin. A four-inch metal shard protruded from her chest, probably lodged into both lungs. Lori had no way to know how deep it was, though it had to be pretty deep based on the steady stream of blood Asher was drooling.

Asher's eyes fluttered and closed. She was going to drown in her own blood within minutes. The young medic, whose first name Lori couldn't recall, appeared as Asher coughed up more blood. Her feet were spread wide, anchoring her to the ground. She rubbed her bony fingers together but didn't move toward Asher. She'd been chatting with the soldiers on the way up and didn't understand that in the field, she didn't have friends, just patients and patients-in-waiting. Two of her patients had just died. The third was about to join them.

The medic had avoided looking at Asher's chest but now leaned forward. Her eyes widened, and her breathing picked up. Great, she was about to have a panic attack. "I can't. I can't help her."

The medic's nametag jolted Lori's memory. She grabbed the medic's collar and pulled her down until her face was inches from Asher's bloody chest. She lowered her voice to calm the medic and spoke into her ear. "Tess, you can do this. Asher's relying on you." Lori stood up and called Pen. "Land between the trucks and the rubble."

The transport floated down through the smoke, churning dust and soot into a sulfuric haze that reeked like death itself. By the time Pen landed, the recruits had contained the tire fire and cleared a path through the remnants of the van. Gold directed the trucks past the smoldering, foam-covered tires and the shallow crater the blast had created.

She approached Gold. "Two heavy transports are on their way." She pointed to the rubble at the other end of the street. "See if there is anything left in there or in the van Pen shot."

"Yes, ma'am."

The recruits filing into the trucks all told the same story with incredulous faces and hunched shoulders. It had not crossed their minds that this was the most likely outcome of every engagement in the field. The dead recruits had unwittingly taught them a valuable lesson.

Four recruits carried Asher's stretcher to the transport. As they staggered forward and struggled to raise her through the door, Asher's life sloshed like water in a drum on a trampoline.

Once Asher was secured, Lori hopped on the transport and sat next to Pen, motioning her up. As they lifted off, the devastation came into focus. Fires burned in three directions. Two more streets were now blocked off to traffic. No one liked them in the Unregulated Territories, because they tore it up whenever they passed through, which was fine because she didn't like the Uregs either. Nothing good ever came out of the place. Only warlords and bodies, and she had no use for either.

Within minutes, they were out of the danger zone and in Marin airspace. She made her way to Asher who was strapped to a cot with an oxygen mask hiding half her face. Despite the tube sticking out of her side, a gurgling sound came each time her chest rose, signaling that more blood than oxygen swished in her lungs. Tess was prodding Asher's side.

"Can you take that shard out?" Lori asked.

Tess leaned over her patient. She flipped on a light above the cot and used two fingers to probe around the wound. She lifted Asher a few inches and applied pressure to her side and back. The flow out of the tube intensified. Tess let Asher back down. "It shredded both lungs, and it's lodged deep. At the rate she's bleeding internally, she won't make it to Marin, but if I take it out, we'll have a sucking chest wound. Both lungs will collapse, and she won't last two minutes." She closed her eyes. "I wish there were something I could do for her, but there isn't."

Tess had prevented Asher from bleeding out with quick action and projected authority as she spoke. She had passed her first field test.

Lori accepted her prognosis. Lung surgery by a medic on a transport didn't make sense. Then again, neither did Asher's still being alive.

Lori pushed a few strands of blood-soaked hair from Asher's face. The calm and innocence she saw belied the violence raging in Asher's lungs. This was why she despised the Uregs. Here, the not-yet-jaded had no chance. The Uregs weren't cruel, just callous, like the universe, and that callousness offended her more than the cruelty of the most vicious warlord. Offended or not, there was nothing she could do for Asher except provide the comfort of human touch for her final breaths. She took Asher's hand. Against all odds, it tightened around hers.

"It'll be okay," she lied and held the hand as she waited for it to go limp.

It never did.

CHAPTER 2

LOST

*"Leadership is a two-way street, loyalty
up and loyalty down."*

−GRACE HOPPER

onging for her sister's forest-green bicycle was one of Lori's first
memories. Unlike her plodding tricycle, that bike moved with
such spirit it might as well have been alive. No matter how much
she begged or cried, her mom's no remained firm, and the bike
stayed out of her reach. That she inherited the bike two years later
had not diminished her hatred for the word that had tormented
her and long denied her her prize.

Later on, as the world crumbled and the response to her
needs determined whether she lived another day, no became a
dangerous word, one that put butterflies in her stomach. Nowadays,
no was rarely uttered in her presence. Few people were in
a position to deny her requests, and she'd learned to phrase her
questions in a manner that eliminated that two-letter word from
the inventory of answers.

Today, her request to see Asher had been denied, and the medical
files she'd requested had failed to materialize. She'd erred in
some way. Her request had been too simple to misstate and her
visits to injured soldiers too frequent to allow a misunderstanding,
which meant the edict to isolate Asher and seal off her files had

come from higher up. Since Lori was the head of Special Forces, higher up was a small place.

With official channels closed, Lori put out a feeler to a discreet field contact. She was disappointed but not surprised to acquire a tail before reaching the hospital exit: a nondescript gray car, pacing her. She drove south and east across Richmond Bridge and left her civilian Humvee in the Rim, a two-mile stretch in East Bay that allowed Marin to interact with the Uregs. The Rim was Marin in name only with establishments that never would have been tolerated on the west side of the bridge. The brass in Marin viewed the Rim as a necessary evil. Lori saw both a safety valve and a windsock that prevented her from being conned by Marin's insularity.

She pulled the hood of her jacket around her face as she stepped out of her Humvee and braced for the cool night. She glided through the empty intersection and took the hill away from the bay, past the relative safety of the Rim and into the unknown of the Uregs. Her tail was still with her, on foot and a block and half back.

Lori didn't flinch at the *crack* of a distant gunshot or react to the muffled *pop* that followed. That combination had only one meaning: the second bullet left the barrel and entered flesh without meeting air. A small-caliber weapon, about two blocks to her left. It was not her concern.

Fifty feet down the sidewalk, two sentries stood watch, equally unmoved by what had become background music in the Uregs. Lori did not make eye contact. The skinny one stood on his right leg, his left knee bent and the sole of his left foot resting flat against the decaying building. The one with the round face leaned against the metal gate. They were the early warning system of the local gang. Their job was not to engage but to remind you the real enforcers were three blocks away. If you were here by accident, it might as well have been three continents.

She'd worked these parts as a young officer and had come to know the local gangs and their routine. She didn't recognize these two, but the shelf life of a sentry wasn't long. You got in when you caught the boss's eye. You got out after a few scrapes by promotion or in a body bag.

Up close, these two looked as though they believed their line of work led somewhere other than an early grave. A few years ago, she'd have pitied their ignorance-fueled optimism. Now she almost envied them.

Still, they'd done their job. She had been warned.

She took the first right and kept her pace while sticking to the middle of the street, giving herself crucial seconds in case anything came around a corner. On the next block, a woman sat on a tree stump ten feet into the overgrown green patch splitting the street. An eagle claw tattoo reached from her hip toward her left breast and disappeared behind a top that didn't cover much.

The woman did not belong here. Her fingernails, still shaped, betrayed that not long ago she'd called a cozier place than a tree stump home. Her glassy eyes poked from a confused, frozen face as though she had walked out of a classy apartment and found herself here, thirty years and three wars removed from her intended destination. As though she couldn't remember whether she should rob Lori or entice her. The woman would have to decide quickly. There were no amateurs in the Uregs, just veterans and corpses.

Lori had taken this detour through the Uregs to confirm the commitment of her tail. She had her answer, because only the most desperate or dedicated would venture into these parts. She took the next right, heading back toward the bay and the Red Spider, her real destination. You could call it a bar, though at most half the customers were there for the drinks. The other half sought to satisfy baser needs. At its core, the Red Spider wasn't in the liquor or sex businesses. It was in the discretion business.

A whiff of charred oak and sour mash greeted her as she walked in. She let her eyes adjust to the light and caught sight of Pras in a booth at the back. As she slid in across from Pras, her tail walked in and strolled past the front bar and velvet curtains to the back bar. The tail wore a thick scarf that made her round face seem smaller than her neck.

Lori slid a small pack across the table, and Pras swiped it with one motion, making it disappear into her tunic. Lori leaned back and pulled her hood halfway back, exposing tufts of shoulder-length red hair. Compared to most of her colleagues' short crop, it expressed as much individualism as it stated she could do as she pleased. Her tail couldn't have lost her if she tried.

"Colonel Rose," Pras said, smiling ear to ear and exposing her overbite. "What an honor to see Your Excellency." Pras had a dark liquid in a narrow ceramic cup. She uncorked a bottle hidden at the end of the table and poured into a second cup before nudging it toward Lori.

Lori ignored the jibe and sniffed the cup. Sharp nail polish remover overpowered her. She took a tentative sip. It tasted as foul as it smelled, but she hadn't come here for the wine. She put the cup down. "What do you have?"

Pras leaned forward. "Just leads. I'll have more in a day."

Pras was discreet and thorough though not cheap. Then again, cheap information was worse than useless. "I need whatever you have now."

Pras nodded and pressed her lips sideways. "Four cases in New Cal, a dozenish in Kern."

"All military?"

She nodded again. "What made you think to look for this shit?"

Lori had hoped she'd been wrong, that there was a simple explanation for the secrecy around Asher's still being alive, that perhaps she hadn't seen what she thought she'd seen. It all evaporated with two nods and a handful of words. She wrapped both hands around the cup but didn't bring it to her lips. "And?"

"And nothing. They're gone, but what's interesting isn't that they disappeared from hospitals after recovering. It's that all their medical records are gone and, in the Kern cases, their entire histories. It's like they never existed."

"But you got them?"

Pras rolled her eyes. "Please."

The missing HR records on the discharged soldiers had just become part of a larger pattern, as had the interference on Asher. She wasn't going to solve any of this tonight.

She took a tentative sip from the liquid Pras insisted on calling wine and put the cup down. The tail moved from mildly irritating to constricting, her mere presence preventing Lori from relaxing even for a few minutes. Any half-decent agent would know there were only two reasons for Lori to be in this booth. One was to get information. The other wasn't, and on that option, they would have agreed on a price by now and moved upstairs. Lori rolled her eyes toward the bar. "Is she still watching?"

Pras glanced up. "Yeah. Pretending not to." She snickered. "Doing a shit job."

"I need to get out of here." Lori leaned forward.

"You want me to keep her busy while you slip out?"

She reached out to take Pras' hand. The skin was rough and leathery, not the hands of someone who earned her keep in the bedroom. But the tail, limited to half a sense in the dim light, couldn't know that. She saw only what she expected to see, which was physical contact. "No, I don't want her to get spooked. Take me upstairs and back."

Pras licked her upper lip and winked. With her big, bright eyes bulging out of her narrow face, she could be charming, even attractive if she didn't hustle you for contraband. They stood, and Lori put a hand around Pras' waist. Pras pushed Lori's hair away from her ear, leaned in to whisper, "One of these days, we'll have to do this for real," and led her up the stairs.

"One of these days," Lori said.

She bolted as soon as they reached the top of the stairwell and called Sierra on her brisk walk to her Humvee.

Sierra answered twenty seconds later. "Colonel."

"Meet me at the hospital."

"Is everything okay?"

"I'm fine, but I don't like what's going on with Asher."

Lori raced across Richmond Bridge at the wheel of her Humvee, slowing down only for the checkpoint. Pras' limited data confirmed that injured soldiers were vanishing in three states. Worse, no one was looking for them. She ground her teeth because she hated mysteries and anything that threatened order, even more so if she couldn't shoot it.

She replayed the Uregs ambush in her mind. Whoever attacked them had stuck to a simple plan: lull them with the thugs, spook them with the fire, blow up the dirty van to scatter them, drop the building to pin them, and swoop in to take out the survivors. It had come too close to working.

But recruits were low-value targets. Why orchestrate all that to get at them? Was it a message? To whom? Her? How would they have known she'd be there?

Sierra? Possibly. Tran? Accomplice or victim?

She made it to the hospital in eighteen minutes and let go of her million unanswered questions. Sierra stood at the entrance, her toned, five-foot-ten frame towering over the reception desk. Sierra was wired to make tactical decisions and take quick action, not play poker. She broadcast her feelings with every twitch of her lips and eyes. Right now, her stretched cheeks and narrow eyes screamed embarrassed. "About Asher."

In the fiasco, Asher making it to the hospital still breathing had been the lone piece of good news. Lori was grateful for not having to explain to Executive Yim how her stepdaughter had been lost during a training exercise. But Sierra's eyes turned into pinholes and remained glued to her toes. She was not embarrassed. Guilty?

"She's gone, isn't she?"

Sierra's eyes widened. "How did you know?"

"When did she come out of surgery?"

Sierra handed her the screen.

Lori scrolled to find the data. "Successful open-lung surgery in forty-five minutes? Are you shitting me?" She flipped to another page. "Doesn't even say who operated on her." She handed the screen back to Sierra. "This thing is useless." She rubbed her neck with one hand to slow her mind. "What do we have?"

Sierra said a lot of words, but they could be summed up by one: nothing. That's what they had with no forced entry, no surveillance footage, and no sign of struggle. An hour after being admitted, Asher had been moved from surgery to intensive care. Two hours later, Asher had vanished and joined Pras' data. Was Asher the lead to cracking the missing soldiers' case, or was she bait to lure Lori deeper into this mess?

"Did you visit Asher earlier tonight, Colonel?"

"I tried, but no. Why?"

"The entry logs to all restricted areas have been wiped except for an ID fragment on the backup log. No time stamp, but the backups only go twenty-four hours." Sierra was not embarrassed or guilty. She was concerned. "Colonel, it matches your ID."

Great. Lori paid Pras with medical supplies she liberated from the hospital. They were nothing Marin would miss but were valuable in the Uregs, almost as valuable as the intel she received in exchange. Her access never raised suspicion, because it was one of hundreds. Having all IDs but hers wiped couldn't be a coincidence.

"How many people knew I'd be in the field today?"

"Up till the moment you left, no one but you and me."

It had taken them a little over an hour to reach their destination, not nearly enough time to set up what they'd faced. She'd been selfish, using a training exercise to scratch her itch from being cooped up in a glass office.

"Two recruits died on my watch."

"With all due respect, Colonel, you saved eighteen recruits today."

That was true only if she accepted the premise that the attack had been random. All the evidence pointed to the contrary. She reached under her hair to massage her neck again. A half-walnut-sized lump of muscle undulated under her fingers but did not come near breaking apart no matter how hard she pulled and pushed. "Since you and I are the only ones who knew I'd be there, one might conclude one of us is responsible for the ambush and Asher's disappearance."

Sierra's lips parted, and her face turned chalk white. Her side neck muscles tightened, turning her head into the top of a triangular volcano about to blow off. She unholstered her sidearm and put it on the reception counter. "If you believe that, I'm not useful to you."

Lori had meant it as a statement of fact, not an accusation. She'd never questioned Sierra's loyalty. She saw no reason to start now. But it said a lot that after all these years, Sierra still didn't know where she stood. The rift Lori had inserted to keep her officers on their toes had become a chasm, and she had no idea how to bridge it. Or whether to.

She let go of her neck and clutched Sierra's gun. The tiny dimples on the handle sucked her palm in as though they wanted to meld with her, begging her to spring into action. Her index finger rested on the barrel, smooth and cool like glass. The barrel urged caution, aware of the power hidden in its belly.

"Good thing I don't believe that." She flipped the gun and held it by the barrel.

Color returned to Sierra's face. She took and holstered her gun and, without missing a beat, launched into an analysis of hospital security: ways in, ways out. She listed the next steps thoroughly, all well thought out and all wrong. This was how they conducted investigations when people disappeared from shitholes in the Uregs when they didn't worry about being set up or being watched by their own.

"Stop. Find Tran." She didn't add the obvious. Tran was either in on this or she was dead. "I still can't believe Asher made it here alive."

"She was lucky."

Yeah, real lucky to be impaled in the chest. Lori pulled up the receiving medic's report. It referred to a clean puncture as though Asher had been pierced by a sharp spear. Lori had seen the metal shards tearing up both lungs. The report did not describe the same patient.

"We'll interrogate all possible suspects. I'll look at who had access to the logs—"

Lori put a hand up. They had to tread lightly, because whatever they'd thought they'd been investigating had just graduated to threatening. "Focus on Tran and the ambush. Keep an eye on the investigation, but let the military police handle Asher's case."

"With all due respect, Colonel, Asher is one of our own. We can't just do nothing."

"That's why I want you to keep an eye on them. I want to know which leads they follow and which they don't. But finding Tran is critical. Either she set us up or someone made her disappear to get one of us into the Uregs. Until you find out which, you can't help Asher."

Sierra nodded but did not look happy, which was fine because Lori wasn't happy either. The knot in the pit of her stomach tightened. She had three mysteries, which was three too many. How had Asher survived? Why were soldiers disappearing from hospitals? Who was watching her? She was stuck with pieces from three puzzles all mixed together. She couldn't act, even through proxies like Pras, without tipping her hand. No, she needed someone with the nose to sniff out absurd leads and unlock the unlikeliest connections, someone who wouldn't give up or be intimidated, someone no one would be watching, someone she could trust. Someone who did not exist.

From the depths of her mind, one name floated up.

He checked all the boxes.

CHAPTER 3

APPOINTMENT

"A friend is one who knows us but loves us anyway."

—JEROME CUMMINGS

Mika Bayley sat at the end of a Uregs bar, elbows on the dented counter, chin resting on his interlocked knuckles. Three bare light bulbs hung over the counter, adding to the gloom more than illuminating the narrow room. This was not a place you came to meet people. It was a place you came to forget about the world. Mika's glass was still full, because he had no intention of drinking this piss-like brew when a treat from Lori waited for him half an hour away. But he needed to kill time, and brooding over a drink usually chased away prying neighbors.

It didn't tonight. The hawker making the rounds reached him and leaned over the bar talking, gesturing, prodding. Black hair slicked back, a denim vest exposing scrawny shoulders, the man projected desperation. Hawkers always worked in pairs, so Mika made a quarter turn to spot the missing partner. Two tables away and bigger, the partner looked bored and missed Mika's scan. Oblivious to it all, the hawker continued his nonsense. Could he interest Mika in designer drugs? Or a lock pick? Or a sniffer that can pick up the scent of a weapons cache? The senselessness of his tired pleas to sell tools he couldn't possibly have was lost on the man.

Evolving sniffers required as much art as science. Too narrow an objective, and the low-level AI became a dumb pattern matcher, like old search engines. Too broad, and it forever chased improbable correlations, lost in a sea of ever-expanding data. Finding the right number and the right breadth of objectives was science. Seeding them with the right clues, or scents, was art. The hounds who balanced all that to unlock anything of value were a rare and expensive breed, not the kind to hang around this bleak bar and hustle strangers for little more than beer money.

"No, thanks," Mika said.

The hawker put his hand on Mika's forearm. "You look like you need a good sniffer."

"Not today," Mika said without looking up.

"I got the best, discreet and powerful. You can find whatever you need."

Mika relaxed his arm and rotated his wrist inward, grabbing and twisting the man's hand. He leaned closer as though they were negotiating. The hawker's partner didn't react, their tussle hidden from his view. "I need peace, and you need a wrist, so how about you move on?"

The man didn't stop. "Trust me, man. I'm just trying to help."

Mika increased the pressure on the hand. The man's shoulders tightened.

"Okay, okay. I'm leaving."

Mika let go, and the man walked toward the next mark, on and on in a circle with no beginning and no end to the lies, hopes, and betrayals. The hawker had tossed out the word "trust" as though it meant something, as though it weren't one more item in short supply in the Uregs. But even that premise wasn't correct. Trust was a meaningless word, an illusory notion. People took care of their own best interests. Period.

That self-evident fact was a revelation to most.

Mika left fifteen minutes later. Two blocks out, what little security the main road offered became a distant memory. He took two quick turns and glanced back. No one was behind him except a body that lay face down in the alley to his right. There was just enough light left to reflect off the blood, to invite a closer look.

It didn't matter who the man had been or what he'd done or not done or to whom he'd done it. What mattered was that trust and skull had shattered here. The blood painting the sidewalk had poured out of the large hole in the back of the man's head, and it had done so recently.

He erased the body from his retina and picked up the pace.

Though six blocks gone, the body pushed him into an extra level of wariness. He skipped the dilapidated converted warehouse that was his destination and walked into the next building. The lobby reeked of wet, musty concrete. Black veins of mold streaked across the walls. He covered his nose with his bandana but kept his eyes on the door. It was a lousy place to spring a trap, but he'd stopped counting on the intelligence of street thugs.

After ten dull minutes, he exited through the back of the lobby into the narrow alley. He doubled back to reach the rear entrance of the brick building he'd skipped. He picked the lock and walked in. The banister was long gone, but the stairs were undamaged.

He climbed up three flights and rhythmically knocked the code on the door. Though another eventful year had passed, he'd once again kept the appointment he'd made as a little boy.

Lori sat on a three-legged stool at the far end of the loft, her back propped against the brick wall. Her right hand rested on the high table next to a gun that would have turned an intruder into a hot pink mess. He hadn't expected a warmer welcome, not in the Uregs, not with a hastily arranged meeting weeks ahead of their yearly appointment.

He hadn't inquired, because you did not do that with Lori. She was small framed, and in a group picture, she might not have stood out. But in real life, everything gravitated toward her, ready to be put in order. Whether you considered her a hero or a war criminal depended on which side of the fence you sat. The few who were on the fence saw a woman whose drive was fueled by a rage burning deep within her, a rage he had watched ignite a long time ago.

Unlike Lori, he could spend a whole night in a crowded room without having anyone recall he'd been there. Lori had told him his smile was his most disarming feature, because his gap teeth destroyed his generic handsomeness and made him memorable. Which is why he rarely smiled in the company of strangers.

He closed the door and faced her with a broad grin.

She stood up and hugged him hard. He pulled his head back but kept his hands on her shoulders. "No new wrinkles, no new scars. A good year then." He kissed her forehead.

"You're not looking closely enough."

She disengaged and reached down into her bag to pull out a bottle. She placed it on the table and extended her right arm, bent at the elbow, palm up, pointing toward the bottle.

"What is it?" He lifted the bottle. "How the hell did you get your hands on this? I haven't seen one of these since—" He looked at it more closely. "Actually, I've never seen one of these."

She sat back down and slapped the stool next to her. "Sit."

"Yes, ma'am."

The moment the words left his lips, he wished he could swallow them back. Lori's shoulders recoiled as though tugged by invisible lines. He knew how much Lori needed to be Lori again without the trappings of power. Not the colonel, and certainly not ma'am.

He sat and made puppy eyes. "Please don't take my present away."

A smile flickered across Lori's narrow face. "I've been thinking about this indulgence of ours. I had every intention of telling you this had to be the last time until…"

"Until next year?" He smiled.

The battle raged between a smile and a scowl on her face. The smile won. They'd been meeting once a year since Lori had moved to Marin over a decade ago. He'd just turned eighteen and hadn't understood what had drawn her to Marin and away from him. He now knew she'd always planned that move but had waited for him to be old enough to give him a choice. He'd chosen not to be a second-class citizen in a world he didn't understand. Still, he'd have followed her had she not joined the army. He couldn't throw his life away to watch Lori throw away hers.

Feeling betrayed and abandoned, he'd vowed to not talk to her again. But when she'd extended an olive branch eight months later and a few weeks before the birthdays they'd always celebrated together, his resolve had melted. Accepting what she'd done and who she'd become was still his proudest achievement. Maybe he wasn't aiming high, but he'd seen worse.

"Until the return of better times," she said. "I have no idea what next year will bring, but I know it's getting more dangerous out there."

If the Kern goons hadn't scared them with their attack three years ago, he didn't see why anything would, but she was talking about a bigger problem, one she hadn't yet decided to share.

"One minute into it, you reminded me why I do this," she added when he didn't reply.

He did it because he missed her, but he wasn't going to state the obvious. He waited.

"Because I've forgotten how to laugh."

"I thought we did it for the fermented, fortified, and aged grape juice."

His words did not elicit a smile. She punched him on the shoulder and tossed him the corkscrew she'd brought. "Here, see if you can still operate one of these."

"How about you laugh all you want and I drink this?"

"Seems I win," she whispered in a barely audible voice.

He put the corkscrew down. She had always been at the center of a storm of her own making, and the clouds following her were getting darker.

She waved as if to flick away an impertinent mosquito. "Open it, will you?"

He relented and cut the wax off the twenty-nine-year-old vintage port Lori had brought.

"Have you found your sail-around-the-world boat yet?" she asked half a bottle later.

He shook his head. "I thought I did six months ago, but the keel bolts were too far gone. I still don't have one that can withstand the Horn or the Indian Ocean."

She chuckled. "I kept my promise to keep you safe. Don't go fuck it up by sinking somewhere in the Southern Hemisphere."

"No danger of that for a while longer."

She stretched back and stroked her neck. She didn't put any force into it, her arm loose, her elbow pointing up. "Yeah. Irony is, you might be safer thousands of miles away than right here." She let go of her neck and waved at the window. "All these lost souls. They all want things to be different, but they don't have any imagination, so they say they want things to be the way they were. But no one has any idea what that means."

He stood and got closer to her, taking in the same moonlit scene. The intersection lay dead, like most things. "I don't know what that means either, but I know one thing. That world is gone and is not coming back. Only a lunatic would not accept that."

"It's too damn depressing, watching people stagger in fear two steps forward and one back. Lunatics." She took a sip. "Restoring order with lunatics is hard work."

He wouldn't know. "No one gives a shit about order." He sat on the floor, cross-legged, and leaned on her stool. Everyone alive was a winner of the genetic lottery. All their order and science hadn't even dented the Purge, the virus that had halved the population every six months for four years. The mathematics of the Purge had left humanity precariously close to the cliff. Then humanity had jumped. As the cities burned or washed away in triggered tsunamis, the four-day war claimed most of the remaining population and nearly all their industrial base.

He'd never understood why it was called the "four-day war." It should have been called the "four-day dying." No one fought. As rumors that the Purge was weaponized emerged, bombs flew, a few first, then retaliation, and then more retaliation. In the end, little remained in the northern landmasses. Twenty years on, they still didn't know how it had all started, not that it mattered anymore.

She took another sip. "A few million lunatics."

With one number, Lori reminded him how close they were to extinction and how they were still shooting their way toward it. With the blasts and EMPs taking out most but not all of the tech, the known world had shrunk to nineteenth-century cities fueled by twentieth-century tech and sprinkled with random twenty-first-century gadgets. The city-states hugged the coast with the Uregs filling the gaps and thinning out as they moved away from power sources. If there were more survivors, they were outside their transport range and not replying to broadcasts.

She sat there, her red hair barely touching her shoulders framing her narrow face, with a distant look in her gray-green eyes. Her hands cradled her elbows, almost fragile. Almost.

He missed her insights, her intensity, being himself and not having to pretend, and talking about his ideas, his fears, without being judged. Mostly he missed talking about nothing.

She grabbed the bottle and trickled the last of it into her glass, rotating the bottle to avoid pouring the sediment. She opened a second bottle and poured him a generous serving. She reached for his hand, giving it a squeeze. She stood, pulled him to his feet, and pointed outside. "What do you see?"

From the back of the loft, all he saw was an empty street, broken glass, boarded windows, and a few rusted self-driving car shells that hadn't moved in two decades. He stayed silent.

"I see a local grocery store with crates of bright-red tomatoes on the sidewalk, the dry-farmed ones we used to get from the farms in the Central Valley," she said.

Even the two of them, so close in so many ways, had divergent memories, so what hope did they have with anyone else?

"I see a little girl holding her mother's hand crossing the street.

A student playing the guitar on the sidewalk, his case open with change in it. A bicyclist wearing a helmet, protecting herself against a fall, not bullets." She pulled him closer and pointed to the second floor of the building across the intersection. "There, I see pots of geraniums. White, pink, red, orange."

He wanted to see all that, but what he saw was a dark, deserted street, one in which you stumbled into bodies with bullet holes in their heads.

Besides, he had no idea what a geranium or a dry-farmed tomato was.

"Prosperity isn't about luxury," she said. "It's not cruise ships or senators or thousands of streaming channels bombarding your every waking moment with distractions. It's about the pointless details you'd never ever think you'd miss until they're gone. Order allows you to enjoy prosperity, enjoy those little things. It allows you to be you, to feel human."

She sat back down on her stool and traced the rim of her glass with her finger. "I remember how happy my mom was when she tended her garden. When I look at a garden, I see dirt and, on a good day, some flowers I can't name, but mostly dirt. Someday, I'd love to find out what it's like to spend endless hours puttering around a small garden talking to flowers, pruning this one, watering that one." She took a breath. "Someday."

Whatever had Lori concerned, it wasn't the flowers she couldn't name or the garden she hadn't planted. They'd known enumerating events that filled a year wasn't a conversation. Neither was reminiscing about a long-dead past. Each year, they picked up right where they had left off as though they had been together only a few days before, as though the whole world wasn't conspiring to pull them apart.

Even after the massacre at Hollister, where Lori's strike had decimated Kern troops and ended the war between Kern and Marin, he had not asked a single question. But that was about ignoring the past. What seemed amiss this time was the future, something Lori could not let go of even for one night. "I'm not supposed to ask but I will. What's bothering you?"

She swirled and sniffed her port. "Sometimes, I worry I'm dead inside."

"What is going on, Lore?"

"People are disappearing and not just from the Uregs. Marin, New Cal, even Kern." She took a sip and looked away. "A soldier disappeared from medical lockdown two nights ago, a young, promising soldier. She wasn't the first one. It scares me that I'm more focused on rooting out the conspiracy behind the disappearances than finding her."

"You're not dead. You're just ruthlessly pragmatic. The conspiracy will lead you to her, right?"

She drained her port. "I just don't know."

Her bright eyes melded the struggles of the resourceful girl, the protective teenager, the doctor's aide, the grieving fugitive, and the Special Forces Colonel. There was no contradiction between Lore, Lori, and Rose. But you had to get behind the wall to see that, and she had to let you. "State secrets. I understand."

"No, that's not it." She stopped. "Well, it is, but that's not the issue here. This," she said, her wrist tipping back and forth between them, "is supposed to be a break from our real lives."

He had plenty of questions too, but they were too mundane to break the rules with. Her concern seemed deeper, and if she felt it was that important, he didn't mind letting her break the rules. Even the good ones. "What's a geranium anyway?"

"You're trying to change the subject."

"That's bad?"

"You're still protecting me, even from myself. Even now."

"I've been accused of worse."

"Yeah, but I'm the one who is supposed to protect you, remember? That's why you offered me oranges."

Oranges. He recalled that day when as an eight-year-old, he had approached Lori with a plan to get them both fed. The memory was so vivid he could smell the oranges.

Lori smiled, most likely transported to that same moment in their past.

"You did pretty well. I'm still here," he said.

"Yeah, well. You're the one who did most of the protecting."

"Nah." She was heading for dangerous territory, to darker days. "Besides, they weren't my oranges."

She grabbed the bottle and poured herself another glass. She reached over and refilled his glass as well. She took her tida out and tapped it. A young woman's face appeared, rotating slowly. Her dark hair was pulled back in a ponytail, a few strands dangling in front of her eyes. She wore a tight, gray turtleneck zipped all the way up. Her smile was more puzzled than amused, urging whoever had taken the picture to get on with it.

"Eva Asher," Lori said, "a Special Forces recruit who was doing well and the stepdaughter of our senate president, Nancy Yim."

Which still didn't tell him why he was staring at her rotating picture.

"She suffered a bad chest wound when we were ambushed in the Uregs. I still don't know how she survived, but against all odds, she pulled through. Then she disappeared from the military hospital. No record of a break-in, no struggle, and no intruders on the security footage, nothing. Someone even made her bed."

He flipped through the limited data. She should have been in an intensive care unit. He flipped again. Multiple gunshot wounds two years ago, a bad fall as a teenager, lacerations from flying through a window as a child. That was a lot of accidents. "Clumsy or unlucky?"

"Don't know about luck, but you can see her accomplishments. She wasn't clumsy."

He agreed with that. An athletic soldier with little regard for her own safety had been injured, had miraculously recovered, and had disappeared. Asher reached through the animated picture to introduce herself. He felt as though he knew her—the smiling woman, not the one in intensive care with shredded lungs. He knew better, but it was hard to not assign personality traits to the face or to the training records. She was serious but playful. Intense yet calm.

"You need what, exactly?"

"I need her found."

He considered why she had to ask. "Smells like an inside job?"

Lori nodded. "She's not the first missing soldier. I need an outsider, not military, not even Marin, good with sniffers, discreet, without an agenda. Someone I trust. Know anyone like that?"

This whole thing smelled wrong. People disappeared in the Uregs all the time, but Marin was supposed to be different. And he'd never set foot in Marin, so he didn't know where he'd start looking for a missing Marin soldier. The dots did not even come close to connecting, but Lori had never asked him for anything, so there was only one answer. "I'll need more than what's here."

She dismissed his professional interest with a single wave. "Not tonight. I'll put you in touch with Pras, my contact who put the missing soldier data together. As for Asher, just take the job when it's offered." She reached up and put her hand on his shoulder. "Be careful."

That went without saying. The lines around her eyes hid more concern than a search for a missing soldier would warrant. He reached for the bottle and refilled both their glasses with the last of the port. She raised hers and took a sip. Mika did the same, enjoying the lasting warmth the ruby liquid provided. Tomorrow, he would embark on a new search, one that would bring him into a world he'd never known with new rules and new dangers, but tonight he let it go.

They sipped port in silence. Her presence was enough to reassure him that all was well.

If only for one night.

CHAPTER 4

OLD INSIGHTS

*"You can never leave footprints that last if you
are always walking on tiptoe."*

—LEYMAH GBOWEE

Amy Chipps, the vice governor of New California, closed her eyes and rubbed her temples. The headache did not go away. Neither did the numbers on her screen when she opened her eyes. Cal City, their capital, was behind schedule. It was third out of four towns in the number of households with running water but first in expending resources. The mayor was not returning her calls, treating her like Governor Eric Fontaine's secretary. That amused her more than it infuriated her, because it was his neck on the line when the clock struck midnight and he failed to meet his targets. Eric was understanding, but he wasn't forgiving.

Eric stood by her door as though he'd read her mind. "Amy, let's take a walk."

She let the numbers melt away and headed for the door. They walked past his car, the same old model she drove, designed before self-driving cars had taken over. The same old model that had become new again when the information grid collapsed and sensors and circuits and GPUs rotted, turning the self-driving cars into expensive doghouses.

They headed toward the bay, passing old office blocks and

older barracks. The Presidio offered a metaphor for New California, a spot that had been repurposed and reinvented many times over. They'd walked four blocks when Eric stopped. "Why are we here, Amy?"

She hoped her confusion didn't show. "You asked me here."

Eric chuckled and pointed to the ground. "I mean, why is Cal City here, here?"

They stood at the northern-most point of the peninsula, an easy-to-defend spot. Eric looked ready to go into one of his lectures. Though he'd rebuilt cities and stitched them into a state, Eric had never shed his professorial past. With his cascading salt-and-pepper hair and metal-rimmed glasses, he belonged to a more civilized world.

"Why is it here, Eric?"

"This place was a fort almost three centuries ago. It's got solid rock, good visibility, and its back to the bay, but if defense had been the only reason, we'd have consolidated in Santa Cruz, like Kern did with LA. No, a state needs more than one town. I needed Cal City to make New Cal big and real, so I went as far as I could from Santa Cruz without antagonizing Kern or Marin."

New California had grown stronger, but it still was a collection of four city-states. Cal City and Santa Cruz anchored the north and south. Mountain View and San Jose linked them up in short hops: four islands of sanity drifting in the sea of violence that was the Unregulated Territories, but that sea of violence provided a hundred-mile buffer between Kern to their south and Marin to their north. "It worked, didn't it?"

"I ended up with Swiss cheese."

She narrowed her eyes to hide her confusion.

"Cheese with holes," Eric said, "and New California consists of the holes, as all my critics like to point out."

Eric had never before discussed his failings or admitted to having critics. Whatever was bothering him was more serious than forts or rock or cheese. "What's on your mind?"

Eric didn't reply but kept walking. He pointed over the bay when they reached the top of a hill. "I crossed that bridge hundreds of times."

The Golden Gate glistened like a haunted mirage at dusk with chunks of roadway missing. It stood tall and defiant like a demented piece of art. On bad days, she saw an alien derelict, there to taunt her with tentacles reaching down from the main cables to snag careless visitors. On good days, she saw an engineering triumph conjured up by forward-looking souls who tamed the future. But she never saw a bridge, a structure meant to connect land and people. "I don't think I ever did."

"That's the difference, isn't it?" Eric said with sad eyes fixed to the sidewalk. She followed his gaze to the two terra cotta pots lining up the alley. Before she could dwell on what differences Eric meant, the smell of basil hit her, but Eric was already gone, speeding away from the scent. "The difference is that I remember everything we lost: bridges, friends, Alyssa's pesto." He paused before whispering, "Alyssa."

She conceded that since she didn't know what she'd lost, maybe she'd lost less, but that line of thinking was pointless. Eric wouldn't have brought her here to talk about his long-dead wife. "Really, what's on your mind?"

"It's getting worse out there. Mountain View still doesn't have running water. San Jose's mayor talks secession. I'm afraid we're going to wake up one morning and find ourselves in the middle of another Marin-Kern shooting war with no one to stand by our side." Eric let out a sigh. "What's the latest on the Uregs violence?"

Eric didn't frighten easily, so she kept an eye on him as she rattled out the facts and let him get to whatever was on his mind at his own pace. "There were six attacks in the Uregs last month. Two shops and another clinic are gone and some compound way east. There are lots of bodies, but no attacker has been killed or caught."

"What do you make of it? Gangs?" he asked but didn't seem interested in her answer.

She understood turf wars, but the latest attacks didn't fit the pattern with dozens of burned, mutilated corpses, including children. "Doubt it. Gangs intimidate to collect money or blow shit up to take over. Blowing up shops doesn't serve any purpose if you don't replace them, and that compound couldn't have owed anyone anything to warrant what happened to them. Don't you have Mika looking into it?"

"You talk to him much?"

She talked to everybody, and he knew it. "Here and there. Why?"

"He's not like us. He's not dedicated to New Cal. Be careful what you share with him."

She didn't like the casual dismissal of an asset. She liked his tone even less. Eric was her boss and her mentor, but he didn't know where the boundaries were. "I can handle myself."

"I know. It's him I don't trust. He disappeared in the Uregs again."

"Isn't that what you pay him for?"

"On the surface, but I've got no way to know who he talks to. For all I know, he's talking to Kern or Marin agents."

"Why do you keep him around?"

He grimaced. "Most of the time, he's useful."

The simple truth was that practical trumped philosophical, but she still didn't see what secret she had that would even be worth Mika's time. "I'll keep that in mind."

His tone softened. "I learned one thing the hard way. As bad as things are, they can always get worse. Do you know we initially worried that the comet would disrupt communication satellites?" He grimaced. "Nine billion corpses later, half the satellites are still functioning. I don't want to worry about satellites."

"What do we worry about?"

"About being a footnote in history."

She had bigger worries than font sizes, and so did he. "What are you not telling me?"

"I've been talking to Chancellor Czernak for a month. She wants a union. A joint state." He stood there as though he'd asked her to audit a water project.

Chancellor Czernak had led Marin from its birth. She was an isolationist. They'd had no official contact in Amy's five years in New Cal or before that according to the records she'd seen. Marin was adamant men could not be trusted with power, that the only way forward was with a women-only government. Now they were discussing a union with New Cal, the only remnants of a functioning mixed society? She took a deep breath through her nose and exhaled, pushing away her exasperation.

Militarily, this painted a bull's eye on New Cal, an invitation for Kern to attack. Politically, this was a surrender. Santa Cruz and Mountain View would probably go for it, because Eric was still a cult hero there. San Jose would agitate, playing the sovereignty card. Cal City could go either way. Herding those councils was going to be migraine-inducing work. What irritated her most, though, wasn't any of that.

She steadied her voice to hide her anger. "What do you want out of this deal?"

"We want a better future."

That wasn't an answer; it was a slogan. "Is their gender segregation nonsense negotiable? What do we have that they want?"

"That's what we need to find out."

She glanced at the Golden Gate, ready to resume its duty, to connect again. Though a hundred years older, the hunk of metal was more malleable than she was. Then again, the bridge was ambivalent about its location, its function. It hadn't chosen either. She had. She believed in New Cal and its ideals. "We can't do this."

He shrugged.

"Why are you doing this?"

If Eric felt disappointment, he didn't let it show. "I watched the world die, Amy. I saw the panic, the riots, and the desperation on screens and right outside my front door. I knew I was infected when I lost Alyssa and Bruce." His voice dropped to a whisper.

"He was only six. I accepted my burden that I'd bear witness to the collapse of civilization."

She waited when he paused.

"When we get a chance to rebuild it all, we have to take it," he said.

There it was. The walk, the history lesson, the personal connection, the frequent use of "we" as though they were one and the same. His job was to push people's buttons. Hers was to know where the buttons were.

"It's a done deal?" she asked.

"It's going to happen. I need you to improve the terms."

"I can't believe you waited a month to tell me."

"I had my reasons."

She locked eyes with him.

"We have a week to prepare for the summit," he said.

"Are you joking?"

"I'm very serious. The framework is set. What we need is to bring the mayors and councils to our side and sell the union. I need all your talents there."

"I don't know that I can do that."

"I know you can." His condescending smile was no doubt meant to be encouraging.

"Okay, I don't know that I want to do that."

Eric's quiet confidence cracked for a second, but he recovered as the smooth governor dislodged the concerned mediator. "Remember what I told you when you joined my staff?"

It had been five years ago when Eric had offered her a nameless job, half a step below errand girl. In a month, she'd asked for more responsibility, and he'd told her to not rush it, that one day she'd run it all. She'd assumed he was placating her, yet here she was.

"Yeah."

"Still holds." He pushed his glasses up and looked at her with his piercing blue eyes as though he could see her inner thoughts. "Now it means something bigger than New Cal."

Right there, he'd pushed another of her buttons. Even when she knew what he was doing, he had a way to tug into her inner fears and desires with just the right pressure.

"Trust me," he said, eyes fixed on hers.

"I'll do what I can."

He smiled again, warmer this time. The twinkle in his eye tried to erase twenty-five years of burden. It was an impossible task.

AMY WALKED TOWARD MACKY'S BAR. SHE NEEDED A DRINK. Staring at the Golden Gate had not provided answers. Her office had turned into a dying friend, one she put off visiting for another night. *Union* was a good word but also a serious one. With one signature, Eric was going to destroy everything she believed in and everything he had said he believed in.

Macky's occupied the top floor of a narrow, three-story warehouse nestled into the wooded hill. Nonperishables were stacked on the first floor, wine and beer barrels on the second, and thirsty customers on the third. The whiff of oats gave way to hops as she ascended the stairs. The place was full with a mix of those indulging in predinner drinks and those who hadn't left their stools in years. A half dozen of Eric's staff she recognized but did not care to know better sat at a table off the bar. Based on their boisterous laughter, they weren't on their first drinks.

She claimed a stool, but Macky waved before she could sit. She put her hands on the counter and leaned forward. Macky, who kept an eye on every volatile glare in his bar, nudged his head to the other end of the bar. "Those two," he said as he pushed a pint of stout toward her.

"Thanks." She didn't know the men but had seen them with Cavana. They were either friends of Cavana or his protection, probably both. "What about them?"

"Nothing serious, yet. A bit of posturing, but they talk shit about New Cal and call the governor King Eric, loudly, with a table of the governor's staff here."

Macky didn't need to say more. He deftly handled drunken disagreements, but he didn't do politics. First Eric, now Macky unloaded their problems on her as though that constituted a solution. Just because it was easier for her to solve the problem didn't mean it was a snap or that it didn't take a toll on her. She took a sip of stout and turned around to go back to work.

She spotted Nando Cavana halfway across the room, surveying the crowd. Mika stood next to him. She walked over, but Mika disappeared before she got through the crowd.

"Hey."

"Ms. Chipps," Cavana's voice boomed, emanating from a chest that could have contained four lungs. It was neither friendly nor hostile. Specks of gray dusted Cavana's short, black beard but hadn't yet spread to his curly hair.

"Settling in?"

"We are managing." Cavana's compound had joined New Cal less than a month ago, and they were still struggling to integrate. He hadn't blinked at Eric's increasingly harsh demands. His crew provided security, self-defense training, and labor, but he held little decision-making power after having been shut out of policy, inspection, and analysis posts. "This," Cavana said, pointing his index up and swirling it. "Seems we did not just move thirty miles but also thirty years."

"New Cal's excesses can be intoxicating."

Cavana chuckled. "From out there, I saw the veneer of civilization, but I did not realize how thin it was or how the wood underneath was rotten to the core."

There were only harmless drunks around them. She took a sip of her beer. "You've been in New Cal, what, three weeks? And you're already declaring us morally rotten?"

"Not just morally." Cavana wasn't smiling.

"Lighten up, Nando. There is a lot wrong with New Cal. There is also a lot that's right." She pointed to Cavana's men at the bar. "This isn't the time or place to air that shit out."

"What is it you think I am doing?"

"Setting a bad example."

Cavana's jaw tightened. "With all due respect, Ms. Chipps, you are out of line."

She pointed to the bar again. "Your men there have been making a scene for a while. Some ignore them, others mouth back. How many drinks before someone takes a swing?"

"Are you saying this is my fault?"

"I'm saying they're doing what they think you want them to do. That if they relaxed and enjoyed themselves, you'd be disappointed."

Cavana's lips curled up into half a smile. "I might be."

"Let me buy you a drink."

Cavana seemed ready to protest, but she turned away and walked to the bar. He was behind her when she reached it. She flagged Macky, pointed to her beer and then to Cavana. She raised her drink to Cavana's men. "Great night, don't you think?"

They gave her gruff nods but did not raise their glasses. Macky pushed a brew to Cavana. He grabbed it, clinked hers, and raised it toward his men. "Cheer up, JJ. This is not a wake." He turned to her. "I will talk to them."

"Thanks."

"But what I said still holds." He ran his hand through his thick hair, his fingers disappearing near his hairline only to resurface halfway up his skull. "Rotten."

She took a step away from the bar but then turned around, set her beer on the counter, and put a hand on Cavana's sleeve. "Do me a favor. Don't focus on trivialities."

"Trivialities?"

"Like how late the bar is open or who drinks too much or whether your men build the water pipeline or audit it. When you pick a fight with Eric, make sure it's a fight worth picking. You'll find a lot more allies than you suspect."

Cavana took a sip and put his beer down before replying. "Recruiting, Ms. Chipps?"

Startled by the man's foresight, she let her eyes linger on him too long.

"I see," Cavana smiled.

"No, you don't. If I were recruiting, you'd be the first to know."

She walked away without waiting for a reply. Eric's staffers were still at the table. A little girl slept in a booth behind them, and Amy felt guilty she couldn't remember her name.

"Amy." She hadn't managed to slip away. Jeremy Cutler, one of Eric's aides and the girl's father stood up, tapping the chair next to him. "Wanna join us?"

"Love to, but I have to run," she lied. A few pints and a few gates helped paint a peaceful family portrait in New Cal. She'd told Cavana they'd made progress, which was true. She'd neglected to mention the road ahead was far longer than she'd have liked if that girl wasn't going to remain an exception. She recalled the girl's name as she reached the door. "Kiss Jeri for me."

She stepped on the porch, catching her breath. Her headache had gotten worse, boosted by Macky's narrow concerns, Cavana's insightful self-interest, and Jeremy's beer-fueled merriment. They all fit into her bins, a caricature of the real world. She'd been so eager to escape she'd left her beer on the counter. She wasn't about to go back to the din of those idle lives to reclaim it. She stared up, letting the blackness reset her eyes.

"Can't get away from work?"

She lowered her gaze. Mika stood by the door, thin, brown hair spilling down his forehead but not reaching his eyes. He did not fit in any of her bins, which was good. He'd asked her out for drinks twice over the last weeks, but she'd given him excuses. Now she wasn't sure why. "I'll take you up on that drink offer, if it's still good."

He squinted, trying to find context. It didn't take long. He disappeared into the bar and reappeared thirty seconds later, halting her introspection with a bottle of wine and two glasses.

"I'd hoped for something more private," he said as he offered her an empty glass.

He was charming and direct, but she'd seen him take apart a so-called security expert with words. She'd been told he was even more ruthless in hand-to-hand combat. Was the disarming look a front? She used Eric's prism to reassess him. He was still charming though more polished. If Eric's warning had any effect, it nudged her toward Mika. "Let's go."

"Where to?"

"To the water."

His eyebrows lifted in surprise. That would take them to the edge of Cal City, to the edge of the pocket of civilization holed up on this confused peninsula.

"Either that or I'm going home. Alone."

She stared into his eyes as she walked past him, an invitation to follow.

------------------------------------ • ------------------------------------

AGAINST HIS BETTER JUDGMENT, MIKA FOLLOWED AMY INTO the night. She stepped confidently and stopped at the edge of a twenty-foot cliff, near a set of rocks that formed three natural benches or two benches and a table. She sat down and extended her glass. He bit the cork sticking out halfway and poured.

The moon's glow reflected off the low-hanging clouds, lighting her face. She wore a matte, three-quarter-inch, silver, California-shaped pendant. Its edges curved inward as though it were rising up like an island on her chest. She sipped her wine. "I love the beauty of the night. It's the only place I can find peace."

He couldn't remember whether he ever thought the night could be peaceful. Maybe out there on the lonely ocean it could be. But not here on land where he'd lost two friends to the night. One to a flash of violence. The other to the inevitable conclusion of events put in motion that night. She was still there once a year but removed, distant. For someone who'd had only two friends, it had been an expensive night.

His mind drifted to the night that bisected his life. A decade and a half ago, while the surviving towns were still deciding whether to band together or pillage and plunder. Most chose poorly.

As did the three thugs who'd accosted them.

The threats and taunts had taken minutes, but the carnage only lasted seconds. When done, four bodies lay by the rusted lamppost. Three had mattered less to him than the lamppost, but the fourth gaped at him accusingly with half a face.

Biting rain pelted them, drowning out sounds, numbing his touch and dimming his vision as though nature were trying to make the violence seem ethereal. But the blood mixing with rainwater and washing down the drain only made it more real.

He had pulled Lori to her feet. She was in a daze, rubbing her bloody hands against her jacket again and again, but that dirtied her jacket more than cleaned her hands. Shouts rang in the distance. He half-dragged, half-carried her for a block before shaking her, pleading with her to focus. He didn't know what they were going to do, but unless she snapped out of it soon, it wouldn't matter. They'd both be dead by morning.

Two more men had come around the corner while he reasoned with Lori, their shots pinging around them, but at least those triggered Lori's flight instincts, and they'd run, and run, and run. With nowhere safe to go, they'd run in circles for a full year.

So, no, he didn't see peace in the night. He pulled himself out of the dark alleys of his own mind.

Can't change the past. Can't erase it either. Damn it, Amy is right. The night is beautiful, the way a crocodile is beautiful from the other side of the river. He pushed the memories away and let Amy anchor him to the here and now.

"Mika?"

He took her hand. "I'd forgotten." He wasn't sure whether he referred to the newfound beauty in the night or the feelings she had stirred in him in the short months since they'd met.

Amy sipped her wine. "What are you mumbling about?"

"Nothing. You know the paperweight on Eric's desk, the three monkeys?" He covered his eyes, his ears, and his mouth. "That's us. Eric can't see where he's going, you can't hear what he's saying, and I can't speak."

"What can't Eric see?"

He twirled the stainless steel ring on his left middle finger, his right thumb pushing it round and round. His permanently swollen knuckle, the product of one dislocation too many, ensured that the ring stayed put. "That he can't put the world back the way it was."

"He's brought us this far."

"It's the next steps I worry about. We're on a roller coaster, and we need an energetic leader who can inspire, who listens. A leader with new ideas that fit the new reality."

"Yeah, like they grow on trees."

"Not on trees." He opened his arms wide without spilling his wine. "Maybe on cliffs though." He took a sip of wine. "Just so we're clear, I'm not talking about me."

She laughed. "I didn't take you for the naïve kind."

"I've been called a lot of things, but naïve? That's a first."

"You think people used to following a white-haired, sixty-year-old man will listen to me? I'm not even thirty."

"If you scare away the old dinosaurs, they will."

"You have no idea how some mayors talk to me, about me. How they say I got this job."

"Since when do you care what they say?"

She drained her glass and held it for him, and he refilled it. She took a long breath and let it out slowly. She took a sip and smacked her lips. "What is it you can't you speak about, again?"

Her earnestness invited trust, but trust didn't come easily to him. He'd run away from the flash of memory so fast that he'd blurted out things he hadn't intended. "About things I shouldn't know about. About deals and unions."

She pushed her hair behind her ear with a flick of her hand. "Am I the last to know?"

"As far as I know, in New Cal, you're the third."

"What are we talking about?"

Good soldier to the end, she wasn't going to be the one spilling the beans. He had no such qualms. He'd found out on his own. It was his information to share. "Marin's union offer."

She grew serious. "I can hear Eric just fine, but do I like what he's saying? Not so much." He mimicked the monkeys again. "They're wrong, and you know it," she said, but there was no venom in the words.

"That's not the point. Either Marin or Kern is going to win at some point."

"So?"

"We need to pick a side now before the winning side swallows us."

"How does picking Marin now help? We're swallowed either way."

"If you pick the right side now, you can have a voice. They won't chew you as much."

"We come out in bigger pieces from the other end?"

That made him snort. "Okay. Poor analogy."

"The right side is Marin?"

He shrugged.

"It is only if you don't look closely," she said. "Marin is even more dishonest than Kern. They hide behind empty words like order, peace, and safety. They'll bully us into submission."

"Exactly. You don't tackle a charging bull. You make it think it's getting what it wants and nudge it away at the last second. Anything else, and it gores you."

"I always thought Kern was the bull. Marin is the poisonous snake."

"That's harsh. Marin isn't as destructive as Kern."

She shook her head. "Kern is an unstable system. If they impose their insanity on us, how long can they hold on to power? How long before pockets of Uregs slip from under them?" He had nothing to say. She pushed on. "The day Kern wins is the day they lose. They can't even run their own house. How are they going to run everything from Marin to LA?"

"They're not going to run it. They're going to burn it."

"Like I said, unstable. I'll bet you resistance will start immediately. Within five years, all of this area will be free, a new New Cal. Marin is different. They have a method to their madness. It'll take generations to overcome their damage."

He chuckled.

"What?" She frowned.

"We got a gender problem. We're defending the wrong sides."

Amy did not smile, but the frown relaxed. "I'm not defending Kern. I'd wipe the sick bastards out if I could, but I'm not warm and fuzzy about the loonies up north either."

Colorfully put, but she was right. He sipped his wine and stared out to the water. The moonlight reflected where the bay opened to the ocean, tracing a path toward the unknown. Though it looked inviting, it led nowhere, a lot like the deal Marin offered.

His attempt to change the topic had worked too well. When he'd played this scene in his mind, it hadn't started with an argument over politics. He pushed Kern and Marin away.

His eye caught the pendant again. It was unassuming and seductive, just like Amy. He moved his gaze from her chest to her dark eyes. He leaned forward, covering half the distance between them. She grabbed the back of his head and pulled him the rest of the way.

As their lips connected, Kern and Marin melted, whisked away by the swinging pendant.

CHAPTER 5

OLD WAYS

"Well-behaved women seldom make history."
—LAUREL THATCHER ULRICH

Lori scanned the bushes one last time, but the tabby was nowhere to be seen this morning. She wrapped the tuna bowl and put it in the fridge. She no longer had the time to walk, so she hopped in her Humvee and reached the military headquarters' underground parking garage in six minutes.

The guards saluted her as she walked into the elevator. She tapped her tida for authorization, and the double chime indicated she'd been recognized. She pushed the button for the top floor and emerged in front of General Dey's office four minutes ahead of schedule.

Being late signaled you couldn't manage your schedule or that you valued your time more than your host's. General Prami Dey deserved more respect than that. She'd been a lieutenant in the US Air Force and now was Marin's chief commander, Lori's boss. But Dey was also Chancellor Czernak's closest confidant, a de facto vice chancellor. The two had built Marin from a refugee camp to the power it was today. Czernak trusted Dey in a way she didn't trust anyone else.

Which made Dey the perfect mentor. Lori had picked up not only the ins and outs of Marin politics from Dey but also how to deal with petty squabbles and jealous rivals.

Dey spotted her and waved her in. "Come in, come in."

A large metal desk monopolized the square office. Six cardboard boxes were stacked on the wall across from the desk. They'd been there for as long as Lori remembered. Whatever they contained had circled from important enough to be packed to useless.

"General." She sat down in front of Dey's desk.

Dey poured two cups of coffee from the pot sitting on a tray at the edge of her desk and pushed one her way. The rich aroma filled the room and reset Lori's sense of smell still reeling from the tuna. As she put three spoons of sugar in her cup, she could have almost believed she was here for a social call. They were two days away from their weekly status meeting, and Dey hadn't stated why she'd summoned Lori.

"You're pretty tough on your recruits."

Lori took a sip of coffee, inviting the sweet brew to insulate her from Dey's words.

"That's good. They need the discipline, but there's a fine line between training them and burning them out. I was too hard as well until I realized a bitter truth," Dey said.

"Truth?"

"The military of my youth is gone. I was in denial for years, but the truth is we are nothing like the Air Force I served in. At best, we're like the part-timers in the reserves."

Lori held her coffee tight, one hand on the handle, the other around the cup. The heat on her palm became uncomfortable, but she held on.

Dey chuckled. "I took a trip to South Africa a few years before the Purge hit. It was the most expensive vacation I ever took, but it was worth every penny. We went to a game reserve where they still had a few big cats, and just driving in their realm was a spiritual experience. The daily life-and-death struggle every living thing faced there made me feel alive. Little did I know that in a few years, we'd all face the same struggle every day. Anyway, one evening, after the sunset game drive, we were drinking with the rangers around the campfire. One told a joke about two rangers practicing tracking in daytime. They follow the trail of an antelope and stumble on a lioness ambling toward them. One ranger sits down, takes off his boots, and puts on his running shoes. The other laughs at him and asks, 'You think you'll outrun a lion in those?' The sitting ranger laces up, stands up, and points to the bulky boots of his mate. 'Of course not,' he says, 'but it's not the lion I intend to outrun.'"

Lori smiled though she'd heard this one before with a bear and two hikers instead of the lion and rangers. "It's not your Air Force we have to fight," she said.

"Exactly. Kern is a mess. If we're the reserves, they're a poorly run militia. They have numbers, but we are miles ahead of them on discipline and organization."

"Good to know."

"Just take it easy on the recruits. We need them trained, but we also need them." Dey took a sip of her coffee and put her cup on her desk. "Anything new on the mess with Asher?"

Though she'd warned Sierra off, Lori had studied the staff interviews and found not one suspect, not one physical clue. "Nothing worth sharing. The police are handling it."

"Yim doesn't trust the police."

Lori didn't blame Yim, but Yim shouldn't have said such a thing to Dey, and Dey shouldn't have said it to Lori. Council harmony kept Marin running, and open discord hinted at a deeper problem. Lori couldn't shake the feeling that she'd missed something in the Uregs, the hospital, or her read of the council.

"This might be related to the missing soldiers I inquired about."

Dey picked up her coffee and pushed her chair back. She took a sip and held her cup in one hand and the saucer in the other. "Let that simmer for now. I don't want the military to become the referee between the senate and judiciary. Particularly not this week."

"If it's connected—"

"Next week. You can dig next week. This week, we will not create mistrust in Marin or in the council."

"Mistrust?"

"Every time you dig, someone high in Marin starts screaming. We can't afford that this week." She put her saucer on the desk and sipped her coffee. "I didn't call you here for a report on Asher or the training incident."

Lori knew calling people to task wasn't how Dey operated. She gave you latitude to do your job, and if you didn't do it, she found someone who did. As for the "training incident," they'd identified and dismantled the gang involved. But they didn't know who'd hired them or who'd tipped them off that Lori would be in command. The gang leader and his top enforcers had been found dead. The rank and file knew nothing.

Dey took a deep breath. "Czernak wants a joint Marin-New California state."

That Lori could help with. Reserve-like or not, Marin had a proper army, Special Forces, high-end jammers, and real weapons. New Cal had militia and a few twenty-year-old tanks. Not that they'd need military power. "We can infiltrate and take over New Cal in twelve hours."

Dey shook her head. "She means politically."

Lori swallowed the first half a dozen curses that crashed in her head. Chancellor Czernak was half cult hero, half myth, but she was all royalty in Marin. She had collected engineers, doctors, scientists, and business leaders while everyone else was still trying to hold on to a dying world. By not waiting for the corpse of the old world to cool, she'd gotten a head start on rebuilding. Marin was the power it was because of Czernak's singular vision. The woman always looked to the future, but this one Lori didn't see.

"Why?"

"She's the chancellor. She doesn't have to tell us why."

For this she did. "The executive council will never go along with it."

The executive council of five ruled Marin. The chancellor, senate president, military chief commander, and attorney general had permanent seats. The fifth seat rotated among the three branches yearly. In two weeks, it would again be the military's turn to have two seats. The system allowed Czernak to run Marin with the support of only one of the branches as long as she timed her issues well. It also prevented anyone from growing too powerful, as alliances needed to survive the yearly council shuffling.

"Shows how little you know. The council is all bark and no bite. It always bends to Czernak's will." She reached for the pot and refilled her coffee. She stretched over her desk and topped up Lori's as well. "You'll soon find out how all that works."

She would?

"I've nominated you to the council," Dey said.

Lori almost choked on her hot and bitter coffee, taking too big a sip and burning the roof of her mouth. Reality hit a few seconds later. There were a dozen more senior candidates, generals with experience and diplomacy skills. "They'll never confirm me."

Dey smiled. "You wouldn't be here if Czernak didn't approve."

The outgoing executive didn't vote. Neither did the nominating member. That left Yim, Lester, and Czernak. It seemed Lori had Czernak's support somehow. "The others?"

"They will do as they're told. You'll be confirmed in a special session tomorrow."

They were rushing for a reason she could not see. Then another concern hit her. She wasn't the model soldier. In fact, if there were a model, she'd be the mold, the opposite image. "You're here to tell me I need to be a good soldier."

"No. I want you to be you, strong willed and fair."

"But?"

"But keep the fire and brimstone in check. A council debate is not unlike a military engagement. You need reliable intelligence, good instincts, and sound tactics. And you need allies. You can't turn every meeting into a bare-knuckled fight."

Without that fire, she failed to see what she brought to the table. "Why not?"

"First off, it'll teach your opponents all your tricks, but more important, it'll alienate your friends. You need to learn how to lose."

"You sure you want me to learn that?"

"I need you to learn which battles are okay to lose and which ones aren't," Dey said.

That was not a skill needed by the head of Special Forces. Coupled with the unsolicited lesson in soldier training, the conversation veered suspiciously toward one where she was being groomed for a future role. She reached over the sugar bowl and put in a heaping spoon to rebalance her coffee. "You're not retiring, are you?"

"See, you're pretty good at this." Dey smiled. "I'm not going to do this forever, and only half my job is military. The rest is about the relationship with the chancellor and to some extent the council. They need to trust you not in terms of loyalty or competence. You earned that a long time ago, but they need to trust that you are like them and that you share their values."

Lori did not share the values of the council, so either she had to change or the council had to change. She didn't put much stock in either.

"What do I bring to the council?"

"Insight. Reality check. There's too much talk of war, but none of them know what it's like. I want them to hear from someone who has won something and knows the cost."

"On that topic, I'm not going to hold back."

"Just pick your battles. Going all out all the time isn't a strategy. Neither is rolling the dice. It works once or twice, but you're guaranteed to lose in the long run."

That again. She couldn't outrun the shadow of her victory. It was a shame she was viewed as dangerous, unreliable even, just because she'd struck a decisive blow to Kern in a battle where she'd used unconventional tactics. Though the council liked to delude itself, peace between Kern and Marin was not an option, just like peace between lions and their prey. To some, Marin was an antelope, conditioned to avoid the predator to survive, but to Lori, it was a buffalo, capable of killing a lion if pushed.

"I'm not going to apologize for Hollister."

"Don't, but we both know you disobeyed direct orders."

"They were terrible orders."

"I get that. That's why I backed you up. You might get away with disobeying orders once in a career. Beyond that, even being right won't save you."

Lori drained her cup, avoiding the top of her mouth as she swallowed. "Thanks for the advice."

Dey's eyes grew cold. "Colonel, just so we're clear. That wasn't advice."

On the walk back, Lori couldn't find the context to grasp all she'd heard. She'd spent the first half of her life struggling against the crushing weight of fear. Fear of the Purge, fear of violence, fear of starving, fear of watching Mika starve. She'd spent the second half of her life struggling to control the growing force of her rage. Rage against injustice, rage against gangs, and rage against Kern. Neither had prepared her for what she faced now.

Union with New Cal, groomed for chief commander, executive. Each one was life altering. Dey had dumped all three on her in fifteen minutes, which meant she was desperate. The New Cal nonsense must have been dumped on her too. She was reacting, not planning. It was possible that whoever had attacked them in the Uregs had also been reacting, perhaps even to the same information. Players from three states, whoever they were, were moving pieces across a half-hidden chess board.

She'd put Mika in the middle of this clusterfuck.

A big, curious data whisperer, so eager to solve puzzles, he lost sight of why he was solving them. Once Mika pulled on the threads, the threads would pull back at him. There'd be no way to stop him from following the answers no matter where they led. And she suspected these led to deep, dark places that didn't like to be poked.

Fuck.

CHAPTER 6

OLD DECEPTION

"I had seen birth and death but had thought they were different."

–T. S. ELIOT

Mika locked his jeep and walked the last four blocks. The Red Spider was in the Rim, a strip by the northeastern edge of the bay that pretended to be Marin but wasn't. The border connecting it to Marin by Richmond Bridge was patrolled. The Uregs side was a border in name only. It was a place where Marin law applied sporadically and rarely when you needed it.

Two men in black leather jackets watched the entrance. Unusual, but no need to be paranoid. The Red Spider had its idiosyncrasies. Mika headed to the back, avoiding the two men. The door to the alley was unlocked. He pulled it open. A cook was slicing something. Mika took a step in and faced a sixty-gallon, cylindrical trashcan two-thirds full of squeezed-out lime halves. Not the cook but the barkeep then, getting ready for another busy night. A waitress sat by the fridge, taking inventory. She noticed him as he stepped in. "Hey, what are you doing back here?" she asked, alarmed.

The barkeep stopped slicing. His grip on the knife tightened. He had short arms but forty pounds on Mika. The barkeep wouldn't be a threat in the open, but in confined quarters, everyone was.

"I'm here to see Pras."

He had gambled that in Pras' line of work, some discretion was expected. It worked. The waitress stood up and pushed open the plastic door to the bar. The barkeep walked to the back door and locked it. Mika moved at the same time, keeping the large wooden table between them.

The waitress pointed to a table along the back wall of the main room, next to one of the only two uncovered windows.

A woman sat alone, her tight track jacket accentuating her muscular arms. She watched him walk toward her with eyes two sizes too big for her gaunt face.

Mika moved a chair to not have his back to the door connecting him to the barkeep and his knife. In another era, the seat would have had a nice view. Now with three-quarters of the boats either sunk or in different stages of decomposing, it looked over a floating trash yard.

"Do you need a beer, or is it just business?" The waitress still stood there.

The woman at the table didn't let him reply. "He needs a beer."

Of course, there was no point using the place as a cover if you didn't pretend to be there for the drinks. Before dark, with daylight filtering in through different shades, the Red Spider had a split personality. Regulars nursed drinks in the front bar. Three women and two men lounged on sofas, barely dressed, in a recessed room partially hidden by crimson velvet curtains. The back bar was closed, and half a dozen patrons were scattered across the tables, discussing deals that mattered to them but no one else. By nightfall, noise and buzz would provide anonymity but not now.

A dark brew that smelled far too strong an hour before lunch sat in front of the woman. "I'll have a pint of wheat," he said, and the waitress disappeared.

"I'm Pras," the woman said, greeting him with a casual wave, the heel of her hand barely getting off the table. "You better be Mika Bayley."

He waved back. "Mee-ka, not My-ka."

Her exaggerated smirk screamed that she didn't care. "Fine. Mee-ka."

"Thanks," he said as the waitress put his beer on the table.

"So," Pras said, "you want hospital records."

He didn't like surprises, and neither did people like Pras. To provide context, he'd sent an outline of what he needed. "Injuries. Missing patients. Access to hospital files."

She reached into her pocket and put a tida on the table. "How about we cut the bullshit?"

He took a sip. The beer was crisp and full of citrus. He took another sip and waited.

"You're looking for Asher," she said.

"I am."

Pras relaxed and flicked her tida. "The data I gave our mutual friend."

Lori had already shown him that. He was here to recruit Pras, not get her data. "Did you know Asher?"

She shook her head.

"Yim?"

She shook her head again. Secrecy surrounded the missing soldiers, but Asher's case couldn't be hidden. If you wanted to grab injured soldiers without fanfare, going after the stepdaughter of the senate president was a stupid move.

"I received access to Marin for three days," he said. It was the most interesting part of his job so far.

Pras smiled, displaying two oversized front teeth. "That's riveting. Not sure either you or Marin will recover."

"Limited to hospital grounds and under escort."

"Why are you here?" Her nod conveyed more contempt than inquiry.

He was there because information was useless unless accompanied by insight, and he didn't have any way of getting insight. "Here's the thing. I poke anything that looks odd until I find something relevant. But I don't know what odd even means in Marin. Where do I start poking?"

"You will be what's odd," she said. "Stick out like a sore thumb."

"Exactly, so how about while they point and stare at Yim's silly investigator, you get the job done?"

She leaned forward, elbows on the table. "What are you asking?"

"Help me get the real hospital records, what's hidden from even the military."

"Why would I do that?"

He tapped his tida and flicked it to her. "Half of what I've been offered."

It took less than a second for her tiered intelligent digital assistant to synchronize with his. Tidas operated on three levels. The lowest level handled all networking and operational issues. The middle layer was the real assistant, acting as an agent of the owner. Its function was that of a concierge, its ability not based on what it knew but on how to get the information it didn't have. The highest layer was where sniffers lived. Having exchanged information with his, Pras' tida displayed his offer. Her brow furrowed. "Since you don't know shit about Marin and I'd do all the work, why would I take half of what I should have received to find Asher?"

Good, Pras was upset at losing the job. Had her objection been ideological, they'd have hit an impasse, but a jilted competitor he could handle. She was now one step away from a jilted partner and another step from a helpful one. "That's not the right question."

"What's the right question?"

"Why would our mutual friend need either of us for anything in Marin or anywhere?"

Pras scowled. Lori's reputation was a wheel chock to pointless bickering.

"How about it? While I distract them, you get in, get the data, and get out."

Pras smiled again. She really had to stop doing that. "I might be convinced."

"Great," he said and threw a set of questions at her. Yim's office had sent the official police records. What he needed was what hadn't made the official records or had been there and got removed or anything that might embarrass Yim: drugs, fights, bribes, or insubordination.

"If your goal is to embarrass Yim or Marin, you got the wrong partner. I'm not a Marin citizen, because life's too boring there, but I won't help you smear them."

He'd thought Pras would know how this worked. She probably did but didn't trust him. He glanced at the boats. Most were in a shameful state. "We can learn a lot from boats. Every day they don't sink is a victory, but the ocean doesn't relent. It's probing every second, looking for a way in. A few years back, I helped an old man work on boats. Three months in, I found out no one was paying him. He did it because a sinking boat was a dead boat. He had seen enough death, so he was fixing the world one boat at a time. I learned a lot about boats, about life, and about myself, including the value of trust, the value of work, and the value of focusing on detail."

He pointed to the docks. "See these boats? What do you think distinguishes them? The one with the blue dodger from the one next to it?" One floated, and the other was just a mast sticking out at an angle. "It's the little things. Were the seacocks bonded? Were the through-hulls reinforced? Was the correctly rated sealant used? You could screw all that up, and the boat could still float for a couple of years but not more. Get all that right, and it might still be here in another decade."

Pras' frown deepened. "Can we get back to Asher?"

"I don't know why Yim didn't hire you. She probably should have, but before I take a job, I need to know why I'm the one they want. Usually, it's because I'm recommended, and I'm recommended because I'm good, and I'm good because I focus on detail. That's the only way to understand the angle and find a solution. Right now, I don't understand the angle."

"An injured soldier goes missing, and you're looking for an angle?"

Mika took another sip of beer. "Why go after Asher? They had to know Yim wouldn't let it drop. Why shine a light on something that had remained buried for months? What does Yim know so that she can't trust her own police?"

Finally, Pras nodded. "While you're distracting them, what am I looking for in the records?"

"I'll be looking for injured, missing soldiers. Asher's background. That's what they'll expect. You will look for any file that's been modified, treatment that's unexpected, transferred patients or soldiers. Look for a bigger canvas. We need to find their angle." He was asking for a lot, but when you needed to find a needle in a haystack, the first step was getting all the hay.

"What do you think we'll find that the Special Forces and police missed?"

"Do they know where Asher is?"

"Obviously not."

"Then obviously they've missed something."

He didn't mind being a trifle annoying. Partners usually were, but he didn't want to piss her off and push her away. He had hit the right balance.

She smiled as though in another universe they'd been in on the same joke. The smile disappeared as her eyes moved to the bar. He followed her gaze. One of the men watching the entrance had walked in. He sat twenty feet away at the closed bar.

Pras tapped her tida, but Mika didn't see whom she'd contacted. She got up. "This is a private area," she told the newcomer.

The man pushed his stool back and stood up, pointing a gun at her. "If you think—"

Three shots to the chest stopped him midsentence. The man collapsed. The barkeep stood in front of the kitchen door. An assault rifle had replaced the lime-slicing knife.

Seconds of silence followed while patrons weighed whether

this was a Red Spider moment or something serious. When they concluded it was a deal gone bad, they returned to their business or their pleasure.

"In the back," Pras said.

The barkeep grabbed the collapsed man's ankles and dragged him to the kitchen. Pras knelt down and checked the man's pockets, finding nothing.

"Was he after you or me?" she asked Mika.

"You," he said with more confidence than he felt.

"We need to find out who the fuck he was and what the fuck he wanted."

"That's usually easier if he's not dead."

Pras' scowl told him that she wasn't in the mood for banter.

"What the devil is going on here?" someone yelled from the main bar. Mika pushed the kitchen door open. Pras was behind him. The second leather-jacketed man walked toward the velvet-curtained room, shouting, "What kind of ratfaced fuck works in this joint?"

Pras took a step forward, but the barkeep pushed her aside, extended his gun-toting arm, and walked toward the man. "If you're not out in three seconds, I'll mow you down."

The man didn't move.

"Two. One."

The man turned and fled. The barkeep chased after him, not to catch him but to make sure he got out and that no more client-upsetting shots needed to be fired.

Pras shook her head and headed back to the kitchen. "What the fuck?" she gasped.

Mika took two quick steps to reach her. Pras' eyes were glued to the floor, as were his, to the spot that had contained a body a minute ago. The spot that was now empty. A wide, bloody smear headed toward the door. It thinned out outside and was replaced with bloody footprints that disappeared around the block. There were no footprints in or around the blood smear in the kitchen.

"You need to lock that damn door," Pras said to the out-of-breath barkeep who'd walked back in.

Mika's eyes stayed on the door, the one the barkeep had locked, the one with the bloody handprints going up. Mika pointed to the blood-stained deadbolt and handle.

"Huh," Pras said. "That's weird."

CHAPTER 7

DISCOVERY

"I need to listen well so that I hear what is not said."

—THULI MADONSELA

B y his third day in Marin, Mika had learned to ignore the stares. Though he had managed to offend Executive Yim with his directness, he had received limited access to Marin records. It was enough to distract their watchers while Pras did the real job.

He took to walking on the hospital grounds, not because he had any place to go but because he could. The more he walked, the less he believed Kern or New Cal operatives could have abducted Asher. The looks he received, the too-polite receptionist, the too-aloof doctor, and the too-hostile soldier all pointed at the differences in their social interactions. It was different enough to expose his alienness to this world.

He'd been racking his brain on how he could have penetrated deep into Marin, eluded guards at multiple checkpoints, and fooled the hospital staff to reach Asher's room, and he came up with nothing. He never even bothered to figure out how he'd have gotten out.

He also pushed to see how far his access extended. Asher's case was not unique. Over the last year, three soldiers had vanished after multiple injuries. Two had stage 4 cancer.

He peeked out of the nurse's break room that had become his office. Four folding chairs stood guard around the laminate-topped round table that doubled as his desk. No one entered the room when he was in it, but someone had to at other times, because the food in the fridge was dwindling. Flint, his minder, sat just outside the door to his right. He couldn't think of a conversation starter that wouldn't sound contrived.

"Is Flint your first name or last name?"

He received a silent glare as answer.

"I have another hour's worth of work." He pointed to the more comfortable chairs in his room. "You can monitor me directly."

She snickered. "You're a strange one, Bayley."

"I've been called worse."

Another forty minutes, and Mika was done. He waved the screen off and packed slowly, giving Flint time to speak.

"What are you after, Bayley?"

He put his backpack on the table. "I figured it was obvious."

"No, I mean what are you really after? 'Cause you got all the data about Asher long ago."

"Did I?"

"Seriously? You know when and where Asher got hurt, how long it took to get her here, and who operated on her. You know what she ate and where she walked. You checked every doctor and nurse who works here, every patient, every food and medical truck that got in or out."

"Your point?"

"You're still digging. None of this is related to her."

"How do you know that?"

"Cancer? Really?"

"You know for sure Asher didn't have cancer."

"Fine," she said. "I don't care as long as you're out of here."

"No, really. Do you know for a fact she didn't have cancer?"

"I know she didn't have a brain tumor, pancreatic cancer, or a bad heart."

"No, but she did have a nasty bout of croup when she was three. It almost killed her." She didn't seem to grasp the implications. He wasn't sure he did either. "I don't know what I'm after, so I follow up on whatever looks odd, and it would be a lot easier if the files I request weren't prescreened."

"Prescreened?"

"Come on, Flint, stop taking me for an idiot. It takes several seconds too long for every query I start. These systems can't be that slow. It's annoying, and it slows me down."

"The three-second delay slows you down?"

"The four irrelevant searches I start for everyone I need slow me down."

She shook her head, part disapproval, part amusement. "You're good at what you do, right? Let's assume you are. How would you have done it?"

Flint didn't believe there was foul play in Asher's disappearance. She probably figured he was indulging Yim and taking her money. "I don't think I could have."

"She was burned out, and she needed out. I'm guessing she doesn't want to be found."

"Possible, but how would you have done it?"

"Are you accusing me now?"

"No more than you were accusing me, but you could have?"

They both knew the answer to that. "In this fantasy of yours, why would I want to do it?"

"That, I have no idea. Those with motive don't have the means, and those with means don't have a motive."

She smiled for the first time. "You're a lousy detective."

He didn't return the smile, as it hit too close to home. "Did you know her?"

"Is this part of your interview?"

"It's a simple question."

"A little."

"What was she like?"

She hesitated but only for a second. "Kept to herself. Nothing stood out."

"Did she have many friends?"

"I don't know. Sometimes she ate alone, sometimes with others."

"Anything else? Was she angry? Scared?"

Flint shook her head.

"Any enemies?"

"Not that I know. It's not like she was around long enough to get into trouble."

"What do you mean?"

"You read her file. Black belt, Special Forces. Always running somewhere. Just when was she going to make enemies?" He didn't reply, so she continued. "I'd check her Uregs gig."

"Uregs gig?"

She smirked. "If you haven't found out about the orphanage, you're really bad at this."

He had. The obvious conclusion pointing at a dead end in Marin was there for all to see, which meant he was not looking in the right places, and he was glad he wasn't the only one who saw a pattern that didn't fit. "Thanks for the chat. Believe it or not, you are the first person I've met in two days who was neither afraid nor offended to have to talk to me."

———————————————

MIKA'S THREE DAYS WERE UP, AND HE HAD LITTLE TO SHOW. HE hoped Pras had more. He'd requested an extension, not because he had a lead but to gauge the reaction. He was surprised to see Ann Lester, Marin's attorney general, walk into the interview room.

"Executive Lester. I was not expecting you."

Her lips curled up. It might have been a smile. "I had a break in my schedule."

That was a transparent lie, but that was the difference between his line of work and Lester's. Her lies did not need to be believable. They just needed to sound official.

"Why did you need to see me, Madam Executive?"

"It was you who needed my signature."

"I needed a signature, but my requests are three levels below your branch, so I'm guessing you wanted to see me for something else."

Her smile warmed a tenth of a degree. "I was right picking you. I need you to do something for me. Off the record."

First Yim, and now Lester. He was getting a lot of business from the Marin council. He chuckled at what Eric would think of his getting paid by two Marin executives but decided he probably wouldn't see the humor in it. "I'm listening."

Lester activated a privacy sniffer. It broadcast their conversation in billions of coded superimposed segments, like writing over and over the same letter. They were effectively shielded. "First, I need you to stop your search for Asher. You just wasted three days of a dozen staffers in the hospital and police. If she can be found, my people will find her."

"Now wait—"

"Let me finish. I understand you owe Executive Yim a reply. Tell her she ran away, that she does not want to be found."

"Is that all?"

"No, that is a simple request. I will double what she pays you to make it all go away."

"I'll think about it," he said though he had no intention of doing so. He'd been ready to dismiss Lori's conspiracy concerns, but she'd been right as always.

"More important, I want you to investigate something for me." She pulled the middle drawer of her desk, took a tida, and slid it between them. Three faces floated up when she tapped it. "These men were seen in the Red Spider. Are you familiar with the place?"

He nodded and pointed at the faces. "Who are they?"

"Kern operatives. I want to know what they are after."

"Aren't Marin agents watching them?"

"They are." She hesitated as though she debated divulging a secret. It felt rehearsed. "Then again, I'm not sure who watches my agents. I want you to keep tabs on them too."

This was getting out of hand. However, it opened a wider

window into Marin. He couldn't pass it up. "No and yes. I won't lie to Executive Yim, but I'll watch these people for you."

"Suit yourself. You are throwing away easy money, but that is fine. I will approve your request but only to follow the agents in and out of the Red Spider. No more hospitals. Clear?"

Pushing would serve no purpose. People like Lester didn't change their minds. He was done with the hospital anyway. What he needed were contacts within the military. He could go after those just as well while shadowing the agents. "Very well. Anything else?"

She shook her head. As he moved to the door, Lester raised a hand. She spoke in a lower voice. "There is a war coming, Mr. Bayley. Choose your allies carefully."

He couldn't tell whether it was a threat or a warning. He leaned toward warning. However, seeing what you wanted to see was a dangerous proposition. It was always what you didn't see that got you, and right now, only one thing was clear.

There was a lot to Ann Lester he didn't see.

<hr />

HE DROVE TO THE ORPHANAGE ON THE RIM. ASHER HAD SPENT more time there than her profile suggested. A smoking man in a black leather jacket sat on the sidewalk across the street. It was the same style of jacket worn by the men at the Red Spider. Mika cataloged the face and stepped into the orphanage. A half-wall separated a rectangular mat from the door. In the back, stairs climbed up toward the dormitories. The walls were barren except for two cityscape pictures and a motivational slogan: *The harder you work, the luckier you get.*

Sometimes you did, and sometimes you didn't.

A dozen barefooted kids tried to mimic the moves the instructor demonstrated on the mat. She wore the traditional gi and hakama more for show than authority. She showed simple throws, and some kids got into it. Still, it was at best organized chaos. None of the kids was good enough to let her put weight into the throws. He stood by the mat until he got the instructor's attention. "I can take some falls."

She studied him for a few seconds and pointed to the mat. He took his jacket and shoes off and walked on the mat. She tapped her left wrist, and he went for a grab. She avoided his reach, grabbed his arm and nudged him forward. It was a cautious throw. He took a roll and got up. Seeing his confident roll, she put a snap of hips into the second throw. He flew, slapping the mat hard as he landed. The students gasped and hollered. After two more, she turned to the students. "Okay, your turn." The students paired up to try the moves.

She walked to him. "I'm Jen. Who might you be?"

"Mika."

"What brings you here?" Before he could answer, she was gone. "No, Lucas. Slow down." She reached for a boy's hand and corrected his hold. In an instant, she was halfway across the room, trapped in a chain reaction of bad holds and worse throws.

His attention shifted to a skinny girl, at most twelve. She stood in the back, not paired with anyone. She had a black eye. He approached her. "What's your name?"

She didn't reply.

He went down to his knees and put his hand on her forearm. She jerked back, trying to pull away, the opposite of what she had to do. He steadied her forearm. "Slow."

She tried the move but only used her arms. She couldn't have nudged, much less thrown, anyone over fifty pounds. He pushed himself up and over, landing on his back after a full spin.

She smiled, more surprised than proud. He got up and faced her. "What's your name?"

"Pit."

He did not hide his surprise. "Pete?"

"Pit," she said. "I'm small and tough."

He grinned. "You are, but let's make you a little tougher."

She nodded, teeth clenched with a seriousness that did not belong on such a young face.

"Okay, Pit. Let's do it again."

He corrected her mechanics, and she tried it a few more times with Mika propelling himself up and over each time. All the kids had stopped and were watching them as was Jen.

Jen clapped twice. "That's enough for today." The kids ran to the back door. So much for discipline. She approached him. "You never told me what you wanted."

He decided to not play games. "I'm looking for Eva Asher."

Her expression hardened, so he wasn't the first to ask. "What do you want with her?"

"I was hired by her family."

"I don't appreciate you coming here and using these kids to get at me."

It wasn't a fair accusation, but he decided not to push back. Any attempt at explaining his approach would push them further down the wrong path. "My apologies, but I thought it was harmless and maybe a little helpful."

She lifted her right arm, stood for a second, and swung, the blade of her hand coming down at his face. He didn't move. Her hand stopped an inch in front of his nose. She finally smiled. "Wait here." She disappeared behind a curtain and reemerged three minutes later, out of her gi and wearing loose pants and a light jacket. "Follow me," she said and walked out the door.

He stepped on the sidewalk and scanned the block. It was empty, the smoking man gone. He caught up to Jen. "Where are we going?"

She didn't reply, just kept a fast pace. They walked three blocks before she spoke again. "You want to know how well I knew Eva?" She stopped in front of a four-story building, unlocked the gate and climbed two flights of stairs. She pushed open the door and pointed to the back of the hallway. "That was her room."

There were two doors to the right of the hallway. One led to a bathroom, the other to a second bedroom. He walked toward Asher's room. The door was ajar.

"How often did she stay here?"

Jen winced. "She lived here."

He had not seen that one coming. Asher, the daughter of Yim's partner, lived in the Rim. Her apartment in Marin had been clean, empty. Sterile. He had assumed it had been scrubbed by the security detail. It had been a cover, an address Asher used to keep up appearances.

"Mind if I look around?"

She moved her hand up, pointing in.

He pushed the door open and stepped into the small, square room. A narrow bed occupied one corner with a dark-blue cover spread over it. He sat at the desk in the opposite corner and thumbed through the pile of junk Asher had accumulated. The signed certificate of her black belt rested at the edge of the desk, propped up against the wall.

He opened her closet to find three pairs of pants, navy, gray, and black T-shirts, and two jackets. One was the turtleneck she wore in the picture he had seen that first day. Her gi sat on top of the bag at the bottom of the closet, while her hakama, neatly folded, lay on an open shelf above the bag. Her black belt hung from a hook inside the closet.

Jen watched him from the doorway. He rummaged through the few items on display. On top of the dresser, a rumpled shirt covered a picture frame. He nudged the shirt to find an image of them, with Jen's arms around Asher's neck, laughing.

"Friend?" There seemed to be more to their relationship.

She shrugged. "Eva is hard to claim or pin down."

That was apparent. He told her what he knew, which wasn't much. She knew even less.

"What is it you're after?"

He was after anything including trouble and friends. "Attitude?"

"Attitude. That's a good one. She first came here when she was fifteen. For three years, she wasted her time. The orphanage ranked somewhere between brushing her teeth and recess for her. She'd come every day for a few weeks, then disappear for weeks. She was more distracted than the kids she was teaching, and you saw the kids. Don't get me started on her own training. No discipline, no focus. I was about to give up on her. Then she got shot in the Uregs. She didn't talk about it, but she came in, shoulder in a sling, longing in her eyes. She looked at the mat like she'd lost something she valued. We weren't even sure she'd be able to train again, but her shoulder healed better than expected, and she dedicated herself to learning and teaching. She was here every day, teaching, training."

Getting shot did that to some. It didn't make Asher an exception. Yet. "Trouble?"

"Not really, but after she got shot, she was more paranoid. Said she was followed."

"Why did she think that?"

Jen reached for her tida and projected images and short clips. A woman with short, straight black hair floated up, watching, looking bored. She walked with the practiced casualness of someone trying to blend in, someone trained for combat. She seemed familiar, like he'd seen her before, but he couldn't place her.

"Eva saw her everywhere. I saw her a few places, so I don't think it was all in her head."

He pointed the images to his own tida and moved on. "Friends?"

A smile returned to Jen's face. "Just a week ago, some drunk assholes harassed a few of the kids. Eva stepped out to put a stop to it and got into a scuffle. Little Pit flew out of the dojo to take on a six-foot guy. All she did was get a black eye in the process. When Eva saw that, she went from trying to pacify the bullies to beating the shit out of them. I had to run out to stop her. Yes, she had friends. Everyone in this orphanage is her friend and her family."

Just like that, Asher—Eva—had become real. Up to now, she'd cut a two-dimensional figure, a ghost drifting in someone else's world. Yim didn't know her own daughter. Pras saw a case, not a person. Her fellow soldiers had shared only the same time and space with her. And the nurses had never observed the vibrant Eva. Her essence had eluded them all. It was here that Eva had connected with the living. She had needed both the freedom to explore and the structure to shape that exploration. The orphanage had given her purpose, and she had given back.

"Where would she go if she had run away?"

A sad smile stretched across Jen's face. "I'd like to think she would have come here."

He saw that. The "Eva ran away" hypothesis was broken now. It made sense only if she had run here. In Marin, they believed it, because they suspected her double life and assumed she'd returned to it. He could see her running away from that life but not from this one. His gaze moved to the door and scanned the corridor.

She must have guessed his thoughts. Tears welled in her eyes. "She didn't."

The perfectly folded hakama, Pit's black eye, this unlikely slice of domestic life, the mysterious tail all pointed to the conclusion he'd been ready to ditch. Despite his inability to figure out how it might have happened, Eva Asher had not left that hospital of her own accord.

FLINT'S ASSUMPTIONS, LESTER'S INTEREST, JEN'S REVELATION all tugged him in different directions. Pras had dug up data that expanded beyond soldiers, linking to unexpected cancer survivors in Marin and the Uregs but mostly deleted files in interesting cases. Marin hiding the fate of its soldiers Mika could believe, but why would anyone delete data from Uregs clinics?

Instead of obsessing, Mika went for a run. Six miles in forty-five minutes. He didn't run fast, but he could run for hours at that pace, and some days he did just to clear his head. When he focused too hard, the big picture disappeared, like squinting hard at an inkblot. You had to let go and free your eyes to see. Running gave him that freedom. This evening, he reached the conclusion that he needed help.

It had been six months since he'd last seen Kevin Jezek but longer since they'd had a real conversation. Protecting data was the advertised component of Kevin's enterprise. As the best of the hounds, breaking codes and stealing data were his specialty.

Mika walked into the narrow courtyard bracketed by metal gates at both ends. A bench sat tucked just inside the roof overhang with a camera mounted above it. The inner gate was locked, and there was no light to betray the occupant's whereabouts. As he grabbed it, the metal handle's chill transported him to their first meeting. He'd walked into a courtyard almost exactly like this thirteen years ago and had waited an hour for Kevin to let him in.

"Mika Bayley," he had said and waved in greeting as the gate had parted.

Kevin Jezek hadn't waved back. His spindly limbs swam in an ensemble of black mock turtleneck, black jeans, and square-toed, black harness boots. His small eyes and straight, black hair held in a loose ponytail completed the surly package. "Who did you say told you I'd help?"

"It's a bit indirect."

"It always is, isn't it?" Kevin let go of the gate and walked into the square office. A hip-high, built-in cabinet ran the length of the right wall, with three gray, plastic chairs scattered in the middle of the room. A closed door to the left hid the rest of the office. Two metal-framed desks formed an L to create a private area past the door, with a mesh chair behind them.

Mika stepped in and closed the door. "Tom Canter said I could trust you."

"He never mentioned you." The voice was cold, but Kevin did not seem threatened.

A cluttered mess of screens and tidas and books—heavy paper-and-print ones—covered every horizontal surface. Mika picked one up from the top of the built-in cabinet. *The Stranger.*

"This ain't a library."

He put the book back. "I need IDs, two."

"What level?"

"Good enough for checkpoints."

"That means fooling Kern sniffers. It'll cost you." Kevin scratched his head. "I think I've seen you before." He moved behind his L-shaped desk and flicked his wrist, scrolling through a few pages on his screen. "There." He spun the square screen Mika's way. It was an arrest warrant for him and Lori. "Price just went up."

"I can't pay you what these IDs are worth."

Kevin glared at him. "Then why the fuck are you here?"

"I need the IDs."

"I don't do payment plans, and even if I did, I wouldn't for you." He jerked a thumb to his screen. "This says you're not going to be alive long enough to make even one payment."

"Wanna bet?"

Kevin snorted as he read the warrant and then whistled. "Says you killed three Kern soldiers, more hardcore than the usual bullshit. They must want you bad. What'd you do?"

"They were thugs, but yeah, it's pretty much spot on."

"Fuck me. You have any idea how much work this is going to take?"

"What?"

"Erasing your presence here, your arrival, and your imminent departure."

"Must be a real burden to have such fulfilling work."

"You're funny for a dead guy. How do you know I didn't call to collect your bounty?"

For an uncomfortable second, he considered it. "You know damn well they'll shoot us both if they get here. You're contaminated now."

"IDs for Tom's two killer friends." He put his hands on his head. "He owes me big."

"He doesn't owe you shit."

"How do you figure that?"

"He's dead."

Kevin stiffened. "You've left a lot of corpses in your wake. Any others I should know about?"

"No, and the dead soldiers are the ones who killed Tom."

Kevin swiped at his screens. They were positioned to prevent customers from peeking, so Mika settled for studying Kevin's almost-impressed face.

"Tom was a good guy. I don't need to know what happened. And I know what Kern fuckheads are like. If you tell me they had it coming, I believe you."

"Do we have a deal?"

Kevin laughed. "A deal? You haven't offered me anything."

"Here is what I have." Mika put a tida on the table. It was a flat, glass-and-metal, rectangular box instead of the ubiquitous computational-glass cylinder.

Kevin tapped it, and a keyboard appeared. "What, you're paying me with antiques?"

"It's been a rough couple of days." Mika keyed in his code, and a number floated up. It was about a quarter what two IDs were worth, but he hoped to bargain his way into getting a new ID for Lori.

Kevin studied the tida for a few more seconds and nudged it back with two fingers. "You keep it. No one should use tidas older than they are." He dug a tida from his drawer and pushed it to Mika. "It will link to you after the first tap. It's got a couple of basic sniffers. They'll pick up most news and let you listen to some chatter on the secure channels." He tapped another screen and pointed to the tida. "A sniffer for so-called locks. Strictly small time. Stores, houses, offices. It'll wipe itself out if it encounters resistance, so if you want it to last, don't go spying on Kern central or robbing banks."

Mika stared at it. "Why?"

"I owed Tom a few favors. Go read that book. Doing this right is going to take time."

A loud *click* from the gate brought Mika back to the present.

"How is Crazy Eric?" Kevin asked as Mika plopped down on the leather chair across from Kevin's desks. The room was longer than Kevin's earlier digs. The L-shaped desk had been replaced by two desks that bisected the room, leaving barely enough space between them for Kevin to get in and out. Two eight-foot tall metal cabinets lined the wall to his right.

Mika chuckled. "Still calling him that?"

"That fuckhead is going to get you all killed, you know." Kevin had always stated that New Cal was a monument to Eric's insanity. It survived in the penumbra of Marin, not openly allied with Marin but protected by proximity. Crazy was one way to describe a state that enjoyed protection without paying for it. Brilliant was another.

"You said this before. We're all still here."

"That's like saying Russian roulette won't kill you after surviving three rounds."

Mika had no reply to that. He moved to the narrow fridge wedged between the cabinets and opened it to grab two bottles of beer. He tossed one to Kevin and opened his.

"You know, only you could do this."

Mika stood, waiting.

"For fuck's sake! I haven't seen you in sodding forever, a war's brewing, shit's blowing up all over the Uregs, and you show up, grab a beer, and act as if we'd chatted last night."

Bracing for the punch line, Mika put his beer on Kevin's desk. "Your point?"

"No point." Kevin smiled. "It was a compliment. I'm glad you stopped by, and I'm glad you can pretend the world around us doesn't exist. Fuck knows we need a few reminders life used to be normal." He opened and sipped his beer. "At least more normal than this. I wish I understood how you do it."

Mika didn't know how he did it since he didn't think that way. He moved from crisis to crisis as they shaped his reality and claimed as many moments in between as he could. He grabbed his beer and sat back down. He took a sip from the refreshing but flavorless brew. Kevin liked his beers light, but he kept them chilled enough for it to not matter.

"I need help to find her." Mika pushed Eva's image between them. He swiped his tida to the woman who'd been following Eva. "This one is likely to know where she is."

Kevin's eyes moved from Eva to the stranger and back to Mika. "I'll look into it."

That meant a deep scan that would reveal anything that left a trace. That was more than good enough. "Thanks." Mika smiled. "What drives business these days?"

Kevin shrugged. "Same as always, you know: weapons, drugs, sniffers, lovers."

"Really? As many people want weapons as lovers?"

Kevin laughed and then grew serious. "Seems everyone wants scramjets."

Of course they did. Speed was the new stealth. The old cruise missiles had become mostly useless. At 600 to 900 mph, even the half hour they took to get where they were going was an eternity. Scramjets reached Mach 9 a few seconds after deployment. You didn't need to hide your punch, just punch fast enough so the other guy couldn't duck.

"Weren't they all used up in the last war?"

Kevin shook his head. "A baker's dozen survived. Marin has six of them. Five are somewhere in the Uregs. If Kern gets their hands on them, Marin's deterrent is gone."

Mika followed the math. "Six for Marin, five buried in the Uregs. I'm missing two."

"So am I. Two scrammies appear and disappear from records. Kern doesn't have them, and Marin doesn't have them."

"New Cal doesn't have them since Eric won't do weapons." Mika smirked.

"I wouldn't be so sure," Kevin said with a hint of a warning in his voice.

"Seriously?"

"New Cal doesn't have them, but I wouldn't be so sure Eric doesn't believe in weapons." Mika raised an eyebrow, and Kevin relented. "I got inquiries about scrammies from New Cal through intermediaries, of course, but I did trace the attempts to the governor's office."

"Who?"

"Chipps."

Either Mika had misread Eric for years or Amy had taken the initiative. He'd have to figure out which and do it quickly. Kevin had shared valuable info, so it was only fair to reciprocate. The biological weapons Mika had found last month had almost become a footnote. "The missing scrammies are a problem because someone needs a delivery mechanism for AHtX."

Kevin's eyes went wide. "AHtX," he said, rhyming it with *latex*. "What the fuck?"

"A new strain, atomized, lighter than air so it floats. It clumps together after a day and comes down."

"Fuck me!"

"The only good news is that it's got a short life span, and it's not contagious. You need to come in contact with the initial spores."

"Not sure I'd use the words *good news* in a sentence with biological weapons, but I see your point." Kevin frowned. "That just makes the bad news worse."

"What bad news?"

Kevin took a large gulp of his beer and put it down. "We're going extinct."

They'd been going extinct for twenty-five years since the comet fragments had crashed near Tromso and dropped the Purge. In theory, extraterrestrial DNA should not have interfered with human DNA. In practice, it had. No one left cared to argue how that had been possible.

"Birth rates are down," Kevin said.

Mika knew that. Everyone knew that. They lived in dangerous, stressful times. Who in their right fucking mind would bring children into this mess? "That's not exactly news."

"Fertility rates are down. Miscarriages are up. Amenorrhea cases are up."

"What's that?"

"No menstruation."

"Why now?"

"It's been getting steadily worse, but we've been too busy making excuses. Nutrition affects menstruation. Heavy exercise affects menstruation. Stress affects pregnancy. Each case can be explained, so it was all chalked up to our screwed-up world."

"That's not it?"

"Nope. If you correct for all that, it's still all subtly going wrong."

That did make it interesting, because most things were going wrong without much subtlety. "Can it be Kern?"

Kevin pressed his lips tight. "You know, you sound just like Lori."

"Leave her out of this."

"Just saying. Sneeze, and it's Kern with her. I get it. She hates the fuckheads and wants to wipe them out, but they're not the only ones out there gunning for us."

Mika rolled his bottle between his palms.

Kevin shrugged. "Whatever, but it's not them this time. They have the same problem, and so does everyone else."

Right. Besides, Kern had never been accused of being too subtle. Down south, they'd galloped back to the sixteenth century, preaching a rigid patriarchy where women had little value other than bearing children. Those trying to escape received public and savage punishment.

In the unregulated territories, mixed populations survived. Most Uregs enclaves lived off the land and made deals with the Kern Republic on quotas and taxes, which didn't always consist of livestock and grain and fruit.

New Cal pretended to live thirty years in the past, as though the Purge had never happened, as though the wars and Kern's rampages were just collective nightmares. Marin, though strictly matriarchal, encouraged teams to venture out at regular intervals. Mika assumed it worked, because men were not picky about when and with whom they exchanged bodily fluids. But if despite the vastly different approaches all four failed at basic reproduction, the culprit had to be biology, not politics. Biology. The dots started connecting: strange recoveries, strange disappearances, and now strange drops in birth rates. No way this was a coincidence.

They'd moved from Eva to scrammies to AHtX to dropping birth rates in a whirlwind that made him dizzy. He felt like a skipping stone, touching down and flying away without grasping any meaning along the way. But it ended only one way for the skipping stone: motionless at the bottom of the sea.

He sipped his beer and tried to view the skipping stone from the seabed's perspective. How did all these sudden disturbances connect? The missing cancer patients and injured soldiers had one thing in common. They were on their deathbeds. An absurd idea popped up, but absurd was all he had. "Kev, have you seen anyone die of illness?"

"Yeah." Kevin snorted. "You know, just about everyone."

"I mean recently." Mika kept his serious eyes on Kevin.

Kevin scratched his head. "Not that I can think of."

"People are healthier than they ought to be."

"So? Those who survived the Purge were on the healthy end of the spectrum."

"What if there was more? Healing fast. Dying less."

Kevin shook his head. "What evidence is there for such crazy shit?"

Mika took his tida out of his pocket. "Data from Marin, Uregs, and New Cal."

Kevin took the tida and waved it by his screen. Numbers and charts appeared. He swiped through a few pages. "What am I looking at?"

"Cancer data, cross-referenced to injury data." Mika pointed to the screen. "Watch the number of deaths, corrected for sloppy recording. They're going down."

Kevin frowned, studying the data. "How does getting shot help with cancer?"

That Mika didn't know, but someone had gone to a lot of trouble to hide the connection.

"How did you get this?"

Mika told him about the innocuous searches he'd started and how Pras had corrupted Marin's monitoring of Mika's searches to access the hidden medical records.

"That's clever. Pras ain't bad for an amateur," Kevin said, which was high praise coming from him. His usual descriptors for hounds ranged from dimwit to incompetent with a lot of colorful terms but not much range. That he approved of Pras and their methods made Mika feel much better about their data. "Wait, wait, wait," he said, pulling up a few charts, overlaying the death and birth rates. There were a few pockets where birth rates were not dropping as fast. Those were the areas with the fewest strange hospital recoveries, the fewest erased files. "Fuck me!"

"The same thing is causing both?"

Kevin nodded. Another mystery. Mika was collecting them like beads now. At least he'd also collected an ally, one whose skills in the sniffer world were without equal. And Kevin's thought-provoking statement may have been wrong, because under one scenario, dropping birth rates didn't lead to extinction.

A scenario in which people stopped dying.

CHAPTER 8

OLD LESSONS

"Any fool can tell the truth, but it requires a man of some sense to know how to lie well."

– SAMUEL BUTLER

A my grabbed her glass and leaned back on her chair, enjoying the privacy Mika's dining room provided. She'd been warned by a colleague at the capitol that Mika couldn't boil an egg, but he'd seared the tuna just right, leaving a pink core. She'd have sacrificed food quality to avoid being in the public eye, but she hadn't had to.

For five days, she'd navigated the ever-changing sea of legal nonsense that would bind them to Marin. She'd coped with mayors, council members, and dozens of staffers on both sides, each triggering her models, crying out to fall into her bins: the ineffective ones who longed for the dead past, the paralyzed ones who feared the future, the opportunistic ones who waited for mistakes. They all craved different times and places. None was concerned with the present.

She cherished the present. It was a time of choice when actions mattered. To act, one had to be free of the past and unafraid to make mistakes. She knew Eric had it tougher. It was impossible for him to not measure their world against how things had been. It wasn't a yardstick that was kind to their accomplishments, but they weren't building the successor to Eric's world. They were building the successor to the world she had grown up in. By that measure, their progress had already been staggering.

She'd wanted a night away from it all, but she couldn't let it go. "I don't think Czernak or anyone else up there cares what we think." She was not hurt or upset, just disappointed. The moment they had accepted to talk, they had been backed into a corner. Czernak had gambled that when forced to choose, they would choose Marin. She'd been right.

"That's why you need to agree with them," Mika said.

His thoughts seemed to go straight but led to unexpected destinations. She knew to not walk into that trap. "We agree with them regardless of what we think? Isn't that a wee bit cynical?"

Mika grabbed the plates and took them to the kitchen. She moved to the sofa in Mika's narrow living room. He still made her uncomfortable. One minute she felt secure in his presence. The next, his words made her question everything. She couldn't tell whether the straight lines she saw were illusions as well. He had not answered her question probably because he lived where cynical met practical.

He came back and sat next to her. He leaned back till his head rested on the wall. "That is one of the lessons my dad taught me," he whispered. "I remember him, not a lot of specifics but conversations here and there. More like a presence than a real person."

"I don't remember my parents." To her, father and mother were words that described strangers like tall or blond. Mika's face told her they did more than that. All she had were her own definitions, and they were empty.

"He took me to a museum once, not far from here with lots of dead animals, unreal, huge monster-like things with teeth the size of my leg," he said. "What I remember best is the grass growing on the roof. It seemed so wrong. They made a big deal of it, like it was some sort of accomplishment to grow grass on a roof. Now stuff grows on everything: roofs, cars, streets. I suppose that roof had a point, but I have no idea what it was. He pulled me aside one night, two years into the virus' rampage. I don't know what he knew, though I suspect he had a pretty good idea. He told me not to argue with anyone in authority. 'Just say yes, but do what you think is right anyway.'"

"How old were you?"

"Eight."

"Let me get this straight. He taught an eight-year-old to lie when it suited him?"

Mika closed his eyes. "That's an ugly way of putting it. There is a fine line between lying and not telling the truth. You still have many options after you agree to something, assuming you're willing to be creative."

"Devious."

He smiled. "I realized much later it wasn't the first part of the statement that was the key to what he meant. He was an administrator. He didn't make the rules. He implemented them. He knew there were times you had to say 'Yes, sir.'"

Neither of them was the "Yes, sir" type, though they coped differently. She fenced with words as long as she could. She didn't lose many arguments, but when she did, she accepted it and moved on. Mika didn't. He won the argument or changed the rules.

"It was the second part he was trying to push through. 'Do what you think is right.'"

"To paraphrase, he told you no matter what you tell the bastards in charge, follow your heart, and do the right thing."

"That sounds so much better than saying he taught me to lie, doesn't it?"

"I guess so," she said, though she couldn't separate the message from the messenger. "You talk like no one means anything to you. Then you talk about your father like he was the most influential person in your life."

"They're just memories. I barely knew him."

"You'd make a good dad. You're patient, and you tell good stories."

He rubbed his chin.

"Sometimes I wonder what it'd feel like to have a family, to watch a baby grow. Have a small, helpless life become the center of my universe. Watch her learn from me and find her own way. The responsibility is terrifying but also intoxicating."

"In a different world, I can see it. In this one, I really don't," he said.

"Don't worry. I'm not crazy, I know that, but that's why the world needs to change."

He took another sip.

Though family was an alien concept to her, belonging wasn't. She'd grown up an outcast, surrounded by those who just wanted the next meal. One could survive like that, but one couldn't live like that. When she'd heard Eric pitch New Cal, she knew she'd found a place she'd fit in.

She'd ignored those who branded her a sell-out for joining New Cal. She knew better. Selling out was giving up. She wanted more. She had no intention of passing through life self-effacing, apologetic, moving from one crisis to another till they defined her life or took it. She had seen the mass graves, the nameless corpses lined up, waiting to be chemically cleansed. She had promised herself she would leave a signpost that said Amy Chipps Was Here.

There was no way of doing that from the Uregs. Within a week, she knew every job could be done the right way or the wrong way. It didn't matter whether it was picking up a lunch or running the power station that kept New California humming. Within a year, she was in the inner circle. Another two, and she'd become Eric's chief of staff. Then last year, Eric told her he was creating the post of vice governor for her. For someone barely twenty-six, it had been quite a promotion.

The office joke was that she was the heir to New California, but jokes aside, she knew where she belonged, which was why Mika confused her. He talked about family but had no need for the concept. Yet he could unravel it all for her by tugging at a few innocuous-looking threads.

MIKA WATCHED AMY DRAIN THE LAST OF HER WINE. IT WAS light and easy to drink. It had rained hard in September last year, so the grapes had been bloated at harvest, resulting in this wispy wine. It tasted nothing like the treasures Lori shared with him. He occasionally stumbled on cellars in abandoned homes or warehouses, but he hadn't in a while. He feared these parts had been picked clean. At least Macky still made drinkable wine. Most others' attempts graduated from fruit juice to vinegar without ever stopping at wine.

Amy got up and walked to the table to grab the bottle. After she filled her glass, she extended the bottle to him, and he lifted his glass. She poured him the last of it and sat next to him on the three-seat sofa. "Say we agree with Czernak. That still leaves us with a problem."

"What's that?"

"We still have to do the right thing, but what the hell is that? Kern can't win. We know that, but is Marin's vision better? I don't think so. What world are we signing up for?"

One with zones, curfews, and ID checks. He'd spent three days there and doubted he'd ever get used to it, but that didn't matter. "You only get to choose from the options you have."

"We can dissolve New California, make it ungovernable, blend it into the Uregs."

"The bury your head in the sand maneuver?"

"If there are bullets flying all about you, it's not such a bad maneuver."

"That's how you get shot in the ass."

Amy's sincere laugh relaxed her eyes. She put her arm around his neck and pulled him closer. "I'm starting to really like you, Mika Bayley."

He rested his head on her shoulder and closed his eyes. She moved her fingers through his hair. He liked the casual intimacy, and for a moment, he forgot about the world. But it didn't last. Just because you forgot about the world didn't mean the world forgot about you.

He opened his eyes. His world was being scrambled by a gigantic eraser moving randomly. He barely noticed patterns that made sense. He paid close attention to those that didn't. Right now so little made sense that he didn't know what to focus on. Amy and scrammies created another pattern violently contradicting his worldview. "I need to ask you something."

She straightened. "What?

"Are you trying to buy missiles for New Cal?"

Her expression did not change. "That's a strange question. Particularly tonight."

"I'm asking anyway."

"No. New Cal is not interested in missiles."

"Then who is?"

"We spend two nights together, and I owe you an explanation for New Cal business?"

"You don't owe me anything."

"I did inquire, yes," she said, her voice calmer.

"Why? How will a few missiles affect the balance of power?"

Over the last minute, her expression shifted from warm smile to cold stare. It settled on cold smile. She scolded him as if he were a dim child. "That's a simple way of looking at it."

"What's a better way?"

"The first missile greatly increases our bargaining power, and the second one doubles it."

"You're pissing in the ocean."

"No. I'm pissing in the pool."

"How's that different?"

"It's noticeable, and it pisses off the pool owner."

It was a fair point, but it was a bad idea if the pool owner had a No Trespassing sign and a shotgun. She was tussling with people who didn't hesitate to shoot early and often, but he wasn't going to change her mind. He had established that Kevin had been right, Eric had not changed, and Amy had turned out to be more ambitious and enterprising than he had suspected. That was more than enough for a two-minute conversation. It was time to ratchet down the hostility. He grabbed another bottle from the hutch.

"More wine?" The flicker of anger was back. He hadn't intended to sound dismissive, but that's how it had come out. "'Cause I need some."

Her furrowed brow relaxed. "Absolutely."

He tossed the cork to the coffee table. It bounced once and rolled on the floor. He filled both their glasses, and she took a sip.

She locked her dark eyes on him, and he felt a deep scan as though she were trying to determine what to do with him. "Are you going to tell Eric?"

Now she surprised him. The lack of trust was insulting, but her concern was genuine. "Why would I do that?"

"Isn't that what he pays you for?"

"I'm not his spymaster. He pays me for specific inquiries. I'd bankrupt New Cal if I told him everything I find." He had known that she was ambitious, protective of Eric, but he hadn't known that protection went beyond what Eric thought he needed. She was attempting to strengthen their hand without his knowledge. It was a dangerous game, both for her and for New Cal. She seemed satisfied, but he wasn't. "However, you have to tell him."

"There is nothing to tell."

"It'll get ugly if Eric hears it from Marin."

"How would they know?"

"I found out."

"Yeah, but you're a resourceful bastard."

That was half compliment, half insult, no apology, and all Amy.

He'd spent an hour talking to fishermen at the harbor where he'd bought the tuna and had watched the boats: sailboats, trawlers, dinghies, self-contained pods of life on an unforgiving ocean. Some came and went. Some hadn't moved in years. Some had sunk in their slips as reminders that any one of a hundred mishaps could kill you. Getting caught unprepared, off guard, was the last thing you wanted out there. Or in here.

She had caught him off guard. Yes, his search for Eva had consumed him. Yes, Kevin's revelation had stunned him, but it still shouldn't have happened. The only explanation was that he was forming a blind spot for Amy.

That was either good news or very, very bad news.

CHAPTER 9

DECONSTRUCTION

"To say nothing, especially when speaking,
is half the art of diplomacy."

—WILL DURANT

Lori sat on the leftmost chair for the Marin delegation and stared at Santa Cruz Mayor Andrea Wender across the curved maple conference table. In pre-Purge days, Wender had been a state senator. She provided credibility as much as pragmatism to the New Cal delegation, and they desperately needed both. Dey sat to Lori's right, then Czernak, and finally Mirkell, a constitutional lawyer, who sat nearest to the thirty-foot, floor-to-ceiling bay window.

Lori suspected Czernak had insisted on even-numbered teams so she did not have to sit in the middle and stare at Fontaine. But no matter where she sat, Czernak monopolized the room. She'd also insisted on this remote mansion in Ross for the symbolism of its architecture. Two wings, one for each delegation, connected to a central hall with twenty-foot ceilings that dwarfed the wings and negotiators. Its attempt to shout "Together we're stronger!" was straight out of pop psychology. It worked, but it also turned security into a nightmare. Nestled at the base of Mt. Tam, the mansion was exposed to anything or anyone who bothered to climb the hill. Electronically and physically scanning a gigantic hillside was a tedious mess.

Fontaine sat across from Dey with Amy Chipps to his left. Lori couldn't decide whether the real reason for the seating arrangement was to elevate the status of Chipps by placing her across the table from Czernak. Lori doubted that but wouldn't put anything past the old chancellor. She knew little of Chipps and even less about the man sitting to her left.

"Nando Cavana joined New Cal four weeks ago," Fontaine said on cue. "He will provide insight into how this treaty will be viewed in the Uregs."

After three hours of oratory, occasionally interrupted by dialogue, the room had been lulled to sleep. Dey had warned Lori this was a dour affair, but she had still expected more.

"Governor Fontaine. Let's recap why we're here." Czernak went to the display that floated in front of the darkened window.

"Please do, Chancellor."

"We're here to discuss how to merge two political entities that seem incompatible, to ensure that the rights of the minority are preserved while the will of the majority is respected, and to discuss the implication of a man's running for office in San Rafael, both for the man running and the women voting, but I also need to know how you'll react when we bomb LA."

Fontaine's eyes bulged. "Did I hear correctly? Bomb LA? The city, not Kern bases, not Kern military installations, but LA?"

"I was speaking metaphorically, Governor, not providing military targets."

"You don't need an ally. You need an accomplice. Is that it?"

Throughout the day, Lori had felt on display. She'd been confirmed to the executive position three days ago in a rush to justify her presence here and as a reminder that Marin had once defeated Kern. She should have bitten her tongue and let Czernak respond, but Fontaine rubbed her the wrong way, and she was tired of being a prop.

"The operation won't—"

"I was talking to her." Fontaine pointed to Czernak.

"And I'm talking to you." Lori hoped her anger didn't bubble into her voice. This was why the union would never work. Fontaine still believed he could browbeat and disparage to get his way. If he'd watched Marin at all over the last decade, it was from a distance, unaware of the deep disdain the Marin populace held for leaders like him. He shifted in his chair to buy time.

She'd pushed him to confront or ignore her. He chose the middle ground, which was the worst option. "Colonel, I am simply trying to get an answer."

"I'd be happy to provide one if you ask a valid question."

Fontaine drew a sharp breath and exhaled. "There is no need to be offensive."

"Governor, I'm trying hard to not be offensive."

"How about we move on?" Fontaine said, pushing the bridge of his glasses up with one finger.

Lori shook her head.

Fontaine's head swiveled back to her. "Do you have a problem with me, Colonel?"

Dey's warning was still fresh in her mind, but learning to lose arguments would have to wait. "If that's your way of telling me we should step outside, I have to decline. I'm under strict orders not to break anyone's neck for the next two days."

"That's enough, Colonel," Czernak said, but if she had wanted to keep things civil, she was too late.

ON THE SECOND DAY OF THE SUMMIT, AMY PUT THE PIECES together. Lori Rose's absence following her confrontation with Eric and Czernak's underplaying of Eric's reaction pointed to one thing: Czernak did not view Eric as a rival. He was her co-conspirator. Their jobs were to sell the union to those on their own side of the table.

Rose had been a late addition to the summit, joining the Marin executive council three days earlier and appearing on the roster the eve of the summit. Amy suspected Czernak had included Rose as a reminder to New Cal that though Marin was extending an olive branch, they also had a fist. That was the problem with fists. They swung, and they did damage.

Rose's reputation as a hard-liner didn't win her any friends in New Cal, but she was revered in Marin for her logic-defying offensive in Hollister. Then-Lieutenant Rose had taken charge of her unit after her commanding officer had been killed, and she had attacked a Kern force of nearly five thousand with fewer than five hundred under her command.

Whether Rose had been ordered to attack or had defied orders was still debated. The outcome was not. Rose had destroyed the Kern battalion, left no survivors, and crippled Kern both tactically and psychologically. Czernak had promoted Rose, which didn't shed any light into what had happened. The aftermath of a nation-defining victory was seldom the time for a public postmortem.

Amy knew Eric's intent had not been hostile, but it wasn't intent that mattered. It was perception, and he'd lost his cool. Though Rose's words had been far more hostile, she'd remained calm. It had all played out like a cliché, reinforcing old stereotypes. Amy had walked in with scorn for Rose and admiration for Eric, but even she couldn't blame Rose for the clash.

The union was a mistake, but not for the reasons Amy had first feared. The hard-liners in Marin weren't going to destroy New Cal with big slashes. Well-intentioned leaders like Eric, who still sought to resuscitate the past, were going to do it for them with a thousand small cuts.

Executive Lester had replaced Rose, but Czernak had not won an ally. Lester objected to minor items, more to make a point than to improve terms. That first Rose and now Lester seemed out of touch with Czernak worried Amy more than Eric's jumping headfirst into this union. Amy had feared she had to grapple with a strong adversary in Marin. Instead, it seemed she faced at least three adversaries, three camps with three agendas to parse.

Czernak scored her first victory with the makeup of the joint ruling council. They agreed on a nine-member council with five seats for Marin's current executives, two for New Cal, and one at-large seat elected by popular vote. The chancellor got to appoint the last member, which allowed Czernak some discretion on how to shape the council.

After the council discussion, Mirkell took over the presentation. Kern appeared in red, Marin a bright blue, and New Cal a lighter shade of blue. "The state will be divided into three zones," Mirkell said. "There will also be a three-tiered system of citizenship with a path to full citizenship for everyone. Full citizens can stand for office and vote in all elections. All current Marin residents will have full citizenship. New California residents will need to apply for it with a sponsor, though a few will receive full citizenship upon the ratification of the constitution."

"What sponsor?" Amy asked.

"A sponsor is any person over the age of twenty-one who was a full citizen when the constitution was ratified or who has been a full citizen for at least two years. Associate citizens can stand for election in local elections and the at-large council seat. They will require an employer or pass to enter Zone 1." She pointed to the screen where most of Marin was lit up. "All New Cal citizens will be granted associate citizenship."

"Gee, thanks," Amy said.

After a pause, Mirkell continued, providing details about residency, work, and travel laws. "Finally, all citizens will be required to carry ID cards showing status."

"Kind of like now? We keep the status quo except you hand out day passes. Is that it?" Amy asked.

"An astute observation," Czernak said, "but this provides a path forward. If you follow employment and sponsorships, integration will proceed faster than you think."

Eric leaned forward, elbows on the table, his left hand cupping his right fist. "What percentage of New Cal residents do you suppose will have full citizenship within five years?"

"We would be pleased if over half acquired full citizenship within five years."

"How about the immediate granting of full citizenships?" Eric asked.

"A thousand. Perhaps two. Business and community leaders and present company."

"This is insane," Amy said.

Czernak glanced to Andrea, then looked back to Amy to ask, "Why do you say that?"

"Because you're discarding half of New Cal before we even start."

"Discarding?"

"Chancellor, let's not mince words. We both know men will be sponsored in lower numbers. This is the same pitch you've been using to recruit women for the last ten years."

"A fair point," Czernak said, "but don't judge this proposal on its first-year impact. Look at it as a buffer for letting go of old allegiances with a New Cal citizen blending into Marin. A disenfranchised Kern citizen can merge into New California and then into Marin. What we provide is a path to a unified state, a state without war and without walled borders."

Amy pushed her chair back and got up. She walked to the screen and waved at it. "This is an elaborate plan. It is thoughtful, and it is detailed. It's even aspirational, but it isn't functional. What do you think will happen to New Cal when you pluck out thousands of its citizens? This may be a desirable future, but it isn't connected to the present. Once you deal with Kern's aggression, this offers nothing to New California. Nothing."

"We allow New California to exist," Dey said.

"You allow it? Really? You allow our water to flow? You allow our electricity to reach our households? You allow us to push back the gangs? What do you *allow*, General Dey?"

"The Kern army is never far. What stops them? Your running water or your militia?"

"That's why I said once you deal with Kern. I fail to see what you offer after that."

"The balance of power isn't going to change."

If they had resorted to threats, their hand was weaker than Amy had suspected. She put her fists on the table and leaned forward. "What then? Destroying New Cal by attrition isn't good enough? You will bomb Cal City after LA if we don't fall in line?"

"That's enough," Eric said. "This is not the place to air our differences."

"What differences? You sold me on the concept of New California. You talked about self-reliance and independence. I didn't know what they meant, but I learned. There is pride in every block of Cal City. You said New California was a lot like old California, always pushing the edge of what was possible. Was all that a lie? Because if you sign off on this, that's what it'll be, a big, fat lie." She straightened and relaxed her fists. "You expect me to sit quietly while you turn everything we worked for into a lie? I don't think so."

Eric's face went white. He was embarrassed at being backed into a corner he hadn't seen coming. He should have.

"You are not here to represent Amy Chipps. You're here to represent New California."

"That's exactly what I'm doing. You? Not so much."

"Stop it. Both of you." Andrea turned to Czernak. "We need a break, Chancellor."

Czernak nodded, but a break now meant they'd be back to dismantling New Cal after coffee.

"I'm sorry, Andrea, but unless Eric backs me on this, I'm done here," Amy said.

"We do need that break," Eric said.

"Very well." Amy walked back to her chair and put her screen in her backpack.

"We're not done, Amy," Eric said.

"I'm afraid we are. As Citizen Chipps, sorry, Associate Citizen

Chipps, I wish you good luck for the rest of this summit. You're going to need it."

"Amy, think of what you're throwing away by walking out."

"I did." Amy made eye contact with Andrea but found neither encouragement nor rebuke. She turned to Eric. "Consider this my resignation."

Her steps got heavy as she neared the door. She wasn't just walking out of a meeting but out of the life she'd spent five years building. But she hadn't had a choice. She only wished she had gotten more of a reaction from Eric or Andrea—or from Czernak who should have given serious consideration to why women like Amy and Andrea were sitting across from her rather than next to her. They all soldiered on, secure in the knowledge that Amy's outburst had been contained by brick and mortar. An official lie would paint over what had transpired, leaving only what Czernak and Eric wanted seen.

She almost didn't notice Cavana follow her, shattering the illusion of containment for all.

Lori monitored the summit from her office with events displayed on twenty-four feeds segmenting her screen. The main hall was off-limits on Czernak's insistence, but the rest of the mansion and surroundings were fair game. The activity had picked up after Chipps and Cavana left an hour earlier. Aides were bustling between wings, trading details that couldn't have mattered to anyone but a bureaucrat. Whatever had happened in the main hall, the energy was gone.

Now the principals were returning to the main hall. Czernak approached a dour Fontaine and a subdued Wender in the corridor where their conversation wasn't shielded. "Governor Fontaine, I was hoping to celebrate the birth of a new nation tonight."

Fontaine nodded as though Czernak had asked him to pick which poison to drink.

"At the rate we are proceeding, in another day, you and I will be negotiating one on one," Czernak said. Her crack at humor elicited a twitch from Fontaine that may have been a smile.

Wender said, "I will stay to the end, Chancellor. However, I will regret not following that brave woman out for the rest of my life."

Whatever Chipps had said or done, Fontaine was too deeply shaken to retake control. He had first lost the high ground with his outburst and had now lost his top lieutenant.

"Why do you say that, Mayor?" Czernak asked.

"Because Amy is right."

"I see," Czernak said, her lips curling down. "Where does that leave us?"

"Nowhere good," Wender said and faced Fontaine. "You told Amy to change her tune that she represented New California. You were half right. She doesn't have to change her tune, but she does represent New Cal. We do not, not anymore. New California left with that woman."

Old-world politician or not, at this moment, Wender believed every word she said. She'd become the tragic figure. She was the one who saw the path they had to take but didn't have the will to follow it, the one who had stayed out of loyalty to a cause she no longer believed in. The one who deserved Lori's compassion.

"Why did you stay?" Czernak asked, pragmatic as ever.

A sad smile stretched across Wender's face. "Because someone still has to put their name on this treaty. Let's go back in and spend an hour arguing whether a new citizen needs to wait two years or eighteen months before sponsoring their spouse. We have nothing better left to do."

They disappeared behind the door, and their conversation cut off.

Lori's attention went back to unlocking Fontaine's motivations as the feeds played in the background. She scrolled from file to file trying to understand the man who'd become a contradiction. The union offered no advancement opportunity for him, no angle to exploit. The image of the stoic governor was real. He was Czernak Lite, a leader who commanded devotion from a legion of grateful citizens. Could he really have been altruistic, ready to put the needs of New Cal ahead of his own? Had she been too hard on him?

Fifteen minutes later, she was no closer to an answer to her Fontaine dilemma.

Czernak walking to the bay window and cupping her chin drew Lori's attention back to the screens. Captured by an external feed, Czernak stood motionless as though she were trying to see a way out of this dead end. She must have seen something other than what she'd expected because she craned her neck and opened her mouth, staring straight out with eyes bulging. Lori leaned forward to see whether another screen displayed what had Czernak so puzzled.

Instead, she saw a flash that turned a third of the feeds blindingly bright.

All feeds cut off.

PART II

CHAPTER 10

LETTER TO GARCIA

"If your dreams do not scare you, they are not big enough."

—ELLEN JOHNSON SIRLEAF

Amy hadn't gone home or to the capitol. They were both tainted now, a product of five years of deceit. She sat on Mika's sofa, feet on the coffee table, her second beer in hand. She took a long sip. "They're dismantling New California," she said as he walked in.

Mika paused, his eyes darting between her beer and the empty bottle on the coffee table. "That was the most likely outcome."

That he'd predicted it didn't make it right. "Yeah, so you said, but you know the sad part? It's Eric who is doing it. He's giving away New California for nothing."

He tossed his jacket on the sofa and grabbed a beer. "He must have his reasons."

Eric's reasons didn't matter. His actions did. He wanted to leave a legacy, and with the right sign from Czernak, he'd decided on a new one. He had betrayed her. She had not followed Eric because it had been practical. She had followed Eric because she had believed in his vision, but visions, as uplifting as they could be, were fragile and dangerous. They didn't collide with pragmatism without shattering. The resulting shards not only hurt the visionary but the converts as well.

To her, a strong, independent New Cal had been a destination, not a stepping stone. Now, Eric was taking them on a path to a different destination, a path she couldn't follow.

"He's given everything away. ID cards, citizenship timeline, council composition, and vice chancellor. Nothing is left that would make this even look like a partnership." She took another sip. "By the way, I'm going to need a new job."

"No. You're very, very good at your job, and a lot of people, me included, feel a lot better knowing you're in that office."

"Then you're all in trouble, 'cause I resigned, and even if I hadn't, I'd be fired."

"Let's not make any rash decisions."

It was too late for that. Eric didn't handle rejection well. "Irrelevant. New Cal is gone. They've invaded without firing a single shot."

"Would you have preferred if they'd invaded shooting?"

She drained the last of her beer. She'd have preferred a sliver of honesty from Eric. "I'd have preferred not being invaded at all, to have real negotiations."

"That was never an option. The summit is just to revive a whiff of old-world pomp."

"How did you end up this cynical?"

"First rule of diplomacy. Never sit at the table until you're sure of the outcome."

She was ready for an argument, but there was no point arguing. He wasn't the one doing the damage. "Anyway, it's done. No more New Cal as soon as they sort out the new state seal."

"What happened to segregation?"

"Three levels of citizenship. Lots of bullshit to say that Marin is still Marin and New Cal is still outside looking in. We'll be associate citizens. Unless Eric gives that up too."

"That's about right. Everything else is window dressing."

"Seriously?" Now he was disappointing her too.

"What did you expect? That they'd open their doors to the Uregs?"

"We're not the Uregs."

"The distinction is pretty muddy from where they stand."

She spun the empty bottle on the table. She wasn't angry, just disappointed. He was trying to be supportive, not belligerent. Lashing out to him served no purpose.

"I don't know what to do with you when you're like this," he said.

She let go of the bottle and narrowed her eyes, inviting him to elaborate.

He reached out, stroking her cheek. "I could caress your face and watch you sleep with your head buried on my chest." He squeezed her hand and leaned in. "Or I could caress your breasts and kiss my way down until I find some other place to bury my head."

"How about both." She stood in front of him, brushing her hand against his chest, her fingernails barely touching him. Her hand wandered down to his belly. She rotated her wrist and with her fingers pointing down, pushed her hand down his pants.

"But not in that order," she whispered.

———

MIKA ENJOYED MAKING COFFEE. IT GAVE HIM NINETY SECONDS TO stop thinking, a pause button for the world while the flavors intensified. He walked back to the bedroom with two cups. Amy was reaching behind her with both hands to pull her hair into a ponytail. Her California-shaped pendant swayed left and right as she moved. He put the cups down and reached over, stopping its motion. It was floaty, almost not there. "You don't take this off, do you?"

She let go of her hair. "Reminds me of what we should be aiming at."

Eyes always on the prize, that was Amy. He put on a T-shirt and walked back to the living room, sipping his coffee. The mess outside the front window greeted him: bags of cement, various lengths of rebar and random lumber all tossed into different piles, leftovers from his new deck.

Amy appeared, fully dressed. She sipped her coffee and pointed to the map. "What's that?"

His screen displayed Eva's possible paths in the Uregs. "Job. Missing girl."

She grimaced. "Let's not talk about it." There wasn't much to talk about. He'd hit dead end after dead end. Amy rescued him from Eva. "Tell me more about your father's lessons."

The words transported him to a different world. "There was one about Garcia."

"What about Garcia?"

"It wasn't about him. It was about a letter that had to be taken to him."

"A letter?"

"Yeah. A letter to Garcia. That's the name of the story."

"Who was Garcia?"

"A general in a faraway place. I don't remember where exactly. This is almost two centuries ago. No instant communication, no sniffers, no tidas." He thought about it. "Well maybe they had the funny ones attached to walls. They needed to get him a message that would change the outcome of a war."

"What war?"

"I don't know. Anyway, if they get the message to Garcia, they win the war. If they don't, they lose the war, but no one knows where Garcia is. One of them says he knows a man who can be trusted, a man who gets things done. They find this man and give him the letter. Their only instruction is to take this letter to Garcia, thousands of miles away in unfriendly territory."

"They don't tell him why?"

"No, they don't tell him anything."

"Figures." He knew what she thought. Some problems transcended time.

"Anyway, this man never asks who Garcia is, why he needs the letter, how he is supposed to find this Garcia, whether there might be another way, whether it is safe or even wise to look for Garcia. He takes the letter and disappears. He crosses oceans and mountains and negotiates enemy lands. Many weeks later, he finds Garcia and delivers the letter."

"The point is supposed to be what? That you can win a war even if you don't have proper communication channels, provided you have a good letter carrier?"

He snorted. "Almost. Do the job you're supposed to do, and do it right. In my more cynical moments, I also see a not-so-subtle message about not asking stupid questions."

She cocked her head, as though she were evaluating an offer. "Yeah, I like this lesson too. I wish I remembered my father or mother."

Mika put his arms around her.

She broke the embrace. "Wait. What's the name of the guy who carried the letter?"

"I don't remember."

"Isn't it strange that the whole story is about the guy who does the right thing and it's titled after the one guy who doesn't do a damn thing? That's history for you. It never remembers the ones who do the real work. History will remember Czernak and Eric, not you."

He was fine with that. It was one of the many reasons he had never seen eye to eye with Eric. Their worldviews were based on fundamentally different ambitions. Eric aimed to shape the world. Mika aimed to understand it. They were like two boats sailing on different tacks. The moment they got close, they both tacked, racing away from each other.

As he turned to check on the latest sniffer data on Eva, a reflection in the distance caught his eye. He switched the screen to his surveillance network, which showed only a coarse picture implying severe hardware failure. He overlaid the sensor count and found it well below the count that should have triggered an alarm. It hadn't.

"Get down!"

Amy dropped in one motion. He focused all remaining sensors to the front. Two heat signatures appeared. "Two, about forty yards out, due south."

Shit. He was still barefooted. Once shooting started, there was going to be glass everywhere. Not having shoes was a silly way to get killed. He grabbed the side of the table and toppled it over. He shoved it on its side without slamming it down. He had picked Brazilian redwood for its beauty and strength. He had also reinforced it with an inch-thick steel plate running under the wood, ending about six inches from the sides. It gave the table a floating look and made it bulletproof.

"I'll be right back." He ran to the bedroom and reemerged with socks and shoes that he had on his feet in ten seconds. He grabbed the jacket from the back of his seat and put it on.

Amy pointed to the side window. "Two more on that side."

He angled the table to provide cover for both the front and side windows. His screen confirmed what Amy had seen. This was an organized assault.

He crawled to the cabinet. He grabbed goggles and put them on as he tossed a pair to Amy. He stuffed two handguns and extra magazines in his jacket and lifted two assault rifles. He stuffed half a dozen mini-grenade spheres in his other pocket. He slid four toward Amy, who pocketed them. He crawled back and handed her a handgun and rifle.

It was 5:00 p.m. This area should have been safe in daylight from gangs and crooks. Was it Kern Special Forces, coming after him for his inquisitiveness at the Red Spider? Why on earth would they attack now, in broad daylight, when they could have done it deep in the night?

He yanked the trapdoor to the basement crawlspace and pointed. Amy jumped in. He'd dug it down to four feet. He regretted not linking it to the carport, but it would provide the protection they needed. He jumped in and pulled the door down.

His tida let him see a rocket-propelled grenade whizzing toward the window. It exploded into fire and smoke, overwhelming his sensors into a white-hot image. The heat and pressure passed over them, enough to shake and rattle but not to hurt them.

It rained bullets.

When the barrage stopped, he counted to ten, popped the door up, and stood up. Amy followed. His tida stitched together the sniffer feed. The two in front kept their distance. The two on the side were now ten feet from the house. He pointed to the direction of the window and made a diving motion with his hand. They had to get out, but they still had one advantage. The attackers must have assumed they were dead. They'd get one shot to improve the odds before they gave up that edge.

The next sixty seconds dragged for an eternity. Finally, his tida picked up activity to the side of the house. He leaned toward Amy and whispered, "Five seconds after I start, shoot at the front of the house whether you see anything or not. Shoot, toss a grenade, shoot, toss a grenade, and keep shooting." He reached over and kissed her. "Shoot whatever moves or doesn't move." He pointed to the side. "Run to that window when I call."

She nodded and took out three grenades. She placed them within reach, neatly spaced. She grabbed the rifle and rested her back against the table. He saw no anger or fear in her eyes, or false bravado, which could be as deadly as fear right now. He saw only determination, which was good, because that they needed.

The zigzagging red light signaled that the first intruder had reached the window. Shards of glass broke. Boots landed on his floor with muffled thumps.

The intruders were now about six feet in, stuck in the narrow hallway. He rolled around the table and fired. He hit the first intruder multiple times. The other intruder returned fire, so Mika tossed a grenade in their direction and ducked back behind the table.

As the grenade detonated, Mika got up and ran, firing the whole way. Amy fired at the same time, aiming at invisible targets to the front. Both intruders were on the hallway floor but still moving. He fired two rounds into their heads.

"Now!" he yelled. Amy came around the table in a blur and was out the window in one smooth motion. He jumped out seconds behind. They landed and rolled in tandem. He came up and aimed toward the front of the house. Amy covered the back.

An explosion inside the house blew out the remaining windows. After the blast, they moved closer to the house, minimizing their angle of exposure to the front. He pointed around the back of the house.

"The jeep," he whispered and took off his goggles.

A man in a crewcut stood by the front door, another about twenty feet back. Mika tossed a grenade and fired. Crewcut collapsed into the house. The other man returned fire. Mika took cover behind the house, but the man had nowhere to go. Mika kept firing until the man dropped. When he heard the jeep start, he ran to it.

Crewcut flew out of the house and tackled him. Mika regained his balance, but the man spun and kicked him in the calves. Crewcut should have been dead, and his chest was blood soaked, but he punched with the force of an ox.

Mika stumbled, and before he steadied himself, Crewcut was on him, punching high and low. On the next low punch, Mika swatted the blow and grabbed the wrist. He got a strong hold and rotated the wrist to gain purchase, but Crewcut's body did not follow the motion of his wrist. Mika applied more pressure, and the wrist cracked. Crewcut's palm now nearly faced up instead of down. The man did not slow down.

The other fist came at Mika, and he couldn't get out of the way. He leaned into it to reduce the impact. As the fist crashed into his nose, Mika tackled Crewcut, slamming him into the house's siding. He drove his forearm to the man's throat and punched him low, but Crewcut just took the blows. Mika grabbed and squeezed the broken wrist, and the man winced but struck Mika in the chest, knocking the wind out of him.

Crewcut took advantage of Mika's stumble and hurled him to the ground. Mika slammed into the pile of lumber and landed on the hard soil. Crewcut jumped on him and swung for his head. The punch landed on his left cheek, and his vision blurred.

Gunfire started again. Amy was firing at something behind him and then at the man on top of him. Blood and flesh flew from Crewcut's arm and shoulder, but the punches kept coming, even as the gunfire drew closer. The fist coming toward his face disintegrated, the wrist and forearm flying away in chunks. A sharp bone sticking out of a bloody stump of a forearm was coming for his face. In a blur, the man was gone.

Mika blinked twice to clear his vision. Amy had tackled Crewcut and pinned him down. Her left hand held the elbow where the bone was extruding. Her right hand was on his throat. Crewcut kicked up, knees aiming for her back. Her hold weakened, but she did not let go.

Mika grabbed a three-foot piece from the pile of rebar. He skipped and took the last three steps in quick succession as if he were approaching a jump. He dropped to his knees and drove the rebar into Crewcut's eye. With all his body weight behind it, the rebar went straight through.

Mika's hands were raw from the friction of the sliding rebar, but he barely registered the pain. The man on the ground thrashed one more time, his head pinned to the ground. He shook as though it was trying to rotate around the rebar.

After a final twitch, Crewcut stopped moving.

Mika took Amy's hand and let her pull him to his feet. He walked back into the house and cataloged what he couldn't live without. It wasn't much.

He leaned on her as they walked to the jeep, his backpack on Amy's shoulder. His ribs screamed in pain as he folded his body to sit. When she shut his door, he took slow, deep breaths to will his pain away.

Amy drove while Mika sat with his eyes closed. His screens were destroyed, but all his data, personal and professional, was scattered and backed up. He could recollect and rebuild his digital world in half a day.

From his analog existence, he had salvaged little: a flute he couldn't play, two ceremonial swords that wouldn't cut, and a charred ebony box that held nothing of value. From an intact house, he'd have walked out with the same items minus the charring on the box.

He ground his teeth, biting down and letting go. The pain was bearable, so his jaw wasn't broken. His nose, however, was in enough pieces that the word broken wouldn't do it justice. His right eye was swollen shut. They hit a pothole, and his ribs screamed at the jolt. The frequency of potholes increased, announcing that they were no longer on New Cal's repaired roads. He didn't open his left eye.

"Where are we going?"

"Compound south of here owes me a few favors. We need a safe place to patch you up, and I need to find out what's going on."

"No calls," he mumbled.

He assumed she had placed a few discreet calls, which was fine while they were still near where they'd been attacked. The farther out they went, the less he wanted to advertise their whereabouts. He suspected she had already thought that through.

She had left out the more important part. She was not taking him to the hospital in Cal City. He'd fretted Amy would cling to the charade that New Cal was real a while longer. With their lives on the line, she had decided to be pragmatic.

"Head to the Rim," he said.

"Why?"

"No matter how many favors they owe you, your pals can't fix this."

Three potholes later, he felt the centrifugal force push him toward the passenger door. As she completed the turn, the bounces from the pothole craters gave way to the constant rattle and shake of dirt-covered, cracked, and crumbling asphalt. They were no longer on the occasionally used road linking the four New Cal cities but on one of the rarely used roads fanning east.

She tapped the steering wheel with her index finger for a moment. "Are we going to talk about what happened?"

"I got the shit beaten out of me, and you saved my ass."

She frowned. "Not what I meant. The man in the front yard stood in a puddle of his own blood, but he still came at me till I shot him in the head, and that asshole on you? He didn't even slow down when I shot him. I shot his arm off, and he almost stabbed you with the bone sticking out of his stump of an arm."

Yeah. That.

"What was that?"

She didn't even know he'd shot Crewcut at least four times in the chest and that the man had fought her with a broken wrist seconds after it shattered. That chest and that hand gripping Amy, they assaulted logic. But the other arm had assaulted reality. There was no rationale that survived watching a man use his shattered ulna to try to spear you in the face.

"I have no idea."

CHAPTER 11

PROMOTION

"Get your facts first, then you can distort them as you please."

—MARK TWAIN

Lori jumped out of her chair and rewound the feeds five seconds to confirm she'd seen what she thought she'd seen. The tail fins and wings of a silver drone appeared on the bottom-right frame before the bright burst and static sequence filled her entire screen. The hills at Ross flashed before her eyes: every bush, every delivery, every rock, every aide was suspect. What a stupid idea the summit had been. But assigning blame had to wait.

She was out the door by the time Sierra howled from across the empty antechamber separating their offices. "What?!" Red faced and eyes nearly squeezed shut with anger, Sierra gesticulated to her tida. "Get the transport ready. Thirty seconds."

As they made eye contact, Sierra yelled, "The feed cut off, but our remote sensors confirmed a drone hit the summit! No casualty report." She caught herself and steadied her voice. "Colonel."

"Communications blackout. No information goes anywhere but here," Lori said, pointing to her tida. "Seal the perimeter." She'd stated basic operating procedures, but this wasn't the time to assume competence, because someone had already fucked up or else they wouldn't be here.

They boarded the transport from the courtyard. Conflicting accounts, oddly thin surveillance data, and eavesdropping on the resolute medical team filled the twelve-minute flight along with the casualty report: Czernak. Dey. Mirkell. Fontaine. Wender. From two hundred feet in the air, the scale of the disaster snapped into focus. A third of the mansion was gone as though a giant dragon had bitten it off, exposing charred wooden framing. A crater stood where the bay window had been. Soot and dirt covered the fake stone façade in black-and-brown blotches, reeking of metallic concrete dust and burnt lavender.

The damage to the structure was unmistakable but irrelevant. The damage to Marin was inconspicuous but substantive. Lori had not seen eye to eye with Czernak on much, but she'd always had great respect for the old politician. Czernak had tricked Marin into lifting its eyes from the floor to look to the future. The scorched ruins of the fifty-year-old mansion made that future hazy again. Lori doubted Czernak's vision would survive her death.

As their transport landed, three officers with solemn faces met them. "Colonel," the one in front said as she saluted.

"Major Kagawa." Lori respected Yuka Kagawa, intelligent and calm, well liked without trying, and now forever linked to this debacle.

"Executive Lester is the only survivor," Kagawa said.

"Walk me through the timeline," Lori said, eyes on her screen.

"The drone hit at 16:48. The assault started eleven seconds later. There were five shooters, part of the catering team setting up the evening reception, two men, three women."

Unbelievable! How the fuck had their background checks been so sloppy? Had the assault team impersonated the caterers? Or had their onsite security fucked up?

Lori nodded for Kagawa to continue.

"The security team stationed outside the main hall engaged them at once. The perimeter team reached the hall ten seconds later, and we contained the assault," Kagawa said.

"Contained" overstated their accomplishments. They walked into what had been the conference room. Charred table bits were embedded in the back wall, witnesses to the force released by the explosion. The room was hot, the rocks still radiating the heat they'd absorbed. She lifted the plastic from the body lying to her right. Dey. The coppery stench of burned flesh greeted her. Dey's wisdom had been replaced with blackened cheeks and a blood-speckled forehead. Lori put the cover back and moved to the next one. Czernak had taken seven bullets, although it was doubtful she'd survived the blast.

Lori stood where she'd sat the day before. Without Fontaine's pigheaded dismissiveness, she'd have been here twenty minutes earlier. The intransigence that always got her in trouble had saved her life. There was a lesson in there somewhere. Whatever it was.

Twenty-four hours removed, she couldn't reconnect with the up-and-coming Executive Rose. The training wheels Dey provided were gone. The steady hand of Czernak on the wheel was gone. Lori was now alone to face whoever had unleashed this on them, which brought her back to the matter at hand. "Major, it says here one of the attackers is still alive?"

"Correct."

Lori turned to Sierra. "No one talks to her. Sedate her. I don't want her to do anything stupid." She turned back to Kagawa. They should have had at least ten seconds of warning even if all sophisticated sensors had failed. But they'd had none. "What happened to the security net?"

"It was functioning. Had the sniffers been down, we would have known. It was selectively ignoring information."

That was a level of hacking that reduced the number of suspects and pointed to inside help. Lori walked to the corpses of the attackers. She pointed to the first one.

"We don't have her in our records." Kagawa said. Lori pointed to another body. "Tyra Harper from New Cal, but for the last year, she was seen frequently in the Rim."

"New Cal?" Lori turned to Sierra. "What do you think?"

Sierra shook her head. "I don't mind pinning this on them, but no way they could have pulled this off on their own."

Lori nodded to Kagawa to continue.

"The two men were traced to the Red Spider two nights ago." That didn't say much. Kagawa extended her screen. "Here is a preliminary list of everyone seen there in the last seventy-two hours along with eight faces we haven't yet identified."

The Red Spider was the perfect cover. Why worry about what someone might be hiding when they were flaunting the fact that they were doing something illegal already? Lori scanned the list. This was getting better by the minute.

Fuck it, Mika. What were you doing at the Red Spider? Lori handed the screen back. "Who saw this list?"

"Other than the two security agents who compiled it, no one yet."

"This list is classified. No one, and I mean no one, has access to it." She pointed to the list. "Everyone on here is a potential suspect, and while you're at it, get us some hounds. I want to know how the net got to have selective amnesia right under our noses."

"Yes, ma'am." Kagawa was subdued, waiting for a reprimand.

"Get me a full reconstruction from the security feed. I need to hear every conversation in that building even if it's a first-year aide relaying complaints about tea temperature."

Kagawa froze as though Lori had asked for the moon.

"Major?"

"The chancellor insisted on privacy."

"And?"

Kagawa's eyes were pointed to her feet. "The main hall was shielded, as were the wings."

The corridors weren't. Emergency security videos would have been triggered, which Kagawa should have known as well. "Full reconstruction," Lori said. If Kagawa was going to be useful, she had to stop blaming herself and start thinking. "For the record, the blame here doesn't stop with local security," Lori said loud enough for the entire team to hear. "We're at fault for trusting our security net, our background checks, our spy network, our policies, our preparation, and for trusting whatever it was we should not have trusted. No. This soup sandwich belongs to us all."

———————

THREE HOURS AFTER THE MOST DEVASTATING ASSAULT ON Marin soil, Lori did not want to meet Lester. Lester lived in a world where words like "peace" and "compromise" became real in the comfort of conference rooms. The cold realities of Lori's world rendered such words meaningless. You did not negotiate with someone holding a gun to your head. Chasing the fading hope that confrontation could be avoided was the sucker's play.

"Come in, Colonel." Lester gestured. Even though Lori didn't like Ann Lester, she was glad to find her alive. She had seen enough corpses for the day. Lester pointed to two leather chairs huddled at the corner of Czernak's windowless briefing room away from the conference table and podium. "Please."

Lori sat, and Lester joined her.

"First order of business, our succession policy is clear, but since we lost both the chancellor and an executive, I want us to be on the same page and avoid any misunderstandings."

Lori nodded, urging Lester to continue.

"Colonel, do you intend on claiming the chancellorship?"

"Absolutely not," Lori said as fast as the words would come out. She had been on the executive council for only ninety-six hours. To say she wasn't ready for this game of accession was an understatement.

"Good. You will issue a statement supporting me, and I will ask for Executive Yim to do the same. The three surviving executives have to show a united front and act as one."

"You have my support."

"Very well. I will release a statement in the morning. I will reassure Marin and let our enemies know we are still here, still strong, and that we will find them and destroy them."

Lori couldn't picture Lester giving such a speech, yet at some point, leaders shed their inhibitions and took the reins. It might have been such a moment, but it felt too rehearsed.

"There is one thing I want you to know," Lester said. "Czernak's last words to me were about you. We were talking a few minutes before the last session. She went into history as she usually did, but in the end, she told me she was concerned about our troops provoking Kern."

"Like how?" A valid question to the person making that statement, but with Lester reporting an earlier conversation, Lori felt cheap as though she were arguing with a corpse.

"Like getting them agitated, making them more aggressive. Anyway, she concluded by saying she had decided to remove you from command."

There it was. The first shot in their power struggle. Lori could never verify the statement, and Lester knew it, but it had a hint of truth to be believable. Disputing it meant insulting either Lester or Czernak, a no-win situation. Opposing Lester publicly was tempting, but where would that lead? She wasn't prepared to lead a coup hours after the chancellor had been assassinated. She kept her voice even, "You're going to follow the chancellor's wishes."

Lester feigned surprise. "Fuck, no. I'm telling you what Czernak said. Remove you? The crazy old coot did not know what was good for her, but I do. I do not want you to lead Special Forces. I want you to lead our entire army." Lester reached into a pocket and pulled out a rectangular box. "That is not a job for a colonel." Lester opened the wooden box and extended it. It contained gold stars. "General Lori Rose. I'm appointing you the chief commander of Marin Armed Forces." She gave Lori an eerie smile. "Congratulations, General."

Lori had expected to be brushed aside or to forge a difficult coexistence. What she hadn't expected was to stand speechless in front of the new chancellor, holding a box containing the stars she had always coveted.

"Thank you," she heard herself say.

"Now, General, what do we know about the attack?"

"Very little. I'll brief you as soon as my team reconstructs the events."

"I have drawn a list of potential suspects and witnesses."

Lori knew how far she could push Dey, but she hadn't established any boundaries with Lester. She chose a muted tone for her warning. "It's dangerous to identify suspects before gathering all the facts. Early conclusions are the most misleading ones."

"Of course, I will let you handle the investigation." Lester tapped her screen. "Here."

It wasn't a list of suspects but of potential enemies. Lori pointed to a name.

"She had motive, and her behavior over the past few days is suspicious," Lester said.

By that logic, they both should be on that list. Lori had left the meeting, which was suspicious. Lester was the lone survivor from the meeting hall, which was suspicious. Some suspicious behaviors made you a suspect. Others led to promotions.

Lori kept reading. All the known hounds were there like Kevin Jezek, of course.

She moved on to the second list. Lester called them witnesses. There were many names from her ranks in there, including Pras and Mika. The list mirrored the one from the Red Spider.

"Who did you say compiled this list?"

"I did. The witness list will grow as we uncover more of the suspects' activities, and I want arrest warrants for the suspects."

"Isn't that premature?"

Lester got impatient. "General, do I need to remind you of the seriousness of what just transpired? Send the arrest orders. As we interrogate these suspects, we can determine their culpability. Right now, I want to prevent them from disappearing."

"What are the charges? We're still trying to keep this under wraps."

"Terrorism, act of war, treason. Pick one that fits for each."

An investigation like this didn't need fanfare. Arresting a dozen high-profile leaders in New Cal and Marin was going to create a circus. But their first official meeting as chancellor and newly minted chief commander wasn't the time to create unnecessary hostility. Lori had to pick her battles, and this was a losing one. Perhaps she'd learned Dey's lesson after all.

"Anything else?"

Lester shook her head. "Let us just get through this day."

Lori walked out more confused than when she had come in. Lester had redefined their relationship with contradictions. She'd assumed power but promoted Lori. She'd asked Lori to handle the investigation but given her a to-do list. She'd talked about conferring with Yim but acted unilaterally.

Lori had been right to worry about Lester but wrong about why. Lester wasn't going to constrain Lori's aggressive tendencies. She was going to channel them to her own purposes. In one short meeting, Lester had demonstrated a natural ability to take control over a conversation and steer it to unpredictable places. If Lori were the gun, Lester appeared to be the mad shooter.

Since Lori had no idea where Lester was pointing, she had to make sure there were few bullets in the chamber.

CHAPTER 12

WITNESS

*"Believe those who are seeking the truth.
Doubt those who find it."*

–ANDRE GIDE

"Stop moving." Amy injected the lightweight foam into his nostril. The foam filled Mika's nasal passages and sinuses, immobilizing his nose. She nudged his nose, triggering another spike of pain. His free hand shot up to grab Amy's wrist, but he willed it to stop before reaching her. She grasped his hand, gave it a squeeze, and moved it back down.

"Almost there. I think everything is where it's supposed to be. Can't promise it'll ever be straight though." She pressed the top of the cartilage back toward the bridge of his nose and injected one last bit of foam. She put thick tape across his nose to immobilize it on the outside as well as she had immobilized it on the inside. "There."

Mika moved his right hand over his face, but he felt only tape through his fingers. His left arm was in a sling, tightly wrapped, after Amy had popped his dislocated shoulder back in place. His right eye was still shut, but overall, he was in better shape than he had feared.

After sunset, they'd reached the cottage he kept in the Rim. They were safe, whatever that meant. He could count the number of people who knew this hideout on one hand if he wore mittens.

Instead of what was wrong with him, it was what wasn't wrong that mattered. His ribs were not broken. They were bruised, and two were most likely cracked but all in the right number of pieces and at the right places, with no sharp edges stabbing him from the inside.

He tried to stay alert but could focus only on the pain signals his brain received from a dozen body parts. He closed his eyes, willing his body into a calmer state even if his mind wouldn't follow.

He woke to the aroma of freshly brewed coffee. He sat up using his good elbow to push his back to the wall. He patted his injured shoulder and moved it as much as the sling allowed, which wasn't much. He barely felt the pain, which was surprising but welcome. He put his hand in front of his good eye. His vision was blurry, but there was good light.

"Leave your eye alone." Amy walked in and handed him a mug of coffee, rotating it so he could grab it by the handle.

"Thanks."

She leaned over and kissed him. When she pulled away, he took a sip of coffee, put the mug on the nightstand, and swung his legs to the side of the bed. He took his nose between his middle finger and thumb, with his index finger resting on the bridge. He gently shook it, moving up and down. He felt no pain.

"So?"

He moved his shoulder in a tight circle, his motion limited by the sling. "Everything that should be moving is, and anything that shouldn't isn't."

"Good, 'cause I need to head out to Cal City."

"I'd rather you didn't," he said, aware it wasn't a winning argument.

"I monitored the news channels." He grimaced. As long as they weren't talking, they were hard to trace, and she knew that. "There was an explosion in Marin. All official channels are dead, so I'm assuming it's linked to the summit."

"The delegation?" he asked, almost afraid to hear the answer. For the first time in a long, long time, he didn't know whether Lori was alive. Just like old days, he'd have to assume she was fine unless he heard otherwise.

"No response. There's a communication blackout. I put a few feelers but got nothing."

That meant Amy was going to New Cal no matter what he said or did. He glanced at his tida. It was past nine. He'd slept almost twelve hours. He stood up. He felt better than he'd expected. He started to take off the sling.

Amy put an arm on his shoulder. "What are you doing?"

"I'm coming with you."

"You can barely move. You'll slow me down."

"Just hand me a new shirt."

She tossed him a shirt. Mika took a sip of his coffee, put it down, and took off his sweaty shirt. She came by his side and flicked her index finger halfway up into the bandage that was holding his ribs tight. Pain shot up his ribs. He jumped, triggering another wave of pain.

"Fine, you say?" Her expression implied she hadn't enjoyed winning this argument.

He grunted, finished putting the shirt on, and put the sling back. A chime interrupted them, and he went to his tida.

She cocked her head. "What is it?"

Nothing good. "Arrest warrants."

"For?"

"You." He kept reading. "What's more interesting is that you are referred to as former vice governor of New California. Whoever posted this knew you resigned."

"That's good, no? Means the delegation is safe."

Maybe it was or maybe not. Eric was either in on this or he was dead, and Marin was weighing in on the New Cal governor succession process. "Or Marin is behind all this."

"Our attackers were men," Amy said. She'd linked the attacks on them and the summit, which was a jump, but then again, this close together, it couldn't have been a coincidence.

"Doesn't mean anything. Marin uses gangs for shit like this."

That brought another problem. "You can't go to Cal City. Until we know what happened in Marin and who wants you in custody, you shouldn't be anywhere they'll look for you."

"Hide here while they dismantle New California? I don't think so. I gave my resignation to Eric. If he's not back, I need to be in Cal City."

Before he could offer a counterargument, his tida chimed again. He tapped it, and his mood soured as he scanned the content.

"What now?" Amy asked.

"Seems I'm a witness. Association with known suspects. I'm called for a deposition."

"Suspects? Me?"

You and every Kern and Marin agent in the Red Spider. Fuck.

"You're not thinking of going are you?"

"Best way to find out what's going on is to listen to the questions they're asking."

"You do what you have to do, and I'll do what I have to do," she said.

The intent on her face left no room for argument. Besides, she was right. Hiding here wasn't going to solve any of their problems. He took slow steps toward her and hugged her. He appreciated that she didn't squeeze back, as the stretch had already triggered pain.

She kissed his forehead. "Be careful."

Leaving Amy in the capitol troubled Mika but only a little. Between the militia and Cavana's men, Amy was safe, short of a Marin assault, and if that happened, nowhere was safe.

The man he'd spotted by the orphanage was leaning on his jeep, smoking again, as Mika walked out. The man made no attempt at stealth, so Mika approached him.

"What do you want?"

The stranger grinned through a cloud of smoke. "Not the right question, is it?"

"Who are you?"

"Still weak. Ask yourself how much closer you'll be if I say Phil instead of Frank."

Normally, Mika could go on forever like this but not today. "Closer to what?"

"To what you really want to know." He took another drag of his cigarette. "Phillips."

Mika couldn't think of what to say, so he pointed to the smoke. "That shit will kill you."

Phillips snorted. "That's the funniest thing I heard in a long, long time."

"You've been watching me."

Phillips nodded, although it hadn't been a question.

Mika waited ten seconds, then stepped into his jeep. "If you have anything to tell me, now is a good time." He tapped the ignition button, and the engine came to life.

Phillips pointed from his eye to his shoulder. "Healing well?"

Mika had been better. "I'm fine."

"I've been watching you because I needed to know whether you were the right kind of man. I needed to know your agenda."

"Didn't know I had one."

"I see that now. Right temperament, right skill set, no agenda, right kinda man."

"Seems you decided to trust me. Why would I trust you?"

"It started."

What had started? The attack on them? The summit?

"There are forces out there you don't even know exist," Phillips said. "The battle lines you see aren't the real ones. For the real fight, I can use someone with your skills."

"Yeah, well, I'm busy."

The grin reappeared. "You're too busy to save the world?"

Mika didn't take the bait. Saving Amy, saving Lori, those were real concerns with real challenges. Saving the world was an abstract concept. "The world will be fine without my help."

Phillips grimaced. "Actually, it needs all the help it can get."

"Sorry. You need to find another acolyte."

"Seriously, don't you want to know why you were attacked?"

"How's that related to saving the world?"

"You're on the right track with the soldiers and the cancer-injury links, but you're poking the wrong people." He flicked his cigarette away. "It's a dangerous world out there."

Mika shook his head. "I knew that when I was eight."

Phillips smiled. "As they say, there is nothing new under the sun." He grew serious. "These guys don't like interference, and they have hard-to-kill allies. You've met a few of them."

"Who are they?"

Phillips grimaced. "Colleagues of a former colleague of mine. If I thought you'd listen, I'd recommend not getting in their way."

This was a hard recommendation to follow since they'd already started shooting at him. "I'll keep that in mind."

"If you do get in their way, shoot for the knees and eyes."

Knees, incapacitate. Eyes, kill. He nodded.

Phillips leaned into the jeep and put a folded piece of paper where the passenger seat met the backrest. "This is the lab you're looking for. You've got data, but you're not paying attention. Check out the viral activity for the injured soldiers. Examine their earlier bouts with illness. It's all linked to the one thing we all share, and try not to get killed, 'cause I really do need the help, and so do you."

The man combined the solemn face of someone spilling invaluable secrets and the words of a raving lunatic. Mika made a note of it all but could not handle more cryptic warnings.

"If you're not going to tell me what's going on, you might want to stop leaning in." He put the jeep in gear and put his good arm on the wheel, inching forward.

"Look, if you change your mind…"

"Not a chance." He pushed forward. Saving the world was an endeavor for fools, and fools who took on grandiose missions didn't live long. Still, Mika had received two bits of useful information. Viral activity was a critical component of what they were after, and the men who'd seemed hard to kill were, in fact, hard to kill.

And they had noticed his interest. Great.

———————————————

THE GUARD VERIFIED MIKA'S PASS AND WAVED HIM ON. HE LEFT his gun in the jeep and walked. When he reached the compound, two guards greeted him, frisked him, and escorted him to Lester. They remained outside the small conference room off the lobby.

The shades were down on the two windows that had to overlook the courtyard. Ann Lester sat behind an oval glass table. Her pearl necklace accentuated how thin her neck was, how fragile. It was shocking they were alone. She either didn't see him as a threat or she'd been insulated from the realities of their world. He couldn't decide which option was more disturbing.

"Take a seat." She waved to a chair across from her. Other than the six chairs around the table, the room was empty. She lifted her eyes and frowned when she saw him. "What happened to you?"

He sank into the chair closest to the door. His arm was still in the sling, but he'd looked far worse last night. She looked tired and had bandages of her own. "Same thing that happens to everyone. You asked me to keep an eye on the Red Spider. I did. Every feed from that place is now being dissected. I thought you'd want to stay far, far away from me."

"You are a material witness. I can talk to you whenever I want." She sighed. "Too many people are implicated in this. I need someone outside the investigation."

"That person is me?"

"We already have a working relationship." She'd grossly overstated their connection. "Though your reports on our security forces have left me underwhelmed."

"I report what I find, Chancellor." To be fair, that hadn't been much. Then again, if she'd wanted him to unravel a conspiracy bold enough to assassinate two heads of state, she should have hired someone with connection to the spy networks of those states.

"Seems you missed a lot."

"Maybe watching your agents at the Red Spider wasn't the right call."

She cupped her chin. "I need you to include our Special Forces in your investigation."

He laughed. "You want me to spy on Colonel Rose?"

She didn't seem to catch the humor, which was a good thing, but the statement was funny on so many levels that it worked no matter how she took it.

"General Rose is now our Chief Commander."

General. Nice. He felt as though he were holding onto a ladder as the helicopter took off. There was a moment, early on, to let go, and once you passed up the opportunity, you were stuck holding on for dear life regardless of the destination. He couldn't decide whether they were already too high. "This might be beyond my expertise and my resources."

"I do not think it is. You will be well compensated. Not to mention you will build a lot of goodwill."

Goodwill was nice, but it wasn't useful against bullets. "What am I looking for?"

"Anything. For example, if there were a coup plot, I would like to know."

Definitely, he was too high to let go of the ladder. He'd become Lester's link to three spy agencies. He chuckled. "Of course you would." The price had just gone up. It was time to test what the goodwill currency was worth. "I want a tangible display of your goodwill."

"Tangible?"

"Yes." He tapped on a screen, bringing up Amy's arrest warrant. "Make this go away."

Her expression did not change. "I cannot do that."

Based on what she was asking, Lester's interpretation of the law was flexible right now. She needed to flex it in his favor. "Chancellor, I know you can."

She made a show of deliberating. "I can make sure she stays at the bottom of the list."

"Fine, and no bounty. That one is non-negotiable."

"Done."

As he waited for his next interview, he had the disturbing feeling Lester had manipulated him too easily.

As far as deals went, this one was very one sided.

CHAPTER 13

OLD MISTAKES

*"Do what you feel in your heart to be right, for
you'll be criticized anyway."*

—ELEANOR ROOSEVELT

Morning light did not improve Lori's mood. The reconstruction that played on her screen was still hiding its secrets. She focused on the preblast sequence: Chipps and Cavana leaving, aides shuffling back and forth, Wender's sincerity deflating Czernak, the coffee arriving, and Czernak walking to the window and staring out.

She rewound to the arrival of the coffee cart fifteen minutes after the session had started. The first day, coffee had been replenished an hour after they'd started. No one onsite had noticed the discrepancy or at least thought it strange enough to question.

"General?" Sierra stood at the door with Kagawa right behind her. Lori had put Sierra in charge of the investigation. Kagawa had been disappointed, itching to solve the case to redeem herself. Lori could have told her it wouldn't help, that the lives lost on her watch were hers to own no matter how the case got resolved. But that wisdom didn't come from getting lectured. It came from sleepless nights and anger and sorrow and reflection. The guilt never went away, but it did fade. Still, guilt stricken or not, Kagawa had been at ground zero and had known the security protocols inside out. She was too valuable to waste, so Lori had put her on Sierra's team.

Lori paused the reconstruction and waved them in. She fast-forwarded, pausing at specific spots: the knock on the door, Lester opening the door for the coffee cart, the blast, the catering team bursting in shooting, and the security team joining the fray.

"Something is wrong here," Lori said, pausing the screen. The simulation, like most statistics, showed her a lot except what she wanted to see. "Two of the attackers got shot far more times than it should have taken to bring them down, and they're still standing, and they're still firing."

"That's what we thought as well, General," Sierra said. "We have heart rates for the last sixty seconds when the emergency recordings started. That section is accurate to over ninety-nine percent. This is as close to what happened as we'll get."

"I don't buy it. That's three shots to the chest with armor-piercing bullets." She froze the screen. "Two in the leg and four more to the chest." She moved it forward in slow motion. "He's still shooting." She paused it again. "Heavy armor?"

Sierra shook her head. "Light armor. There were eleven bullets in the corpse." Sierra pointed to the heart rate and replayed the key twenty seconds. The heart rate went up. The bullets hit him, and he kept shooting with his heart rate dropping. After the second barrage of shots, the rate dropped to twenty. The man kept shooting. He stumbled out when two bullets hit his face.

"That's where we lose the bio data." Sierra said.

"Assuming I buy it, which I don't, what do you make of it?"

"Here's his file," Sierra said.

Kern soldier, injured eighteen months ago and presumed dead until he surfaced at the Red Spider three days ago. Were these the missing soldiers linked to Asher? Recovering from fatal injuries was one thing, functioning after getting shot twelve times was another.

"Give me a rundown on each of the five."

Sierra ran through their files. There were two Kern agents and three New Cal militia. A New Cal-Kern collaboration would complicate things. Sierra was clenching and unclenching her jaw, making her cheeks pulse, which meant it was going to get worse. "The equipment is Marin. The drone is from our base in Beale and was never reported stolen, and there's no way they could have disabled the security without inside help." Sierra flipped to a new screen. Tran's face appeared. "Tran was at Beale last week."

Marin involvement was bad enough, but Tran was Special Forces. This had been planned right under their noses. Still, there were simpler ways to kill Czernak and Fontaine, so what was the real game here? "Has the surviving agent talked?" Lori asked.

"That's another problem. She won't shut up," Sierra said. "She babbles on and on. We're letting her in case she says something useful along the way."

"Anything I should know?"

"There is one segment sandwiched between threats and bragging that might mean something." With that, she tapped the screen, and a woman in restraints appeared. She had dark hair, pulled back, framing a red, round face. Beads of sweat were visible on her forehead. Her eyes were bloodshot.

Sierra's voice came from off-screen. "You're proud of working with Kern?"

"Kern? Kern is irrelevant. Proud? You have no idea! I'm not proud, and I'm not happy, but I'm human, and I did what I had to. What about you? What are you? Do you know? Do you know? Huh? Crazy fucks. You're irrelevant. Lost somewhere between the tiger and the dodo. How many tigers are there? Oh, not many. Slid into oblivion in captivity. Like you. Caged, dangerous animals. You should all be in captivity." Spit flew from her lips. "You freaks are a dead end, an evolutionary dead end, like the dodo and like the tiger. Fuck you all. You think you have me, but I'm human, and I know who I am. Who are you? Huh? What are you? Do you know? Do you know?"

Sierra paused the screen. "She's been repeating this garbage nonstop. This is the most coherent version."

Lori didn't need one more complication, but what she needed didn't seem to matter. The nonsensical reconstruction defied the laws of physics and biology. Having a lunatic talk too much just fit the pattern. The knock on the door stopped Lori from speculating further. "Yes."

One of her guards stepped in. "The next witness is on his way, but he will be a few minutes late. Mr. Bayley was called to meet the chancellor and just got out."

Lori waved, dismissing the guard. Lester's interest was becoming suffocating. The last thing Lori needed was for Lester to dig at Mika's past, because even with her random swings, she was eventually going to hit something.

Mika walked in ten minutes later, and Kagawa closed the door behind them. It wasn't Mika's reactions that scared her in recording this interview. It was hers. He stood by the door with a black eye, taped nose, and shoulder in a sling. To hide her concern, she pointed to Sierra sitting to her left. "This is Colonel Rendon. She leads the investigation," she pointed to Kagawa, "and Major Kagawa."

Kagawa walked around the narrow table and sat to her right. Mika sat across from them, three feet away from the table.

"The proceedings will be recorded. Please state your name," Kagawa said.

"Mika Bayley."

"For the record, you are not a suspect. You are a material witness. You might possess information that can help the investigation." Mika nodded, and Kagawa continued. "How did you get injured, Mr. Bayley?"

"I fell off a bar stool."

Kagawa raised an eyebrow. "A bar stool?"

He raised his hand to his chest. "A high one. Well, a few others fell with me, and let's say we exchanged a few punches on the way up."

Kagawa went over Mika's link to the New Cal delegation, his knowledge of their activities, and his opinions on Fontaine. He gave simple answers that were neither lies nor insightful. He mixed sarcasm and honesty to appear cooperative. His answers gave the impression of moving forward, but they were going nowhere.

"The nature of your relationship with Ms. Chipps?" Kagawa asked.

His lips twitched for a split second but he recovered. "Cordial."

"What does that mean?"

Mika reached over and touched a screen. "May I?"

Kagawa pushed it toward him. He swiped and, after a few moments, turned the screen back to her. "Here." It was displaying a dictionary.

Sierra pushed her chair back. "You think this is funny?"

Mika smiled wide with his lips pressed together.

"Do you have sexual relations with Ms. Chipps?" Kagawa asked.

"What's that got to do with anything?"

"Trying to establish your connection to the suspect."

Mika leaned forward and stared into Kagawa's eyes. "No."

"You seem very certain."

"Yeah. I think I'd remember something like that."

"Let's move on," Lori said.

Kagawa tapped her screen. "Very well. Two nights ago, you were at the Red Spider."

He leaned back in his chair and took a deep breath. "Is that a question?"

"What were you doing there?"

Mika grinned wide without parting his lips. "Have you been to the Red Spider, Major?"

"No."

"Clearly, because if you had, you wouldn't be asking."

"Humor me."

"I was having a drink."

"By yourself?"

"Mostly."

"What does that mean?"

Mika gestured at the dictionary page on the screen. "I went there alone, but I did talk to a few people at the bar."

"Do you recall who?"

"Not particularly."

Kagawa swiped at the screen. "Can you confirm whether these suspects were there?"

"Possibly."

Kagawa flicked through pictures in quick succession.

"No, no, no, no, no." He paused at the image of Tran. "Yes."

"You're sure?" Kagawa asked.

Mika half shrugged. "Yes." Kagawa clicked and flashed more faces. "No, no, and no."

Kagawa brought back Tran's picture. "Who is she?"

"I have no idea."

Kagawa waited for him to continue.

"You asked if I saw her. I did, but I never talked to her, and I don't know who she is."

"You're sure she was there two nights ago?"

"Yes."

"Did you leave the Red Spider alone?"

"Yes."

"Is that usual?"

"No, but that night, the Red Spider was in a funky mood. There were these people walking around asking whether anyone wanted to help them blow up a mansion in Marin. It wasn't the most arousing barroom conversation."

Sierra leapt out of her chair. "If you don't answer the questions, I will make you."

"Then ask me a question worth answering."

Lori motioned Sierra back to her seat, but Sierra crossed her arms and moved to the corner of the room.

"What is your relationship with Mr. Cavana?" Kagawa asked.

"I don't sleep with him either."

Sierra took two quick steps and grabbed the armrests of Mika's chair, filling the space between them. "Answer the question."

"I did."

"Do you know where Mr. Cavana is?" Kagawa asked, peering around Sierra.

He shook his head. "No."

"How about Ms. Chipps?"

"Nope."

"You expect us to believe you?" Sierra asked.

Mika spun the ring on his left middle finger, propelling it with his right thumb and index finger. The flat, stainless-steel ring with black waves etched on its band had belonged to his father. Lori knew Mika had carried it in his pocket for a decade, his fingers never filling up to his fathers' thickness until he'd broken his finger in two places and dislocated his middle knuckle. Now the lump on his knuckle acted as a stop for the loose ring. When he was stressed, that ring vibrated at a dizzying frequency. When relaxed, he whirled it at a slow, deliberate pace, distracting anyone caught staring at it. Like now.

"No, I don't expect you to believe me." Mika turned to Lori and spoke clearly for the recording. "I don't give a fuck whether you believe me or not."

"Let the record show that the witness is being uncooperative," Kagawa said.

"Great observation, but since you call this an investigation, instead of asking me inane questions, you might consider, oh I don't know, doing some actual investigating."

"That'll be all. Thank you, Mr. Bayley," Lori said. Other than get Sierra riled up, they'd achieved nothing. She tapped her screen, and a guard appeared by the door. Mika stood and walked out, shaking his head.

"I need an hour in a proper interrogation room," Sierra said before the door closed.

"No."

"He's lying."

"Obviously," Lori said.

"He is lying about Cavana and Chipps, and he's lying about his injuries," Kagawa said. "However, he recognized Tran, and we suspected Tran was in the Red Spider at least three times over the last month, so he's probably telling the truth there."

Lori stood. Mika had not done her any favors, but the real problem was that they had no tangible leads. "I'm tired of tiptoeing around this. Get the last survivor to talk. We need a lead."

Sierra frowned.

"What?"

"She's fragile. Not all there. If I push, I'm afraid she'll disintegrate."

"I don't care if she's fine fucking china. Either she breaks or she breaks."

CHAPTER 14

REGRETS

"A friend in power is a friend lost."

−HENRY B. ADAMS

ori listened to reports as she walked to meet Lester. Two attacks had occurred in one morning. A drone had taken out the Red Spider along with half the block in a military operation, planned and executed to precision. To her relief, Pras wasn't listed on the casualty report.

The other attack had targeted a gang in the Uregs with the same force and precision. The body count was higher there, but what bothered her more were the whispers of angels of death coming to claim the last humans. She dismissed such talk, but her mind wandered to the simulation at Ross where the attackers had defied the laws of nature. She didn't believe in angels of death, but she was starting to fret about the unkillable soldiers.

She corrected herself instantly. Not unkillable, hard to kill. There was a huge difference.

Yim sat at one end of the sleek, black sofa that had replaced the two leather armchairs in the chancellor's office. Lori sat at the other end. Redecorating the office was a strange way to settle into the role, but that's what Lester had chosen. "Chancellor Lester, President Yim."

"How could this have happened again?" Lester asked before Lori's back hit the cushion.

Lori crossed her legs. She was growing tired of Lester's insinuation that there was a magical solution to their problems. "With all due respect, Chancellor, the Uregs are a big place."

"Is it the same people who hit Ross?"

Some towns became synonymous with catastrophe. They rose to stardom and claimed the spotlight against their will: Pearl Harbor, Hiroshima, Tromso, and Ross now joined them. Two heads of state had been assassinated there, throwing their world into chaos. Lori very much doubted anything would ever happen in Ross that would let it live down this stain.

"Same weaponry, yes, but we don't know much more yet."

"What about the targets?"

"The Red Spider is obvious. The gang that was hit had done several missions for us."

"We work with gangs?" Lester hissed.

Lori shrugged. "Some gangs work for us. Some gangs work for Kern."

Lester shook her head. "It is Kern or a gang working for them?"

"Can't tell just yet."

"What can you tell, General?"

Lori focused on the simple question, not the implication of how little progress she'd made. "Two of the perps are from Kern. The rest are from New Cal. There is also evidence of Marin involvement."

Yim's eyes shot up, and her mouth opened. Lester sat a little more rigidly. "What do you mean?"

"The drones were ours but never reported stolen. They were signed out by soldiers recorded as dead or missing. Someone entered Marin, broke into a secure base, unlocked the armory, and walked out with drones. None of that could have happened without inside help."

"That is ridiculous," Lester said.

"They selectively disabled the security net, which is possible only if they knew what the net was doing. They got on the grounds by impersonating the vetted catering team."

"Expand the list of suspects. Include all personnel who could have enabled that."

What was it with Lester and lists anyway? "We're on it."

"Good, but speed up the arrests. The hounds are still out there. For all we know, they are erasing their involvement as we speak."

Lori nodded.

"We need to start hitting back," Lester said. "We cannot sit here and take more body blows. General, draw me some targets, and let us hit something."

She was glad Yim was in the room, because what she wanted to hit was Lester's nose. The transformation from dove to hawk was stuck in rooster mode.

"We will," Lori said, "once we know who did it."

"Very well. General, the gloves are off. I have come to your point of view. It is us or them. There is no coexisting. I know Dey and Czernak's plans aimed to minimize casualties. Just so we are clear, I'm not interested in minimizing anything. Do whatever it takes, kill whoever it takes, destroy whatever city is in the way. I want Kern wiped from the face of the earth."

Yim had nodded when Lester had first shown steel, but she now had a look of frozen horror.

"Understood." Lori cleared her throat. "One more thing. New Cal didn't take the news of Ross well. Do you have a strategy for how to deal with them?"

Lester shook her head. "Right now, there is a threatening hyena that is pissing me off. Go shoot that hyena between the eyes. As for the poodle yapping at my feet, toss it a bone, and let it yap. I will stomp on it when I'm done with the hyena."

———

THREE HOURS REMOVED FROM LESTER'S INELEGANT AGGRESSION, Lori had the outline of a plan for neutralizing Kern. No matter how she approached the attack, though, she could not keep the casualties within reason. She let go of her analysis and glanced at the screen that covered the interviews. Kagawa and Sierra kept going, witness after witness. The choreographed dance of officers, witnesses, and guards had created the illusion of motion but resulted in little progress.

She stepped out into the corridor but skipped the interview room and kept walking. Two narrow tables lined the corridor, covered with cheese sandwiches, a crockpot of black beans, and stale coffee no amount of sugar could fix. She headed to the kitchenette at the end of the corridor and ran a can of black beans under hot water for two minutes. If too cold, the congealed fat and starches coated her mouth with an unpalatable film. Too hot, like those in the crockpot, and the beans pretended to be real food, disappointing her with their watery broth and soft texture. The beans were at their best at room temperature where their deficiencies were muted.

Chewing on a spoonful, she walked back to her office. It was dark out. From the window that covered half the wall across from her door, she could barely spot the outline of the senate building across the square. She was nearly done with the can when a knock pulled her attention away from the screen where Sierra was grilling another witness. "Yes."

A guard Lori didn't recognize pushed the door open and leaned in. "General, there is a witness here to see you."

There was no one on her schedule. Witnesses tended to run away from her, not toward her. It wasn't hard to guess who this witness might be. "Send him in."

The guard nodded and opened the door wide. Mika waltzed in. The guard stood there unsure of whether to stay or go.

"That'll be all."

She stepped out and closed the door behind her. Lori deployed a privacy sniffer and tossed it on her desk. It was ironic that after years of meeting in stealth in dangerous places, here they were inside the protected walls of Marin, but they hadn't talked. She had merely been civil toward him. He hadn't even been that.

"Doesn't anyone talk without one of those around here?" he said.

"A bar fight? Really?"

"A little more serious. It may have been the same people who hit Ross. We handled it."

"And? You didn't think that was relevant information?" Mika looked away, escaping her gaze. She knew he did not lie to her, but he did not always tell the truth either. She moved toward him and clasped his shoulders. "You're okay?"

"I'll be fine."

She stepped back, leaning on her desk. "Anything on Asher or the missing soldiers?"

He plopped down on one of the two wingback chairs that butted against the wall across from her desk. "Two of the three soldiers who disappeared from Marin had aggressive tumors, but the third one didn't, so it might be nothing."

Her eyebrows moved up. "Which one didn't?"

"Edberg. According to her records, she was healthy as a horse until she got shot."

"Edberg?" She went to her screen and flipped through the files. "Thought so. Edberg was clinically depressed. She tried to commit suicide two years ago."

"That's not in her records."

She shrugged.

"How?"

She read off her screen. "Opioids."

"I'll check the timeline. Pras has a new theory that isolates two labs in the Uregs as possible staging posts for missing soldiers, but I haven't heard from her since yesterday."

"Pras was at the Red Spider when the drone hit, but she's not on the casualty list."

He crossed his legs and put his head on the backrest.

"What is it?"

He shot a look at the privacy sniffer. "Lester wants me to stop looking for Asher. She offered to double my pay to close the case."

"Not the worst idea. This is turning into a shitshow."

"Not a chance." He leaned forward, eyes on the floor. "She also wants me to spy on you."

She hopped on her desk and let her legs swing. "Doesn't add up."

He seemed to seize on her uncertainty. "You still think it was Kern?"

Kern hadn't claimed credit or offered condolences. They hadn't even raised an eyebrow when Kern agents were arrested in the Rim and the Uregs. "I don't know what to think."

"I cannot find a single scenario where their current strategy makes sense, and that bothers me," he said.

"You always gave them more credit than they deserved. Most likely, whoever did this didn't tell Kern Central, and Spindler is deciding whether to congratulate him or execute him."

"You never gave them enough credit. My outlook is safer than yours."

"How do you figure that?"

"If I'm wrong..." He shrugged with his palms up and head tilted sideways. "If you're wrong, they'll hurt you when you least expect it."

Her head moved in a tight figure eight, neither nod nor shake.

"You don't believe it's Kern," he said.

"I don't know what to believe. I can't discount anything, neither Kern's involvement nor the lack of Kern's involvement." She grimaced. "Could have done without your performance this afternoon."

"I don't like the arrest warrants."

"Those are from the chancellor's office. We play the hand we're dealt."

"No, you don't. You always pick your own cards."

She shook her head but didn't hide the half smile he'd coaxed out of her. "Half my staff thinks you know more than you let on, and I can't tell them to not waste their time, because that'd be suspicious."

"I don't think Rendon likes me very much."

"She doesn't trust you."

Mika straightened and leaned forward.

"Sierra wants the entire world to be like Marin. It's a simple power structure. She understands it and trusts it."

"You don't sound very impressed."

"I think the world of her. What she wants makes sense from a certain point of view, but yeah, I have a broader perspective."

"Yet you want the same thing she does."

"No, I don't. You think Marin is like New Cal, but with women in charge? It's nothing like that. Sierra grew up in a different world than you. She is part of the power structure. Sure, there are men at many jobs, but they have to work hard to blend in, twice as hard to justify their being here. How many men did you see when you were jaunting around the hospital?"

"Not many."

"Exactly. Sierra has met two types of men: Marin men who want to earn her respect and men she's had to fight. Guess which category she'd put you in?"

"Let's not forget you put me in the middle of this mess."

She scowled and whispered, "That was a mistake."

He kept his eyes on her.

"How about we try this again? Did you know any more of the faces Kagawa showed you?"

He took a deep breath and exhaled slowly from his nose. "Pras, obviously, but beyond her, no."

"Do you know where Chipps is?" she said.

"Yes."

"Where does that leave us?"

He became still, a despondent statue with unblinking eyes.

"There's a war brewing, Mika, and I'm not going to lose that war."

"How about not starting it then?"

"Start?" The flash of anger made her voice rise in pitch and volume. "Our existence is cause for war for Kern. How do you live with that?" She took a breath to calm herself down. "Do you know how many villages Kern raided, how many women, and for that matter men, they killed in the Uregs last year?"

He didn't answer.

"I didn't think so. Sixteen raids were recorded with three hundred and eighty dead, nearly two thousand missing. Do I need to remind you what happens to the missing?"

He squinted as though he were trying to change the focus of his eyes. "You always had the anger, but there used to be so much more. You used to be generous and funny."

"That was a different world. Not much left to be funny about."

He stood, cradling his hurt elbow. "No, it wasn't. The teenager who promised to protect me lived in a fucked-up world. She fought for survival every day, but she found enough in life to make it worth living. What's happened to you?"

"You, of all people, should not be asking me that."

"I am because I see power, and I see determination, but mostly I see hate, and hate isn't enough. Doesn't work. Didn't work."

She tapped the desk with her heels at an increasing frequency.

"I watched you cross that line once. I don't want you to repeat it on a bigger scale."

She stopped tapping. "Not the same thing," she said but didn't even believe it herself.

"What comes after you see this through?"

She pointed to the horizon through the window. A gibbous moon was rising over the hills behind the senate, lighting up the dispersed clouds. With the thin cloud cover, the air had a translucent, unreal feel. Lori touched the back of his hand with her finger but then recoiled. "I want to walk on those hills and talk about the view, not about fortifying gun batteries. I want young women to go through life without worrying about—"

"Don't." He put his good arm on her shoulder, dropping to her elbow. "This isn't the way, Lore," he whispered. "This isn't the way."

She stiffened and withdrew her arm.

"You know, it wasn't just not finding the perfect boat that kept me here." He tugged at the sling holding his arm in place. "Not sure how to say this."

She tilted her head, inviting the words she knew she wasn't going to like.

"I figured if I'm around, you might think twice about burning it all."

"You overestimate my influence in Marin."

"I don't think I do."

"So," she said, pinning him with her eyes, "my crazy temper kept you here all these years, but now, it's what?"

He averted his eyes.

"It's Chipps, isn't it?"

Mika remained still and didn't even breathe.

She smiled. "Does she agree with you?"

He narrowed his eyes, confusion plastered on his face.

"Chipps. Does she think I'm crazy?"

"Don't take it personally. She thinks you're all crazy."

She laughed and snorted, disarmed by his candor. "She suits you, Mika. You'll make a great power couple."

"Was it that obvious?"

"No, but I know you. You don't react like that. You were protective of her."

Mika relented and talked about Chipps. He didn't say much, sticking to dinners and drinks, but that he talked at all spoke volumes. The tension on his face gave way to contentment and then to peace. He looked like a man who'd found what he'd been missing.

His ebullience spread to her, and she smiled. "It's serious?"

He didn't nod, but his nondenial was a screaming answer.

Her smile widened. "Good for you."

"How are you holding up?"

She took a deep breath. "Do you think this is who I wanted to be? A hunter?"

"You regret moving to Marin?"

"Regret is a useless word. Can't go back to see how things would have turned out had I done this instead of that. We get one crack at this. We made, I mean, I made a choice, and it led me here. I live with the consequences of that choice every day." She lowered her voice. "I went by the old neighborhood a few months ago. The market is still there. I recognized a few old merchants. I was out of uniform, but they were still scared of me. No one met my eye. They all scurried out of my way as if I were from a different reality, a disrupting force they didn't know what to do with."

"Don't tell me you miss that life."

"Miss it? I couldn't get away fast enough. It's not what I became that scares me. It's what I would have become had I stayed. What I do miss, though, is looking to the future with hope."

"There is always New Cal." He grinned. "Big on hope, short on delivery."

She smirked back. "Anyway, if I regret anything, it's hiding you all these years. Once a year is not enough. Crumbs, that's what that is. Seeing you these last few weeks, even across political divides, and through arguments, it reminds me of how things used to be, how they could have been, and how they could still be."

He blinked twice.

"I've lost you once. I'm not going to lose you again. No matter how this ends, whatever we build, it is going to have room for you to bring Chipps to my house for drinks," she said.

He stepped closer and hugged her. This time, she let him.

CHAPTER 15

OLD FRIENDS

"You get to choose what monsters you want to slay."

—CARRIE FISHER

Mika reached Kevin's compound by sunset, but it had been torched from the inside. He headed into the Uregs to find Kevin, cataloging what he knew. Each soldier who'd disappeared had been seriously injured, had a life-threatening illness, or had attempted suicide. The viral activity had jumped at each step, and the soldiers had recovered and then disappeared.

He'd operated with the assumption that whoever had hit the summit had gone after Amy to eliminate the New Cal leadership and taken out the Red Spider to hide their tracks, but now he had another angle. What if they were targeting Kevin, Pras, and him for their inquiries about the recoveries? It wasn't comforting that the two options weren't mutually exclusive.

At least he now knew where he'd seen the woman following Eva. It was in the Red Spider. She'd been the face Lori's team had asked about.

Mika got to the bungalow Kevin retreated to when spooked after a ninety-minute drive.

He parked under the carport and walked around the structure. Kevin's truck was hidden under tarp in the back. At dusk, with the shutters closed, the place looked abandoned, but his tida unlocked the back door. A sofa lined the wall to his right. A square table separated the living space from a sink and a wall of cabinets to his left that might have passed for a kitchen.

Years of neglect combined with the sudden appearance of electronics made the living room look as though the old place had died and a new place was growing in the same space. The dirty shirts and half-eaten dinners made it smell like it too. But there was so little there that the disorder wasn't overbearing.

Lit by the blue of his screens, Kevin was slumped in a chair by the table, his hair out of his ponytail and unkempt. His trimmed, three-day beard was pushing five, but he wasn't hurt.

Mika stepped in and bolted the door. "Are you okay?"

Kevin roused himself and yawned. "Yeah. I worried when I heard your place was hit. But you look fine."

Mika had no idea how he looked, but his ribs and shoulder felt fine. "I'd return the compliment, but you look like shit." He turned the lights on, moved a packing box from the sofa, but changed his mind and sat on the chair across Kevin.

"Told you crazy Eric was going to get you all killed," Kevin said, squinting.

Mika grimaced and pushed the destruction and broken bodies out of his mind.

"Speaking of crazies, how's our good Colonel Rose? I bet she's itching for a fight."

Kevin was the only person he could talk to about Lori and not feel as though he were betraying her. "She's always been close to the edge," Mika said. "I'm afraid she's about to go over it."

"It was always a matter of time. You just figured that out?"

He shook his head, unwilling to agree out loud.

"Just remember. To her, everyone is a piece on the board, hers to use and discard."

"You don't believe that," Mika said.

"I do. Even you. Sure, you're a valuable piece but still a piece. Don't you forget it."

"Yeah, yeah. Anything on Eva or the other woman?"

Kevin scratched his head. "You know, I had much more interesting news for you, but if you insist." He swiped at the screen, and the mystery woman's face floated up wearing a Marin Special Forces beret. "Lieutenant Judy Tran. Works for no other than our good old Lori Rose."

Mika swallowed slowly. "They asked me about her during the Ross investigation, but I didn't realize why."

"Tran vanished nearly two weeks ago. Special Forces has been on her trail since."

"Still trying to parse how Lori could miss something like that."

Kevin chuckled. "Hard to believe, ain't it? Lori's slipping."

"Eva?"

Kevin shook his head. "Three likely staging posts on the way out of Marin. Average of a half dozen destinations from each. I can't narrow it down further without more data."

By the time he chased each lead, Eva would be a memory if she weren't already. He put the piece of paper with the coordinates Phillips had given him on the table. "Do these help?"

Kevin punched in the numbers and set his sniffers to work. "Let's give it a few minutes."

While the probabilities of Eva's potential paths fluctuated, Mika's mind went to the men who'd attacked his house. There'd been an economy of motion to the man he'd fought. Precise. Mechanical. He tapped his tida, playing a reconstruction from his sensors. "Did the guys who came after you look anything like this?"

Kevin zoomed in on the attacker who had nearly killed Mika. He superimposed the attackers from his compound: a four-man team all moving the same way.

"Who are these guys?" Mika asked.

"They're not Kern, and they're no gang, but they're the ones who hit Ross."

"Why do you say that?"

"Because one of the guys who attacked me and this guy here," he pointed to the screen, "were in a Uregs compound with the Ross attackers two days ago."

Whoever had hit the summit was coming after them for their interest in the medical data, and it wasn't a rogue Kern general.

Phillips' words kept tugging at him: *It's all linked to the one thing we all share.*

"How much have you dug into the Purge?" Mika asked.

"As much as anyone, you know. That damn virus has such a short genetic code it's insulting we let it kill that many."

"That's not the point. Why are we alive?"

Kevin gave a short laugh, mouth closed, his chest shaking. "You want what, a clever answer?"

"I'm serious."

"'Cause we were immune." Mika waited, but Kevin raised his hands. "It's all I got."

"Okay, so hear me out. What if someone figured it out, what the Purge did? What it still might be doing?"

"Are you saying the Purge is back?"

"I'm saying maybe it never left. Maybe someone figured out how to use the virus to generate a chemical that makes hard-to-kill soldiers with low fertility as a side effect."

Kevin shook his head. "Why bring the Purge into this? Why not just a new drug?"

"The Purge is the one thing we all share."

Kevin scratched his beard and looked at him blankly.

"I've been digging, Kev. This shit is everywhere: Marin, New Cal, even Kern. How can a drug reach that many places? Who could manufacture that much of any drug? How could anyone deliver it? To both Kern and Marin? Air? Water? It doesn't add up. There is no trace of facilities or any distribution mechanism. Nothing, yet it's everywhere."

"Still doesn't mean it's the Purge."

"Purge concentrations surge after a major shock such as an

injury, a biological stress, particularly when those are coupled. And when Purge activity reaches a certain level, the patients disappear." He sighed in frustration. "I wish I could trust any of this."

Kevin grinned. "Told you I had something before you interrupted me with the Eva nonsense."

"What do you have?"

"You can trust the data. All of it. The Purge activity is real as are the cancer recoveries."

"What makes you say that?"

There was as much pride as mischief in the smile. "I validated it on a bigger sample."

"How?"

"Forget the original cancer data and the few cases of gruesome injuries. With small samples, it's hard to tell whether the data were tampered with, particularly when you assume poor recording. I went for something that would affect most people."

"What? Like the flu?"

"Nah, no one goes to clinics for shit like that. Something simple, annoying, and painful if not dealt with but common." Mika kept staring, so Kevin relented. "Dental records."

"Dental?"

"Yeah. Cavities."

"So?"

"So dentists are an endangered species. In pre-Purge days, the average number of cavities for an adult was between three and four."

"With the sorry state of recording, how would you even notice drops in that rate?"

"True, you wouldn't notice small drops, but I normalized for as many factors as I could. Cavity rates should be higher, closer to numbers from a century ago, but instead, we're at barely one cavity per adult. And that drop is identical to the drop in cancer mortality and to the drop in birth rates."

One of Kevin's sniffers chimed, drawing their attention to the screen. Most of Eva's potential paths out of Marin had become thin red lines with tiny probabilities. One was thick green: a compound at the edge of the Rim linking to a lab in northern Kern.

"Seems those coordinates and my data like to dance," Kevin said.

"That's where she is?"

Kevin pointed to the screen and shrugged. "Only with ninety-three percent probability."

Whatever that lab was, it linked to Pras' data, to Phillips' coordinates, and to Eva like an arrow.

"That's not a place you want to go without backup. I mean, serious, armed backup," Kevin said.

"Do you have access to missiles?"

Kevin's eyes widened. "Scrammies?"

"No. Cruisers will do."

"Yeah, I can swing that."

"Aim them at this lab." Mika pointed. "I'll provide cancel codes every four hours. If you lose track of me, well, you know what to do."

"You're really going there?"

"Whatever it is, it's significant."

"The missiles are for?"

"If I'm not out four hours after going in, I'm not coming out on my own."

Kevin fidgeted. For a high-stakes data thief, he had an astonishingly weak stomach. "You know, I'm afraid we're on the right track."

Mika nodded but narrowed his eyes. "Why?"

"They're trying to kill us."

CHAPTER 16

NEW WAYS

"Power can be taken, but not given."

–GLORIA STEINEM

The growing crowd in the streets of Cal City forced Amy to take stock of what she felt.

She was angry with Marin for hiding Eric and Andrea's death for two days, for making the news public without contacting her first, and for sending an impersonal condolences message. But mostly, she was angry with them for allowing it to happen.

She also felt sorrow. Eric's loss had left an enormous hole in New Cal, but she had lost more than a governor. She'd lost her mentor, the person who had pushed her to reach a potential no one but him had seen. She couldn't believe he wouldn't pop out of his office and say something asinine, something that only after reflection would turn out to be insightful. That her last words to him had been hurtful deepened her sorrow.

She felt frustration and desperation. Trying to keep New California functioning, she'd come to realize how Eric had held things together with spit and glue and sheer strength of will. New Cal had lost its first governor and maybe the only governor it would have.

That thought triggered determination. Eric had his faults, but his vision deserved better than to be discarded without a fight.

New California didn't need a sad and frustrated leader. She would grieve for him when she could. Today, she had room for only anger and determination with a hint of desperation thrown in to keep her on her toes.

Because New Cal was disintegrating.

The militia leaders had been loyal to Eric, but now they were more angry and confused than she was with loyalties stretched thin. Randy Halsan, Cal City's mayor, had claimed to be the new governor, adding fuel to the fire, and though Amy suspected she would get the support of Santa Cruz and Mountain View in time, she didn't have it now.

Between her staff and a dozen security guards, there were about thirty people in the capitol. After being barricaded for a day and a half, offices had turned into dormitories and the break room into a kitchen. Amy had agreed to talk to Halsan because in another day the stench of desperation would overpower the sweat that already permeated the air.

"We're connected, Governor," Ferg said, and Halsan's image appeared on Amy's screen, sitting at a desk in front of a picture of him shaking hands with Eric. Subtle. With his pressed white shirt, navy tie, and vest, the man pretended a sophistication he couldn't attain. A tuft of hair clung to the middle of his forehead, fighting a losing battle against the receding hairline that made his pudgy face seem even rounder that it was.

"Ms. Chipps, this has gone on far enough. We need to resume the rule of law."

"We do, Mayor. I agreed to this talk to stop you from breaking New California law. Withdraw your forces and return the control of the militia to this office."

"Ms. Chipps, you are a wanted fugitive. I am offering you the courtesy of staying under house arrest until we determine the circumstances leading to your arrest warrant."

"You want to enforce a politically motivated Marin warrant? I don't think so."

Halsan shook his head. "That's irrelevant. What isn't is that you resigned. You cannot reclaim a title you voluntarily gave up."

She wagged a finger. "I suggest you consult your legal team. I never submitted a resignation letter, and the governor never accepted one. I am the governor of New California, and I cannot be subject to arrest warrants from other political entities. Read our constitution."

He smiled, all teeth. "An interesting and elaborate fiction. Your resignation occurred during diplomatic negotiations. As a consequence, the Marin chancellor did not consider you to be vice governor two days ago. Neither does she recognize you as governor today. As the longest-tenured mayor, I am now the acting governor of New California, and out of goodwill for your previous contributions, I'm willing to allow you to remain in your home while our legal teams sort this out, but this offer is valid only if you take it in the next two hours."

"And then what, Mayor?"

"My forces will seize the capitol and charge everyone in there with sedition."

"Mayor, I recommend you consider your words carefully. Threatening the governor is still a crime."

"Two hours. My patience has limits, Ms. Chipps."

"You are blocking access to the capitol. Withdraw the militia."

He chuckled. "Ms. Chipps, you are not in a position to make demands. You have no supplies and limited firepower. Your attempt to take control has failed."

"Mayor, you have illegally appropriated the New California defense force. The other cities will not stand for it."

"Ms. Chipps, do you see the Santa Cruz militia here? I don't. That's because they know you are making a power grab. Once this is over, we will hold elections. You are welcome to run, assuming you are cleared of the pending charges. Two hours." Halsan cut the connection.

"You're not considering this are you, Governor?" Bogdan Kiril, the leader of the militia unit protecting the capitol, stood by the door. He'd been shaken by Ross, but there was nothing he could have done. Even the full might of Marin had not been enough to avoid the massacre.

"I'm thinking about it."

"No, no, no. If he attacks, we'll push him back. He has the superior force, but we're entrenched."

"I don't want more blood."

"We can't cave now."

She hated that word. "He knows too much. He's getting updates on our situation."

Kiril grimaced. "We can still hold the fort."

"I know you can, but at what cost?"

He looked away. "We all knew what we signed up for."

She appreciated Kiril's support. He'd had been loyal to Eric, and to his eternal credit, he had transferred that loyalty to her without questions. She shook her head. "No. No one dies so I stay in this office."

"He can't legitimize his power if he blasts his way in and leaves thirty corpses. No way is he willing to do that."

"Maybe not, but Halsan might think a dozen corpses acceptable, particularly if he can pin the deaths on me. We need a strategy that'll work long term. It's one thing to push him back for a few hours, but what then?"

"Santa Cruz, even Marin—they're all waiting to see who will prevail. If we can hold him long enough, we'll look like we're winning, and then we'll win."

"I can't gamble all your lives that the cavalry will arrive in time."

He frowned. "What's the alternative?

She shrugged, wishing she could have summoned Eric's magic with words.

An hour later, she was working on a half-formed plan when commotion and shouting resonated from the front entrance. They were still away from Halsan's deadline, but she'd suspected he'd move before the time was up. She dropped her screen and headed downstairs.

Two men in Halsan's favored gray uniforms stood outside the door with their hands in the air, faces covered in bandanas. Her guards had the door covered. Kiril motioned the door open. "Walk real slow, and let me see your faces."

The men walked in and took their bandanas off.

"Who the fuck are you?" Kiril asked.

"Nando Cavana. Who the fuck are you?" Cavana grinned.

Amy stepped between the two to stop the pissing contest. "Hello, Nando."

"Ms. Chipps." Cavana smiled. "I mean, Governor Chipps."

Kiril walked around her and faced Cavana. "How did you get past the siege?"

Cavana shrugged. "That is what I do, but right now, it is who you are that concerns me."

"Bogdan Kiril." He gestured around. "Everyone here with a gun is with me." He pointed his thumb to Cavana but turned to Amy. "Governor, do you trust him?"

This was not a time for a nuanced answer. She looked straight into Cavana's eyes. He did not look away. She turned to Kiril. "Fully."

The tension in Kiril's face disappeared. "Okay then. Not sure walking into a siege is the best move, but we can use all the help we can get. What is it you're good at?"

"Defending compounds against thugs." Cavana smiled again. "I am also pretty good at sneaking past checkpoints."

"Like a smuggler?"

Cavana ran his left hand through his curly hair. "You can say that."

"Great. That's what we needed, a damned smuggler."

"Glad we agree." Cavana was still smiling.

"Bogdan," Amy warned.

"It is fine," Cavana said. "I am not easily offended." He turned to Kiril. "Keep in mind smugglers get an edge by predicting how people react under stress and then exploit that edge, and there is a lot of stress right now, both in here and out there. For example, right now, the mayor is planning an offensive, but the men and women in the militia are confused. They do not know why they are here. They have an eye out to prevent people from leaving, but they are careless about people getting in. They will wise up soon, but they have not yet. Case in point." He pointed at himself.

"What's wrong with their siege?" Amy asked.

"It is set too far back. It allows them to see anyone coming out, but without enough open space behind them, they cannot see what is coming in until it's right on them. If, say, a truck sped toward the roadblock from behind, they would have no idea what to do, particularly if it had the insignia of the mayor's office and it were leaking some nasty, smelly shit. Most if not all of these poorly trained militia do not want to be here. They are under stress, so all they will think is will the truck explode? Will they shoot? Are they on our side? When the truck passes by them, they will move on to oh crap, we are going to blow up the capitol! And what is that nasty-smelling shit it's spewing? Is it toxic? Shit, is it going to get on me? Is it going to blow up near me? The few officers worth the title, and there are not many, will see through this, but by the time they decide to act, it will be too late. There will be a scattering of shots, but unless they get really, really lucky, they will not hit anything that will slow the truck down. So—"

"What the fuck are you rambling about?" Kiril asked.

"All that behavioral crap I just unloaded on you? That was just a guess." Cavana looked at his watch. "Want to see if I am right?" He whispered to the man he'd walked in with and started up the stairs. They all followed. Cavana walked halfway up the corridor and into a south-facing room. He headed to the window. "There." He pointed down the street straight out to the barricade.

There was nothing there. Before she could point that out, the man who'd arrived with Cavana returned and whispered in Cavana's ear. "JJ here says right after my little show down there, as everyone was running up here, one person moved to a closet and tried to make a call. JJ stopped him. You would not happen to have a mole, would you?"

Amy's eyes met Kiril's. The man was impressed and didn't seem to know whether to be relieved or pissed. She smiled and ratcheted the tension down.

"Anyway," Cavana said, pointing out the window again. "Here it is."

A large truck appeared in the distance, speeding toward them. It had Cal City sanitation markings. Something green was leaking from it and leaving a bright, reflective line behind it. The men at the barricade dove out of the way when they realized the truck wasn't going to stop. It crashed through the roadblock and continued up the hill. A few shots rang out, but the truck didn't stop. The metal gates of the outer perimeter opened when the truck reached them.

The truck continued at full speed and, once inside the perimeter, skidded to a stop by bouncing off the concrete wall. It reversed and disappeared into the underground garage.

Cavana smiled at Kiril. "I understand you do not have much use for smugglers. If you also do not have use for food or guns or soldiers, we can hop back on the truck and drive away. Either way, you can keep the mole."

CHAPTER 17

FOUND

"A half truth, like half a brick, is always more forcible as an argument than a whole one. It carries better."

−STEPHEN LEACOCK

Mika spent the night at Kevin's compound rather than heading back to Cal City. The capitol was Amy's playground. He hated the place, but he'd be back there in a day to show support. Until then, though, they both had jobs to do. He left early in the morning and rode his bike as far as San Simeon. He gave a wide berth to the castle. He'd never found it pretty, but it had become a new shade of hideous since a Kern-leaning gang had appropriated it.

He spotted three Kern patrols in over a hundred miles. That was too light a footprint, but it wasn't their numbers that bothered him. They usually watched the road. Today, they watched the coast. He avoided them and continued on foot and covered more ground than he'd planned.

He reached Morro Bay by sunset. The walk had taken its toll on his busted-up ribs, but the hard part was done. Now he had to watch what and who went in and what and who went out of the facility. Unable to keep his eyes open, he set up sentries and turned in.

He woke up at first light and allowed himself a stretch to test his tender ribs. His power-pack-heated morning coffee brought him back to life. He settled into a shallow crease on the last bump before the ridge peaked a quarter mile to his south. The lab was half a mile down the ridge. It had a walled perimeter, a tower, and heavy artillery. It was more military base than lab. He was lying flat in his spot at the edge of the ridge with his scope glued to his eyes when the crack of a breaking dry branch startled him.

He let go of the scope and launched himself sideways in one motion, rolling up to face the direction of the sound with his gun drawn. There was no one there.

"Put the gun down and stand up. Real slow," said a voice followed by a two-second pause. "Hands on your head."

Two shots landed on either side of him. He put the gun down and stood. A man in a Kern uniform walked out from his right. A sniper stood ten yards behind with a rifle trained on Mika.

The man got closer. "On the ground."

The man's boot on his cheek pinned him to the ground. The cold metal locked his wrists together. He had been too focused on the sentries that didn't make sense and had missed their approach. Because he had been eager to get answers, he had pushed his luck.

And his luck had pushed back.

* * *

MIKA CLOSED HIS EYES TIGHTLY AND LET GO. HE DID THIS TWO more times and focused on the face at the door. It was the man from the hill.

Mika had spent the last half hour being beaten by two eager soldiers. They'd taken him to a cell in the basement, tied him to a chair, and alternated asking him questions and punching him. It wasn't an effective interrogation routine, but it had taken a toll on his already-bruised ribs.

The man walked in and dragged a chair to five feet from Mika. He sat and leaned forward, elbows on his knees, dangerously calm. "It doesn't have to be this hard. Who are you?"

Mika blinked a few more times.

"You were in Kern territory. You work for New Cal or for a gang that works for Marin, which makes you a spy. I'm going to ask you some questions, and trust me, you will answer them. Don't ask yourself whether you should try to resist and prolong the process. Ask yourself whether you want to annoy me enough that I shoot you when we're done." He waited for it to sink in. "Got it?"

"Can't even promise a good outcome as a carrot?"

The man didn't smile. "There are no good outcomes. It's a bullet to the back of the head or a labor camp." He moved his chair closer. "Who are you?"

"Mike."

The man leaned over and punched Mika hard in the left kidney. So much for saving them.

"Let me tell you how this works. I ask the questions, and you give full answers. Do we understand each other?"

The man leaned over and punched him higher on the side right below the ribcage.

"Do we understand each other?"

Mika nodded, though the motion made his head hurt.

"Mike what?"

"Mike Burress."

"Who sent you here?"

"Well, you can hit me again, but the answer is no one."

The man hit him again but not hard enough to do damage. "Who sent you?" The man punched him again, harder this time, smashing his knuckles into the side of his mouth. "Who sent you?"

He could take quite a bit of this, and they would escalate the pain, and he could probably tolerate that for a while as well. The physical pain wasn't the main threat. It was the gaps between the bouts, the anticipation of pain that got to you. His resolve would get tested between sessions in little offers, little concessions, and from that, they would determine how he was holding up, how much he feared the next wave of pain. And use that against him.

Between the tiredness and the expectation of future pain, it wasn't his body that would break first. It was his mind. If played to its conclusion, his mind would acknowledge there was no point in resisting, so under normal circumstances, he would eventually crack.

But he was safe from that assault on his sanity. They had only a few hours, so they had only the threat of physical pain, and that he could handle. There was no eventually here, there was only now.

"No one sent me here, but I'll tell you why I'm here."

The man was about to punch him again but stopped. "Oh?"

"I'm looking for a woman."

"Really? Who?" He laughed. "What does she look like?"

"Twenty. Dark hair. Small nose. About five eight, athletic build." He paused. "Pretty."

The man's eyebrows came up. Mika had nailed it.

"What do you want with this woman?"

He shrugged. The man stepped up and punched him on his bad eye, then on his mouth.

"Girlfriend." He spat blood.

The man laughed. "You're here for your girlfriend?"

"She's here?"

"What's her name?"

"Eva."

He nodded. "What were you going to do after you found her?"

"I was hoping she'd be somewhere less fortified."

His statement was too sincere to get a reaction. The man got up, walked out, and returned about two hours later. He rotated Mika's chair ninety degrees so he faced the side wall. "We're going to play a new game." The man tapped a screen. The opaque glass became clear, exposing a twin room. Eva was shackled to a chair in the center, same as he was. A man with a cap stood in the room. He put a hood over Eva's head. The cloth barely moved as she inhaled. Her slow breaths hinted at a calm that did not correlate with her situation.

"Who are you?"

"Mike Burress."

"Who sent you?"

"No one."

The man touched his screen. "Go ahead, Tony."

The capped man took a knife with a thin, ten-inch blade from the table. He stabbed Eva in the left shoulder. She flinched, but it was a muted reaction. She must have been drugged.

"What the fuck!"

"Who sent you?"

"No one."

"The other one, Tony."

Tony plunged another knife to Eva's right shoulder. "She's running out of shoulders."

"What do you want me to say?"

"The problem is your story doesn't check out."

"How so?"

"She's from the Rim."

"So am I."

"How did you meet?"

"In the orphanage. Down by the old docks."

"I'm afraid you convinced me."

Mika blinked tight and opened his eyes. "Afraid?"

The man tapped his knuckles on the glass. "We're done, Tony."

Tony took a gun from his belt and pointed it at Eva. He fired three quick shots into Eva's chest. She fell backward as the glass darkened again.

"The fuck did you do that for?"

"You convinced me. You're nobody, and she's nobody. I have no use for either of you."

"Well, I lied. She was not my girlfriend."

"Kinda late for a confession." Tony walked in, gun raised.

"I'm a special agent with Kern intelligence," Mika said.

"You expect me to believe that?"

"Well, it's the truth."

"You have ten seconds."

"Think, man. How could I have been in those hills? How could I have come this close to the lab? Heck, how would I even have known about this lab? What about Eva? She was nobody's girlfriend. She'd been sent here to disappear from high up. Most of her file is classified. I know you know at least that much."

"Suppose I believe you, Mike Burress. What then?

"That's not my name. I'm Major Michael Winston."

The man snickered. "Now you're reaching."

"And you're in deep shit."

"Why? Because you'll make some calls and make things difficult for me?" He sneered.

"Not exactly."

"Mike, or whatever your name is, why am I in trouble?"

"What time is it?"

"What?"

"What time is it?"

"Why would I tell you that?"

"You were about to shoot me. Now you're worried about telling me the time?"

The man glanced at his tida. "It's three thirty-five."

"You're in trouble, because they'll be here in ten minutes."

"I've had enough of this nonsense."

"Ten minutes. I have critical information. What went on at the Red Spider."

The man flinched at the mention of the name.

"If I'm telling the truth, you're about to make a mistake. If I'm lying, you'll find out shortly. You can shoot me then."

"What's this information?"

"Fuck you. You think I'd trust you with that?"

The man leaned over and punched Mika on his right cheek.

"Go ahead, keep punching. You and I both know there is nothing you can do to make me talk in ten minutes."

The man put his hand on Mika's face as though he was grabbing a ball. His palm pressed on Mika's nose. His index and middle fingers slid down from Mika's forehead. The fingers found his eyes. "Tempting." His fingers applied pressure but then eased up.

Mika let go the breath he'd been holding. "By the way, I suggest you pull in all your men from the perimeter fences and towers. No point in engaging the incoming force."

"No point?"

"We're all on the same side, so why get into a firefight?"

"Because I don't like you, and I'm sure I'm not going to like your special agent friends, and I can handle a few armed men."

"It's not going to be a few."

"You call yourself an officer." The man sneered in disgust. "Blabbing about the size of the incoming force. Tony, get everyone outside to watch the perimeter in case this piece of shit isn't lying."

Mika shook his head. "Suit yourself, but it's a bad idea."

"You know, you were an annoyance a few minutes ago, but now you're starting to piss me off." Both men walked out.

The feeling was mutual. Everyone had let Eva go. He had not. Some ironies he could have done without.

About twenty minutes later, Mika felt the low rumble of the first explosion, followed by the commotion and higher pitches of secondary blasts. He had no idea how many men were out in the open, but he doubted anyone outside would have survived the ferocity of the attack he heard.

The next person coming through the door would do so with murderous intent. He hopped to a position behind the door. He couldn't move fast or well, but the confusion of the empty room might buy him a few precious seconds.

As the door opened, he launched himself at it, smashing a man between the door and frame. The man fell inward. Mika flung himself, landing on the man's head with the back of the chair. The man stopped moving.

Mika rolled over and grabbed the knife from the man's belt. The angle between his hand and string didn't give him much purchase, so cutting his bindings was slow work. When the string snapped, he grabbed the man's gun and flipped the man over. It was the man who had shot Eva, Tony. He didn't move, but Mika still fired a shot at his face.

He put on the man's jacket and walked to the corridor. There was a row of cells. He checked each, but they were empty. Eva's body was gone, but her blood was still there.

He stumbled up the stairs and spotted a room where the roof had caved in. His tida with its chipped edge lay on a desk. He pocketed it and walked out into the courtyard. Kevin had not been economical with his ordnance. Fires raged everywhere, and three buildings had been reduced to rubble. Two men dragged an injured soldier away from the burning perimeter fence. Bodies lay crumpled against a low wall to his left. He made his way toward one of the bodies, grabbed the dead man's rifle, and kept moving. He spotted an undamaged vehicle halfway across the base and headed for it. No one challenged him or paid him any attention as he climbed inside.

He was two miles out when a puff of smoke appeared ahead. The whistling sound of a handheld launcher followed. He yanked the wheel, driving off the road, but regained control before rolling the truck. He slammed on the brakes and had almost stopped when an oncoming tree completed the task for him.

This was not his day. He jumped out and took a few steps away from the truck. Two men and a woman walked his way, guns out. Mika relaxed when they got closer. "Enrico!" he called, recognizing the mercenary.

"Who's there?"

"It's Mika."

"Mika. Sorry about that, man. Thought it was a pendejo from Kern."

Mika walked out of the ditch but kept his hand on the rifle. "What are you doing here?"

"Our old pal Kevin is paying me handsomely to bail out your sorry ass," Enrico said.

With his quarter-inch buzz cut, high cheekbones, and hazel eyes, Enrico put the most adorned merchandise at the Red Spider to shame. His loose jacket hid his toned muscles but not the charisma that made him the leader of the most sought-after mercenary team in the Uregs. "He said he'd contracted air support, but he didn't say he'd blow the whole goddamn base to kingdom come. I was worried we'd have to scrape you off with a spatula."

Mika sized up the posse in front him. Enrico and the man held assault rifles. The woman had a sniper's rifle strapped to her back. They were well armed but no match against a Kern garrison. "You three were going to get me out of that base?"

Enrico pointed to the woman. "Ella here can shoot a fly from two hundred feet."

Ella nodded. Mike returned the nod and waited because that still didn't add up. Enrico made a circle with his index finger and thumb and brought them to his lips. He let out a long whistle followed by two short ones. Armed men and women came out of the forest. Mika counted about thirty before relaxing.

They drove west in a convoy. Mika couldn't reach Amy, but Enrico assured him there'd been no fighting in Cal City. For now that had to be good enough.

Enrico's two scouts on bikes were ahead, sending back every minute, "The road is clear."

By the time they got back to it, the base had been empty. Eva's body was gone as were the soldiers. Mika pushed thoughts of Eva away and focused on the deserted road. "Something is not right here. I don't like it when things are too easy."

Enrico frowned at him. "Easy?"

"We should have seen patrols by now and checkpoints."

"You really wanna find patrols?"

He shook his head. As they got near the southern edge of Los Padres Forest, Mika patted Enrico's forearm and raised his palm.

His bruised kidneys couldn't take any more of the bouncing. "We need a break."

Enrico tapped the driver's shoulder, and they stopped. Mika's abdominal pain was getting worse, so he gritted his teeth as he stepped off the truck. He felt Enrico's gaze following him. Based on how he felt, he didn't want to guess how he looked, but he could no longer ignore the pressure in his bladder. He stumbled to the nearest tree and unzipped his pants.

Pain shot up through his body, an electrical impulse bouncing inside him as though trying to get out. He grimaced and put a hand on the tree to steady himself. A red trickle came out. The pain intensified. He leaned further forward and rested his forearm on the tree, then his head on his forearm, momentarily stopping his fight with gravity. He pulled his shirt up. His abdomen was covered by a large purple blot.

"You okay, boss?" That Enrico had followed him meant he hadn't hidden his misery as well as he'd thought.

"Fine." He finished and zipped up.

Enrico was staring out to the distant ocean from a hill framed by tall firs. Mika took a few steps and stood next to Enrico. The views of the Pacific were breathtaking, but he had always been suspicious of these waters in Southern California. Up north, the wild coastline reminded visitors the waters were dangerous. There was a savage beauty to them, both scary and inviting, but here, nature mellowed just enough to mask the dangers of waters still cold and deadly.

They stood high above one of the oldest towns on the coast, established as a mission nearly three centuries ago near one of the oldest harbors. Mika pointed to the binoculars hanging from Enrico's belt. Enrico handed them over, and Mika trained them toward the coastline.

"Have you been here before?"

Enrico shrugged. "Not here here but yeah. I've been in these parts."

He handed the binoculars back, pointing to the water. "Anything different?"

Enrico shook his head.

"How about the boats?"

"Now that you mention it, the harbor is emptier than usual."

"Yep." Mika walked back to the truck. Santa Barbara harbor had always had some of the largest boats on the coast, but now it was half empty with the larger vessels gone. "It's not just the boats. No patrols and no roadblocks for forty miles? The base I was in was practically empty. There were at most twenty people there where it should have been two hundred. Where is everybody?"

Enrico shrugged. "LA?"

"Maybe."

Back in the truck, Mika opened his eyes as they rolled to a stop. His tida said he'd dozed off for fifteen minutes. Enrico was talking to two men, expression frozen somewhere between temptation and disapproval. Mika stepped off the truck.

Burt Jasser and Jeremy Cutler stood next to Enrico. They were an odd couple with Burt's muscular frame towering a foot over Jeremy's plump body. Burt had been a field officer for Eric. He could have been competent had he not had such a high opinion of his own skills. After Ross, he had taken over special ops for New Cal, which was like saying he was in control of a dingy in a storm. Jeremy was a clerk. He did not belong in the field. Someone was desperate and thin on resources, because he knew Amy had not sent them here.

"What brings you here?" Mika asked Burt.

"There's a Marin battalion on its way. We need to blow a bunker before they get here."

"What's in the bunker?"

"Scrammies. We can't let them fall into Marin hands," Burt said.

Mika shook his head in disbelief. Burt wasn't a good liar, because he neither respected his audience's intelligence nor had any himself to make up a good story or a plausible one.

"We don't have time for this," Burt said. "Let us go, and we'll take care of it."

Mika leaned close to Enrico's ear. "Where did you find them?"

Enrico took a few steps away. "The scouts spotted them heading north. They found this on them." He handed Mika a detonator.

Long-range, top-notch detonator. "Why wait? Why didn't they blow it already?"

"Hey!" Burt yelled. "Hand it back, that's mine."

Two of Enrico's sentries came running. One whispered in Enrico's ear. "Six heavy transports landing on the pads," Enrico said. "Marin."

"Fuck." Each transport carried twenty soldiers. No matter what was going on, over a hundred Marin troops were about to descend on them.

"Told you." Burt seemed vindicated. "Now hand it over."

Mika shook his head.

When Enrico didn't intervene, Burt lunged at him. Mika took a step forward, swatting Burt's arms and then punching Burt in the head. Burt fell, but Mika dropped the detonator. It rolled to Enrico, who picked it up and studied it as though it were a precious life-form.

"Blow it!" Burt ordered.

Mika panted from his brief struggle with Burt. He felt hot, and his headache was getting worse. He blinked twice and focused. "There are over a hundred people there. The landing pads are sitting on top of the bunker. The whole bunker will go up, including the transports."

"So?" Burt snarled. "You cannot let Marin get their hands on scrammies. They can kill thousands with those. A hundred seems like a fair price to pay to prevent that."

"Arithmetic," Mika said. "Not the best subject for this situation."

"C'mon, man. It's us or them, and I choose us."

"Us? Who is us? New Cal, or are we now Kern too?"

Burt shook his head. "Fuck Kern, and fuck Marin." He turned to Enrico. "Just do it."

"Let's get out of here," Mika said. "The last thing we need is a firefight."

"No!" Burt was back on his feet and had drawn his gun.

"Put that thing down."

Burt took a step forward and shifted his aim from Mika to Enrico. "The detonator, now."

Burt's head exploded, bits of brain and blood spraying to their right.

Ella stood thirty feet to their left, her extended arm holding a pistol with a suppressor. In his infinite wisdom, Burt had not considered the implications of pointing a gun at the leader of a gang in front of thirty of his followers. It had been his last mistake.

The *pop* had been loud but was not likely to alert the Marin contingent. At that moment, Jeremy ran toward the trees. Ella tracked him with her pistol. Mika took steps toward her and put his hand on her gun, nudging it down without appearing threatening.

Her arm followed Jeremy's path, but she waited for confirmation. Mika's thoughts went to little Jeri, running around Macky's deck, smiling and screaming and sleeping in the booth, oblivious to the world she lived in. Fuck. What was wrong with people? How had Jeremy made the trek from working in an office to playing field operative with Burt?

"What's the point?" he asked Enrico. "Where is he going to go?"

Enrico nodded, and Ella lowered her pistol, but Mika hadn't done Jeremy any favors. The place was going to be crawling with Marin troops soon enough, and Jeremy did not have the tools to survive in this environment.

"We need to get the hell out of here now, or it's going to get ugly," Mika said.

"Burt may have been a moron, but he did make a valid point. What if they kill thousands with those missiles?"

"I don't think there are any scrammies. I bet it was a trap to lure these transports here." Enrico extended his arm, offering him the detonator. Mika took it. "Why?"

"Why did I not do it?"

Mika shook his head. "You didn't do it because you're not a cold-blooded mass murderer, but why did you give it to me?"

"So I can sleep tonight."

"How so?"

"See, boss, I've killed many. Fourteen personally. Probably two, three times that if you count my crew." His chin moved in Burt's direction. "Like that, but it was always a response to threat. I can't just flip a switch and wipe out a hundred lives. If I push that button, ain't no way I can sleep tonight." He swallowed. "But what if Burt is right and you're wrong? I don't push that button, and they kill thousands. If I think of that, ain't no way I can sleep tonight."

Enrico cracked a crooked smile, half a lip going up and half going down. "Don't pay me enough to make these calls." He walked away, giving instructions as he moved.

They were nearly on the last truck out when two Marin soldiers walked into the clearing, hands over their heads, escorted by three of Enrico's crew. Shit. They now had at most ten minutes before the team failed to check in and this place turned into a warzone.

The quick, quiet retreat he had hoped for evaporated. He leaned closer to Enrico. "Very soft touch," he whispered. "There's a hundred of them, and they have air support."

Enrico pointed to a tree by the side. "Secure them."

Two of his men tied the soldiers' hand behind their backs. "Sit down," the older one said, and one of the captured soldiers complied. The younger man tied her ankles.

The older man got closer to the soldier who had not moved. "I said sit down."

She glared at him but did not move.

He brandished his knife and moved it closer to her face. "We can do this different ways." He moved the knife lower, lingering over her throat and resting on her chest. He slashed down, cutting a three-inch vertical strip on her jacket. A trickle of blood appeared on the fabric.

Mika moved closer, ready to grab the knife, but stopped as a shout rang. "Hey, Nate."

Ella walked their way, eyes on Nate. "You need help with that?"

Nate pushed the soldier down. He turned to the younger man who had tied the other soldiers. "Make sure they don't go nowhere." He walked away.

Mika crouched in front of the soldier who had challenged Nate. She showed no emotions, no fear, no anger, and she was not hurt. Nate had just nicked her. "I'm Mika. Who is in charge of this operation?" She did not reply. "The bunker is booby trapped, but I'm sure you know that, and I really need to talk to your commanding officer. I have a message for Colonel Rendon."

The soldier's neck jerked up. "Who are you?"

"Told you. Can you get her a message? It's important."

She looked him up and down. "Are you trying to be cryptic?"

He stood up and walked to Enrico. "You need to get out of here."

"Yeah, but those two are coming with us."

"You don't want hostages. Trust me on this."

"Why?" Enrico was caught between his Uregs logic and the new reality. In the Uregs, taking these hostages was the right move, but here, facing a unit of Marin Special Forces, it was the deadly move.

"Because they won't bargain, and at some point you'll get frustrated, and someone will do something stupid, and it'll get personal, and they'll chase you until the end of time."

"You sound like you're not coming."

He shook his head. "I need to check a few things in LA."

"Are you crazy?"

He probably was. "I need one of the bikes."

"C'mon, boss."

"Well, if I don't bring it back, you can add it to my tab."

"If you don't bring it back, you'll be dead."

He tapped his tida to push a spot on the map between them. "I left mine here. Grab it on your way up. It's newer than your bikes. If I don't bring yours back, you can keep it."

Enrico shook his head and then gave him one nod toward the bike. "Try not to get killed."

Enrico's crew disappeared within minutes. Mika walked toward the Marin soldiers and addressed the leader. "Don't tackle me. I just want to talk."

"How would I tackle you with my hands tied behind my back?"

"Your hands aren't tied."

As he suspected, she'd already worked them free. She moved her hands forward and started tugging at her ankle binds. "Why did they leave us here?"

"I convinced them your buddies would be upset if they did anything to you."

She wrapped the string around her knuckles. "That goes for you too."

He tossed her his knife. She cut the ties on her ankles and cut the wrist bindings of the other soldier. She handed the knife to the soldier and stood. "Who are you?"

"Told you. My name is Mika." The transports, their behavior all screamed Special Forces. "Is Rendon here?"

The soldier cut her bindings and hopped up. They faced him, though their eyes darted behind him.

"Why do you want to know?" As Mika turned, Rendon walked toward them accompanied by three soldiers whose guns were trained on his chest.

"The bunker is booby trapped," Mika said.

"Tell me something I don't know."

There were six of them. Could one of them be a spy? "A private word?"

She approached Mika. "You got ten seconds before I haul your ass in and for a real interrogation this time."

He tossed her the detonator. "They were waiting for you to arrive to blow it up."

She grabbed the detonator and frowned.

He leaned closer. "Also, the Kern army is gone."

"Gone?" She pursed her lips as though she'd tasted something sour. "Where?"

"I don't know."

"You gotta do better than that."

"I need to check out a lead. Give me four hours."

"And then what?"

"I'll contact you with what I have."

"What are you playing at, Bayley?"

"No play, just trying to save your ass." He smiled, though no amount of smiling would erase his antics during his interview. He was betting that a lot had happened since then and that on the list of things that upset Rendon, he had dropped down a fair bit.

She turned to the soldier who had challenged Nate. "What happened here, Sergeant?" She got a full summary including Nate's antics, Mika's reaction, and his role in Enrico leaving them here. "Any reason we should keep him for questioning?"

The sergeant grimaced. "I can say yes if you want me to, ma'am."

"Simple question."

"Then no."

Rendon tossed him a tida. He caught it midair. "Direct encoded line. You have two hours."

He hopped on the bike and started it. "I'll call you in three," he said, splitting the difference. As Rendon nodded, he gunned it and disappeared into the forest.

Three hours after leaving Rendon, he reached the vantage point he'd been seeking. There was no more doubt in his mind. The empty bases and the lack of patrols all pointed to the same thing. The Kern army was gone.

The sentries watching the ocean snapped into shape. He knew where the Kern army was going and how. It was a daring plan, but it was Kern's bad luck that he'd always been fascinated by the sea. He'd scoured these parts to find the perfect ocean-going sailboat for his always-two-years-away trip around the world. He knew where the big ships were, how often they moved, and what it took to move them. Los Angeles harbor had been home to three old cruise ships that could accommodate tanks, transports, and thousands of soldiers. It had also sheltered dozens of ships that could take hundreds of soldiers and hundreds of boats that could take dozens, but now, the setting sun reflected on the water between the docks.

Los Angeles harbor was empty.

CHAPTER 18

GOVERNOR

"Being powerful is like being a lady. If you have to tell people you are, you aren't."

—MARGARET THATCHER

Cavana's stunt had bought Amy not only time but also leverage. Four snipers were now on the roof, and with Halsan's information source cut off, they'd put the mayor at a disadvantage for the first time. Plus they now knew the force surrounding them consisted of three platoons, only half of the Cal City militia. That was the good news. The better news was that Andrea's successor had agreed that he couldn't leave New Cal in the hands of an overzealous mayor. A hundred armed troops were coming north from Santa Cruz and would be there within the hour.

The best news was that crowds outside were growing—well outside the barricades but there, and crowds meant witnesses. Having seen the cracks in the resolve of the troops around them, Amy was going to take a sledgehammer to them. With one decision, she had finally managed to get Cavana and Kiril to agree: they both opposed her stepping outside.

She'd been editing sections of her speech and didn't hear Cavana walk in.

"Here," he said, as he put a light armor vest and hardshell helmet on the table.

Her eyes moved from him to the table. "Are you serious?"

"Very. It is fine to be brave, but no reason to be stupid."

She narrowed her eyes. In private, his directness occasionally drifted too far.

"Eighty percent of sniper shots hit you in the chest. Half the rest hit you in the head, so if you insist on putting yourself in the line of fire, at least wear these and improve your odds."

It was Cavana talking, but it was Mika's argument she heard. She smiled. "Where do they teach you to talk like that?"

"Please put the vest on."

She relented and lifted it. It was lighter than she'd expected. She put it back on the table. She held the helmet by its ear cups, her eyes on the dangling chinstrap. "I'll look ridiculous."

"You will look a lot worse if you are dead. Trust me, I have seen head shots, and it is not pretty."

When she stepped out there, she was going to do so as Governor Chipps. Eric had taught her that looking the part made the part. She put a hand on Cavana's forearm. "I appreciate what you're trying to do, but no one follows a governor who's afraid to face her own people. The vest I'll wear. The helmet? Not so much."

He stood up with a satisfied smirk as though the vest had been his only intent.

"Any words of wisdom?" she asked. "On the tone I need to hit?"

He extended his right hand, palm flat, thumb pointing up. She cocked her head, questioning. "That is how we used to greet each other, before we lost billions to the Purge. Before we concluded that maybe touching the palm and fingers of a stranger was not the best idea."

"You have a point?"

"The past is past. The customs of that world don't make sense here. You have good instincts. Trust them."

"Noted. Now go pester Kiril. I have a speech to finish."

He smiled, showing more teeth than she'd thought possible. "Yes, ma'am."

THE HASTILY ASSEMBLED PODIUM STOOD TWENTY FEET OUTSIDE the capitol. She walked with purpose, her eyes on nothing but the path between her feet and the podium. She wasn't worried about getting shot. She was worried about tripping.

A dozen of Cavana's people came out with her as did half of her staff in a show of support, but it was also an act of defiance. Two different sets of people were behind her, and even if they were not sharing her risk, they were taking a real one standing there within sniper range.

She climbed the steps and faced the barricades two hundred feet away. The broadcast would go to anyone in New Cal or Marin with a screen, which was everyone. She pretended to address a state, but her eyes were on the men and women behind the barricades.

"New Californians," she said, and her voice cracked. She swallowed and whisked a few strands of hair behind her ear. "It is with deep sadness that I address you today as your governor. My presence on this podium is a reminder that the giant who built this city, this state, is no longer among us. I could promise you that I'll try to fill his shoes, but it would be an empty promise. I know that I cannot, but I can promise you to work day and night to make sure his dreams become our reality.

"I've been warned that my presence here is unwise, that my safety is at stake, but safety is an illusion. I don't need illusions, and I don't think you do either, so I won't sell you any.

"I am ready to speak, and I know you are ready to hear me. For three days, we have stared at each other through these barricades through the scopes of our guns, and just like staring at a mirror, we've seen the barrel pointing back at us.

"Divided, confused, weak, afraid. That's what others see when they look at us.

"Divided, we're nothing but more gangs from the Unregulated

Territories. Divided, our strength comes from the number of mercenaries we can afford.

"I reject that. I reject that we're another gang. I reject that we need mercenaries. I reject that we're confused. I reject that we're weak, and most of all, I reject that we're afraid of each other, afraid of the future. Accepting any of that is an insult to the memory of the men and women who gave their lives to forge a better future for us all.

"Three days." She waved three fingers. "We've wasted three days here, squabbling while the murderers who took our leaders have gone underground. That ends today.

"Our leaders are not dead. They live as long as their words resonate in our minds. If you allow me an indulgence, I will share a few of those words with you."

She moved her eyes from side to side but could not read the mood of the crowd. People moved behind the barricades, trying to get closer, only to be blocked by the militia. The Santa Cruz contingent had arrived half an hour ago. They were behind the barricades and standing to her right, out of the fray.

"I am Governor Eric Fontaine, who said, 'It's all right to let the world put a few marks on you as long as in return you put your mark on the world.' The world took him at his word and put its mark on him, but Fontaine had the last laugh, because he put a New California-sized mark on the world, and I say to you today, you will remove that mark over my dead body."

She turned toward the Santa Cruz contingent. "I am Mayor Andrea Wender, who said, 'Ideas are dangerous. Once they take root, they cannot be snuffed by killing the messenger.' Mayor Wender was right. The idea that we are more than a collection of towns, that we can rebuild a state spanning this whole coast cannot be snuffed, and in the faces I see in the distance, I know that idea is as strong today as it was three days ago."

She lowered her voice. "I am Chancellor Rachel Czernak, who said, 'The future of our civilization cannot depend on the whims of a puny fringe.' She was right seven years ago when she uttered those words. She was right four days ago, and she is right today. The fringe might change, but the lesson won't. We will not be hostage to the whims of the few. We will not let them control our future. Not here. Not today. Not ever."

The motion behind the barricades ratcheted up. The militia were not scuffling with the crowd trying to push through as she'd first thought. They were scuffling with each other.

"I am Amy Chipps, and I say if you see division or confusion or weakness or fear, look again. We are united by our ambition. We grow stronger with every kind word, every good deed. We are not afraid of guns, and we are definitely not afraid of the future.

"We are survivors. We are descendants of a people that nearly went extinct many times over. Seventy thousand years ago, there were only ten thousand adult humans left on the planet. What did they do? They became nine billion. Compared to them, we have it easy."

She moved her head from her left to the right, pausing at each of the roadblocks. "Words. I only have words to offer you today. No promises, no illusion. Words and a demand, Mr. Mayor." She raised her right hand, index finger pointing up, and brought her hand down with each of her next four words. "Take. Down. These. Barricades."

Her face moved to the Santa Cruz wing and back toward the Cal City crowd ahead of her. "Friends, our future is in your hands. History is watching. It will recall this day. I ask you to make sure it says something worth remembering, something that will make us all proud." She let her gaze fall on the sentries at the barricades. "I'm counting on you. I am counting on New California. Thank you."

Applause came from behind her and from the distance. She assumed she had reached the citizens who had gathered behind the roadblocks. She had, but half the troops in the barricades were also applauding. Several moved forward past their own roadblocks and walked toward the capitol. The citizens behind them pushed forward and joined them.

She heard shouts but no shots.

———————

AMY SAT IN HER OFFICE AND RUBBED HER TEMPLES. IN THE thirty minutes following her speech, four militia leaders had pledged their support to her. Mountain View and Santa Cruz had officially recognized her as governor. That was not a bad return for six minutes on stage.

Her next guest, Colonel Rendon, was going to be the first Marin official she would receive. Cavana had argued against it. As head of state, her equivalent would have been Chancellor Lester. Though Amy understood protocol, the value of anyone in Marin's recognizing her legitimacy far outweighed protocol.

Cavana's head popped through the door. "Great job, Governor. Who was your inspiration?"

"The fact that we're still here is all the inspiration I needed."

"Oh, okay."

"What?"

"I figured you were quoting some famous writer or something."

She shook her head. "No, just me. Just some thoughts."

"They were good thoughts." He walked away, looking embarrassed.

She was still staring at the open door when Ferg knocked and introduced Colonel Sierra Rendon.

Rendon was taller than she'd expected. On their only screen conversation, she'd been plain spoken and without the bluster Amy had come to expect from an executive officer. She had pictured Rendon as a smallish woman who excelled in organizational skills. Faced with the fit, confident soldier who greeted her, she chastised herself. After spending the first three minutes exchanging compliments and sipping coffee, Amy put her elbows on her desk, clasped her hands, and leaned forward. "Colonel, you said you had official business?"

Rendon put her cup down and leaned back. "I can make some up." She waited a few seconds. "General Rose thought it would be helpful if we had an official meeting."

"Why is General Rose extending this courtesy?"

"She'd like a functioning New Cal and an ally in office."

"Very well. Is there anything you'd like to talk about while we pretend to talk business?"

Rendon shook her head. Amy went back to studying the backgrounds of the militia leaders who had pledged their loyalty to her. She needed them, but she had a greater need of keeping alive the promise that things would get better. Eric had been good at providing that type of inspiration, but that worked only if you delivered, and she hadn't delivered much. She glanced at Rendon sitting there still as a statue.

Amy cocked her head. "Why are you really here, Colonel?"

"General Rose thought it—"

"Would be helpful, yes, but why? What do you care if it's me or Halsan in this chair?"

"The general wanted to thank you for the warning about the Kern army movement."

Amy nodded to buy time.

"Bayley's tip was solid," Rendon said.

Of course it had to be Mika. He never did the expected, but he always did something. Mostly, it was something useful, but a direct line to Rose's XO? That was one secret too far. Any question would imply she hadn't known, so she tapped her screen, bringing back the militia breakdown to distract herself.

Rendon stood up and straightened her jacket. "May I speak off the record?"

Amy nodded again.

"That pendant was a nice touch. You hypnotized half my troops. They couldn't keep their eyes off of it or stop talking about it."

Amy brought her hand to her chest and held the pendant. "A memento."

Rendon smiled. "Works fine either way as a map from the past and a roadmap to the future. Nice symbolism, and the speech was inspiring too."

Amy flicked her hair behind her ear to distract herself from the compliments.

"It captured the moment just right. You must have a great speechwriting team."

Amy chuckled. She did not remember anyone telling Eric such things. "I don't have speechwriters."

"Oh." Rendon's eyes widened.

"I wrote it myself thirty minutes before I delivered it."

Rendon moved to the door but paused. "Mostly, I don't vote, but I'd vote for you."

It was Amy's turn to smile. "Are you joining New Cal, Colonel?"

"No. I meant for Chancellor of Marin."

Rendon walked out, leaving Amy to stare at a closing door and opening horizons.

CHAPTER 19

NEW DECEPTION

"Those who know do not speak. Those who speak do not know."

—LAO TSU

Swaths of green extended from the coast to the ocean, painting areas they'd explored and found empty. An ominous gray signaling the unknown still covered most of the ocean. Lori was convinced that every minute they wasted, the Kern army crept another mile closer. Wherever it was. After viewing the south and east as their vulnerable borders for a decade, Lori feared their sentries north weren't up to the task. She'd put Kagawa back in the field to scout.

Lori couldn't afford to lose competent people to self-doubt or a witch hunt. It was now clear the assault at Ross was the culmination of a deep conspiracy spanning three states. Kagawa's security wasn't to blame, and in fact, their quick action had saved scores of lives.

Sierra scanned the charts as Kagawa's reports filtered in. "Still nothing."

"What's our footprint?"

Sierra glanced at her screen. "We have dispatched three transports, six trucks, and two dozen troops."

The insight they'd received from Mika the night before rang true to her. It had just the right element of desperation she'd expect from Kern. In spite of not having seen any evidence of militarized ships or missing Kern troops, Lori had started discreetly moving troops. But the Pacific was a big ocean, and even a militarized fleet capable of delivering thousands of troops was a speck on it. "Keep at it."

"One question, General."

"Yes?"

"How much of this data can we trust?"

"The harbor data seem accurate. Missing troops are estimates. Don't trust anything you don't verify, and keep looking for possible landing spots."

"We will confirm the missing ships in two hours."

"Keep the troops moving."

"General, it is not my place to question your decisions, but if this is a trap—"

"You mean if those ships are empty?"

"If those ships are still in Southern California—"

"They aren't."

"General, I understand Bayley is not a known Kern collaborator, but I find it suspicious that he stumbled on such harbor information. Why would anyone notice missing ships?"

Mika's love for the sea and boats was no secret to anyone who knew him. They'd spent months hiding in those parts with Mika passing the time counting ships. It had driven her crazy, but it was who he was.

"Colonel, do you trust me?"

"General!"

"I'll take that as a yes. Those ships are out there somewhere. Let's focus on finding them and determining how many troops they carry."

"Yes, ma'am."

Lori pointed to the northern shore of the Golden Gate. "We need heavy guns here." She pointed to the south. "And here."

"In New Cal?"

Lori nodded. "Go talk to your new pal, the governor, and make her see the value in this."

"Do I have anything to offer, ma'am?"

"We'll protect them as well," she said, creating a new treaty as she spoke.

Sierra didn't move or speak.

"Now, Colonel. Dismissed."

LORI WALKED ALONG THE LINE OF TRUCKS WAITING BY THE southern edge of the one-lane road hugging the cliff above Baker Beach. It had taken Sierra two hours to convince Chipps to cooperate. Lori had had no doubt. Between Sierra's praise and Mika's protectiveness, Lori felt as though she knew Chipps: stubborn but someone who understood who the real enemy was.

Lori's troops were entrenching heavy guns along the mile-long stretch of cliffs west of the Golden Gate Bridge, guarding the entrance to the bay. Their progress had been halted by a smattering of soldiers in gray-blue uniforms. They'd appeared minutes ago, blocking the path of her trucks. She approached them. "What's going on here?"

"You cannot use this road," the balding man in a suit said. He stood in front of the truck with half a dozen armed guards.

Lori got closer and recognized the uniforms as Cal City militia. "Why not?"

"This road belongs to Cal City."

"We just cleared this with the governor."

The man shook his head. "If you dealt with the usurper in the capitol, your agreement has no standing." He puffed up his chest. "In fact, why haven't you arrested her yet?"

"Who are you?"

"I'm the mayor of this city and governor of New Cal. I cannot allow you to pass."

So this was Halsan. "Mayor, do I look like I give a fuck what you will allow?"

Halsan's jaw tightened and a bead of sweat appeared on his forehead. "We are allies. You cannot just trample our sovereignty."

Lori signaled the truck forward. The truck edged forward, but the man didn't move.

"You cannot do this. We are not at war."

He seemed to think telling her what she could not do was a strategy. "We will be in five seconds if you don't get the fuck out of my way." She tapped the side of the truck and yelled over the rumbling engine, "Move!"

"You will hear about this!" Halsan shouted but stepped aside as the truck gathered momentum. "I will speak to the chancellor!"

Take a number. The world was never short on its fool supply. No sooner you dealt with one, another popped up to take their place. But this fool had been a little too bold, too entitled. She'd have to keep tabs on this fool.

------------------------------*------------------------------

NOT FIGHTING ON MULTIPLE FRONTS HAD BEEN THE FIRST lesson drilled into Lori, but every action she took opened a new front and exposed new enemies: the Kern army on the loose, the Asher affair, the frame-up attempt, Halsan, and the Ross investigation. Enough fronts to lose sleep over.

Sierra had concluded the Ross attack had not been perpetrated by Kern, but that raised more questions than it answered. Lori wasn't even sure whether the surviving assailant had cracked or lost her mind. They were getting a stream of leads from her, implicating half the military, but names were names, and though most turned out worthless, some held value.

One such name was the hound responsible for leaving traces of Lori's ID at Asher's disappearance. They'd found her dead, shot in the head, hours after she'd been named. Then there was the soldier presumed dead for two years who'd been alive enough to accompany Tran to liberate the drones used at Ross. Some leads pointed to General Herrera, Lester's favorite officer, but they were too circumstantial to act upon. She first had to find which way the manipulation graph flowed.

"General?" Sierra held the door, leaning into Lori's office and blocking the way in.

"Yes?"

"The chancellor insisted on seeing you."

Lori had expected this but not this soon. "Put her on the screen."

Sierra nudged her head back with her eyes looking up. Lester was here.

"General Rose," Lester barged in, pushing Sierra aside. "We need to talk."

Lori took a deep breath to delay speaking. She gestured for Sierra to stay. Every interaction she had with Lester had the makings of a rebellion. Each one could be explained individually, but they were converging toward a dangerous picture. She wanted Sierra to see each step so the final one wouldn't rattle her, assuming anything would rattle Sierra.

Lester glanced at Sierra and sat down across from Lori's desk. "What are you doing out in New Cal?"

Lori had missed something. Again. A call, yes, but a visit? An hour after she'd returned from New Cal? So Halsan had a direct line to Lester, interesting and disturbing.

"Nothing you should worry about. Simple troop movement."

"Do not insult me, General. When our troops cross into New Cal, I need to know."

"We have reliable intel that the Kern army is attempting to outflank us. I recalled all reserve units." The chancellor's body language gave nothing away. "I recommend you declare martial law so we can execute critical troop movement." Lori still got no response, though the edge of Lester's lips drooped. "Also, I need access to all weaponry, including the scramjets."

Lester moved from displeased to disgusted. "That is a lot of firepower."

"We might be facing an offensive on Marin soil. I need all the power we have."

"Outflank?"

"Yes. We have reason to believe they plan to attack from the north."

Lester raised an eyebrow. Lori assumed Lester was trying to determine what that meant. They'd never discussed naval warfare or thought of the sea as a potential front.

"Where is this force now?" Lester asked.

"We are trying to locate it."

"Let me get this straight. You want me to declare martial law and hand you our most precious weapons because of a threat to the existence of Marin, and you do not know what that threat is or where it is coming from?"

Put like that, Lori understood Lester's disbelief. "We have reliable intelligence."

Lester remained silent for fifteen seconds. "I know I asked you to deal with Kern, but we do not need to play these games. I will not declare martial law or hand over the scramjets. Now keep mobilizing, but the troops are moving south. I want an assault on Kern in forty-eight hours."

"Chancellor, we need to—"

"I just gave you a direct order."

"Yes, ma'am." Lori suspected she hadn't kept the contempt from her voice.

Lester stood up and glared at her. "Do not make me regret promoting you."

Lori also stood. "Yes, Chancellor."

Lester stormed off, leaving Lori standing in her own office with orders she couldn't follow. Sierra closed the door. Lori suspected Sierra had a high tolerance for nonsense because she understood its purpose. Machines needed oil to operate smoothly. Politics needed nonsense.

"Should I reverse troop movement?" Sierra asked.

Dey's edict about how often you could disobey a direct order was correct. And she'd already reached her full count. "The chancellor said nothing about heavy weapons. Keep the artillery moving as scheduled, and if some troops need to move with them, that's fine too."

Sierra did not react.

"I learned a valuable lesson from an old friend. There's no point arguing with authority when you know you're right. Our job is to defend Marin, and that's what we're going to do. I cannot let the safety of Marin be compromised to comply with orders. Do you have a problem with that?"

Sierra reached for the door handle. "I will coordinate the movement of artillery. Is there anything else?"

"Get me three scrammies."

"Three?"

"I'll meet the chancellor halfway."

Lori needed someone to talk to. With Dey gone, she'd lost her mentor. General Lisa Kuipers was her senior in both age and military service. They talked strategy, though Kuipers was incapable of thinking like a Kern commander. That's probably why Czernak had passed her over. Lori did not know why Lester had, but the more she got to know Lester, the less she understood her actions. That Lester had picked her instead of Kuipers made her question not only her own values but also her role in the game Lester was playing.

Kuipers wasn't here either.

"Sierra, you're here to tell me if I'm making a mistake."

Sierra let the door handle go. "Like when I questioned the reliability of Bayley's intel?"

"Yes, like that. I heard you. I just didn't change my mind. I need to hear you again."

"Putting gun batteries south of the Golden Gate is sound strategy, but till we learn more about the Kern troops, I urge restraint and caution."

Lori tapped on her desk. She had not expected Sierra to contradict her, but she had wanted to ask in case she had missed something obvious. The knock on the door interrupted her thoughts.

"Yes?"

A communications officer appeared, uttering the words Lori had both been planning for and dreading since she'd gotten Mika's message. "We've made contact with the Kern troops."

"And?"

"Transport SC-2 was shot down over Fort Bragg by Kern forces."

So much for restraint or caution.

CHAPTER 20

OLD SCARS

"It's a shallow life that doesn't give a person a few scars."

–GARRISON KEILLOR

The news that Mika was in the capitol reached Amy before Mika did. She scanned the security footage. He waltzed into the building, talked to the guards, and stepped into the elevator. It all was so easy.

He emerged on her floor on screen, and then there he was in her office, in the flesh, as though nothing had happened over the last few days. She stood, and as they made eye contact, her ire gave way to concern. Mika's face was hidden behind new scars. Here they were, two souls refusing to bow to the forces bent on destroying them. She was no longer sure such souls were meant for each other.

He stood motionless, eight feet away. After a few seconds, she let the tension in her face melt and allowed a smile to appear. He took a step and put his arms around her. "I'm proud of you. I don't think anyone is wondering who the governor is anymore."

"Aren't you going to ask me who wrote my speech?"

"Why would I do that?"

"Everyone else does."

"Really? Defiance and promise, nods to past and future but firmly rooted in the present. It had your fingerprints all over it."

She appreciated the compliment, but it still nagged her that he hadn't been there. That bothered her, but so did his dry lips and sweaty brow. "Are you all right?"

"I'm okay." He hesitated. "I'm sorry I wasn't here—not that you needed me."

"We're managing."

He wiped his forehead with the back of his hand and sat down on the chair across her desk. "What's Marin doing in the cliffs?"

She sat on her desk and squinted, but it focused only her eyes, not her conflicting thoughts. "Seems General Rose needs access to our cliffs and promises to defend us against Kern aggression."

Mika smiled as though he'd expected it, so even that wasn't what it appeared to be.

She was still discovering the man behind the façade. She liked the clarity of his mind, always a step ahead of disaster, and how he managed to keep a lighter side. Did she see the real Mika in the few moments when they were alone? Was the real Mika the cocky data stalker? Another knock interrupted her.

"What?" she snapped.

Cavana pushed her office door open. "Governor."

"Can't it wait?"

Cavana shook his head. "It is Santa Cruz. You need to talk to them, or they walk."

She hopped off her desk and spoke to Mika. "Don't go anywhere."

Cavana's footsteps did not follow her. "I would not cross her if I were you," she heard him say to Mika, and he didn't sound like he was joking.

She pressed on with half a smile.

───────────※───────────

THE BRIGHT LIGHTS HAD TRIGGERED HIS HEADACHE, SO MIKA dimmed the lights and closed the curtains. He shut his eyes and rested his head on the back of the chair to relieve the tension on his face. He dozed off.

He opened his eyes. It had been forty minutes. He felt even more tired than before he'd slept. He got up, but the room spun around him. He steadied himself on the chair and grabbed a glass of water. He'd just sat back down when Amy opened the door. She too looked tired. She sat across from him, and any hope he'd had this would be a light conversation disappeared when she spoke.

"Who is Lori Rose?"

He focused on her eyes. Fierce, strong, and more belligerent with each second he remained silent. The cold answer was that she was the chief commander of Marin's armed forces. The partial truth was that she was the doctor's aide he knew a lifetime ago. The insightful truth was that she was the girl he met at a market two lifetimes ago, the teenager who could carry a sack of oranges. The painful truth was that she was the vulnerable woman with whom he had run and hidden after Tom had been murdered in cold blood. None of them, though, defined Lori.

"An old friend," he heard himself say. *Yes, like that's going to do it.*

"Were you lovers?"

An amusing thought, but he had the good sense not to laugh. "God no."

"Why not?"

There had been a time he'd wanted that. Lori had grown into a graceful woman while he was still a lanky teenager. She'd gently but firmly resisted his awkward advances, and there had been a time when Lori had needed that, but just as Lori had known his crush would not have survived her moods, he had known that needing was not the same as wanting.

The rage in Lori burned deep. He was the ice to her fire, a force that resisted her impulses, a presence she wasn't willing to burn. A relationship would have stoked the fire, turning it into a blaze that would have consumed them both.

"It would have never worked. I won't lie to you. I care for her.

Being across the bridge used to bother me, but I got over it. She chose her path, and I chose mine."

Amy played with her tida, holding it between her index and middle fingers and tapping it with her thumb. "Look, I can deal with old lovers, and I can deal with friends, but I need to know what it is I'm dealing with."

"What do you want from me?"

"I can't believe you just asked me that." She shook her head. "I want you to be honest with me. I want to understand you, but any time we get near anything personal, you clam up."

"I'm pretty simple. I want to know what the fuck happened to the world."

"Why? Everyone wants to move forward. Why are you stuck in the past?"

The past? The Purge wasn't in the past. It was everywhere, on every face. They were all linked, but then again, he didn't agree that everyone wanted to move forward. It wasn't her words that connected with him. It was her passion. It was almost contagious. Almost.

"I think I'm falling for you." He surprised himself at how easily the words came out.

"I wish I knew what that meant and what I'm getting into."

"I'm sorry. When I think of events that shaped me, a few stand out. Wounds that go deep, so deep that you think they'll never heal. In time, they all do. All you're left with is scars, reminding you of the raw pain but also of the healing. In some cases, the healing can be more painful than the wound." He pulled his shirt down, exposing a three-inch scar on his right shoulder. "I let a knife get too close to me once. It almost killed me." He let his fingers move over the scar. "I remember his face as he stabbed me. Concentration and anger were all mixed up. I got stitched up and worked out bit by bit until I got my strength back. The stabbing and the rehab are linked in my mind, the two sides of this scar." He pulled his shirt back up.

She opened her mouth but didn't speak. He waited.

"We're not talking about your shoulder, are we?" she asked.

"I'm sorry these scars are bubbling up now."

"Which side of the scar was she on?"

"Both," he said.

"Hurt you and healed you?"

She had but not in that order.

The initial wound had been deeper for Lori, and her healing had fashioned General Rose. Her scar had caused his wound, the one that hadn't closed yet. Lori had shielded herself from everyone, including Mika. Amy wanted answers and needed assurances. He was happy giving her the latter, but without the right answers, they'd be hollow.

"When did you meet her?"

"I was a little over eight. In and out of orphanages. I hated those places. The volunteers kept dropping dead. The food trucks never arrived, because the drivers were dead. They were more depressing and dangerous than being on your own, so I ran away enough times that they stopped coming after me. I survived by going to shelters and stealing food at markets. I saw Lori at a market. Her eyes scanned everyone and every counter. She was a survivor, so I told her I'd help her get food if she'd let me stay with her."

"How did you know she had a safe place to stay?"

"Her clothes fit, and she didn't have bags under her eyes."

"That meant what?"

"Kids at the shelters shared clothes from the racks. They never fit. I knew she didn't stay in a shelter, but those on their own have to be on guard all the time. They yawned all the time, always tired. She didn't, so she had to have a safe place to sleep."

She studied him as though there was something wrong with him. "What kind of an eight-year-old were you?"

He shrugged. "The kind who got to be a nine-year-old."

"Fair enough. How were you going to get her food?"

"That was the easy part. One of the warehouses had a bent

metal gate. Even when it was closed, I was small enough to squeeze through. The second floor was full of bulk food. Oats, rice, and occasionally even oranges, but I couldn't carry enough to be worth the risk. There was a tree across the fence. I needed to get a moving clothesline going, so I got in, she tossed me the line, I looped it and tossed it back. We got enough food in half an hour to last a month, and I doubt they even noticed it was missing."

Amy frowned, and he knew why. She had asked about scars, and they were talking about orange thieves. "What is it between you two, Mika?"

It was a part of him that had been so well sealed he didn't even know where to start unwrapping it. He went to her and wrapped his arms around her. He leaned over and kissed her neck.

Amy broke his hold. "You're not making this easy." She moved to the door. She stopped and waited as though she expected him to offer more. He remained silent, so she walked out, leaving him alone in her office. He did not want to lose her, but if she insisted on too many details, he was most likely going to.

Mika stood by the window. Everyone out there operated on a high with the anticipation that something significant was about to happen. He feared that no one was going to like it when something did finally happen. He put his hand on his left kidney and stroked the skin. He gritted his teeth and stepped out. He needed to get away from the capitol, away from the sense of foreboding.

He walked, though he had nowhere to go.

He found himself at the harbor. At high tide, the four floating docks jutting out to sea were almost level with the walking path anchored by concrete pillars. He took a step toward the boats but found it hard to keep his balance. The wood under his foot felt soft, elastic, as though it stretched and bounced with his steps.

The walk had intensified his pain. He sat on a bench, overlooking the boats. These were peaceful boats, unlike the ones out there, bringing impending doom.

He was sweating far more than an easy walk should have warranted. He couldn't remember why he was at the docks.

He leaned back and vomited over the bench. He took slow breaths until his queasiness subsided. He sat back, facing the docks. The docks split in two with boats multiplying.

A sailboat lunged at him. He tilted his head back to let it fly over him. When he faced the docks again, the boat was still there.

He took another deep breath. His vision blurred, and a diffused white spot appeared in his field of vision. The boats disappeared, seared by the white spot.

He leaned back on the bench and closed his eyes. The pain had spread from his side to his back. He exhaled, trying to push the pain out alongside his breath. It did not work.

He collapsed forward, and his face hit the worn dock. It was not nearly elastic enough.

Disconnected from external stimuli, his mind slowed. As darkness engulfed him, his thoughts found Amy and the way she'd left him. He tried to recall her face, her scent, but he could not.

His last conscious thought was surprise. He smelled tobacco on the wet wood pressed against his nose.

CHAPTER 21

OLD WORRIES

*"Bitterness is like cancer. It eats upon the host.
But anger is like fire. It burns it all clean."*

—MAYA ANGELOU

I n another day, Lori would have had the troops to face the Kern army up north. It was a bitter joke that Mika had provided crucial intel too late for her to use it effectively.

A twenty-foot screen monopolized the narrow end of the rectangular command center on the top floor of the military headquarters, displaying a map centered on Marin. Data and tactical analysis boxes were superimposed over the coastline. Half the Kern fleet had landed in Fort Bragg and had already fortified defenses. That only half the ships had shown up was an even bigger problem. The estimated six thousand on shore were already more than the full force they'd been expecting, more than they could handle.

Kern's footprint stretched over twenty miles from Fort Bragg to the mouth of the Navarro River. The first armored vehicles were pushing inland. Lori suspected they'd take the ridge all the way to the north end of Anderson Valley. Once their full army was in that valley, they would be impossible to stop.

Sierra set out their options. They were limited. The closest Marin unit was a light armored reconnaissance company forty miles south of Anderson Valley. Lori had ordered them north to block Kern's entry into the valley. That was a race not just against the clock but also against logic.

Any real help was at least two hours away.

"We've found the rest of the fleet!" an officer called from across the room.

"On screen."

Cones appeared on the water, heading directly for the mouth of the Navarro River. Now that they had secured the coast, there was no need for them to disembark as far as Fort Bragg.

"How many?"

"At least three thousand, perhaps four."

None of their estimates had shown that Kern possessed this much manpower or firepower. If that force made it to Anderson Valley, Marin was lost. She spoke so only Sierra could hear. "Get me a dozen transports fueled and armed with missiles, ready to go."

"General, those ships have anti-aircraft defenses."

"I'm well aware of that," Lori snapped. She found an officer on a headset. "Where is Kuipers?"

The officer swiped at her screen. "In the building. She'll be here in ninety seconds as will Generals Gardner and Herrera."

In less than thirty minutes, the floor had transformed from a quietly efficient military headquarters into a war room. Com officers lined one wall leading to the large display ensuring Lori had a direct line to each unit in the field. The opposite wall contained four high tables, each the domain of a different general's officers. The cacophony of a dozen conversations turned the forty-by-sixty-foot command center into a cramped and oppressive cave.

The transformation was more drastic outside. Declaration Square had become a staging area. Recalled reserves arrived by the minute, heavy trucks picked up their loads, Humvees darted around in all directions. Beyond the square, transports swallowed troops by the dozen. It was all too calm, too precise—nothing like the panicked mess that must have unfolded that first winter. She couldn't tell whether that constituted progress.

A thin rope even protected the boulders from the choreographed chaos as though they were the fragile ones, not the soft sacks of flesh and bone she was hurtling north.

First Lori had to make sure everyone understood the stakes, and then she had to convince them they had the upper hand. She faced her officers and waved to the map on the screen. "Let's forget everything we know about supply lines and long-term strategy. This engagement hinges on one thing: either they make it out into the valley in the next two days or they don't."

Kuipers, the most senior officer in the room, nodded. "How do you propose to stop them? We have under two hundred troops in engagement distance."

The exact numbers appeared on the screen. A company of 170 with six heavy guns, Kagawa's twenty-four scouts with three transports, against an army with air support.

"Who is in charge of that company?" General Gardner asked.

"Captain Morales was," Sierra said. "Major Kagawa has taken command. We can send armed transports to provide limited air support, but to move heavy artillery, we need two hours."

"Which Major Kagawa doesn't have," Kuipers said.

Sierra blinked. "She can delay them for two hours."

"How?" asked Gardner.

Lori knew what Sierra was thinking. It was the sort of tactic that occurred only to a certain type of people. Some said those people did not value life. They were wrong. It meant they understood how everything was linked and appreciated one's place in that chain. Sometimes you had a starring role, sometimes a bit part.

Sierra pointed to three spots along the ridge before it opened into Anderson Valley. "These are the narrowest points on their path. Thirty, forty feet, so the armored vehicles need to move in single file. That's where we hit them."

They all knew what would ensue. Sierra verbalized it anyway. "Each strike will delay the Kern army about fifteen minutes. We have six heavy guns and three transports within range."

Kuipers closed her eyes. Sierra didn't need to expand on the tactics. The transports were scouts, defenseless against Kern missiles, and each of the strikes would result in returned fire. They were setting the exchange rate: lives for minutes. With the hand they were dealt, it wasn't a favorable rate. Kuipers' silence told Lori what the old general was thinking. Kuipers had found fault in Sierra's ethics, not her tactics, and unless Kuipers could come up with a better option, she'd express her displeasure with silence.

Lori sympathized with Kuipers, but she didn't have the luxury of considering morality with their existence in the balance. "Sierra, get me Major Kagawa."

"Are you sure you want to talk to her?" asked Kuipers.

"Very." Lori pitched her head forward and dug her index and middle fingers into a lump of muscle in her neck. The muscle didn't give, because no amount of kneading could release this tension. She let go of her neck when Kagawa appeared on screen. Kagawa's picture looked still.

"General Rose."

"Major." The soldier's somber face told her she'd absorbed the tactical analysis. She knew what was expected of her. "I wish I could say reinforcements will reach you in time."

"I understand, General."

"I know what I'm asking, Major." She took a deep breath. "Yuka, I am not ordering you to fight. I am ordering you to die."

The silence on the other end stretched.

"You can count on us, General," Kagawa said. "We will not let you down."

"I know."

"How long do we have?"

"Twenty minutes."

"We will be ready."

"I don't doubt it, Yuka. I don't doubt it."

"We need to prepare." Kagawa waited for a few seconds. "It's been an honor, General."

"The honor is mine." Lori meant it. She'd thought Kagawa would be defined by Ross, spend her life trying to redeem a career gone off the rails. She'd never thought Kagawa would succeed, much less in a week. Fate was fickle, giving them a chance at redemption but extracting a heavy toll. Lori's jaw was clenched so hard her molars ached.

Kuipers put a hand on her arm. Lori appreciated the gesture but moved away. She had told 194 soldiers they'd probably never see their loved ones again. She wasn't the one who needed comforting.

The troops now moved north and west with all discretion removed from the equation. It still wasn't fast enough, but it beat the slow charade they had been playing the previous evening.

The expected call from the chancellor drew Lori away from the strategy table. Lester's face displaced the map on the giant screen. "General, I recall ordering you to not move troops north."

"Chancellor, there is an army of six thousand men to our north."

"I am aware of that, General."

All activity ceased. Lori had operated from the assumption that Lester had been in the dark. An ill-informed politician clinging to the illusion that safety could be achieved with words. "Chancellor, they shot our transport."

"General, this is why there is a chain of command. I have been negotiating with Kern commanders for a week. The forces to our north are defecting. They shot the transport in self-defense. That one is on you for disobeying a direct order. Kern troops to our north will support the Marin-New Cal federation. The only army still loyal to Kern Central is in Bakersfield."

Doubt crept in Lori's mind for the first time since she'd been fighting Kern. If Lester was right, Lori was about to attack friendly forces. But the tactical analysis did not match what she heard. There was no reason for a friendly force to seek the valley or to shoot a scout down. Words were no substitute for deeds. She knew that everyone in the room wanted to believe the Kern force was friendly. She did not allow herself to be distracted.

"One moment, Chancellor." Lori froze the link.

By her reckoning, she had less than three minutes before the chancellor fired her or arrested her.

She walked to Sierra and lowered her voice. "The day we were ambushed in the Uregs and lost Asher, when did you call Lester to cancel my lunch?"

"Immediately after I left your office."

Lester, or someone in her office, had known Lori would be in the Uregs hours before they'd gotten there. There was their leak. That made trusting Lester's words instead of the troop movement even more difficult. Impossible, in fact. It still made what Lori had to do excruciating. She was about to go against everything she stood for. Order? Smashed. Chain of command? Broken. Career? Gone, and yet she felt at ease. Lori walked back to the screen but faced the room where a dozen high-ranking officers were coordinating their forces. "I need your full attention." She waited for the heads to lift.

She took two steps to clear her head. "You've all heard my conversation with the chancellor. I do not believe the Kern army is there to defect, but I'm willing to consider the possibility. If anyone can point to any activity that suggests their movement is not offensive or that they could have shot our transport in self-defense, I need to hear it now."

"The chancellor said that—" Herrera started.

Lori raised a hand to stop her. "Words. I want actions. Is there anything the Kern army did that can be interpreted as anything but hostile?"

"You do not get to make that call," Herrera said and took a step toward her.

Sierra intercepted Herrera. Her gun was drawn. "General."

Herrera's officers went for their guns, but they were too late. Sierra's team had them covered.

"Let's not do this," Lori said. Herrera's officers let go of their guns. "Did you contact the chancellor?" Lori asked Herrera.

Herrera nodded. "Aren't you going to ask why I did it?"

"I don't care why you did it." Lori turned to Sierra. "Please escort the general out."

Lori waited until Herrera and her officers walked out. "Okay then. We've all known that if we lose this war, we will be executed. Now I am about to give orders that will contradict the chancellor. That means that if you follow them, even if we win the war, you will be court-martialed. This is your last chance to leave. But if you stay, I need your full dedication regardless of the personal cost." No one moved, so Lori turned to Kuipers. "General, I need you to tell me if I'm making a mistake. For the last time, any chance that force might be friendly?"

Kuipers' eyes moved from the map to the displays as though looking at it one more time would make it say something new. She shook her head.

The screen facing the main table had been chiming nonstop since she had cut off the connection. She waved, and the chancellor reappeared. Lori patched her to the main screen.

"Was there a technical problem?" Lester hissed.

"No. No problem, Chancellor. I needed to confer with my officers."

"General, you received a direct order. I do not recall asking for an analysis."

"I'm sorry, Chancellor. I cannot allow you to jeopardize the safety of Marin. The army you say is defecting moves in a threatening manner. A defecting force would have remained north. This one shot a scout transport and is moving inland, trying to reach terrain that would provide a direct path to Marin. Their actions can't be interpreted as anything but hostile."

"General Rose, you are relieved of command. General Herrera, place General Rose under arrest." When nothing happened, Lester spoke again. "General Kuipers."

Kuipers did not reply.

Lester's eyes moved around. "General Gardner." The scene repeated. "Promoting you was the worst mistake I ever made," Lester said. "I should have listened to Czernak. General Kuipers,

I have evidence linking Rose to the weapons used to assassinate Chancellor Czernak and to the disappearance of multiple soldiers just to start this war. I order you to arrest General Rose."

Kuipers turned to Lori for an instant, turned back to the screen, and shook her head. "I'm sorry, Chancellor, I will not do that."

Lester's tone grew colder. "I am charging everyone in that room with inciting a war. A court-martial will be convened to determine your culpability, and if you are found—"

"I think," Lori said, "we can dispense with the threats. Now, Chancellor, if you'll excuse us, we have the defense of Marin to coordinate." She came eye to eye with Kuipers. The old general didn't need an explanation. Not now.

Kuipers nodded, and Lori nodded back.

Lori gave the word to start the offensive on the second fleet. The transports were already in the air, and the scramjets were now within two hundred miles of the fleet. Lori knew that the fleet's defenses would be sufficient to overcome ordinary missiles, but there was no defense against a scramjet coming at you at 7,000 mph.

Once the fortified ships were taken out, ordinary missiles would pick out the rest.

"General, this is my final warning. Do not engage. We are not at war."

She had almost forgotten Lester was still on the line. She felt a strange echo, hearing the same five words the Cal City mayor had uttered. But repeating them didn't make them true.

She tapped the screen, sending the codes authorizing each unit to engage. That meant the transports released their scramjets, the light transports released their missiles, and Kagawa's forces shelled the ridge.

The arrow was in flight. She couldn't shake the feeling she'd started pulling on the bowstring with her unanswered inquiries about missing soldiers, leading to Asher, leading to Ross, leading here, step by step. Her next words were as much for her audience in the room as they were for Lester. "We are now."

PART III

BLAZE

CHAPTER 22

NEW WORRIES

"The truth is rarely pure and never simple."

—OSCAR WILDE

Though Marin policies puzzled her, Amy couldn't dismiss the chancellor's request to mediate talks with Kern defectors, but the term confused her. *Defecting* implied the possibility of a new life. She couldn't see how Marin offered that to a Kern officer, but that was probably where she came in. New Cal provided an alternative acceptable to both parties.

She'd tried to find Mika before leaving, but he'd disappeared again. After their spat, she suspected he needed time and space, but right about now, she could have used his insight, because the disorganized mess they were flying over didn't fit her model of a menacing Kern battalion.

"I'd like to talk to Kern soldiers," she said.

"We can call a few once we land," Cavana said.

"I mean now."

They were on a light transport configured for passengers with five rows of three seats in the main cabin. Kiril and Cavana sat in the front row and Amy in the second. Four of Cavana's men occupied the two back rows. Amy stood and walked toward the cockpit along the double doors on the starboard side. "Can we land there?" she asked the pilot, pointing to a hill. They were over twenty miles from the compound that had become a makeshift Marin base.

The pilot nodded.

"Do it." She sat back down.

"Governor, I do not think this is a good idea." As her new advisor, Cavana's job was to question her moves. Hers was to not ignore things that were out of place.

Two soldiers in Kern uniforms approached them as they landed into a clearing a hundred yards away from the nearest activity. Amy stepped off after Cavana. "Who is the commanding officer here?" she asked when the approaching soldiers got within thirty feet.

One of the soldiers pointed to a tent in the distance. He had a scruffy beard, and his uniform didn't fit.

"All the officers left fifteen minutes ago," the other one said. He wore sunglasses and a bandana under his cap.

More armed men were approaching. Cavana's team moved into a defensive in position, but if it came to a firefight, they were severely undergunned.

"We should go," Cavana muttered.

They walked back to the transport. As they took off, she instructed the pilot to circle the camp. The chaos extended farther than she'd thought, but what bothered her most was that the soldiers had answered her, accepting her authority. Even allowing for the fact that they were in a defector camp, that was a jarring departure for indoctrinated Kern soldiers.

As they landed in the Marin camp and Amy stepped out, an officer greeted her with a hand wave. "Colonel Mary Milner." They exchanged a few words that didn't mean anything.

"Is the Kern contingent here?" Amy asked as they walked to the compound.

Milner shook her head. "They're delayed. Should be here in another hour."

That was a long time to travel a few miles. "Have you interacted with them yet?"

Milner shook her head. "Very little."

"Notice anything out of place, anything that doesn't add up?"

Milner took a few seconds too long to say no. One of Milner's officers looked away.

Amy turned to Cavana. "Nando, take your crew and visit the Kern camp. See what you can find out."

"Our orders are not to interact with the Kern battalion," Milner said.

"I understand, but those orders do not bind me."

"Governor," Milner said, "I cannot provide you with an escort or allow you to enter their camp."

Amy addressed Cavana. "Quick and discreet. Be back in an hour." She turned back to Milner. "My advisor will board that transport. Whether he visits the Kern camp or I join him and head back to New Cal is up to you."

"Governor, this isn't the time."

"Colonel, I accept there is some risk in everything we do, but I like to understand the risks, and I don't like it when the people I call allies lie to me. I saw the Kern troops on our way here, or I should say I didn't see them. Instead, I found a ragtag bunch who couldn't fight their way out of a jam with an Uregs gang. Right now, I don't know why we're here, and I need to know. Cavana is going to pay that camp a visit."

"Fine." Milner relented but was not pleased. "I don't see how anything he sees will help. Those officers will still need New Cal citizenship in return for staying out of the firefight. There is nothing you can do about it."

Amy shook her head. "Colonel. I'll mediate, assuming there is anyone or anything to mediate, but don't tell me what I can and cannot do. I'm here to offer a way out of the mess your leaders created."

Milner stood defiantly, neither offended enough to argue nor ready to explain what she knew. "I'm just following orders."

It took Cavana only forty-five minutes to call Amy back. She tapped her tida and listened. "Are you sure?" she said.

He was.

"Okay, get back here."

Milner was surrounded by her officers, huddled around a screen in the back room that had become her command center. She was frowning with the expression of a player trying to find the winning play at a card game.

"Is everything all right?" Amy asked.

"Still nothing from the Kern contingent," Milner said.

Whatever had Milner rattled wasn't the missing Kern defectors. "I don't think they're coming. Cavana confirmed what I suspected. That's not a Kern battalion out there."

Milner frowned. "That's a hell of a jump from a few minutes of inspection."

"Suit yourself, but as soon as he's back, we're leaving."

Milner walked toward her, grabbed her elbow, and moved her away from earshot. "What do you propose I do with a thousand armed Kern soldiers?"

"That's the point. They're not Kern soldiers. It looks like they were plucked from the Uregs and given uniforms. When we leave, they'll probably go back home, wherever that is."

"Probably? I have orders. I can't disobey them because you have a hunch."

Amy shook her arm free. "You can do whatever you like, but if I were you, I'd worry about where the real Kern soldiers are, because they sure as hell aren't here."

Milner's eyes brightened as though she'd found her winning move. "You're right, governor, you should leave." Milner turned to an officer. "Get me General Rose right now."

"Can't get through," the officer said as rumbling filled the room.

Amy stepped outside. Two Marin heavy transports were coming toward them. Kiril followed her and frowned as he spotted the transports.

"What's wrong?" Amy asked.

"They don't look like they're on a landing approach."

One of Lambert's officers stood by the door. Amy approached her. "Major Chastain?"

The woman nodded.

"Where are those two transports coming from?"

Chastain tapped her screen. "Strange."

It was not a word Amy liked hearing this far in the Uregs.

Chastain dropped her screen and pulled her gun. At that moment, Kiril dove and tackled Amy. As they landed, the building behind them turned into a fireball. Amy scampered to the side of the building, diving behind it. More explosions shook the ground, and gunfire followed. It wasn't the crack of handguns but the teeth-rattling thumping of heavy machine guns.

After a few moments of silence, Amy crouched. The holes on the side of the building were larger than the windows had been. She coughed, barely able to breathe from the heavy smoke and dust that filled the air. As her vision cleared, she spotted Kiril. He hadn't made it around the building. He lay in a pool of blood, lifeless eyes open and staring up.

Amy stumbled to the opening on the wall and peered inside what was left of the structure. Bodies in various stages of dismemberment specked the building and courtyard. Her eyes found Milner lying several feet away. Half her torso had been torn away.

Amy closed her eyes, clenched her jaw, and reopened her eyes. The scene did not change. One body stirred. Chastain. As Amy crawled toward her, three goggled figures appeared.

"She's alive," someone said. The words came in echoes as her ears were still ringing.

Two of the figures moved closer, both armed. "So is this one."

Handcuffs clicked on Chastain. Amy felt hands, and another set of cuffs clicked behind her. She was still dazed from the explosions and smoke when they put a hood over her head, pulled her to her feet, and pushed her into a transport.

CHAPTER 23

OLD RULES

"I learned a long time ago that there is something worse than missing the goal and that's not pulling the trigger."

—MIA HAMM

Lori sat in the back of the transport as they flew north, analyzing every decision she'd made for the third time. Below her, the convoy of heavy artillery and troop-engorged trucks marched north with the precision and resolve of ants who'd found food. She kept her eyes on her screen as bits of information filtered from units scattered across hundreds of miles.

With the war barely an hour old, she had received confirmation that thousands of lives had been lost. The raid on the second Kern fleet had produced an occurrence that seldom, if ever, happened in war: everything had gone exactly according to plan. The two large ships had sunk within minutes of getting hit by the scrammies. Left unprotected, the midsize ones had been battered by the ensuing missile barrage.

She did not know how the Kern contingent on land would react to the news, but the odds had tilted toward only moderately bad.

Kuipers had remained in C&C. General Gardner had taken a third of their forces and was heading north toward Redwood Valley. And there was only one place for her to be—the frontlines in

Anderson Valley—but she didn't rush. To make the right decisions, she had to see, smell, and hear the battle.

The most surprising news had come from the capital. Lester had ordered the deployment of defensive forces to the north. There were two ways to interpret that. It was possible that Lester had been fooled by Kern. It was equally possible that Lester had grasped the simple truth that arresting the chief commander of her armed forces during a war would get her shot.

Either Lester was a fool or she was dangerous. Lori almost wished it were the latter to spare herself the agony of admitting letting a fool become chancellor. But then again, it would be far easier to deal with a fool down the road.

Fool or not, Lester would neither forget nor forgive. Lori had a reprieve as long as they were fighting. Once the fighting stopped, the troops were going to turn on each other, loyalties tested by allegiances to the chancellor or the chief commander.

She pushed the thoughts away. Those were calculations for the reality in which she succeeded. In the one where she didn't, none of it mattered.

She studied the progress of Gardner's forces as the heavy rain hit her windshield. To win, she had to be unpredictable, and if there was one thing Kern would predict, it was a major Marin stand at the mouth of Anderson Valley. Still, she aimed to concentrate all her firepower on the narrowest passage the Kern army would use. It was a good plan, but it had a major flaw. At the current progress of the Kern army, her forces would be two hours too late.

Kagawa had slowed the Kern war machine. As the storm raged, Lori was glad to see that weather was on her side. The harder it rained, the slower the Kern army moved over the ridge.

She wasn't deluded enough to attribute the favorable weather to anything other than luck, but as far as allies went, she could do a lot worse than Lady Luck. As the chopper nudged northwest, she stared out to sea, transfixed by the power raging within that dark mass.

Mika had been the one who loved the sea. He'd taken her sailing, inside the bay on a mild day, but every time the boat had climbed a swell, she had felt as though they were about to fall off the side of a mountain. And they had only to climb it and fall again. The short time it had taken Mika to bring them back to shore had felt like a trans-Pacific cruise. She had alternated between emptying her insides over the lifelines and curling into a fetal position in the cockpit. She had not had the strength to move an arm much less march onto a battlefield or wield a weapon. The misery had lasted long after she had set foot on solid ground.

The second time, she had tried the pills Mika had ensured would make her feel better. They had helped a little, but she had sworn to never go back to sea. She was glad she wasn't one of the fools who'd come to her shores in these waters.

The thought froze in her mind.

She'd been such an idiot. She was planning to face a well-prepared invading army, but the army she faced had been through this roller coaster for days, going out far enough to appear to come to them from the west. She had a decisive but temporary edge.

She turned to Sierra and broke her own protocol for radio silence. "I need to speak to Gardner, Eze, and Herrera immediately."

"General Gardner." Lori nodded as Gardner appeared on her screen. Gardner nodded back with the intensity of someone interrupted by an unwelcome distraction. A veteran of the first Kern war, she showed no concern at facing a battle for the survival of Marin.

"I need you to head straight for these new targets and hit them as soon as they get within range." Lori paused to allow Gardner to absorb her new orders. Gardner's eyes moved away to the coordinates being projected on the map. "By my estimates, you should engage them in forty minutes."

Gardner's brow furrowed.

"General, I'm aware of how these orders sound, but we have an opportunity I do not want to miss. Can you confirm you can engage within forty minutes?"

Gardner must have been inspecting her logistics, because she didn't reply for ten seconds. "Yes, but if we do so, we cannot help when the Kern army comes over the ridge."

"I'm aware of that, but I suspect the force up the ridge is weaker than we believe."

Gardner paused. "Very well."

Lori broke the connection. Her communication with Gardner had mostly been nonverbal. Josie Eze was a good soldier but also a thinker. She was going to expect to understand.

Sierra activated the next call. "Colonel Eze is ready for you."

"General, I did not expect to hear from you," Eze said.

"I need you to start the offensive now."

"Now? General, we don't have the numbers yet."

Lori put her hand near the back of the second peak on the ridge on her map and relayed it to Eze. "Focus our fire here."

Eze looked pained. "That's where their fortified artillery is. We lost two transports trying to take them out. The response to Major Kagawa's strikes came from that spot."

Why do people always argue with me about these things? It was probably because her orders always bordered on insane.

Eze interpreted her silence as a license to argue. "This spot is narrower." She pointed to a spot closer to their position. "We can hold them there."

"Colonel, I'm not trying to hold them. I'm trying to destroy them. We're going to hit them where they least expect it." She put her hand on the heavily fortified ridge on the map. "Initiate the assault on this spot, now."

"Yes, ma'am."

Lori moved to her next call. She suspected she was the last person Herrera expected to hear from. She had to gauge whether Herrera was sticking to the chain of command or actively support-ing Lester. If the latter, she would have to protect her southern flank from Marin forces, which was distasteful for more than tactical reasons.

Herrera appeared on her chiming screen. "General Rose."

"I know we don't see eye to eye right now, so I'll be brief. I have one more order for you."

"General, I'm neither inclined nor in a position to accept orders from you."

"Nevertheless, here it is. Deploy your forces to the north of the city to defend the capital in case my forces fail to stop the Kern offensive."

Herrera grimaced. "I won't follow your orders, but I am already setting up the defense of the capital."

Lori rubbed her chin and softened her expression as much as she could, but she knew it wasn't much. "Good to hear. Also, you better do some soul searching, because you'll receive orders to engage Marin troops soon."

Herrera's eyebrows shot up. "General, I told you I will not follow your orders."

"Those orders are not going to come from me. Good day, General."

Lori went over her strategy one more time. She was about to spread her troops thin and open two fronts, a dangerous maneuver under any circumstance but doubly so while on the defensive. She had little margin for error, but then again, that margin had never existed.

"Colonel Eze." Lori made her way to the front lines in Anderson Valley. Smoke drifted up from the ridge in four stacks as though four small volcanoes lived under these long-dead mountains and belched their last meal of soot and burned leaves. Broken redwoods were strewn in the distance, littering the valley like hundreds of discarded matchsticks. "Report."

"Major Kagawa's forces held the line, General. We are pounding the ridge as you instructed. No Kern heavy artillery has taken position in the valley yet."

Lori rubbed her chin. "Major Kagawa?"

Eze shook her head. "Major Kagawa was lost during the third wave of the assault."

"Casualties?"

Eze grimaced. "Two thirds of Kagawa's forces are unaccounted for."

Lori moved to the tent that passed for the command center. Three folding tables had been put together to create one large surface. A generator hummed right outside, powering the entire center. Lori grabbed one of the screens scattered on the makeshift conference table and scrolled through the reports as Eze continued her summary.

Eze's assault had taken out three artillery units. Though the losses head been heavy, they'd been fewer than she had feared. That confirmed that they had found Kern's underbelly, and now she would keep pounding at it and see what would spill out.

As the second day of the battle drew to a close, Lori considered her long-term strategy. She had that luxury because Gardner's raid had devastated the Kern army. As Lori had suspected, the troops at the rear had not been battle ready, and when Gardner had begun inflicting heavier and heavier losses, Kern had recalled its heavy transports to defend its rear.

Which had allowed Eze's forces to push up the ridge. Half the Kern army was stuck on the narrow ridge, being pounded by artillery fire and unforgiving weather. Aided by the heavy rains, a lot more than soil was washing down the hillside. The other half was shrinking as it retreated north. They were a fraction of the force that had landed only forty-eight hours ago.

Her screen was chiming. It was Kuipers. Lori waved it on. "Yes, General?"

Kuipers was standing in the war room, surrounded by officers. They were more chipper than she was. They had witnessed the great Marin stand from headquarters. That always lifted spirits. What Lori had seen was a lot of body parts accompanied by the stench of rotting corpses. It tended to dim one's enthusiasm for victory.

"Lori!" Kuipers exclaimed. "I had no doubt you would pull this off. It is what you do."

Lori was running on coffee and adrenaline, riding a roller coaster of fleeting triumphs peppered with disheartening losses. She'd taken four thirty-minute naps in the last forty-eight hours. Her gaze searched the surroundings, trying to find something that would focus her mind. She found nothing. That they all thought this was what she did haunted her more than what she had done. But it was too early to celebrate.

"About a quarter of the Kern army is still to our north." Granted, it was trying to disappear, but still.

Kuipers shook her head. "It's over, Lori. Let's push for peace now while we still have the moral high ground."

If Lori held the moral high ground, they were in serious trouble. She wasn't interested in moral grounds, high or low. She was tired. Tired of war, tired of killing, but she knew, with no uncertainty, this cycle would repeat if she didn't get to the root of it. Seven years ago, they had stood exactly at this place after their victory in Hollister, and here they were again.

"I'm sorry, Lisa, but we tried that once, and it got us nowhere. I cannot spend the rest of my life fearing and devising defenses for the next Kern offensive. This has to end."

End was an idea that, when applied to Kern, confused her because she was a hunter, and for the first time in her life, she faced the possibility of becoming a hunter without prey, of living without fear and rage. It should have been uplifting, but it left her oddly despondent. Remove her dogged determination to destroy Kern, and she didn't know what was left of her.

Lori cut the connection, letting her nebulous thoughts dissolve with Kuipers' image, and focused on the facts. Marin had lost a soldier for every five they'd killed in the valley and one to every seven on the shores. The losses sickened her, but the numbers didn't lie. Kern had finally run out of troops and time.

It still wasn't over. There were still Kern commanders to her north and her south, and she didn't know what they wanted. The euphoria of victory had already sapped the will from Kuipers. They were no closer to finding out why Kern had become aggressive again, what Lester's orders meant, or who the perpetrators of Ross were.

These things could not be independent, but she couldn't find the connections while Lester watched over Lori's shoulder. She had to get out from under that watchful eye.

Then she had to pluck that eye.

CHAPTER 24

NEW SCARS

*"The world breaks everyone, and afterward many
are strong at the broken places."*

—ERNEST HEMINGWAY

B *urning.*
Flames blazed in his veins, boiled his blood. Ice on his chest.
The ice sublimated, but the flames did not subside.
Bleeding and burning.
*Blood trickled down his arm. Circles of blood. The flow did not
stop. Blood froze, and the ice turned red. He was in a tub of red ice.*
Sweating and bleeding and burning.
*Sweat dripped into his eyes. The blood thinned, mixed with sweat,
and moved like water.*
Thirsty.

Mika opened his eyes to a small room. He was lying on a long
sofa he did not recognize. He pushed himself up and saw two more
chairs and a coffee table, functional but sterile. His tida and gun
rested on the table. The blinds were up, but little light filtered in
through the tall firs.

His thirst hadn't been a dream. His mouth was so dry he
couldn't complete the swallowing motion. His larynx moved up
but did not come down. There was a water container on the coffee
table. As he reached for it, his triceps tightened but did not cramp.

He took two sips, letting the water move around his mouth before swallowing. He took bigger gulps and downed half the container.

Burning.

How and where had that been? Where was he? He'd been on the docks, then in a gray jeep, bouncing up and down a mountain road. There had been a man with a leather jacket.

You need to relax.

The man's face floated in his consciousness: Phillips.

That was no dream. He had tried to relax, but the burning had not gone away. He remembered waking to drink. How many times had he done that?

Bleeding.

He couldn't possibly have lost the amount of blood his memory told him he'd lost. He drank the rest of the water and stood to confront the two doors at the far end of the living space. The first room held a desk, two screens, and a closet. Monochromatic shirts, stack of pants, and three leather jackets lined the closet racks. He moved to the next room, and the pungent sniff of castor oil greeted him as he pushed the door open.

Pras lay on the bed, wires disappearing into her arms and chest and linking her to screens. She was sweating but alive. Mostly. Gray tape covered her right shoulder and hip. A dozen three-inch scars extended from her wrists to shoulders. The readouts meant nothing to him, so he backed away. He reached for the door handle, and his sleeve crept back, exposing a scar. He rolled up his sleeve. He had the same set of scars as Pras, a ladder from his wrist to his shoulder.

Circles of blood.

The scars were too old to account for his dreams, yet they hadn't been there before.

Before what?

Images floated in his mind: the Kern cell, Amy, the docks. His hand went to his side, and he lifted his shirt. He remembered a large, red bruise and the sharp pain each step had caused. It was now yellow and brown, fading. He prodded it. There was some tenderness but no pain as though he'd been injured weeks ago, but his mind insisted it had been yesterday.

He tapped his tida, and the date floated up.

Shit.

He blinked, but the numbers didn't budge. He had passed out five days and eleven hours ago, which meant both his mind and body were wrong. He reached for his face, and his fingers met stubble that seemed about five days old. At least part of his body agreed with the lost time.

He tapped his tida. He was only an hour away from the Marin compound that had been a stopover to the Kern base that Kevin's missiles had destroyed. It was the only clue he had left, but a clue for what? Eva was gone. The base was gone.

He called Amy but got no answer, so he continued to explore. He stepped on the porch. The decking felt solid, but the railing had seen better days. A narrow driveway lined up with pine trees extended for thirty feet before the unpaved road meandered left and disappeared down the mountain. A pickup truck was parked in the driveway, facing out. The wireless key stood in the cup holder between the front seats. It was tempting. Instead, he went for a run. He started slow, coddling his ribs, but he felt strong, his lungs pumping, his legs humming, so he kept going.

Phillips wasn't back when he returned forty-five minutes later. Pras was still sleeping or in a coma. It was hard to tell. He cleaned up and got dressed. As he picked up his gun and tida, he caught the distance his tida claimed he'd covered: 8.9 miles, which meant almost five-minute miles. For someone who'd been stuck at seven-and-a-half-minute miles forever? While half dead? Had his tida lost its mind?

He stepped out to connect to something real. The dry deck creaked under his foot. He crouched and ran his fingers on the wood. The clear stain had peeled in places, leaving the wood exposed to the elements. He rubbed his thumb to the tip of his middle finger, and the smooth dust slid between his fingers like hundreds of tiny ball bearings. Nothing beyond the faint aroma of the pine cones all around him reached his nose. He touched his fingers to his tongue but tasted nothing. He wiped his fingers on his pants and stood up.

The truck beckoned, daring him to explore. The sensible thing to do was to wait for Phillips. But how long would that be? Another hour? A day? His supernatural run tag-teamed with the new scars on his arm to proclaim it was too late to be sensible. He hopped in the truck and headed to the compound.

He left the truck a quarter mile out and walked. He'd memorized the layout on the way over: two one-story buildings connected by a covered walkway in the back of the property. A paved courtyard split the buildings. It was easily defensible but not overly fortified. Two Humvees were parked in the courtyard behind the chained gate. A dim light shone in the east barrack.

He circled around. Two soldiers stood guard in the back with three in the front. He hopped the wall on the west side of the compound, avoided the motion sensors, and picked the lock of the dark building. He made his way to the basement and found the underground corridor connecting the two buildings. He went up the stairway in the occupied building and opened the fire doors. A rumble filled the empty corridor, and light spilled from a door halfway down.

He drew his gun and walked to the door that let the noise and light escape. It was a lab with tables lining the back wall and a row of high benches bisecting the room. A musky onion scent permeated the place. The rumbling stemmed from two self-standing, four-foot fans running at full speed. Two fluorescent tubes hanging from the concrete ceiling barely lit the space. Jeremy Cutler, Eric's clerk, was handcuffed to a chair with a bright spotlight shining on his ashen face, sporting a sweat-soaked shirt with vomit stains.

Rendon walked around Jeremy's chair with a syringe in her hand. He'd had a split second for a quick exit, but it was too late. She reached for her gun with her free hand.

"Don't." He pointed his gun at her. Had she recognized him in the dim light?

"Shoot her," Jeremy croaked, removing any pretense Mika's face was hidden.

As he took two more steps, Lori walked in from a side door, reading a screen. "That also checks out. That's definitely where they keep the bulk—"

She stopped as she took in the scene.

"Shoot," Jeremy said, straining against his handcuffs.

Mika scratched his beard with the barrel of his gun.

Lori, immaculately dressed, glanced at her screen as though she were going over a purchase order. Her face did not betray any recognition or hint at how to proceed.

Jeremy shook and coughed. Mika took another step in and saw Jeremy clearly for the first time. His face was part red, part green, and his eyes had a milky yellow film crisscrossed by the red of bursting blood vessels. His mind had been ripped apart by the combination of hallucinogens and truth serums. He'd never be whole again, not that there was any chance he'd walk out of here.

"Step away from him."

Rendon raised the syringe on her left hand. "I need to give him this, or he will die in thirty seconds, and it won't be pretty."

It wasn't pretty now. Jeremy was more dead than alive though he made lot of noise for a dead guy. They could keep him talking, convulsing, passing out just to wake him up and repeat the process. Jeremy coughed again as though he had to spit a fist-sized furball. He caught his breath long enough to croak, "Shoot, man."

It was his fault Jeremy was here. Had he let Enrico's sniper shoot him, he'd have saved them all a lot of trouble. Mika raised his gun and fired. Rendon's right arm moved up instinctively as though she could block the bullet. She didn't need to. The bullet hit the syringe, and the amber liquid exploded.

"Fuck," Rendon said, but Lori didn't flinch.

Jeremy took shallow breaths in quick succession and whistled like an angry tea kettle. He coughed blood, and a foamy, yellow-green drool appeared on his chin before his convulsions increased in frequency.

Rendon grabbed Jeremy's chin, but Lori intervened. "Let it go."

After two more shakes, Jeremy stopped moving and collapsed forward, spewing blood from his mouth and nose.

Rendon moved between Lori and Mika, shielding Lori.

"Sierra, step outside, and just so we're clear, no one comes in here until I say so."

"General, he's got a gun and—"

"Now, and figure out how he walked into this room. So much for security." Rendon didn't move. "I mean it. The head of anyone walking in here, for whatever reason, will end up on a pike. That includes yours. Clear?"

Mika stepped out of the way. Rendon's eyes could have started a fire had they hit anything flammable. He suspected it was more because of the rebuke she had received than the danger he posed. She was an explosion flailing against a containment field.

"If anything happens to the general, I'll cut you to tiny pieces," Rendon whispered.

For both their sakes, he hoped her containment field would hold another five seconds.

Lori spoke the instant the door closed. "What the fuck are you doing here?"

He tucked his gun into his jacket. "This is what you do now?"

She glared at him for a moment. "Why are you here?"

He took a deep breath. "The truth is I don't know."

Her eyes demanded an answer.

"Eva Asher moved through here."

Her eyebrows edged up. "Only Special Forces use this place."

"Maybe your forces took Eva. Maybe Tran?"

Her head swiveled at the name, but she nodded.

"Tran was following Eva. I'd been racking my brain to figure out where I'd seen her until Kagawa showed me her Red Spider picture. But Eva was shot in a Kern cell. Why would Tran have taken her to a Kern base?"

"Tran disappeared the day Asher got injured in the ambush. The fault lines within Marin and Kern collaborators in my ranks?" She pointed to the lifeless body. "They connect to shitheads like him."

"If I walked down the corridor, what else would I find?"

"Don't walk down the corridor." She shook her head. "You're unbelievable. What were you going to do if Asher had been here? Take out a Special Forces unit?"

"Eva's dead."

She shook her head, eyes closed, but it took only three seconds for her to reset. Disapproval and resignation fused into her next words. "Why did you walk in here?"

He couldn't keep his eyes off Jeremy. "It wasn't to kill a friend."

"He wasn't your friend."

That was true. He hadn't particularly liked or disliked Jeremy, but they'd shared a few drinks, so he could loosely use the word. Anyone whose four-year-old you knew was more friend than foe. "No?"

"No. He worked with Tran, and he betrayed New Cal."

"Betrayed how?"

When she didn't answer, his eyes moved from her to Jeremy to the floor in front of Jeremy where blood and green spittle were pooling. It was impossible to ignore what they'd done to Jeremy or what Phillips had done to him. "Can you do a blood test here?"

She pointed to the side door she'd used to enter the large lab. "In there."

He followed her. The cups on the desk reminded him he was thirsty again. He filled one and drank, then filled another one and sat. He rolled up his sleeve and exposed his scars.

She grabbed his arm. "How did you get these?"

"I don't know."

Her thumb dug into his palm. "Don't play games with me."

"I'm not, Lore."

She relented and pushed the needle in, drawing two vials of blood. She moved to the back of the room and put the vials in the centrifuge on the bench. As the device whirred and clicked, she came back and pointed to his arm.

He rubbed his scars. "Sounds like you've seen these before."

She nodded. "On one of the fuckers we killed in Ross."

Great.

He told her what he remembered: his jaunt to the Kern lab, his interrogation, his busted kidneys, peeing blood, the docks, waking up today, the missing days, Pras. The rest was disconnected images, scenes from hazy dreams, and a lot of burning and ice.

"These don't look five days old." She put her hand in his collar and pushed his shirt down, exposing his right shoulder. "What the fuck?"

He looked down. The scar on his shoulder was gone, the knife wound erased. She ran her fingers over his skin. "How is this possible?"

He nudged her hand away and prodded where his collarbone met his shoulder. The familiar hard bump was gone, replaced with smooth, unbroken skin. He sighed and reached for the cup of water. He drained it, and fear gripped him. Losing an old scar and gaining new ones were ethereal concerns. The pressure on his bladder wasn't. "Bathroom?"

She pointed. He put a hand on the back wall of the bathroom, anticipating the pain. A slight burn accompanied the first trickle, but it went away. His pee was as dark as an old trumpet, but there was no sign of blood, and it flowed without pain. He'd never felt this much joy peeing.

Lori's eyes were glued to the screen when he walked out, her right hand rubbing the left side of her neck. With her elbow pointed forward, she was putting her full strength into it, which meant she didn't like what the screen displayed. He leaned over her shoulder and understood why. There was little ambiguity in what the flashing red numbers said.

New scar or old scar, he should be dead. "That can't be right."

Lori waved at the screen, overlaying the next set of results. "These concentrations mean there's over 9 mg of ricin in your bloodstream. That's enough to kill half a dozen men."

"That explains the burning," he mumbled.

"This explains something to you?"

"All I remember is burning, bleeding, and sweating. Now at least I know why that is."

Lori pointed to another chart. "This says your kidneys are functioning normally."

"There's a tree in Kern that would disagree with that."

He lifted his shirt, exposing his abdomen. She put a finger on his side, first pushing softly, then harder up his ribs. He felt nothing. The bruises had mostly faded, and the cracked ribs from ten days ago were a distant memory as though they'd happened to someone else.

"Why are you here?" he asked again.

"I don't understand some alliances. Might have learned more had you not eliminated our best lead."

He couldn't picture a scenario where Jeremy was her best lead.

"Kern is in shambles," she said. "The top-down fear is gone, replaced by confusion and ambition. It's like half a dozen rebellions are unfolding in fast-forward. Everyone says they're in charge, but no one is. Key players are on the run. Some want to talk. Some want to shoot. This is our best chance to end this war, but I need to understand what they're after."

When Lori talked about ending the war, she was referring to the total destruction of Kern. It wasn't an argument worth having with her. He feared she would never be done. There would always be one more Kern officer to find. "At some point, this war of yours has to stop."

"War of mine?" She narrowed her eyes. "Fuck off."

She had slipped back into the reality where the angry General Rose roamed. Her anger was focused on a concept, but you couldn't wage war against a concept. You could shoot people, and you could blow up places. At some point the concept was gone, but you'd still be shooting. She was fast approaching that point. More likely, she was already past it.

At least she was being true to herself. Her trajectory was always going to lead here. Just as Eric's trajectory was always going to lead where it had. Mika had become a spectator. Neither peacemaker nor warrior, he was a figure caught between the two ideas, using but not embracing either, drifting in and out between competing realities. It had gotten him exactly nowhere.

There was little else to say. Lori's shield was back up, and she had moved on. It was his turn to do the same. He headed out, greeted by Jeremy's corpse, a silent reminder. He wanted to pretend he'd had no choice, but he knew that wasn't true. He walked past it, trying not to look at it, but he didn't succeed. The messy puddle on the floor had already acquired a coppery brown hue.

Jeremy was a warning that with one wrong move, he, Lori, or Amy could end up in that exact spot. They did not live in a forgiving world.

"Stop."

He did, startled by the urgency in Lori's voice. She got between him and the door to the corridor. She knocked and opened it slowly. The soldiers covering the door were itching for a fight. It was a good thing he hadn't walked out on his own.

It was reassuring to know that despite her cold façade, Lori still had one foot firmly rooted in the here and now and one eye still looking after him.

———————————

"Sit down." Lori didn't wait for Sierra to do so. "I want all entry records to this compound for the last two weeks."

"Other than Bayley—"

"Just do it, and while you're at it, I want to know where Governor Chipps is and what it would take to extract her."

Sierra fidgeted. "Permission to speak freely."

Lori wasn't going to like what was coming. Still, she had to hear this. She squeezed her tida. It felt heavy in her hand as though burdened by Mika's blood test. "Granted."

"We need all our resources to root out the Kern generals in hiding. This compound isn't critical, and I want to help Chipps too, but we need to finish taking apart the Kern military."

"Perhaps, but do it anyway. I want to be ready just in case."

"It's Bayley, isn't it?"

"What are you mumbling about?"

"Did he ask you to find Chipps?"

"I didn't tell him she was missing."

"Seems he's always around when you make questionable decisions."

Lori swallowed. It was more dissent than Sierra had ever displayed, but it was also true, and Lori didn't want to squash the conversation without letting Sierra air out her grievance. Sierra had always been her handle on the troops. If Sierra questioned her decisions, so would everyone else, and unlike Sierra's, she didn't have everyone else's blind trust.

"What do you suggest we do about it?"

Sierra's tone had just enough anger to not sound funny. "I could shoot him if it'll make you think more clearly."

Lori reached for her gun and held it up for Sierra to see. "Just so we're clear. I'm emptying this into the next wiseass who makes that joke." She waited a few second for the words to sink in. "Do me a favor. Never go there again." She swallowed again. "Ever."

CHAPTER 25

IMMORTAL

"Some pirates achieved immortality by great deeds...but the captain had long ago decided that he would, on the whole, prefer to achieve immortality by not dying."

–TERRY PRATCHET

Mika pulled into Phillips' hideout. Two vehicles that hadn't been there when he'd left were parked in the driveway: the gray jeep from his memory and a green army truck that boxed it in. The front door was ajar. He pushed it open.

Two bodies lay on the floor. One had a large hole where his face had been. The second one's head had rolled sideways with only partial skin keeping it attached to the body.

Phillips sat on the floor with his back against the three-legged remnant of the sofa on which Mika had woken. Phillips blinked, head propped up by the collapsed backrest. His left leg traced an angle above the knee that did not belong on a human body. He'd been gut shot and sat in a pool of his own blood. His right hand still held a gun, barely, as the right arm was loosely attached to the shoulder.

Mika knelt next to Phillips. The way he lay, his back was most likely broken.

"It's all right." Phillips breathed heavily. "I know what you want to know."

"What happened here?"

"No, that's not what you want to know. But I'll tell you. What had to happen happened." He waved at the body directly in front of him. "You win some, you lose some. First two, I shot. The third one got to me. Fortunately, the wanker relied on youth, strength, and an unhealthy trust in being a tough-to-kill son of a bitch."

Mika's eyes moved from the broken body to Phillips. "And you?"

"Me?" Phillips choked a laugh. "I relied on being a tougher-to-kill son of a bitch."

Mika surveyed the scene again. "I see only two bodies."

"Thought I got all three." Phillips grimaced. "Bloody hell. Wasn't there a body right outside?"

Mika shook his head. "Should I look for one?"

"No time. You need to get us out of here before they come to clean up this mess."

"If I move you, you'll never walk again. I'm not sure I can get you anywhere before the blood loss kills you."

"Wrong on both counts. Look, I know what I must look like, and if I had minutes left, I'd tell you what I know, but trust me on this, I'm not dying. Grab Pras. Let's get out of here, and we'll talk."

Mika put an arm behind Phillips to lift him up.

"No, no, no. First you need to operate. There is a kit in the bathroom."

"You're serious?"

Phillips nodded. Mika walked to the bathroom and scanned the cabinet. There was a midsize, black pouch. He opened it to confirm it was the right one and returned to the room.

"We have about ten minutes before these guys miss their check-in and another fifteen before the drone gets here. We don't have a lot of time, but you don't have to rush either. The skin-colored stuff is for anything under half an inch deep. The gray stuff is for the big holes."

"I guess we don't need the skin-colored stuff." He put two gray sheets on Phillips' chest and ribs. The sheets dug in at the edges, and a few drops of blood dribbled. The sheets tightened, forming a seal and providing support. Mika flicked the patch in front of the ribs with his index finger, and it felt like hard plastic. "What is this stuff?"

"That's the third question you asked, and it still isn't the right one."

Phillips was right, so he moved to what mattered. "What did you do to me?"

"Obviously, I helped you heal."

"The Purge is doing all this?"

Phillips tried to nod but mostly shook.

"Why did you give me those coordinates?"

"You know how sometimes you wake up, and you have this feeling that you know something, something really important?" Phillips waited for a second but not long enough for Mika to reply. "But you don't know what you think you know. You assume it's the dream, but the dream is out of reach, all blurry. Then midday, without warning, the dream crystallizes, and you're no closer to solving your little mystery. The dream, it turns out, had nothing worth remembering. You know what I mean?"

Mika didn't. He pointed to his own scars. "Something is seriously wrong with this."

"Oh, something is definitely seriously wrong but not in the way you think." Phillips pointed to the medical pouch. "Do you mind?"

Mika put three of the large gray sheets on Phillips' lower back, covering the area from the bottom of his ribcage to his spine and from his tailbone to midway up his back. Mika was wallpapering over earthquake damage, but the sheets hardened and dug in. The man appeared almost alive—not particularly human, but alive.

Phillips flexed his chest and moved it side to side. He lifted his left arm, tried to reach to his back, but barely made it to his left ear. "You need to operate on my right shoulder."

Phillips' right shoulder was his only undamaged part. "What's wrong with it?"

"There is a small tida in there."

Mika looked for surgical cuts. "I don't see any scars."

"Right. It's two inches below the collarbone and about an inch from my spine. Cut it open, and dig for it."

Mika resisted the urge to ask whether Phillips were serious. He pushed his fingers over the skin, moving side to side, but he couldn't feel anything. He took a scalpel and cut in, exposing flesh and muscle. "What's it for?"

"Collects biodata to help fine-tune the healing process, but someone is monitoring mine. My location. I suspected it, but now I know. By the way, you have one too."

Mika was about to ask about the healing part but stopped. "What?"

"You have one too, in your left arm."

"What the hell for?"

"I just told you, to fine-tune the biodata." He pointed his chin to his shoulder. "Do you mind?"

Mika put a glove on and pushed his index finger inside, poking in different directions. After a few rotations, his finger hit a hard object that wasn't bone. "Are you okay?"

"You started already?" Phillips grunted.

Mika grabbed curved, serrated forceps from the pouch. He pushed in, and more blood rippled out. He tugged the hard material, and after three attempts, he pulled the mini tida out, an inch long and a quarter of an inch in diameter cylinder. He put it on a table leg remnant.

"Now we can use the skin-colored patch," Mika said.

"Hardly worth it for a scratch, but sure."

Mika pointed to Pras' room. "Can we move her?"

Phillips nodded. "You're gonna have to carry her. With what I gave her, she won't wake up for another two hours. Just unplug her, grab the screen and medical pouch." He took two shallow breaths. "Dump whatever is in the top drawer into the backpack. The rest can burn."

Mika came out carrying Pras with one arm under her waist, the other under her knees. She was heavier than he'd guessed. He strained to balance and avoided banging her head on the bedroom door frame by inches. Phillips stood up, grabbed his gun from the table, and hopped to the front door on one leg. He stopped next to the body with the broken neck, put the gun to the man's eye, and pulled the trigger.

Phillips reached the jeep, opened the door, and pointed to the backseat. "Lay her down," he said before his face went slack. He drew his gun and aimed at Mika in one motion. Mika froze. Pras' shapeless weight prevented him from ducking.

Mika swiveled and stumbled, not accounting for Pras' shifting weight. He'd turned halfway when a gun went off behind him and again. Phillips fired three times. That Phillips could walk was shocking. That he could spin and shoot with agility was astonishing.

Mika completed his turn. A bloody-chested man was slumped against the side of the house, holding a gun.

Phillips hopped to him. "I'm sorry it came to this." He fired into the man's eye. He hopped back and frowned. "You can put her down now."

They were only steps from the jeep. Mika didn't want to have to pick Pras up again. "I can make it," he said and glanced down. Shit. Blood was pooling by his feet.

A bullet had entered above Pras' ear and left through the top of her skull. He took two steps to get away from the blood, lowered her to the ground, and crouched. She was gone.

Phillips ignored Pras and put a hand on Mika's side, prodding. "You've been shot."

Blood streaked down Mika's side, but it had to be Pras'. He had been shot once before in the thigh. It had felt like he'd been jabbed by a red-hot poker. The scorching pain had short-circuited his thoughts, leaving him dazed for seconds. The searing had given way to throbbing as though his flesh were being plucked by metal shears.

The only thing he felt now was sorrow for Pras. He reached for his oblique. The blood was his. Phillips shoved Mika's hand away, feeling his side.

"Exit wound. Good," Phillips said and grabbed the backpack. He slapped a gray sheet on the wound.

Mika's obliques froze, and a hundred small tacks bit into his skin. His side stung and gave way to cold numbness.

"Bullet went through. You'll be good in an hour." Phillips walked to the jeep.

"What did you do?" Mika asked, but the stinging returned. Stinging, cold, and numbness cycled in quick succession. If Mika felt shock, it was to the casualness of Phillips' response to Mika's bullet wound and Pras' lifeless body.

MIKA DROVE WITH PHILLIPS SLEEPING AS HIS PASSENGER. HE'D gotten little information other than how Phillips had picked up Pras from the debris at the Red Spider. All that just to leave her behind to be consumed by the drone strike. Mika couldn't even express indignation, as the man had passed out the moment they'd started driving.

Ten minutes into the drive, Mika's tida chimed. To his surprise, Lori floated in front of his vision.

"I need you to back Sierra up on a mission."

"What?"

"Long story. She received direct orders from Lester, and I don't like it."

"How about she doesn't go?"

"Doesn't work that way. Besides, I need to know what Lester's after."

Typical Lori. She drilled and prodded to remove all that didn't fit to expose something that might and found a way to turn any situation to her advantage. "You're out of the loop?"

"My relationship with the chancellor is a little dicey right now."

"What's the mission?"

"I don't know."

"You're okay with this?"

Lori took too long to answer. "No, but she's still the chancellor."

"At some point—"

"At some point, one of us is going to get shot."

"Are we going to survive this mission?"

Lori's expression froze. "What?"

"I mean, without killing each other." He laughed. Lori didn't, probably because she had a healthier grasp of the real risk.

"Head here." A point appeared on his map about eighty miles east of where he was. "That's one of my personal safe houses. Sierra will be there in three hours."

"I can be there in two."

"Good, and no sniffers on your way there. I don't want anyone to get wind of this."

He didn't like that. He hadn't gotten a reply from Amy. He had no idea what she thought he'd been doing, and it was going to be hard enough to explain as it was without delaying another half a day.

"Fine."

"Watch your back." She added before breaking the link, "And watch Sierra's back."

The connection was gone before he could reply. From the little he had seen, Rendon's back not only had eyes, it had sharp, spiked, poisonous blades discouraging anyone from coming anywhere near it. It didn't need watching.

That Lori had even verbalized that warning was bad news indeed.

PHILLIPS RESTED ON THE BED IN THE SAFE HOUSE, HIDDEN among ruins in an abandoned town. He had tried to clean up with moderate success. He still looked like a cross between a zombie and a damaged mannequin put together from spare parts, but at least he looked as though he might last the night. They had a little under an hour before Rendon arrived, so after a few quick checks to make sure his sentries were up, Mika returned to the room with a cup of tea. He hadn't thought far enough to figure out how Phillips would drink it.

Phillips' left arm was in a sling, hiding multiple fractures. He held his tea with his right hand and moved his right arm up without bending the elbow immobilized by the gray material. He moved his shoulder out and leaned forward to bring his lips to the cup.

Mika sat across from him. "Okay, here's where we are. A conspiracy reaching across Marin, New Cal, and Kern is erasing all medical data related to miracle recoveries. Eva's staying alive spooked this group. Her recovery would have brought up uncomfortable questions, so she disappeared. Kidnapped by Marin Special Forces, she ended up in a Kern Cell. The conspiracy reaches pretty far, most likely all the way to the top of Marin."

He stopped to see Phillips' reaction, but there wasn't any. "How am I doing so far?"

Phillips nodded.

The missing soldiers, the cancer patients, Eva—they were data to build a case. Mika's fingers brushed against the gray sheet covering his side. He was now part of the case data, but the full plot still eluded him.

"The hard-to-kill soldiers are this group's foot soldiers. The dropping birth rates are connected to recoveries. Unless our data's very faulty, the same thing is causing both, and since there is no way anyone could manufacture, distribute, and dispense a drug at this scale, this is linked to the Purge. Someone is manipulating it, but I can't figure out how." He pulled his sleeve up and exposed his fading scars. He rapped his knuckles on the gray sheet. "You know how, because you did it to me."

Phillips lifted his immobilized left hand and slapped it three times with his right hand in a comical attempt at clapping that didn't produce any sound. "Well done."

"What am I missing?"

"Not much, actually. Your data's real, and you're right about manipulating PRG."

PRG. Mika hadn't heard anyone refer to the virus by its actual name in a long time.

"I figured. No one would have made that shit up. So?"

"You're right, the patient data doesn't make sense statistically. See, averages are useful but not when two fundamentally different things are mixed. Then they muddy the water."

"What are you talking about?"

"See, PRG does not work like a normal virus."

"How's that?"

"Essentially, a virus injects its DNA into the host's cells with the intent of making more copies of itself. PRG rewrites the host's DNA, and once it does that, it moves to the next cell."

"How does that matter?"

"There is no runaway duplication. PRG makes only enough of itself to change the host one cell at a time, and then it stops."

"Change the host? As in making it dead?"

"Not at all. In fact, it's going for the exact opposite."

"People are still dying."

"That's where averages led you astray. Look, two types of people survived the Purge: those who killed the virus and those the virus didn't kill."

"You're nine billion corpses too late for word play."

"Look, it's simple. Some people just beat the virus. Their immune system killed the thing. Genetic diversity is useful that way. Those people are clean, pure homo sapiens."

"Pure homo sapiens?"

"Yeah, the garden variety human. The get-born-reproduce-and-die kind."

Thoughts flew and crashed in his head. "There is another kind?"

Phillips coughed, and his cough turned into a laugh. "You. Me. About seventy percent of survivors, we're one for three on that count."

"One for three?"

"We were born. See, PRG was trying to repair us all. In us, it succeeded, but in most, it failed miserably."

Mika snorted. "Most of the hosts didn't need repairing until this thing hit them."

"Look, I didn't say it was good at it, but if you want to be pedantic, we were all terminally ill. You, for example, had about eighty years left to live."

"That's not funny."

"Not meant to be. Functionally, if you're trying to stop people from dying, whether the host will die in five minutes or fifty years, it's the same problem. It was trying to repair us, to modify us. It still is, but clearly, something went wrong."

Mika shook his head. "Modify how?" He reconsidered. "Okay, I run faster than I used to, but I'm guessing this thing didn't kill nine billion people so I can break a five-minute mile."

"No, but it's increasing hemoglobin mass so you get more oxygen flow to the muscles."

"That means what?"

"Never mind, that's a side effect. The main purpose is to remove genetic defects, boost repair mechanisms, switch off division in cancerous cells, and fix telomeres."

He thought about his bloody piss, pulp of a kidney, and getting shot. "Trauma?"

"Every repair triggers new levels of repair. Eventually, it can repair anything."

He had to hear himself say, "You're saying we're not going to die."

"Not entirely correct but close."

"Fuck."

His mind moved to Lori and Amy. What if they'd just beat the virus? "Wait. How and when does the repair mechanism switch on?"

"It switched on the moment you were infected at a background level. We're all a little healthier, a little more youthful than we ought to be. It works in jumps. It repairs more and more as long as the jumps aren't too drastic." He laughed. "Basically, getting shot or stabbed works well."

"Yeah. Worked real well for those three you shot in the eye."

"Look, there are limits, but they can be pushed. Keep your head attached, don't get tossed off rooftops, don't get shot in the eye, and you just might live forever."

Phillips had been shot in the gut, had a broken back, a smashed collarbone, a snapped femur, and a knee with no ligaments and was still breathing. "You must have been shot a lot."

"You don't think I got this way by accident, do you? All those guys you've seen around the Uregs? The hard-to-kill, leather-clad wankers who call themselves the avenging angels? They're all the product of an elaborate program that starts with small injuries, adds a little poison, inflicts bigger injuries, adds more poison, and keeps going on and on and on."

"That's what you did to me."

Phillips nodded. "One of your kidneys was done, and the other was seriously damaged. You wouldn't have made it."

"*What* did you do?"

"The cuts to your arms were to stimulate blood production. The poison was to trigger the virus' repair mechanisms. It was touch and go for a while, but you had enough function left on one kidney to ride it out."

"I remember sweating, coughing, and a lot of blood."

"Yeah, ricin makes you sweat like hell. Your body temperature was over 105."

"Shouldn't that have killed me?"

Phillips laughed again. "Look, not having functioning kidneys should have killed you. A quarter of the ricin should have killed you. But don't get cocky, you're not that hard to kill yet."

Mika had no scale to interpret that statement, but he remembered how he'd felt in the docks. He'd come a long way. "How is this related to infertility?"

"Seems PRG doesn't think we need any offspring."

"This is what you meant by right kinda man?" Phillips could have gotten him killed. Could have gotten Amy killed. "You knew they'd be coming after us, and you didn't warn me."

"Quit your whining. Look at you, all healed and indignant."

Mika didn't respond.

"I did keep an eye on you. I tried to keep you away from them. I didn't count on your being dumb enough to go looking for trouble." He grabbed a thin vial from the supplies they had saved from his house. He tossed it over. "Here. Today's dose."

"Not a chance. I can't afford to hallucinate for another week."

"Relax. That's a follow-up dose. It'll clear your system in two hours, and in the meantime, you'll have a mild fever."

A follow-up dose of ricin. A fever for a few hours. *We're something else.*

They had moved to a new reality, but the secrecy and hostility implied it wasn't necessarily a better one or a peaceful one.

"I take it these pure humans don't like us."

"When have different people ever lived in peace? Think how terrifying it must feel. You can't heal, but others can. Wouldn't you be scared? Envious?" He shook his head. "They despise us. They want one single, strong state to control us. Enslave us as long we're useful, dispose of us when we're not."

"Wait, wait, wait. You talk about pure humans, yet all I see in the front lines are hard-to-kill fuckers like you. Nothing pure about you."

"Long story." Phillips yawned and put his head down. He straightened up again. "There was a program that supplied hard-to-kill soldiers to those who paid well. Kern was first in line, and then came the Puries. Raid a Marin base here, take out an outpost there."

"Assassinate Czernak and Fontaine."

"That too."

One thing didn't add up. "Why are there so few of you?"

Phillips frowned. "It's not like they gave the blueprint to anyone. They pretended to have discovered a new drug that gives these powers. Two injections every day, but it was poison, different versions of what I used on you, along with useless but complex proteins that'd take years to analyze. The poison kicked the virus into hyperdrive, but in the doses they used, the subjects would die without the antidote. They had to come back every day to get the antidote, and the scientists in Kern kept chasing wrong leads."

"Fuck."

"Yeah, but some subjects overcame the poison and escaped. After that, they cycled through them faster."

"Cycled through? You mean killed them?"

"To these people, we're not human. We're not even weapons. We're bullets. They load us, point us, and when the clip is empty, toss us away, and go load a new clip."

Mika ran his fingertips over the gray plastic covering his obliques. This was getting well beyond what he could handle. "We need to get you to New Cal."

Phillips put his tea down. "Let's not. Marin's top is rotten right now, and they have claws deep into New Cal." He closed his eyes. "Can't trust anyone."

In a matter of seconds, Phillips' breathing deepened, becoming louder than sighs, softer than snores. Mika put a blanket on Phillips. The man didn't stir.

On trust, he didn't entirely agree with Phillips. The Puries had built an organization that cut across borders. He had to do the same. New Cal, Uregs, and Marin working together was a hard sell, but when he thought of Amy, Kevin, and Lori, it sounded almost plausible.

But it was dangerous to consider only how something might succeed. He also had to consider how it might fail, and when he thought of Amy, Kevin, Lori with that point of view, he felt less buoyant. Those three in any combination were like jet fuel. They contained the potential for great achievement and enough incendiary power for a spectacular fireball.

CHAPTER 26

NEW FRIENDS

"It's the friends you can call up at four a.m. that matter."

—MARLENE DIETRICH

Rendon had rebuffed Mika's attempts at conversation, alternating giving him cold stares and monosyllabic answers for 150 miles. He didn't blame her. His mere presence in this Humvee must have shattered years of Marin conditioning. Their interaction to date would not inspire confidence either, which meant she had to be racking her brain trying to figure out why Lori had put up with his antics during the investigation and not shot him as an intruder at the Special Forces compound or, for that matter, asked him to accompany her today.

He knew he was as much an enigma as an annoyance to her, but he hadn't found a way to leverage that curiosity. He gave up and closed his eyes, letting his head rest on the seatback.

"Why are you here?" she asked minutes later.

"I'm not sure."

"Really?"

"Apparently, I was the only option within hundreds of miles."

She winced. "Proximity isn't a great argument when I trust you as much as I'd trust a random Kern soldier."

He opened his eyes and straightened. "That's terrible logic."

"How do you figure?"

"Either your boss is careless and wasteful with her critical assets or she has a good reason to put us together. You should probably trust me a bit more than a Kern soldier."

"Why would I do that?"

"'Cause your boss does. Her you trust, right?"

She slammed on the brakes. The Humvee came to a stop by the ditch running along the side of the road. "I don't know what game you're playing, but I'm not interested."

Mika cocked his gun and handed it to Rendon. He opened his door, stepped out, and walked five steps along the ditch.

"We don't have time for this."

"One minute. That's all I need."

She came around the Humvee. "What now?"

Mika closed his eyes and reached for her hand. He brought her gun-holding hand to his forehead. "Go ahead and pull the trigger. No one will know." He brought his hand down with the cold metal pressed on his forehead.

"Tempting," she said.

A few seconds later, the pressure went away, but the cold sensation remained. He opened his eyes. "See?"

"See what?"

"I trusted you wouldn't shoot, because no matter what you think of me, in the back of your mind, you know there is a reason your boss put us together."

She only grunted assent.

He reached for his gun, and she let him have it. "Your turn." He raised the gun slowly. "Close your eyes."

She took a deep breath and let it out through her nose. She kept her eyes on him.

"Fine," he said and touched the gun to her forehead. "You would never, ever have let a random Kern soldier do this." He put the gun down and walked to the Humvee. She stepped in as he said, "Can we at least agree that neither of us wants to explain to Lori how we got the other one killed?"

"Really? We're on a first-name basis with the general now?"

He took a deep breath. "General Rose. Same question."

"Agreed," she said as she shut the door and put the Humvee in gear.

"Why are *you* here?" he asked as they got back on the road.

"I was ordered by the chancellor."

"I thought the chain of command was broken."

"It's frayed."

"Here's a simpler question. What's your cargo?"

"Nothing that concerns you."

She kept her eyes on the road, and he kept his eyes on her. "You don't know, do you?"

She shook her head.

"This is worse than I thought."

"I don't know what's in the crate, and I don't care what's in the crate. The sooner we deliver the damn thing, the sooner we can go our separate ways. Got it?"

A silent twenty minutes later, they pulled into the remnants of what must have passed as the center of this one-street town. She stopped when the street narrowed for a block, giving the illusion of charm. It must have been artificial in the best of times. Now it was desolate.

A dim light escaped from the bar, providing the only sign that they were in the right spot. She stepped out, walked in front of the Humvee, and approached the four-foot-wide, metal-framed door. Other than one square window next to the door, the front of the bar was siding all the way to a steel garage door thirty feet away. The door opened before she reached it, and two bouncers blocked her way in. The broad-shouldered one was Mika's size and wore a skullcap. The other man was a half foot shorter with small eyes poking out of a round face.

"Delivery for Cabaye," Rendon said.

Roundface said something quiet to his collar, put a finger to his earpiece, and pointed at Mika. "Who is that?"

"My partner." She spat the word like it tasted the way your mouth did the morning after getting drunk.

Roundface pointed to the steel garage door. "Back the truck there."

Mika waited for Rendon to nod, then hopped into the driver's seat and backed up to the door.

"Mr. Cabaye wants a word with you," Roundface told Rendon.

"I'm pressed for time. Unload the package, and we'll be out of here."

He listened to his earpiece. "Mr. Cabaye insists. He says you should understand."

She remained silent. These were not bouncers, since there was no one to bounce. Then again, he was pretty sure they weren't carrying bar supplies.

Mika climbed out of the Humvee and walked their way.

Roundface put a hand up. "Only her."

"Not a chance."

He again listened to his earpiece. "Suit yourself, but I need your weapons."

She handed Roundface her gun, and Mika did too. Skullcap stepped up and patted them both down. They followed Roundface with Skullcap trailing them. The bar had five tables in two staggered rows to their right and a long bar counter to their left. A man sat at the middle table by the wall, and another two sat at the counter.

They walked through a black-framed sliding screen door and down a set of metal stairs. Mika counted eleven steps on the way down. The stairwell opened into a large rectangular room. Booths lined both sides with an octagonal stage in the middle. The stage was empty, although the leather straps dangling from the ceiling and protruding from the floor confirmed this wasn't a dancing stage. The hot, fetid air completed the oppressiveness.

Somewhere during his scan, he stopped thinking of the place as a bar. The privacy curtains for all but the last booth to his left were open. There were restraints on the walls. The booths had metal examination chairs with stirrups. Soft, red light poured out of the only concealed booth. The humming of a compressor was interrupted by clicks every few seconds. He craned his neck but couldn't see in.

Roundface knocked as they reached the door in the back. A man in a three-piece suit opened the door. The man Mika assumed was Cabaye was seated behind a wood desk, his feet on the desk. Double-frosted glass doors across from where they'd entered filled a third of the wall behind the desk. "Thank you, Maclin," Cabaye said to the man in the suit.

Mika replayed the last few minutes but couldn't pinpoint a crucial mistake. Most likely, the accumulation of small mistakes had led them here. Rendon had a somber scowl and a pulsating jaw in stark contrast to the calm but displeased driver he'd engaged in partial conversation for the last few hours.

"Ms. Rendon." Cabaye gestured to the two chairs.

She didn't sit down. "If we can speed this up, we'll be on our way."

"In light of how delicate your cargo is, I need to verify it's safe. You understand?"

"No, I don't understand."

Cabaye flashed a fake smile. "It seems we have a problem with the cargo." He turned to Mika. "If you can give them a hand, we'll be done faster." He gave one upward nod to Skullcap.

"Got it," Skullcap said and reached for Mika's elbow.

Mika shook his elbow to break the connection but stepped out ahead of Skullcap.

As the door closed behind them, Skullcap shoved Mika forward. He didn't like leaving Rendon behind, but being separated had one advantage: now he had only one guard to deal with. When they reached the stairwell, Skullcap pointed to a door next to the stairs.

"That's not where the truck is," Mika said.

Skullcap pushed the gun into his back. "Open the door."

Mika did. It was a narrow corridor ending at a fire door with metal stairs to the right heading down. He took a few short steps, preserving his natural motion but slowing down to let Skullcap get closer. As the door closed, Mika spun clockwise and drove his right elbow up straight into the gun at his back. He caught Skullcap as he was leaning back to close the door. The gun flew up. Mika whipped his arm around the Skullcap's neck, grabbing the chin. He reached over with his left arm and grabbed Skullcap's forehead. His arms moved as one, breaking the guard's neck.

He grabbed the gun, put on the man's jacket and skullcap, and wrapped the guard's earpiece around his ear. It wouldn't fool anyone for long, but it'd buy him a second or two.

He dragged the body through the corridor.

"Is it done, Lenny?" his earpiece asked.

"Done," he said as plainly as he could.

"I'll tell the boss. Dump the body in the back, and come back down."

"Got it," he said as Lenny had done earlier. He opened the fire door. The dumpster was ten feet away. All he had to do was dump Lenny and walk away. His mind drifted to Pras' limp body. She came to life in his mind and spoke through a full-toothed smile: *Don't lose another partner.* And when Lori had asked him to watch Rendon's back, she probably hadn't meant, *Play games about trust in the truck, but leave her in the hands of homicidal psychopaths, and run at the first sign of trouble.* He took off one of the guard's shoes and used it to prop the door open.

He went through the dead man's pockets and found a key card. He dumped the body in the dumpster, walked back in, and tossed the shoe out. He followed the stairs down two floors. They ended at another metal door with a one-foot-square window at eye level. The room behind it was about forty feet deep and twenty-five wide. Elevator doors took up the far right corner. A dozen screens were scattered on two rows of desks running along the room's long axis. Clinical diagnostic kits, test tubes, centrifuges, and blood analyzers were spread on benches lining the walls.

Mika counted three armed guards, three technicians or scientists, and, based on the black turtleneck he wore and the four
screens on his desk, one hound. Mika swiped the card. It lit green,
but it also required a code. He typed the same code three times and
got a red screen locking him out. He waved his card by the window,
leaning back and sideways to expose a skullcapped silhouette. He
exhaled on the window to fog it up.

A guard opened the door. "Lenny, you're a moron."

They were not the best last words. Mika shot him in the head,
stepped in, and shot the other two guards before they drew their
guns. Two of the techs charged him. He shot them too. The last
tech grabbed a gun from her desk. Mika fired first.

"Get your hands where I can see them," he said to the man
hiding behind the four screens.

The man lifted his hands up. "I just work here."

"What's your name?" Mika received a blank stare. "What's your
name?"

"Fabrice."

"Okay, Fabrice, you're a hound, right?"

Fabrice blinked twice. When Mika pointed his gun to Fabrice's
face, he nodded.

"Turn off all cameras in this room now."

Fabrice gestured to his screen.

"Great job you got here."

"I had no choice," Fabrice said.

"We all have a choice."

"Yeah, great choice. Work here or stop breathing."

Mika didn't let Fabrice's excuses distract him. "Bring the main
servers down."

Fabrice did so.

"Now call upstairs, and tell Cabaye you think all the systems
are compromised. Ask him to come down."

Fabrice squeezed his eyes closed and took quick, shallow
breaths.

"You're worried about Cabaye? Don't be silly. In a few minutes, you might be the only one left alive here."

Fabrice still didn't move. Logic sometimes worked. Sharp pain and logic worked better. He grabbed Fabrice's hand and yanked the middle finger. Fabrice yelped and pulled his hand back. His middle finger was now sticking out at a sixty-degree angle to the rest of his fingers.

"I'm serious." Mika grabbed another finger.

Fabrice tapped his screen. "Mr. Cabaye, our systems are down."

The speakers came to life. "Damn it. What now?"

"I think we're compromised. Our secure server is down."

"Get it back up, you idiot."

"Sir, we need system-level passwords to reset. Everything is going crazy."

"Yes, yes. I'll be right down."

Mika moved his hand across his throat in a slashing gesture. Fabrice hit another key. "We're disconnected."

"Well done." He pointed to the screen in front of Fabrice. "Put the feed from Cabaye's office on here. Last five minutes."

Fabrice's trembling hand moved toward the screen but didn't select the feed.

"Now," Mika said, and Fabrice tapped the screen. Mika watched himself step out of the office. Rendon's shoulders recoiled as the barrel of Maclin's gun touched the base of her skull.

"Sit down," Maclin told her.

Cabaye listened to his earpiece. "Seems your partner fell into a dumpster with a bullet in his head. Happens sometimes."

Rendon remained stone faced.

"I see a lack of empathy, Ms. Rendon."

"I didn't know him that well."

"I see. We might dispense with this charade then. Maclin, please secure our cargo."

"You managed to get the cargo?"

This time Cabaye laughed. "Oh yes."

A leather strip came over Rendon's head and tightened around her throat. She tilted back, balanced on the back legs of the chair. She reached for the garrote with her right hand but couldn't dig under it. Her left hand slapped and grabbed his forearm and elbow, but Maclin's hold was too strong. Her cheeks turned red, and she kicked forward, her foot crashing against the heavy desk.

Cabaye came around the desk, grabbed her right wrist, pulled it forward across her body, and handcuffed it to the left armrest of the chair. "You see, Ms. Rendon, you were the cargo." He waited for a reaction from her, but she seemed busy trying to breathe.

Mika sped up the feed. Rendon kicked up but did not hit anything. Cabaye picked up a yolk-colored, eight-inch finish nail gun. He brought the nail gun to the inside of her right thigh and fired. She grunted and kicked away again with her left leg.

She tried to twist, but Maclin pulled hard, and she lifted out of the chair, back arched. The recoil of Cabaye's firing three times was followed by her silent scream. Cabaye put the nail gun down on his desk. He opened a drawer and picked up a larger nail gun.

He brought the gun to the top of her right thigh and fired.

From the way Rendon shook, the nail must have gone straight through her femur.

Mika slowed the feed down to normal speed. Rendon made a half-scream, half-choking sound as though her throat weren't wide enough to let the air out from her lungs. She spat blood, probably from biting her tongue.

Cabaye put his finger to his earpiece and went to a screen. "Damn it." Silence. "What now?"

"Get it back up, you idiot." More silence. "Yes, yes, I'll be right down."

He headed to the frosted-glass doors, and Maclin followed him. Rendon fell backward, coughing and spitting.

Mika swiped the screen to pause before the elevator doors opened, exposing Cabaye and Maclin.

"What the fuck is going on here?" Cabaye yelled as he walked in. "A monkey can run these systems better than you idiots."

Mika had his gun trained on them. "Hands where I can see them."

"What, you're not dead yet?"

After what he'd just seen, Mika had lost his appetite for banter. He wanted answers, but he'd settle for corpses. He pointed to a chair. "Sit." He turned to Maclin. "Don't move."

Cabaye reached the chair and sat. "Now what?"

"You tell me," Mika said. "Why is Rendon here?"

Cabaye squinted but didn't reply.

"What did you do to her?"

Maclin took two steps toward Mika. Mika lowered his aim and fired, connecting with Maclin's thigh. Maclin stumbled and fell, clutching his leg. "The fuck is wrong with you?" he yelled.

"I said don't move. You moved. Next time, I'll aim higher."

Mika spotted motion from the corner of his eye. One of the guards he'd shot in the chest stood up and aimed for him. They fired at the same time. Mika shot the guard in the head. The guard's bullet grazed Mika's left arm. In the distraction, Cabaye rushed for the elevator.

Maclin lunged at him. Mika rolled backward, tossing Maclin over him. They rolled, but Mika's roll was tighter. He came out of it first and fired. Maclin fell back.

By the time Mika got up, the elevator doors had closed. He'd been an idiot not using his new knowledge. No matter what he had seen, his instincts still clung to old realities like *people who got shot stayed shot.* He walked over to the guards and fired one bullet in each face. He reached Maclin, who wasn't moving. He shot him in the eye too just in case.

His biceps throbbed, but it was a nick. He grabbed Fabrice by the elbow and lifted him to his feet. "Any explosives here?"

Fabrice pointed to a locker. Mika opened it and pocketed three grenades and another handgun. He swiped at the screen he'd paused when Cabaye had come down and moved it at triple speed.

Cabaye and Maclin disappeared into the double doors behind the desk. Rendon rolled around, getting on her hands and knees. She winced as she crouched, which at high speed looked like a twitch. Her leg must have screamed with pain with every move she made. He wanted to go to her but needed to know which way she'd headed.

Roundface hovered over Rendon, gun trained on her.

Rendon coughed, shaking as she crawled around the chair. Her whole body was crouched between the four legs of the chair. She launched herself toward the guard, using the chair as a battering ram. He fired, but the chair connected with his wrist and pushed his gun up. Rendon drove the chair into him hard. The top of the seat connected with the guard's midriff, and he doubled over. They tumbled sideways. She lifted the half chair still attached to her wrist and brought it down on his face. He stopped moving.

She got to her feet but couldn't free her wrist from the metal underside of the armrest. She pushed Roundface's gun against the chain, lowered her head behind his leg, and fired. The chain gave way.

She dug into her thigh, but Mika couldn't tell whether she got any nails out. She stumbled back to the desk and rested for a few seconds before hopping out of the office, dragging her right leg as dead weight. Mika winced at the pain he knew she bore.

"Swap the feed," Mika said.

"We need to go."

"Swap the feed," Mika said, and Fabrice scrolled to another view.

The room with the octagonal stage came on screen. It took him a few seconds to realize Rendon had moved toward the occupied booth with the clicking sounds rather than the stairway up.

In the booth, a naked, tattooed woman with shoulder-length, black hair sat on a low medical table. Her head hung forward, hiding her face. Two leather straps fastened her blood-stained arms to the metal bed frame. Three IV drips were connected to her right forearm. A man knelt in front of her with a device that looked like a large tattoo gun. He brought the device to her shoulder, and the woman twitched.

Rendon must have made a sound, because the man put the device down and turned around. As they made eye contact, she fired twice into his face, and he fell back. Rendon unfastened the leather straps from the woman's arms. The woman folded forward and crashed on the floor before Rendon could catch her and before Mika could discern the woman's face.

Mika rushed to the door, but it was locked. "Unlock this door."

Fabrice waved at his screens. "It's the containment protocol. I'm being overruled."

Mika took two steps back, fired on the locks, and kicked the door open. He raced up the stairwell and reached the corridor where he had snapped Lenny's neck ten minutes or an eternity ago. He was about to run up to the bar level when he froze.

Eva stood in front of the booth, with disoriented eyes fixed on the stairwell. He tried to reconcile what he'd seen in the Kern lab with the healthy body in front of him. He couldn't. He'd been staring at her bare chest too long, not because she was beautiful but because her smooth skin bore no signs of having been shot. She pointed up the stairwell.

Before he could decide whether to reach for Eva or chase after Rendon, gunfire erupted from the bar above.

"That's enough!" Cabaye screamed from the top of the stairs. "Close the door, you bitch!"

Mika set a grenade to two seconds, tossed it up the stairwell, and retreated behind the wall.

"Or I'll—"

The explosion cut him off. The walls in the stairway were blown out to the studs, but the metal stairs had held up. Mika took the smoke-filled steps two at a time. Broken glass and the smell of alcohol permeated the main room. Nothing moved. Cabaye was sprawled on the floor halfway across the bar, closer to the outside door than the stairs. His head and limbs traced unnatural angles.

One man was folded over the bar, bleeding into the metal footrest. Another lay on the floor by the door, missing half a face.

Rendon and the third man who'd been in the bar were gone.

The front door was off its hinges, and a figure stumbled forward and fell. A guard came from behind their Humvee and aimed at the figure outside. Mika fired, and the guard collapsed. Mika got to the door to find Rendon sprawled on the ground, no longer moving. He reached for Rendon's shoulders and pulled her inside. Streaks of blood stained her pants. Eva came up and sat next to Rendon, cross-legged. She cradled Rendon's head in her lap.

"We got you. You're safe," Mika said as Rendon's eyes fluttered.

"Good, you're alive," Rendon whispered without opening her eyes.

He reached for Rendon's hand. "What?"

She opened her eyes, but her eyelids drooped. "I didn't want to explain to the general how I got you killed."

He smiled. "That makes two of us."

Her eyes closed, and she went limp, but the hint of a smile stretched on her weary face.

Mika grabbed Fabrice's arm. "Get some water and a first aid kit."

"I'm not going down there."

"Now."

Fabrice shook his head. "We are under lockdown. That means the lab's self-destruct protocols have been activated."

As Fabrice spoke, the floor undulated. Mika felt like he was riding a bull whose insides had exploded, which also meant all the medical data had just been incinerated.

"Go to the office. There must be something there." He pointed to Eva. "Find something for her to wear."

Fabrice stood his ground for a few more seconds before sulking away.

Rendon's pants were dark brown and sticky, the nail on top of the thigh having gone straight through. He reached to unbutton her pants. Eva's hand landed on his wrist, ready to take him on.

"Eva, I'm Mika, and I've been looking for you."

She jumped at hearing her name but didn't let go of his wrist.

"That's Sierra." He pointed. "Now, Eva, I'm going to lower her pants so we can see what's wrong with her."

"I know what's wrong with her," she said.

Her hand was still on his wrist. She pulled it closer and rested it on her inner thigh, right above her knee. She moved his hand up, brushing it against her own flesh. His knuckles moved over metal, rippling like scales. He pulled his hand back. The dark spots he had thought were tattoos were nail heads.

"Help me help her," he said, forcing his mind away from her markings.

They lowered Rendon's pants. He breathed his relief as they found less blood than he'd feared. Had Rendon passed out from blood loss, there would have been nothing they could have done for her here. Pain they could deal with.

He probed Rendon's thigh with his fingertips. Blood came out of four holes on the inner thigh, which was good. On the top of her thigh, though, there was a purple blot but no blood. With that nail still lodged into her femur, every step would have been agony, and she had gotten up the stairs and fought her way out, taking out at least three guards. He was glad that at least for one day they were on the same side.

Fabrice reappeared with a toolbag and a few rumpled jackets and shirts under his arm. Mika went behind the counter and opened the metal refrigerator built into the counter. Light-amber liquid poured out as every bottle had been smashed. He opened the low fridge on the back wall and found two clear, unbroken bottles wedged between two shelves. He uncapped and sniffed the first one. It was vodka.

He walked back to Rendon. He poured the alcohol on his knife and made an inch-long incision to expose the nail a half-inch down into her flesh. He took a set of curved pliers from the toolbox and poured vodka on them too. He tugged at the nail, but it didn't budge. He put one hand above her knee and pulled harder. The nail came out along with a trickle of blood. He wished he'd kept some of Phillips' magical tape. He poured the vodka on the wound, ripped a shirt into shreds, and pressed it to her thigh.

A gunshot jerked him back as he tied the last square knot to hold the bandage in place. Fabrice was on the floor, missing half a head. Eva crouched a few steps away, holding the gun with relaxed arms. She put the gun down and picked a green army jacket from the pile. She put it on and then picked up the gun and put it in her pocket. It wasn't exactly modest, but it covered her. Mostly. She sat back down, bit her lower lip, and brushed a few hairs from Rendon's face as though nothing had happened.

"He just worked here," Mika muttered.

"He should have worked somewhere else." There was no defiance or satisfaction or anger or craving of revenge in her voice, just the steady steel of having balanced the books.

He knew nothing about Fabrice other than the fact he'd been the only one who hadn't reached for a gun in the basement. She had been here long enough to know. He had no right to question her.

But all the data was gone, and now so was Fabrice, his last link to that data.

They used blankets for a makeshift cot for Rendon in the Humvee's back. Eva hopped into the passenger seat and didn't speak.

Lester had shown her hand. The attempt to get rid of Rendon had been blatant, and it had failed. It was sweet irony that after warning him off, Lester had led him directly to Eva.

Because Eva had been through the process Phillips had described, but she wasn't a ghost from the Uregs, an unlikable outsider like Phillips, or a long-missing Kern soldier.

She was more important than all the data Cabaye had destroyed, because she was a sweet child of Marin.

And she was data.

CHAPTER 27

NEW RULES

*"If some persons died and others did not die,
death would be a terrible affliction."*

—JEAN DE LA BRUYERE

I t was past ten when Lori reached her safe house in the Uregs. Mika's invitation had been cryptic but with enough urgency to force her to drop the hunt for Kern commanders if only for a night. Sierra sat on a sofa, her leg bandaged. Kevin gestured at his screens by the dining table.

Asher was there. Alive.

Mika talked to a man Lori didn't recognize. The man looked hurt but rose as they made eye contact. He drew his gun and spoke to Mika. "What the fuck did you do?"

Sierra drew simultaneously, aiming at the man. Mika jumped to his feet, arms extended, palms facing out, as though he was pushing back two walls. "Easy. Put the gun down, Phillips."

Phillips did not let go of the gun. "Bloody hell! I told you no one from Marin. I told you the rot goes to the top, and you bring the top here."

"I got it the first time," Mika said.

Phillips pointed at Lori with his free hand but spoke to Mika. "You do know who she is, right, or are you dumber than your frozen expression suggests right now?"

"Right now, technically, she's not Marin."

"Technically? How technical do you need to get before Colonel Rose isn't Marin?"

"Less technical than when you argued the Purge wasn't trying to kill us."

What does that mean? Lori hated being the latecomer, the one not privy to the in joke. The subtle eye contact she noticed between Asher and Phillips, and Sierra and Mika, hinted at alliances she didn't grasp. Tacking on throwaway references to the Purge wasn't helping.

"Bloody hell," Phillips said, eyes and gun still on Lori.

Mika put his hand on Phillips' gun and pushed it down. As Mika moved toward Sierra, Phillips raised his arm and fired. Lori's leg erupted in fire as though sliced by a burning knife. Lori caught the chair in front of her and let out a breath. She put a hand up, but the room had already burst into chaos. Mika tackled Sierra as she fired. Her shot went high, and they flew into the wall. As they rolled, Sierra's gun barrel found Mika's exposed gut. Lori held her breath as though the gunshot that would take Mika's life was waiting for her to exhale.

The shot never came. Sierra's grip on the gun loosened as they landed. Twelve hours ago, Sierra would have finished that fight.

As they came out of the roll, Sierra steadied herself for another shot at Phillips, but Mika slapped her arm. "Can we not shoot anyone for thirty seconds?"

Phillips put his gun on the coffee table and put his hands up. Asher took the gun and walked back. Lori couldn't tell whether Asher intended to shoot or protect Phillips. Sierra took shallow breaths, exhausted. Mika extended her a hand. Twelve hours ago, he wouldn't have cared. He pulled Sierra up, and she rested her back on the wall. She lowered but kept the gun.

"Let me explain," Phillips said.

Lori pushed up against the chair and straightened, making sure she had their attention. Blood streaked from her leg, but it hadn't even reached the floor. "Please do."

"The bullet essentially grazed your thigh. There should be no bone or artery damage. Only muscle, and that'll heal."

She reached down and probed her thigh, confirming the diagnosis. "The point?"

"Look, it will heal, but the question is how fast."

"Fuck." Mika said. "There are other ways to find out."

"Not on our timeline."

As far as explanations went, it left a lot to desire. She was done indulging them and had to understand what had happened here. Now. "Mika's thirty seconds are up. If someone doesn't start making sense, I'll ask these ladies to start shooting." She pointed to Sierra and Asher with her bloody hand, but she turned to Phillips. "Guess where they're likely to start."

"I'll explain," Mika said, stepping in front of Phillips, "but let's look at that leg of yours first."

A few minutes later, Lori rested her leg on the coffee table with a loose bandage on her thigh. With her adrenaline receding, the throbbing had intensified. Phillips scanned her leg, establishing the extent of the injury, before she took a shot of a local painkiller.

"I've been looking for Eva for over two weeks," Mika said once they'd settled in. She'd asked him to start because everyone here was connected to him. "She disappeared from a Marin hospital, but based on her files, she should have been dead, not missing. I had nothing on her, so I looked for similar cases. I dug into missing soldiers, into miraculous recoveries, into cancer survivors. Eva wasn't the only one who should have been dead. About a week ago, I shot a man in the chest, and he kept coming at me. I broke his wrist, and he kept punching. It was no longer medical files that defied logic but flesh and bone."

Lori read more skepticism than agreement on the faces around her. She turned to Asher. "When you got injured, I feared the worst. I was so glad you made it to the hospital I didn't question it, but I should have."

"Exactly," Mika said. "Family and friends are fine with miracles. They don't question them, and the files disappear before anyone else can dig into them, but Pras found the files, and a pattern emerged. The records get more erratic as prognoses get worse." He frowned. "They killed Pras and tried to kill us to hide a disturbing fact. Fewer people die from so-called fatal injuries and illnesses than ever before."

Lori filed her sorrow for Pras away to be unlocked some other time. She'd mourn everyone when she could.

"It wasn't a new drug that gave these abilities," Mika said, "it was the Purge. The reason for the missing soldiers. The reason for our health. Purge activity jumps, patients recover, and they disappear." He kept going, describing two types of survivors: those with and without the virus.

She tried to find fault in his logic, but she couldn't. "Wait a minute. Does that mean every newborn is a..." She paused, trying to remember the word Mika had used. "What did you call them? Are all newborns Puries?"

Phillips shook his head. "No. Until the virus is triggered, the reproductive cycle still works. If I had to guess, I'd say that's the cause of some of the gruesome murders in the Uregs."

"This is encouraging. No, it's better than that. It's great news," Kevin said.

Lori shook her head. "This is a disaster."

"Not going extinct is a disaster?"

"What we might have to do is the disaster. If those whose virus hasn't been triggered can become pregnant, what do you think will happen to them?"

There was silence. None of them had thought about that, because they were all too focused on the detail to see the big picture. Keep girls protected so they don't hurt themselves, keep them isolated so they don't catch any disease, and breed them early so they don't run the risk of activating the virus. She didn't voice her nightmare, fearing that words might give it shape.

"A gentler version of Kern," Kevin said, having gotten there as well.

His insensitivity turned her sorrow into anger. "Gentler? Seriously? If this is true, all these young women will become incubators just like in Kern. We're going to become Kern."

Everyone always said she worried too much. That was because there was an unending supply of things to worry about. She let go of the dropping birth rates. *Immortal* was a simple word but a difficult concept for the human brain to grasp.

They'd broken with anything connecting them to their reality. She felt like she was holding a plastic anemometer in a hurricane. She needed to talk, to provide a counterbalance to the deluge of implausible but likely true information she'd received.

"I believe you," she said, "because as crazy as it all sounds, it explains most of what I've seen recently on the battlefield and the policy front, but why do you conclude the Purge wasn't meant to kill us?"

Mika pointed to Phillips. "That's your story."

Phillips nodded. "Basically, it comes to Occam's razor. It's far more likely that something meant to make us healthier went wrong and killed us than something meant to kill us made us healthier."

"I'm not sure I'd use the word healthier to describe nine billion corpses." The timeline still bothered her. "Why now? I mean, the Purge appeared twenty-five years ago and disappeared five years later. Why would these hard-to-kill soldiers appear over the last year?"

"Actually, it was slowly working the whole time, but you're right, something happened recently." Phillips cringed as though pain jabbed at him. Lori knew it wasn't the injuries he'd sustained. "As the population dwindled, three surviving scientists uncovered what the Purge was doing. The four-day war hit, and everyone blamed science for the Purge. They ran and hid, hounded by FBI agents first, angry mobs next, and Kern agents after that.

"About two years ago, one of them decided he was done hiding. He set up a lab, took in hurt soldiers from Kern and even Marin, and healed them. The soldiers had military training. He gave them biological training." Phillips brought his fingertips together and flicked them out. "*Poof.* He had a loyal squad, willing to do anything for him. He used them to build a powerbase, but Kern noticed, so he made a deal. In exchange for land and protection, he provided indestructible soldiers."

"No one questioned the ethics of creating a new type of human?" asked Kevin.

"To be fair, he wasn't creating new humans. The Purge already had done that. He was accelerating the process, but to your point, ethics come and go. Politics is permanent."

Kevin wasn't impressed. "It always takes one lunatic to start a fire. Just saying."

"Actually, it turned out to be a blessing. A new group approached him to get soldiers. A little digging, and he found out it was the Puries, humans without the Purge. They knew about the split and had been gathering pure humans in the Uregs. They'd been hiding all these years, infiltrating Kern and Marin, manipulating behind the scenes, but now they wanted more. The scientist reached out to his two colleagues to expand his operation. One decided to join him. Together, they supplied teams of supersoldiers to the Puries, which takes us to last year with the attacks in the Uregs, clinics, gangs. All were hits sanctioned by the Puries to hide data or destroy evidence, or cause panic, or trigger moves that helped them consolidate power."

"They hit Ross," Lori said. It was the only conclusion. The reason they couldn't unravel the mystery was that they were looking at the usual suspects, the wrong suspects.

Phillips nodded.

She closed her eyes. It all made sense, and none of it made sense. There was no lid on this. "A world where some are nearly immortal and others aren't. This won't end well."

"Two species competing for the same habitat," Kevin said. "At least one will go extinct."

She opened her eyes. "Species?"

"What do you want to call it? One side can reproduce and die. The other can't do either without a lot of help. I'd say you're already past the split," Kevin said.

"He's right," Phillips said. "See, the Puries are torn between wiping us out and using us as lab rats to see whether they can generate a drug that works on them."

"Will that work?" she asked.

Phillips shook his head. "God knows they've tortured us enough to find out." His gaze found Asher. "Nothing worked so far, and I doubt it ever will. Some deals you can't change, but they'll keep trying."

She did not disagree, but she had a bigger worry. "You have an answer for everything. Perhaps all you said is true, but it's also possible this is an elaborate hoax to turn the tide in a war that Kern is losing, so—"

"Now wait—"

She raised her hand. "You know what the Purge does, what it isn't, and who used it to create supersoldiers. You claim to know there's a side that has hooks into Marin, a side I didn't even know existed until half an hour ago. I'm going to ask you two more questions. Who are you, and what do you not know?"

Phillips frowned. "Not the right time for this."

She kept her eyes on him.

Phillips answered her second question. "I don't know how this virus can exist."

"Well, it does. What's the problem?"

"It's too perfect, too well adapted to what it does. Also, it seems incomplete."

Perfect. Another word she wouldn't have used to describe the Purge. Phillips seemed to understand and admire the virus. She couldn't decide whether he was thoughtful or deranged. "What do you mean, incomplete?"

"It's almost symmetrical, a simple, twisting corkscrew, but one end seems lopped off."

"And?"

He winced.

The hysteria, the nonstop theories of the early days hit her. The scientists had been baffled by the virus using the same set of amino acids as all life on Earth, but she didn't recall any major disagreement on its origin. It had survived in the cold of space and landed on Earth with the comet. "You're saying someone created this?"

"I don't see how." Phillips' lips slackened. "I'm stumped, and I've been at it a while."

The deep regret in his voice triggered alarm bells. "How long?" she asked.

He looked like a man who'd borne the weight of this cataclysm on his shoulder for an eternity. "Long enough."

"How long?"

He lowered his voice as though that would change the meaning. "Twenty-six long years."

That made her laugh. "What? You must have been a kid. I was eleven when the Purge hit. Fifteen when the four-day war burned everything. You don't look older than I do."

"I am."

"You're what?"

"I'm sixty-four."

She tilted her head forward and grabbed the knot on the back of neck, kneading as hard as she could. The lump didn't budge.

"The mechanism repairs everything," he said, forcing her to let go of her neck and process his words. "Slowly at first, then efficiently, and finally so well you don't even notice you're no longer changing."

"You knew all along."

"We weren't exactly popular. Half the world blamed us for the Purge, so we kept a low profile." He turned to Mika. "Giving you hints and helping you heal is one thing, but if I'd walked up to you and said I'm an old scientist and I know what the virus does, you would have thought I was nuts. That is, if you hadn't shot me first, but everything I told you is true."

"You're one of the three scientists." Kevin said.

He nodded. "Two left now. One of them had come to kill me when Mika showed up."

"Where is the third one?" Mika asked.

"I honestly don't know. Probably deep in the Uregs."

She didn't know which part was harder to believe: that the Purge might be artificial or that it was healing them. "What the fuck have you guys been doing all these years?"

"Lying low and trying to prevent our extinction."

Kevin smirked. "How's that working out?"

"Not bad, actually," Phillips said. "We're still not extinct."

With those words, Lori realized Phillips did not belong in her world. Mika, Sierra, and Asher were part of the new reality, having grown up in the post-Purge world. Along with Czernak, Dey, and Fontaine, Phillips belonged to a world where nine billion souls had toiled. He was an alien who did not accept what the world had become. Lori was part of a tiny generation that lived with one foot in each world, a generation so thin it couldn't even be called a generation.

"I'm not buying it," she said. "The Purge spread when some activists got past the quarantine and into the Tromso contact site. It came from the comet. No one created it."

"That's the official story," Phillips said with a condescending smile. "It's not true." He took a deep breath. "There is no way anyone could have gone past the military quarantine, much less a bunch of civilians, and a year after the comet contact? No way, no how. The Purge got loose because someone in a lab fucked up. Once it got out, they framed a stupid group who'd been agitating for access and transparency. The story took on a life of its own."

"You're saying they infected and killed dozens of civilians to plant a story?"

"Billions were about to die. You think they gave a fuck about a few dozen more?"

"Why? Why frame a few conspiracy nuts if the Purge was already loose?"

"What else were they going to do? Raise their hands and say our bad, we just played with something we don't understand and fucked up, by the way, we might all die? They wanted to avoid a global war. In the end, they couldn't even do that."

"The four-day war." Lori brushed her hand over her bandaged thigh. She felt nothing.

He nodded. "Even that war confirms Tromso was a cover story. Only four nukes were used in the whole war, and where did they land? Tromso? No. At Shasta, the Baltic Sea, Chengdu, and Irkutsk—the US, European, Chinese, and Russian labs that studied the comet fragments. That neither the US nor Russia retaliated or escalated nuclear strikes tells you all you need to know. Basically, they were glad someone else nuked their facility so they didn't have to do it themselves."

"Un-fucking-believable. You and all the fuckers like you have been playing with this thing, but you have no idea how it works or where it came from. That's fucking brilliant."

"It wasn't a priority." Phillips sounded like a man who'd forgotten to unplug the iron and was trying to explain how the fire had been destined to happen sooner or later.

"What was?"

"What do you do when lightning strikes and starts a fire? You put the fire out, that's what. Now if you've observed a few lightning strikes and you happen to be the bright kind, what do you do?" He waited. "You focus on what gets hit and design a lightning rod. Your priorities are to contain the damage and, if possible, avoid future damage. The physics of lightning? Who or what created lightning? The answer is who the fuck cares as long as you got a lightning rod."

"I'd care," Kevin said. "That's a poor analogy, you know. Lightning is natural."

Phillips closed his eyes. "Look, there's no point getting stuck on an irrelevant detail like whether lightning is natural or not while the thing is busy wiping you out."

Kevin didn't back down. "You chose the analogy, and it's not irrelevant. If your enemies used lightning as a weapon, finding out how it worked would be critical."

Trying to steer this conversation was like trying to steer a tire over ice. "How do you control the process?" Lori asked.

"Control?" Phillips looked puzzled.

She pointed to Asher and then Phillips. "Yeah, how do I end up with you?"

Kevin snorted. "Ethics and politics. That was what, three minutes ago?"

Lori raised a hand, stopping Kevin. She pointed to Phillips again.

"Gradual physical and biological stress," he said. "Accumulation of injuries, interspersed with a biotrigger. A little poison, a tiny injury, a little more poison, a bigger injury, a bigger dose of poison, and so on. The healing chart looks like a slanted staircase."

"The key to longevity is getting shot a lot. Brilliant." She paused. "What kind of poison?"

"Initially, any poison will do. The best recipes escalate the dosage and potency of the poison to keep your immune system stressed but not overwhelmed. The first recorded cases were cancer patients getting into accidents, but any nasty biological agent will do in the right dose."

"Kern has a stash of AHtX. Nasty enough for you?" Mika asked.

Kern has a bioweapon? Any other day, that would have dominated her agenda, but she let go. She could only concentrate on one problem at a time. "Will that do it?"

Phillips took his time replying—she saw the struggle, the uncertainty on whether this was still a hypothetical question. "If you're asking me whether it can make a whole population of supersoldiers overnight, the answer is no. It would be too big a jump, so it'll kill the subjects. Theoretically, if you had already trained soldiers—" He stopped. "You'd have to be crazy to even try."

"If I were Kern and losing, I'd try anything."

"Don't say that," Mika snapped. "Don't ever say that."

"You don't have to worry about that," Phillips said.

"Why not?"

"Because Kern doesn't have the AHtX. The Puries do." Phillips continued before Lori could assess the new threat. "Are you going to continue a war that started under false assumptions?"

"The sooner the war ends, the sooner we can deal with this mess," she said.

"Are you fighting the right war, or are you now a front for the Puries?" Mika asked.

"That is a good question," Phillips said.

The dam that held her anger broke. "Him," she pointed to Mika, "I trust. You I don't. Don't ever suggest what I should or should not do."

"Look, I'm not interested in telling you what to do. Fight whatever war you think you're fighting, but Mika has a point, and yelling at me isn't going to change that."

There was a kernel of logic in what they were saying. But running the tactical analysis in her head, she still ended up in the same place. Take out Kern Command. Contain the northern front. Deal with the Puries mess in Marin. In that order. "I'll keep that in mind." She stood and stretched. Her leg ached. "I'm going to get some rest."

Phillips stood. "It's time to look at that leg of yours."

Mika whispered in Kevin's ear and put his hand on his gun. So he was nervous after all.

"What are we looking for?" Lori asked.

Phillips walked toward her. He knelt next to her, eyes on Sierra, who also had her hand on her gun. "Don't shoot the messenger."

"We'll see," Sierra said.

Phillips took the bandage off and moved a tida over her thigh, the same way he had done after he had shot her. She had no idea what she'd expected, but it looked like a fresh wound. Phillips had his index finger and thumb together and moved them apart, blowing up two red numbers to float in the air, 13:42 ± 7:38, and 1.4% in green below them.

Phillips stood. "The first number gives the average time it would have taken the wound to get to this point in a Purie, followed by the expected range for ninety-five percent of them. That is, the injury appears to have been inflicted thirteen hours and forty-two minutes ago, and ninety-five percent of Puries will fall within seven hours and thirty-eight minutes of that. The good news is that I shot Colonel Rose less than three hours ago, well outside that range."

"General," Sierra said.

"Oh, yes, General Rose. The last number says that given her current state, there is at most a one point four percent probability General Rose does not carry the PRG virus, which is good enough for me."

"How does this change anything?" Lori asked.

"For starters, you can all exhale, because I don't have to blow up this place anymore."

LORI WALKED TO THE KITCHEN TO STOP HERSELF FROM SHOOT-ing Phillips. She needed time and distance to process the implication that their strings were being pulled by an unknown puppet master. She got the kettle going, waited for it to ding, and poured near-boiling water over the coffee pods, filling the room with a nutty cocoa smell. Lucky for her, whoever had packed the supply crate had considered good coffee to be essential.

She emptied three sugar pouches into her coffee mug, stirred, and walked back to the living room. "Okay. Let's discuss this theory that the Puries are running this war."

Phillips had his eyes closed, but he rose to full wakefulness in a second. "Nothing to discuss. Lester is a Purie, so Marin is out of your control. Spindler's second in command is a Purie, so Kern is one assassination away or one lost battle away, which you're working on."

"Any evidence? Something besides shooting people and watching them heal?"

"It's everywhere. How else do you explain the ease of your victory at Anderson Valley?"

She swallowed the first six curses that came to her lips. "Ease?" Kagawa's face floated in front of her eyes, and her control slipped away, letting her voice rise. "You weren't there. You didn't see the bodies piling up on either side. Don't talk about things you know nothing about."

Phillips frowned, appearing surprised that his words had elicited a reaction. "I'm sorry. I didn't mean to disparage your efforts or minimize your losses."

She took a deep breath and let him continue uninterrupted.

"Look, you did surprise them," he said, "and your victory was quicker and more decisive than they'd expected, but Kern's offensive was a disaster from the get-go. The commanders didn't trust one another. They received conflicting orders and had no supply lines. It was a distraction, not an occupation attempt."

It hadn't looked that way from the strategy table, but if she was honest, even with her insight and Kagawa's initial stand, she'd expected a fiercer, longer battle. Distraction from what? She knew the answer. It was from Ross, from Lester, from what they were doing behind the scenes.

"Look at where we are," Phillips said. "Lester is entrenched. Spindler is weak. The Puries have no interest in anyone's winning this war. As long as you're fighting, no one is looking too far. Right after Hollister, if you'd pushed, you would have crushed Kern. They were too busy blaming each other to fight you, but you didn't push."

"It was deemed too risky."

"Purie influence in Marin. Three years ago, when Kern was becoming too aggressive? The power plant blew up, setting them back years. Move, counter move. And last week? The assault at Ross pegged you back on the ambition front and installed Lester as chancellor."

"I believe you. There is no other way to explain Lester's actions at Anderson Valley."

"Exactly." He softened. "Look, they've been keeping you in the dark since the beginning. The hospital records Mika has been chasing were part of this puzzle. The Puries have known about the split for almost a decade. Fortunately, they didn't figure out how to manipulate the process and get indestructible soldiers on their own. But since they've been working with my colleagues, anyone with too many injuries disappears. Eva? Gone. Hospital records? Erased."

"There's one other thing," Sierra said.

Lori lifted an eyebrow. "Yes?"

"The reconstruction from Ross. We focused on the biodata from the attackers, but there was one other inconsistency. Lester was in the back when the drone crashed. She let go of the coffee pot and crouched right before the blast. I assumed it was a glitch in the reconstruction, a split-second delay in the two sides of the room's sensors connecting. But what if it wasn't? What if she knew the drone was coming and had gone to the back and ducked to protect herself?"

"You didn't think this was important enough to put on your report?" Lori asked.

Sierra shook her head. "With all due respect, General, it was too important to put on the report. I couldn't accuse the chancellor of murder and treason without proof. With the credibility of the reconstruction in question after the biodata, I thought it best to keep this to myself."

"Shit." The data from the attackers was real, and so were Lester's actions. There had been nothing wrong with the reconstruction except their own preconceptions. Lester was the link between the ambush in the Uregs, Asher's disappearance, and now this. Lester hadn't seized upon the opportunity to take over. She'd orchestrated the whole damn thing.

"Okay," Lori said. "I believe you both, but that doesn't change a whole lot. We still have to clean up Kern. That means something different now, but whoever is pulling the strings, Kern soldiers out there are still armed, and they're still shooting."

"Cleaning up Marin might not be a bad idea either," Phillips said.

She shook her head. Going after Lester would create chaos in Marin and most likely split the armed forces. Sure, Kern was in disarray, but if they came together, they could threaten a divided Marin. She wouldn't give them the opportunity. If the Puries' strategy had been to keep either side from winning, she would upset the apple cart by first winning the war decisively.

"I know where Lester is. I know what she is. She can't do any damage in a few days, particularly since she doesn't know we know. We'll watch her and learn far more than we ever could by taking her down."

Mika frowned, but Sierra seemed relieved.

"I have one final question," Phillips said.

"Now what?"

Phillips turned to Mika. "I'm having a hard time with Chipps' story. The events of the last months can be explained when you factor in the Purie influence. The random attacks, Ross, erratic Kern policy, Lester's actions were all consistent."

Mika's face tightened, his jaw clamping down hard, but Phillips ignored the cues.

"Chipps' story isn't. She survived Ross, conveniently leaving earlier in the day. She survived the attack in Mika's house, and then she survived the bloodbath with the defectors. I'll chalk up one to coincidence, but three close calls? Why isn't anyone asking the obvious?"

No one spoke.

"Is she a Purie?" Phillips asked. "Is she working with Lester? Both Marin and Kern have been infiltrated right at the top by people with believable stories and an impossible-to-verify Uregs background. Why not New Cal? She fits the pattern."

Anger and worry were jockeying for supremacy on Mika's face. Lori spoke before Mika could. "You really have a way with words."

"Seriously, you're worried about his feelings? I'm trying to prevent genocide, so I'd say my priority trumps his. Chalk up my directness to being posthuman."

She sized up the word. It fit. Interacting with Phillips and Asher had not felt right. Their body language and their demeanor had been off. She'd thought of Phillips as an alien for his link to Czernak's world, but she'd been wrong. He was an alien far more literally. They were all on a path to redefine what it meant to be human, and Phillips and Asher were well ahead of the pack down that path.

"Just make sure your posthuman arguments don't become posthumous," she said.

"Funny," Phillips said, stone faced.

"Stop!" Mika hollered. "What bloodbath? Where is Amy?"

"She was in a Uregs compound meeting Kern defectors before heading to Marin for a new summit," Lori said. "The compound was hit, leaving fourteen corpses from Marin and New Cal. Chipps and Chastain are still missing. We assumed it was Kern, but at this point, it's just as likely it was the Puries."

"Who is Chastain?" Mika asked.

"Major Helen Chastain. Executive officer of Colonel Milner, the commanding officer of the Marin unit that was hit," Sierra said.

"When?"

"Right before sunset on the second day of hostilities."

Mika narrowed his eyes. "Four days?"

"There is nothing you could have done," Lori said.

He shook his head. "That wasn't your call to make."

"Let's get back to Chipps," Phillips said. "Did the Puries capture or rescue her?"

"You don't know?" Lori asked.

Phillips shrugged. "Obviously not."

"Too bad she's not here so you can shoot her too," Lori snapped.

"She's what, twenty-five?" Phillips asked. "Young enough to be a post-Purge baby."

"She's twenty-seven." Mika's tone was cool.

"You verified this how?" Phillips asked.

"Does it matter?" Mika yelled. "She is somewhere in Kern, and you want to discuss how old she is? Your fucking reasoning would have made a lot more sense but for her." He pointed to Asher. "I saw her shot full of holes, which shoots your post-Purge babies are Puries argument full of holes."

Phillips didn't back down. "That's your argument? A counter-example of one?"

"Don't start with me on statistics."

"Okay, let's not, and let's forget her age and the three close calls. How about injuries? Any odd behavior?" Phillips asked.

Mika's eyes edged toward Kevin. It wasn't a question, but it was something—a query, perhaps, or a request.

Phillips missed the exchange. "Does she still menstruate?"

"That's enough." Lori stepped between Phillips and Mika. "We will find her, and if you're right, and if she was involved in the Ross attack, I'll shoot her myself, but for now, you're going to shut up, because we sure as hell won't be using menstruation as evidence of anything. This isn't the sixteenth century, and we're not burning witches."

Her gaze settled on Mika again. He looked more disappointed than angry, but she knew that wouldn't last.

"I can't believe you kept this from me." Mika dropped any pretense they didn't share a past. He squeezed the back of a wood-framed chair, knuckles going white from the pressure he applied. A little more of this and either the chair or his hand was going to break.

She could not justify her actions, but she wanted to reason with him, but she couldn't even try while they had an audience. "Everyone out."

Sierra headed toward the rooms in the back. Phillips and Asher stood. Kevin remained seated.

"You too, Kevin."

"Fuck off, Lori." Kevin stayed in his seat and kept tapping at his screen.

The horror on Sierra's face would have made her laugh another time. After a few seconds of indecision, Sierra stepped out.

Mika squeezed his eyes shut, his jaw flexing out. She knew how hard he was squeezing, trying to make the world stop. Massaging his temples was the only way to help him let go, which she couldn't do.

Kevin relented and got up, but he stopped in front of Mika. "Told you," he said. "Pieces." He turned to Lori and glared before walking out. She couldn't tell whether it was pity or disappointment in his eyes.

Mika spoke the moment the door closed. "Shoot her yourself? Seriously?"

"I didn't like his tone either, and fresh off wrapping up a gender war, I don't want to start a species war. But he did have a point."

"No, he didn't."

"Now, I believe you when you say you trust her, but you can't dismiss his points."

"Cavana backs her story for how they walked out of the negotiations, and I know what happened when we were attacked."

"She still has her period, doesn't she?"

He nodded.

"Doesn't mean anything, but what about the odd behavior? He didn't answer. "I saw you look at Kevin. However damaging you think what you're hiding is, I'm imagining worse."

"I didn't want Kevin blurting out that New Cal was trying to buy scrammies out of context."

"New Cal or Chipps?"

"New Cal," he said though not convincingly. "So you know, she didn't just survive the attack at my house. She shot and tackled the freak who was about to skewer me. Had she been three seconds late, we wouldn't be having this conversation. Keep that in mind when you talk about shooting her."

"I said what he wanted to hear."

"Where is she?"

"I don't know."

"So we find out, and we go get her."

"*We* do no such thing."

"We what?"

"Mika, I'm days away from taking out Kern Central Command and cleaning up Marin. Once I take care of Lester, it'll be a lot easier to find Chipps."

"By then, there may not be anything left of her to find."

"I need to piece together a few leads, and we won't have to worry about Kern or Lester."

"She is not a piece!"

"If we get distracted, Kern rebuilds its power base, and we're back to square one."

"She's not a distraction either."

"Stop clubbing me with my own words," she said.

"Then stop using words that make me want to club you."

"If we delay, the whole thing crashes and burns."

"Let it burn. I don't give a fuck," he said.

"You were always the one who said we have to stop fighting to save humanity."

"Maybe humanity doesn't deserve to be saved."

"You don't mean that."

Her attempt to engage his rational side met an empty stare. "Why not? You do."

"*You* can't," she said. "One of us has to have a moral compass, and that's you."

"My compass is pointing to Amy."

"Mika, you're the pragmatic one. You don't know who took her or where she is, and even if you did, then what? This isn't like sneaking into a compound in the Rim. It's a war zone out there. If you start running around in the middle of it, you're going to get yourself killed."

"You knew I'd go after her. That's why you didn't tell me at the compound. You told me to not call anyone, sent me to the Uregs with Sierra, and now you're asking me to wait more?"

He held his ring for a moment and then oscillated it, his thumb pushing it up and down fast enough to start a fire. Anger and desperation danced on his face, and he opened and closed his mouth three times. The man who found the right word for every situation was struggling for words. "Kev told me we were all pieces to you," he said, letting go of his ring. "I didn't believe him. You told me you thought you were dead inside. I didn't believe you." His face relaxed as though all the muscles had let go. "You were both right." He moved to the door but turned around. "Maybe it was best we saw each other once a year, so I could pretend to still know you."

To prevent herself from replying, she walked to the transport. She rhythmically punched the starting sequence and displayed the latest reports from the front.

Through the transport's window, she spied Mika intercept Sierra, who was walking to the transport. Lori couldn't hear them, but the intensity on their faces and in their movements spoke volumes. They acted like two old friends parting ways, but she knew better. They were two soldiers trading favors. She was almost glad the glass separating them made their conversation inaccessible to her.

Mika put her hand on Sierra's forearm and leaned closer. This closeness explained what had transpired when she'd walked into the safe house an eternity ago, a closeness she had pushed away. Sierra nodded and pulled back. She turned and gave the transport a furtive look. Lori knew they were now talking about her. Her most trusted confidant and her oldest, and perhaps only, friend. She doubted they were extolling her virtues.

As Mika walked back to the house, Lori wondered whether she had anything left to say to him. She couldn't think of a single word. Promises and apologies weren't her style. In any case, she couldn't promise what he wanted, and apologies always sounded hollow.

There was only one apology that would work. She had to send him one of his favorite bottles of wine. Hand delivered by Chipps.

He disappeared inside the house. He didn't look back. The solid thump of Sierra's closing the door severed her last connection to this scene. Mika was now beyond her reality, sealed away outside her sphere of influence.

Until today, Mika had disagreed with her on principle. Now it was personal, and if Phillips was right, it was going to get worse. For the first time, she wasn't sure their relationship would survive her actions or inaction or what actions she might have to take. She suspected it might not, and that thought scared her more than the entire Kern army ever had.

As the transport rose, she took a deep breath and held it. She chewed the air, fearing the release, the moment the breath would escape, rushing away from her. She held it in a little more, reaching the edge of discomfort. As the safe house shrank away from her, she exhaled.

In her mind's eye, she pictured tiny bubbles of air moving away in an expanding cone, getting farther and farther away from her. Then they were gone, forever lost.

Unless she altered her plan, Mika was going to retrace the path of those air bubbles.

CHAPTER 28

OLD ENEMIES

"Courage is not not being afraid. It's being afraid and doing it anyways."

—GINA BIANCHINI

The brick cell was ten feet deep and eight wide. The door had a one-foot-square opening with one-inch steel bars splitting it into quarters. That window funneled in the only natural light coming in from the corridor. There were two cots on either side of the cell and a metal toilet and sink on the back wall. The plumbing worked but not fast enough to prevent the urine smell from permeating the cell.

Amy sat on her cot as Chastain did push-ups in the center of the cell. Amy had avoided reflecting on Eric's death, but that hadn't been a conscious choice. She'd been running from crisis to crisis, trying to stay alive and keep New Cal functioning, but now, sitting in a damp cell and staring at the wall, it was impossible to avoid thinking about him.

She'd said the dead would live in the memories of the survivors, but that was a lie. They were gone. There was a finality to it no thoughts or words could erase.

"We're not going to die here," Amy said.

Chastain exhaled as her body moved up. She held her position at the top of the push-up, arms fully extended. She swiveled her head, did three more push-ups, and stopped. She put her knees down and grabbed her right elbow in her left hand to stretch her shoulder. "What can possibly make you say that?"

"We haven't been moved," Amy said. "The roads aren't safe, or they don't know what to do with us."

"So? Lady, you Neuts couldn't find a bloody grounded tanker in a shallow bay. You think your people can find us? Assuming they do, what then?"

"How about a wager?" Amy asked. "If we make it out of here, you owe me dinner with good wine."

"If we don't?"

"I owe you dinner."

"What the hell kind of bet is that?"

Amy raised her palms up and cocked her head to one side.

Chastain shook her head and started another set of push-ups. There wasn't enough room for both of them to work out, so Amy stretched at the foot of her bed. She dropped her shoulders and twisted to her right, putting her palms together. After five long breaths, she switched sides.

Helen finished her set and sat up, leaning on her cot. "You know what I don't get? Why you'd think that talking to Kern defectors was a good idea."

Amy didn't reply.

"Politicians. No responsibility for anything, right? You think up grandiose ideas, and this is what happens when they meet reality."

Amy ignored the taunt but focused on the verdict. She did not consider herself a politician, but Eric was gone. She had to face the fact that she was now the governor. "You're saying we're here because of my decisions?"

"Somebody sure as hell fucked up, and when people like you fuck up, people like me die."

"Yet here you are, in one piece, unlike Kiril and all those bodies we left in the Uregs."

Chastain stood, ready for a fight.

Amy raised a hand. "Sorry. That was uncalled for."

Chastain sat back down. "Those were good soldiers."

"What was the news from Marin that had all you on the edge?"

Chastain must have realized the futility of secrets here. "Kern army sighting near Marin. It's all fucked up."

Chastain's anger was palpable, but so was her despair. It was a mix that sapped all logic, forcing the host to lash out at whoever was nearby. Amy was familiar with that reaction from her days in the Uregs. "As a soldier, I expected you to be more accepting of impending death," Amy said.

"Death? Lady, of all the things that may happen to us in the next few days, death is the only one I am looking forward to."

"I'm looking forward to getting out of here."

Chastain shook her head. "Yeah, but I live in the real world."

Amy grated her fingertips on the rough brick and considered the source of Chastain's despair. It hit her. Chastain's reaction was the normal one. It was her detached outlook that was out of place. She focused on the facts. "We're missing the bigger question here," Amy said.

"What's that?"

"How come a Marin transport attacked us and yet we're in a Kern cell?"

"They hijacked the transport."

"Doesn't track. Marin pilots let these so-called defectors take over a transport? I don't think so. Besides, I heard a woman's voice in the transport."

"So? We weren't the only ones they took."

"She wasn't in the back of the transport. She was in the front, barking orders."

"If that's true, New Cal was involved."

"You're quick to jump to conclusions."

"Who else?"

It was a good question, but she'd also heard loud arguments when they'd landed. The more Amy replayed the events, the less it all made sense. If she had wanted to lure herself into a trap, this was exactly the kind of meeting she would have used as bait. That sounded like paranoia, and in this cell, she didn't need paranoia to know someone was out to get her.

The cold certainty of their fate hit her, and she lost the urge to continue with the charade of conversation.

DAYLIGHT FILTERED INTO THEIR CELL FROM THE DOOR WINDOW. They'd made it through one more night unharmed, which was an unexpected relief.

"Awake?" Amy asked.

Chastain didn't reply for nearly a minute. "Yeah, now."

Amy sat up on her cot. "Can you think of any reason you were set up?"

"What are you talking about?" Chastain sounded barely awake.

"Might General Rose try to get rid of Colonel Milner? Or you for that matter?"

"If she did, she would do it a lot more directly than by sending me here. That much I know."

"How well do you know her?"

Chastain rolled to face her. "How well?"

"Do you talk to her? Do you have drinks with her?"

Chastain laughed, almost snorting. "General Rose? Are you for real? I say yes ma'am when she gives an order and get out of her way when our paths cross, which isn't often. I know enough to know that I don't want to spend any more time with her than I have to."

"Do you ever hear stories? About her friends? Her past?"

Chastain was silent for a minute. "She doesn't have many friends."

"Partners? Women? Men?"

Chastain didn't answer.

"How about Sierra Rendon?"

"Rendon is cool."

"Ever had beer with her?"

"Yeah, a couple of times. She was a little ahead of me, but we have mutual friends."

"Any stories about Rose from her?"

"God, you really don't have a clue, do you? Rendon worships the general. She's more likely to chop off her right arm than spread rumors about the general or chop off the tongue of anyone who would spread rumors about the general."

Amy hadn't expected a revelation, but she'd expected more. She bit a cuticle from her thumb and pulverized it between her front teeth.

"Okay, I'll bite," Chastain said. "How do we get out of here?"

"I don't know yet, but we need to stay alert till the situation out there changes. It's likely your bosses have figured out what happened at the compound and know where we are."

"Not likely. If I made a list of key Marin assets, we'd be so far down the list we'd need eight screens to reach us." She smirked. "No offense."

"Figured."

Chastain's dour face returned. "How the fuck do you suppose we'll get out of here?"

"Why does hope bother you so much?"

"I don't mind hope. It's the illusion of hope that bothers me."

Amy accepted that premise. She tapped the back wall with her knuckles. "This wall is solid." She ran her fingers along the wall on Chastain's side. "So is this one." She pointed across. "That one, on the other hand, has at least three weak bricks near the bottom." She pulled her cot away from the wall. "The mortar is weak, and the bricks are cracked." She wiggled one, and it moved side to side.

"Your escape plan is to move to the adjacent cell? Brilliant."

"Why so hostile?"

"Do me a favor, and shut the fuck up. Best-case scenario, they take care of us here, and I really hope that means a bullet to the head. Worst-case scenario, we are moved to LA. At that point, it's a slow, painful, and degrading slide into oblivion with bad news followed by worse news, so please stop talking. I don't need to listen to your inane chatter."

Amy picked at the bricks. She had almost dislodged a brick when the door unlocked. She jumped back and pushed her cot against the wall.

"You." The soldier pointed to her. He was barely eighteen if that. Strands of brown beard flecked his jaw line but did not yet connect to his wispy mustache. "Come with me."

She stretched her neck, first to the left, then to the right. She got up and walked to the door. As she reached the door, Chastain stood up. Her earlier anger was now focused on the soldier. The soldier noticed Chastain's movement. Amy put her hand on Chastain's shoulder. She was all for taking their chances, but there had to be a chance to take. This wasn't the time. She put gentle pressure on Chastain's shoulder, pushing her down.

"Wrists," the guard said, and Amy extended her arms. He cuffed her and guided her out. They walked along a narrow corridor and reached the stairwell. She'd been hooded when they'd been brought here. They were in a U-shaped building with a courtyard in the middle. They reached the second floor on the bottom of the U. The soldier stopped in front of a door near the middle of the corridor and knocked under a sign that read Cl. Felix Ranford.

Ranford sat at a metal-framed desk to her left with two brown armchairs across from it. Opposite the door, a square window offered expansive mountain views. She hadn't realized how far east they'd gone. An octagonal cabinet stood in front of the window.

"That'll be all, Private Buck." Ranford had a sharp chin and a thin face that exaggerated the size of his eyes. Buck saluted and walked out.

Ranford gestured to a chair across from his desk. Amy sat down. He grabbed a tida and tossed it to her. She barely caught it, the handcuffs constraining her motion. She swiped her hand on the computational glass, and the privacy symbol lit up. She tossed it back on the desk.

"You want me to believe this is private?"

"You can believe whatever you want, but we are shielded."

"Why?"

"Because my orders concerning you make little sense."

"You want me to help you sort them out?"

"In a matter of speaking. Do you know standard procedure with prisoners like you?"

That depended greatly on what "like you" meant. Hostage? Asset? Woman of child-bearing age? Prospects weren't good for Kern prisoners, but some prospects were worse than others. Still, she wasn't about to offer him any ideas. She shook her head.

"Interrogate the prisoner in the first twenty-four hours. If there is value, ship 'em to a facility in Kern." He didn't have to say what happened if there was no value in the prisoner.

They'd been here three days. "Am I supposed to thank you?"

"I'm not interested in thanks. I'd just like to understand my orders."

"What are they?"

"Minimize contact and hand you to a special unit coming tomorrow. Does that make sense to you?"

"Is this part of the interrogation?"

"Please don't insult me. I'm asking you a simple question. Why would you be the subject to such an unorthodox order?"

"I can't think of any reason."

His eyes drilled into her.

"Who do you think I am?"

"You are Amy Chipps, the former vice governor of New California. Some consider you the governor of New Cal, but your claim to the title is tenuous."

"Not that tenuous." She smiled. "The governor can't disappear, but Amy Chipps can?"

Ranford shook his head. "No, that's not it. Three days ago, a fancy title like governor wouldn't have fazed anyone."

She rubbed the skin under her metal handcuffs.

Ranford's eyes widened. "You don't know, do you?"

"Know what?"

Ranford gave her a sad smile. "Ms. Chipps, soon after you were captured, Kern forces engaged Marin. To say the operation was a disaster would be an understatement. Marin wiped out our northern flank, and the remnants of the army broke up and dispersed into the Uregs. Kern is in disarray. Some commanders are marching up. Some are retreating to defend LA."

"Northern flank?"

"Central Command decided that since there hadn't been a naval engagement in our lifetimes, Marin wouldn't expect an invading fleet. Turns out they did." He looked disgusted. "We lost thousands on northbound ships and even more ashore."

"Marching up, you said?"

"Idiots. Only an idiot would launch an offensive on someone else's timeline."

Rose had won another battle with Kern, one that had destabilized it—again. At some point she'd have to figure out what made that woman tick, but right now, Rose was neither a concern nor a priority. She keyed on Ranford's predicament. He really didn't know what to do with her. She was somewhere between a complication and a Get Out of Jail Free card.

"Where will this special unit take us?"

"I don't know, which is why I can't decide what to do with you."

"It's possible your indecision is coming from your conscience. I suggest you listen to it."

"Are you mocking me, Ms. Chipps?"

"No. I just have a low threshold for bullshit."

He stood. "We're done here. I'd hoped to find some clues about what they wanted out of you or who they might be. I thought you might be curious as well. I was mistaken."

"I didn't mean to offend you," she said, "but it's hard to take anything you say at face value."

"We're not all monsters, Ms. Chipps."

"When your guards pulled me out of the cell, I braced myself for many outcomes, but a heart to heart about the political realities of Kern wasn't one of them."

"Would you prefer I acted in more predictable ways?"

"I'd prefer to understand what's going on. Right now, I don't."

"Insulting the person in charge is your best strategy?"

"In charge of what?"

A flash of anger appeared on his face, but it gave way to amusement. "You have a wanton disregard for your own safety."

"I figure I'm playing with house money. What do I have to lose?"

Ranford walked toward the window. He bent forward, opened the octagonal cabinet, and emerged holding two glasses and a bottle of brandy. He put them on his desk, pushed a tida toward her, and pointed to his wrist. Amy touched the tida to the handcuffs. They clicked open. She put the tida back on the desk and rubbed her wrists.

"I'm going to pretend you walked through that door under different circumstances." He poured a generous serving in each glass and pushed one in her direction. He took his glass and walked back to his chair. "I'll start with something easy. What's most unusual about your circumstance isn't what happened since you got here or where I'm supposed to ship you. What's most unusual is that you're here in the first place."

"I thought that was the obvious part. You overwhelmed the base's defenses."

"Except it wasn't us. We had no forces in that area. You were delivered to us."

She leaned back in her chair and crossed her legs. "Delivered? By whom?"

"Not entirely sure. By all appearances, Marin forces."

She swirled her drink. "Do you collaborate with Marin often?"

"Never before, and I wouldn't say collaborate. They dropped you off."

"You didn't ask why?"

He took a sip of his drink. "I had two choices: start shooting or accept their offer."

"I wasn't trying to rattle you earlier when I asked what you were in charge of. I'm asking whether you're still a cog in the Kern war machine or the military governor of a well-armed Uregs compound."

"Things haven't yet fallen apart to that point, Ms. Chipps."

"Are they about to?"

He hesitated longer than a Kern colonel should have. "No, I wouldn't say so."

"That's too bad. You'd make a good military governor."

"First insults, then flattery. I'm afraid neither affects me much."

She drained her drink and waited.

The man sitting across from her didn't seem to know what to do or what he wanted. Ranford seemed stuck in a play he didn't like, repeating the lines to make it through another night, except someone had flipped the script. He looked like a man who heard lines that didn't mesh with his yet still stuck to his lines. The discord between Ranford and his surroundings grew by the minute, turning the assertive Kern colonel into a conflicted man.

"One more thing. Privates Buck and Grear are the two guards who escorted you here. They will take turns outside your cell. Do not trust any other guard."

"Trust?"

"If you see anyone else, Ms. Chipps, I did not send them. Am I making myself clear?"

Whoever had dropped her here had allies inside, but Ranford wasn't one of them. As she walked to her cell, she considered her options. They were limited, but she now knew there were two sides here.

Chastain stood as Amy walked into the cell. "Are you all right?"

Amy sat on her cot. Trying to explain what had happened would have been difficult, and she suspected they were monitored. "I'm fine."

"If you say so."

Amy pulled her cot back and sat by the wall. She leaned forward and picked at the bricks. Chastain stepped over the cot and sat down. She ran her fingers on the wall. She put her hand on Amy's shoulder, but Amy continued picking at the brick. There was little they could do to influence what happened out there, but there was something she could do to influence what might happen here, particularly if their next visitor wasn't Buck or Grear.

Chastain retreated to her cot.

It was slow work. After about ninety minutes, Amy got up from the corner she had been hunched over. She had blood on her fingers and knuckles, and her hand was clenched into a fist. She sat on her cot. "Just so we're clear." She waited to make sure she had Chastain's attention. "I never intended to escape to the next cell or anywhere else." She opened her fist, revealing a third of a brick. She squeezed it and relaxed her hold. She did not have to verbalize her next thought.

CHAPTER 29

PRICE

"The price of anything is the amount of life you exchange for it."

−HENRY DAVID THOREAU

ori's transport had left, taking with it Mika's last hope that Lori could be redeemed. Still, it was too easy for him to blame it all on Lori. Amy's putting herself in the middle of Kern defectors and Marin executives was as inevitable as Lori's war.

However, he did blame Lori for hiding Amy's disappearance. The accusation had been there, in the back of his mind, that maybe she didn't want Amy found, that it would be more convenient if Amy never came back, more convenient for Marin, and more convenient for Lori.

No permutation of those thoughts had produced a sentence he could utter. No matter how many times he played that conversation in his head, it ended in the same cul-de-sac. He had come dangerously close to saying things that could never be unsaid.

His restraint didn't mean he was about to forgive her or that his anger was dissipating.

Kevin and Phillips were the only ones left in the safe house. Kevin gestured at his screens, gear scattered all over the table. It all looked too normal, though Mika no longer knew what that meant. He'd been awake eighteen hours after having slept five days. His body was worn out, but his mind was oddly alert. He sat next to Kevin and pulled his sleeve back to expose his left forearm. "Kev, there is a tida in here. Whatever it broadcasts, make sure Lori gets it."

"Give it to her yourself. I'm done with her."

"Just do it." Mika lowered his voice. "Please."

"You know, you ought to talk to her."

"What are you, a counselor?"

"Just saying."

He put a hand up. "Not now."

"Anything else?" Kevin rhythmically tapped the tabletop.

"I need some lock picks."

"What kind?"

"The kind I could never afford."

Kevin didn't reply, so Mika told him what he had in mind, what he'd told Rendon.

Kevin kept tapping at an increasing frequency. "Are you crazy?"

"I need your help. But I don't need advice."

Kevin's tapping stopped. "Rendon agreed to help?"

Mika nodded.

"She's going to keep this from Lori?"

He nodded again.

"What makes you think she won't sell you out?"

"She tried the I-don't-give-a-fuck routine, but she couldn't pull it off because she knows I'm right." It wasn't lost on him that twelve hours ago, Rendon would have shot him given half a chance. Now after their ill-fated adventure in Cabaye's compound, she wanted to help him, except in doing so, she most likely was going to get him killed. That was irony for you.

"She'll do her part. I need you to do yours."

"I must be crazy for even considering this. You're going to get yourself killed." Kevin frowned. "Not that I care, but you're going to get Rendon killed, because once Lori finds out, she'll skin her alive."

"My guess is she'll get to keep her skin."

His tida chimed. There it was: the watch schedule, security setup, and a list of guards he could trust, as Rendon had promised.

"So?"

Kevin scratched his head, then nodded.

"Thanks."

He sent a short thank you to Rendon.

The reply was immediate. *Don't thank me. We both know I can get you in, but I can't get you out.*

As he approached Marin, Mika went over his strategy again. He was trying to keep busy, because at the first hint of quiet, his thoughts meandered to Amy, which led him to visualize the many ways she could be getting hurt. Unfortunately, he was very creative.

He had grasped the impossibility of finding Amy the moment Rendon had given him the details of how she'd been taken. His reality did not accept a situation where Marin cooperated with Kern, but his reality had been obliterated. The new reality was a stranger to him with loyalties, alliances, and debts that no longer obeyed the rules he had come to know.

It was unlikely that Kern forces had followed their defectors, assuming they were real, that far north. As many questions as were raised by a Marin strike on its own base, it also answered a few, which left only one address, one person, who stood at the center of the new reality—one person who had played both sides against the middle this whole time.

He approached Lester's compound without confrontation courtesy of Rendon's security briefing and Kevin's genius at evolving lock picks and identities. At the perimeter security, he presented his tida. He was a weapons expert here to see the chancellor. The only problem was that there would be no matching record on the guard's files.

"Who did you say made this appointment?" she asked, leaning in.

"Eva Asher."

He put his hands on the wheel and waited. The whole mission, and his life, were now in the hands of a perfect stranger. Rendon had pinpointed this time window to ensure the guard on duty could be trusted. Two days earlier, he would have never trusted Rendon with this or anything else for that matter. Now his trust tree had a new branch.

"Ah, yes." She waved him in.

The light in the top corner of the five-story building was on. Good. Lester was sticking to her routine. He headed to the alley separating the twin buildings.

Rendon had isolated the second building's fire escape as the best entry point, explaining that the presence of triple security consisting of video surveillance, digital locks, and sentries ensured that none of the three was taken as seriously as they should have been.

He watched the activity for fifteen minutes to confirm the routine had not changed. The sentry monitoring the alley stood by the door. He activated the sniffer that would replay the last hour of footage in a randomized sequence and moved in. The sentry did not notice him until it was too late. He fired two quick shots with the tranq gun, each delivering enough to put down a charging, five-hundred-pound black bear. She buckled forward with a blank expression. He touched the lock picks to the door.

Once he got the blinking green light, he moved the guard into the stairwell. She'd be out at least two hours, which was more then he needed. He'd be long gone by then or dead.

He flew up the five flights of stairs to reach the top. The stairway opened into the asphalt roof. An elevator shaft jutted out in the middle, pretending to be a cabin on a gray prairie. He stepped around the haphazardly scattered vent pipes and HVAC units to reach the edge of the roof.

Lester's building was sixty feet away. Mika activated the suction bonds and tossed his grapple over the gap between the buildings. The grapple landed with a soft thud and attached itself to the roof's floor in thousands of spots. He tugged on it and secured his side.

He grabbed the line, wrapped his ankles around it, and clipped his safety tether before starting across.

The line was too low to allow him to clear the ledge. When he reached the building, he unwrapped his ankles and kicked up to put a foot over the ledge. He let go of the line and pulled himself over the half wall. He released the suction bonds and tossed the line back across. In the unlikely event someone walked one of the roofs, he figured it would be this one.

He stepped into the stairwell and walked down to the lobby. He let the tida download the glitch. Kevin's picks could pick these locks as well, but he could not physically open the door without causing an intrusion alert. They were magnetically monitored, so he had to wait for the guards to turn the system off and on in response to the glitch.

He walked back up to the fifth floor. The glitch had to be detected by now. The door in the lobby whizzed. If the guard decided to walk up, it would all fall apart. There were no footsteps.

"Lobby secure!" the guard called.

The doors unlocked and relocked one at a time. "Second floor secure."

"Third floor secure."

"Fourth floor secure."

The door opened, and a hand waved him in. "Fifth floor secure." He stepped into the hallway, and the door locked behind him. Flint's index finger went to her lips as she listened to her earpiece. Seeing her, he felt relief even though that was an irrational response. He had no more reason to trust Flint than the guard at the checkpoint. The source of trust here was their link to Rendon, not a short chat at the Marin hospital weeks ago.

Flint spoke to her collar. "The damn cat is scratching the door again." She waited. "Sure, as long as you'll be the one coming up to clean it, I don't care where she pees either." She pushed the door open pointing him in. He moved forward but felt a hand on his forearm, stopping him. "Kelly." She waved a deliberate greeting. "Flint is my last name."

He waved back. "Kelly." He leaned into her ear and pointed to Lester's office door. "No matter what happens, don't open that door." She nodded and closed the front door.

Mika stepped into the antechamber leading to Lester's office. He stuck his knife behind the door's molding to pry it loose and stuffed thin layers of explosive putty around the door. He squeezed a bead of conductive gel connecting the explosives to the door handle and pushed the molding back into place. Within ten seconds, the beads had become invisible. He knocked.

"What?" Lester shouted.

He opened the door and touched his tida to the handle to lock it and turn the whole mechanism into a detonator. The office was about twenty feet deep and thirty wide. He entered from a door six feet from the corner on the long side. The space in front of him was open with a floor-to-ceiling window straight across from the door. A solid oak desk took center stage along the long wall, a third of the way into the room. The desktop was empty but for a screen and a bronze ostrich neck and head sculpture.

Bookcases lined the wall to his left, rounding the corner and extending behind the desk all the way to the window. A sleek leather sofa stood to his left across from the desk. Between the sofa and the desk, a square, wood-top coffee table with metal legs tried to create the illusion of warmth. It did not succeed.

Lester sat at the desk. "What do you—" She lifted her head. "This is unexpected."

He closed the door. "Move away from the desk."

She seemed more amused than concerned. "What are you doing, Bayley?"

He moved closer. "Move away from the desk."

"Or what? You are going to shoot me?"

He pulled his handgun. There were no tranqs here. "If I have to."

"Are you stupid? One shot, and every door in this building locks. You will not make it out of this room, much less this floor."

"Maybe. But that won't bring you back, will it?"

"Playing the martyr?" She gave him a cold smile. "Does not suit you."

He motioned her away with the gun. She shook her head but walked around her desk, passed in front of him, and sank into the leather sofa. Mika leaned on her desk, covering both Lester and the door. "Now you're going to call Yim and tell her you're resigning. Call it a sabbatical, call it burnout. With the war and all, it's not that far-fetched a story."

She laughed. "What the hell is wrong with you?"

"And you're going to tell me where Chipps is."

Lester's laughter sputtered to a stop. "Is that what this is about? How sadly predictable. I told you I would protect her if you did what I asked, which I was still doing."

"There was no reason to get her involved."

"Please. She involved herself when she took over for Fontaine. You involved her when you worked for Yim. You cannot play power games and ask to be left out when things get hot."

"You should have left her alone."

"What? You feel betrayed?" She shook her head. "Either you use people or people use you. Hell, you use people for a living. She is a pawn." She shook her head. "So are you."

"What does that make you?"

She was silent for ten seconds. "Fuck!" she exploded. "You are such an idiot. I cannot believe I thought you could be useful. Here is a clue. Fontaine, Czernak, and Dey are dead. Rendon, if she is not beyond the veil, she is under it. Now Rose, she does seem to have nine lives, does she not? It will not matter. She is going to spend her remaining lives running and hiding from her own troops. New Cal? Gone. Kern? Going. Marin?" She lifted her hand, cupping an imaginary ball. "In my palm. What does that make me? It makes me the fucking queen of your universe."

He grinned. "You disappoint me. I thought you were after something more than power."

"Oh but I am. Power is the currency. Everything, and I do mean everything, has a price, and power is the ultimate bank account." She leaned back on the sofa, putting her arms across the back. She focused her gaze on him. "After all, it is all about choices. Take Chipps, for example. What is her life worth? What are you willing to pay for it?"

She waited, but he remained silent.

"Stuck in a cell in the Uregs, hidden by mountains. Her power account is empty, so her options are limited to dying quickly or dying painfully. Even that she doesn't get to choose. Since you're being such a prick, in her case, I'm going to choose the latter. I do hope she has a high pain threshold. I'd hate for her to die in a day or two when she can entertain for so much longer."

He took a deep breath, held it, and exhaled through his nose. He put his hand in his jacket and double tapped the tida, the signal to prioritize the last sixty seconds in the tida in his arm. He had confirmation, as near as he could get, that Amy was not working with Lester. The clue to narrow her location was a bonus, though he doubted Kevin needed that.

"Are you trying to get me to shoot you?"

"Anger. Almost human, but you are not, are you? You and all the freaks like you. You're an evolutionary dead end, a side shoot of the human tree. You started human but got twisted. You are soulless, walking, talking machines. Feeling machines? I'm not even sure about that. And machines can be turned off, and worse, they can get corrupted."

"Yes, I see your point. You're pure and corruption proof."

"I will remember your humor when you are begging me to put a bullet in your skull, which is really thick. After all of this, you still do not get it. You act like we are all one big happy human race. Guess what? You are no longer part of it. What do those billions of ticking bombs do inside you right now? They stitch you up if I cut you. They cure you if you catch a cold. How fucking nice! What happens when they decide to block a few arteries around your heart? Or dam a blood vessel in your brain? Or create endorphins right inside your brain? Or give instructions to blow up your neighbor? How funny do you think you will be then?"

She waited, but he'd learned long ago not to argue with fanatics.

"Speechless, I see. If you freaks had any decency, you would take a leap over the Golden Gate and let the human race have a chance at survival."

After watching Phillips' broken body recover, he didn't think a drop from the Golden Gate would have fazed him. "Do you believe a word you say?"

She didn't reply.

"If we don't jump, you're going to push us."

"Somebody has to."

He chuckled. "You're not a genocidal maniac with delusions of queenhood. No, you're the reluctant hero, who has to do what no one else can. And she must bear her burden alone."

She pursed her lips in disgust. "Keep laughing while you can."

"I don't get one thing. Why hit the negotiations? Why not let the Marin-Kern war run its course? Was the Czernak-Fontaine meeting that threatening?"

"Please. Two derelicts howling into the wind as the world passed them by. What were they going to achieve? Tacking New Cal to Marin does not exactly tip the scales, does it?"

"Why kill them? Why now?"

Lester sneered and shook her head. Her eyes grew colder. "Why do you even ask? Do you live in the same world I do? The one where the indestructible bastards roam the Uregs?"

"Weren't you the ones who unleashed them?"

She shook her head. "You do not get it. A few are useful, but they are like zombies. Half-dead fuckers who do not just destroy but hold the key to make everyone like themselves."

"They're a sideshow."

"Sideshow?" She laughed. "They are you, and you are them. Look in the mirror. That is who you are. The sooner you admit that to yourself, the closer we will be to a solution."

"How many Evas disappear in your solution?"

"As many as necessary."

"To do what?"

"To stave off extinction."

"All the burned villages in the Uregs, all the murdered kids. Those helped how?"

She didn't blink. Even by the standards of their insane world, those murders had been particularly gruesome. They had blamed Kern, but now he knew better. The attacks that defied logic had been to eliminate those who healed too well. "They were not kids. They were soulless abominations, dangerous, sick machines. Machines that would have destroyed the human race."

He shook his head. "It won't work."

"Why, because you will stop me? Do not make me laugh."

"No, because secrecy was your best weapon."

She did not reply for fifteen seconds but rallied. "Are we done?"

"That call to Yim—"

A knock on the door was followed by a voice. "Ma'am?"

He straightened and aimed the gun straight at her head. "Tell her to not disturb you," he whispered. "If that door opens, I swear I'll blow your head off."

The knock intensified. "I'm busy!" Lester called. "What is it?"

"I have new numbers from the front lines."

"Do not bother me with shit like that!"

The footsteps moved away, but his attention remained on the door and the near miss. "Don't—" he said, but his thoughts got short-circuited as pain shot through his body.

His muscles refused to obey his brain. His grip loosened, and the gun slipped away. He collapsed forward. He tried to extend his arms to soften his landing, but nothing moved. He crashed on the coffee table, his chest hitting the edge, and his head bouncing on the tabletop.

WHEN HE CAME TO, HIS FACE RESTED ON THE EDGE OF THE coffee table. None of his muscles moved. He felt a warm puddle on his cheek, covering his right eye. He assumed he had split his head on the table.

He heard Lester's voice. "...a security team in my quarters now. No, wait. Get me General Herrera. I want everyone in this building to stay where they are. If anyone gets out, I will execute every last fucking one of you. Clear?"

He assumed it was clear. Footsteps approached him. He twitched as she kicked him in the ribs, but there was surprisingly little pain.

"How the fuck did you get in here?"

He grunted, so Lester moved into his field of vision between the sofa and the table. She grabbed his chin, moving it sideways. "Awake? Crap, you dented my coffee table." She let go of his head, and it fell back on the table. "You should have quit while you were ahead or at least while you were away." She laughed at her own joke. She walked around him and left his field of vision. He tried to move his head, but his head didn't comply. He willed his muscles to move. Nothing even twitched.

"General Herrera," Lester said, "I need a security team in my quarters, now." She must not have liked the response. Her voice rose. "No, it is not fucking all right. Cannot trust anyone." A few seconds of silence. "Fine, but I want Tran in here in ten minutes and with her own team."

She reappeared in front of him and sat. His head rested right in front of her. She pulled his head forward until his face was hanging off the edge of the coffee table. "Those two electrodes that dug in your back? They are doing a high voltage tango with your muscles. Just in case." She tapped one more time. He convulsed for three seconds. "That should last a while. What do we have here?" She patted him and found the tida. "You were recording this? Even you had to know once you walked through that door that you were not walking out again. You had to know you cannot broadcast from here since we are shielded. Seriously, how dumb are you?"

She put the tida on the table next to his cheek. She grabbed the ostrich sculpture from her desk and brought its heavy base on the tida at a slight angle. The tida cracked. She hit it a second time, and it splintered into three dozen pieces.

She walked back out his field of vision, and he heard a drawer open. His head moved enough to follow her. He flexed his toes and fingers, and though they were sluggish, they moved. Just a tad. She came back and put one knee down. She held a knife with a four-inch blade.

She grabbed his left wrist and turned his palm up. "Look at this," she said as she noticed the now-nearly invisible scars. "Not all innocent after all. Did you figure this out on your own, or did you get help?"

He tried to move his mouth, but his jaw did not cooperate. He pushed his tongue against his teeth and managed only a smacking sound. Not a problem yet, as he had nothing to say.

"No matter." She pushed the knife in between the two tendons running to his left hand, a third of the way between his wrist and elbow. It went in easily. He watched blood run down his hand. "You were so eager to be a hero. Here is an opportunity, Bayley." She grabbed his right hand and moved it to the knife's handle. She closed his fingers into a fist around the handle.

"Go ahead. Cut up and down a couple of times, and you will shred that artery real good. I will give you a few seconds to decide."

He relaxed his right hand and gripped the handle in his palm. His hand wasn't steady, but at least it moved. The blade was less than three inches from the tida embedded in his arm. He squeezed the handle and pulled the knife out. Still no pain. He let go, and the knife fell to the floor. He rolled to his left and fell from the coffee table onto the carpeted floor. Blood dripped from his wrist, but it was a trickle. She hadn't nicked the artery.

"Pathetic." She tapped the screen, and he convulsed again. "Now that we have gotten to know each other, I know this partnership would not have worked. You are like all the others. No stomach to do what needs to be done." She kicked him in the ribs. "Prolonging a life beyond its value."

"Which is it?" He slurred the words.

"What?"

He stammered, forcing each syllable. "F-f-freak to jump b-bridge or partner?"

She walked over to him and kicked him in the thigh. She stepped on his face, the sole of her boot pressing down on his cheek. "What?" She brought her heel down on his exposed ribs. "Fucker."

The cracking sound was probably louder in his ear than in the room, but two of his ribs were now broken. His pain receptors decided this was a good time to start working again, which didn't help him concentrate. He rolled over and faced the carpet.

Lester walked to her desk and tapped on the screen. "No changes in the guard schedule. Whoever helped you was always on the team. Unbelievable." She walked to him and kicked his ribs again. "Who let you in?"

He curled up tighter, willing his ribs to stop sending jolts of electricity to his brain.

She grabbed his face and dug her nails into his cheek. "Answer me. Who let you in?" He did not speak. She pressed harder, but it wasn't much of a motivator. Next to his ribs, he hardly felt his cheeks. He moved his lips, and she relaxed her hold.

"Eva," he uttered.

She let go of his face. "You think that is funny?" She kicked him on the back of his leg, stepped over him and kicked him in the stomach. "You can go where Eva went."

He coughed blood and curled up tighter.

"What now?" he croaked.

She seemed to debate between zapping him and answering him. She crouched in front of him. "Now you will go into a nice lab, but they will not try to make you unbreakable. Oh no, they will make you break. You will heal, and then you will break again."

"Not ambitious."

"You are correct. That is just the fun part, but waste not, want not. You never know. The Purge might reveal its secrets."

He laughed, but it came out as a cough. "Not so pure, huh? Want the forbidden fruit?"

"Not forbidden. Contaminated. I want to control the Purge, not the other way around."

"And the AHtX?"

She arched her eyebrows, and wrinkles appeared on her forehead. For the first time, he'd surprised her, but she recovered. "That is not your concern." She turned to her screen and blinked. "Tran. Where the hell are you? This fucker is bleeding all over my carpet."

"Securing the lobby. My team is on their way up. They'll be there in sixty seconds."

"About fucking time." She walked to the window, screen in hand.

He reached back and pulled the electrodes out. He dragged himself toward the door.

"You think healing fast is good? Just wait. We will see whether you can repair your body fast enough to not go mad from the pain." She glanced at him. "I'm betting not."

He kept moving toward her, toward the door.

She stopped tapping on her screen. "Where do you think you are going?"

He focused on moving his elbows to drag his body along. He forced himself forward a few more feet. He was now exactly between Lester and the door. Every muscle in his body screamed at him to stop moving. He ignored them and willed himself to his hands and knees. He steadied himself and pushed back, sitting on his heels, tasting blood as he swallowed. He hurt all over, and he was tired. All he wanted to do was curl up and sleep. It wouldn't be long now.

His last words to Lori had been hurtful, but with all the thoughts that had danced in his mind, they'd been innocuous enough. He owed her an apology anyway, not for what he had said but for what he had almost said.

His last words to Amy had been kinder but less expressive. He had evaded her questions and minimized her concerns. But it wasn't Lori he was protecting. It was the memory of the woman she'd been, a memory he had to let go and accept Lori for who she was. For Lori's sake and his and Amy's.

He took a deep breath, even though his broken ribs screamed at him to not do it, but pain was a signal he could ignore for a few more seconds. He would not let this lunatic get her hands on Amy or Lori or anyone else. Lester misinterpreted his intent. She still thought he was trying to get away, to survive. He'd always known everything had a price. He'd taken the knife out of his wrist because he'd been unwilling to write Lester a blank check. Now he knew the price.

The sixty-second arrival promised by the guard had to be up by now. He waited for the click on the door handle. That was his ten-second warning. The lock would hold for that long unless they hit it with something.

Lester stopped tapping again. "Seriously, you do know you are not getting out that door, right?"

His internal countdown had reached five. Four. Three. He stopped counting. "How about the fucking window then?" He launched himself at her.

The door behind him exploded. He flew forward with far more force than his unsteady legs could have generated. His back burned as the overheated air caught him and propelled him toward Lester. His head bounced off her chest, but his right shoulder connected. He grabbed her in a bear hug as they were lifted up and swept away by the blast.

Lester's expression danced between confusion and horror. Understanding flashed across her face as her back slammed into the window, but the window didn't need their weight to blow out as the expanding blast wave reached it first. Her lips moved, and from the spit flying from her mouth, he guessed she was screaming at him. With his eardrums blown, he didn't hear a thing. He felt the air rush past his cheeks as they flew into the cool night.

Phillips' words echoed in his mind. *Don't get tossed out of rooftops, and you'll live forever.* He hadn't been tossed out of a rooftop, but he suspected Phillips' warning concerned the landing, not the cause or floor of departure. But it didn't matter. He had come to find out what Amy was or wasn't and, if possible, force Lester out of office. He hadn't meant it this literally, but on the cosmic score sheet, he was two for two.

Shards of glass danced around them, keeping a respectful distance like a shoal of minnows floating around a larger predator, but it wasn't fear that had them sticking together, tracing the same trajectory he was. It was gravity.

As light from the floors they passed reflected on them, the shards swam in and out of his field of vision, blindingly bright in one moment, invisible the next.

A lot like his feelings for Amy were.

He closed his eyes, and in his dark, silent world, he visualized the tida in his arm broadcasting what had transpired in Lester's office to Kevin. There was more than enough there to confirm that Amy had never worked with Lester, which meant he no longer had to worry about what Lori might do to Amy.

He chose to believe that Kevin would find Amy and that Lori would rescue her. A smile stretched across his face. He pitied the fool who'd be holding Amy when Lori came knocking.

He was still smiling when they landed on solid concrete five stories below.

PART IV

ASHES

CHAPTER 30

NEW LESSONS

"If you don't risk anything, you risk even more."

—ERICA JONG

A s they flew low over the Uregs, Lori marveled at nature's healing powers. Forests gave way to bush-strewn grassland for a hundred miles. Occasional ruins pinpointed towns that had long been dead, but even those were sparse. The land between the coastal range and the Sierras was empty, not as though it had recently emptied but as though it had never been used.

She let go of the landscape and focused on her prioritized target list. Kern Central command was on top. The Puries' base with AHtX right below it. The part of her steeped in Kern wars was compelled to sever Kern's head. The part that had grasped the new dangers clamored to eliminate Lester and the Purie threat. A chime brought all of her back to the cockpit.

Chipps' whereabouts were in a coded message from Kevin. She called up the analysis Sierra had conducted. They matched, so she read further. Chipps had been abducted by Lester, handed over to Kern, and was not likely to be involved in Ross. All good, but Chipps still was a distant third on her list. Her mind wandered to Mika. She wasn't used to seeing him angry, but to be fair, she wasn't used to seeing him at all anymore.

Drinking one night a year had reinforced the images they'd

kept in their minds, but the last few weeks had shattered those images. Mika was the same stubborn boy underneath but with a much stronger grasp of how he fit into the lives of those around him. She had no illusion that Mika had walked away with anything remotely flattering about her. The rage that had given her strength was now controlling her. He had seen that in a few short meetings.

Flying high over the Uregs, it hit her. Her list was inverted, and Sierra had been wrong about what they wanted and needed to do. Lori wanted to clean up Kern. She needed to take out Lester and the Purie threat, but she *had* to save Chipps so she could save herself, assuming that was still possible.

She glanced at the targets again. Kern Command was to their south, the Purie stronghold to their east. Both were time critical, but not today. She tapped the map. "New mission. Extraction."

Sierra waited a moment longer than usual, but she punched in the new orders.

A thin, tall man in a Kern colonel uniform appeared on her screen as they approached the base. The man blinked. She suspected her face was not one he'd expected to see.

"This is a restricted area," he said. "Withdraw."

"Or what?"

When he didn't make an idle threat, she said, "You must see by now that I can get what I want by force, so I'll make you an offer."

"Proceed."

"You have two guests. I'd like them back. If they're unharmed, we leave. Period."

"That's a one-sided deal."

"No, it's not. In return, I offer to not turn your base into a smoldering catacomb."

"I'll consider—"

His image vanished. She spun to Sierra. "What the hell happened?"

"Nothing's wrong on our end," Sierra said. "Picking up gunfire," she said as a younger officer appeared on the screen. Beads of sweat were streaking down on his round, red face.

"No deal. We will defend our prisoners whatever the cost."

Lori glared at the man for ten seconds without blinking. "My good man, clearly you've been given incorrect pricing information." She paused, letting the implication sink in. Her eyes pierced him as though she were reaching through the screen into his mind. "You seem intent on standing in my way. I assure you there are far safer places for you to stand."

The connection broke off again.

"They lost power," Sierra said.

Seriously? Lori was tempted to go in, but there would be a cost to that, a cost in lives she wasn't willing to pay. Yet.

"Incoming," Sierra said.

The interceptors had been ready, and all eight transports launched their preprogrammed flares and missiles. The incoming missile blew up well before it reached them. Within seconds, three of the anti-aircraft batteries went up in smoke. The fourth was hit, though it remained standing if only momentarily. A second burst took it out seconds later.

The first man reappeared. "Ranford here. We have regained control of the tower. I did not authorize the assault." He sounded almost apologetic. Her power display had dispelled any thought of fighting back or at least crystallized the consequences of doing so.

"Colonel, I expect your guests are safe?"

"Verifying."

"Please do."

She cut off the connection. Her politeness was not sincere, nor was it intended to be. "Move us on top of them. The moment you sniff a sign of Chipps or Chastain, I want the extraction team on the ground."

THE DOOR TO AMY'S CELL OPENED. "UP AGAINST THE WALL."
Not Buck or Grear. Not good.

Chastain stood but did not take a step. Amy remained seated. She squeezed the half-brick hidden behind her thigh. The explosions had shaken their cells. The implication was clear. Chastain owed her dinner. Though before she could collect, they had to stay alive for another few minutes.

"Didn't you hear me?" the soldier barked as he took a step into the cell. His gun was drawn, and he was agitated. Amy stood up. A second soldier stood right outside their cell.

"Okay, okay, easy."

"Move to that wall." He motioned with the gun. "Stop talking." Sweat was forming on his forehead. Amy shuffled sideways, hiding the brick. "Turn around."

No. Most of these so-called soldiers could shoot her from behind. Only the well-trained ones could pull the trigger while she stared into their eyes. "Are you sure you want to do this?"

"Shut up!" He pointed the gun at her head. He blinked several times but kept the gun on her. Amy took half a step to her right. It wouldn't help her if he decided to shoot her, but she didn't want to get shot accidentally. "Don't move!"

Chastain chose that moment to dive at him. He fired as she reached him. They tumbled out. The second guard's gaze followed the motion. That gave Amy time to step up and throw the brick. From about seven feet, it connected with his temple, and he stumbled back, hitting the door. She lunged at him, reaching him as he was trying to regain his balance. As they landed, she slammed his head into the concrete floor. He did not move again. She grabbed his gun and turned around.

Chastain lay on top of the guard who was out cold. She rolled over and crouched, one extended arm steadying her against the wall. Blood pooled by her side.

"The stairs," Chastain hissed through gritted teeth.

Two more Kern soldiers, both armed, had entered the corridor. "Are you okay?" asked the first one as he hurried toward them.

What on earth?

"We need to get you out of here," the second one said.

Yes, that was a good plan, but Chastain had folded forward, her chest resting on her knees and her head dangling. Amy knelt next to her.

Chastain coughed and spat blood. "No time. For this."

"Stop talking," Amy said. The color had been drained from Chastain's face. The bullet had entered midway between her hip and shoulder on her right side. Amy did not see an exit wound. She turned to the soldiers. "We have to carry her or hold this position, but she can't walk."

"We need to go now."

"Why are you here?" she yelled.

She'd startled him, but he recovered. "To get you out."

"That implied we both had to be alive, no?" His eyes moved to Chastain and back. "Then you're about to fail." She stepped into the cell, ripped the bed sheet, and pushed a piece of it into Chastain's wound. She stretched another length of the cloth and tied it around Chastain's waist. The pressure wouldn't hold for long, but it didn't need to. She lowered Chastain to the cot. She pointed to the cot. "Grab that end."

The second soldier stepped in and grabbed the back of the cot that now doubled as a stretcher. They ran into the narrow corridor taking them toward the corner staircase, and the corridor exploded behind them.

———— * ————

"Now," Lori ordered as one inner corner of the U-shaped building went up in smoke. She punched the channel. "Colonel Ranford, we are done waiting, and I hope for your sake that no one I'm interested in finding was near that explosion."

The transports had executed their dance the moment Lori had given the order. Two hovered over the two wings, and two landed in the courtyard. Three remained high above, spraying the complex with gunfire. If anything moved, it didn't move for long. Lori's transport hovered atop the narrow part of the base connecting the two wings, ready to pounce at a moment's notice.

Ground teams emerged from the transports on the ground and dispersed into the complex.

"We've got them." A short silence followed. "We require immediate medical assistance."

Lori motioned the transport down. "Status?"

Silence. She waited. "Chastain was shot. Not good."

"Chipps?"

More silence. She was not sure she wanted an answer.

"Unconscious."

Six minutes later, she was on the ground, the compound under her team's control. Ranford and his officers stood by her transport. Ranford's men had regained the upper hand against the insurgents but not engaged Lori's forces.

"I want the ones responsible for the uprising," Lori said.

"It was an internal matter, and we handled it."

She shook her head and walked toward the medic who was examining Chastain. "Prognosis?"

The medic stood as Lori reached her. "Chipps has a concussion. She needs rest, but she'll recover."

Lori nodded in relief. Perhaps there was hope for them all after all. "Chastain?"

The medic's face soured. "If we could operate right away, I'd like her chances, but since we're three hours away, I'd say she's fifty-fifty at best."

"Any marks on either of them?"

"No. Neither was touched."

Lori walked back. She had not dared expect anything but was relieved and pleasantly surprised. She addressed Ranford again. "I'm waiting, Colonel."

"You said you'd leave if you got what you came for."

"I came for two healthy women, which I don't have, so no, I don't have what I came for, and no, this is not an internal matter."

Ranford nodded to one of his officers, who walked away to join Lori's officers. Sierra approached her with gritted teeth, tida in hand.

"What is it?" Lori said.

"A barrage of missiles is headed our way. Enough to turn this base into rubble."

Lori turned to Ranford. "Do you have anti-missile defenses left?"

Ranford shook his head. "I didn't hold back. This is all that's left," he said and waved toward the smoking towers along the perimeter of the base.

"How long?" she asked Sierra.

"Eight minutes."

"Where from?"

"Marin. Based on trajectory, it has to be Beale."

Lori did the math. The missiles had been launched shortly after they'd engaged Ranford's defense. She turned to Ranford. "Colonel, there was never any mention of this base in Marin. Half an hour after I show up, Marin decides to take you out." She glanced at Ranford's troops, surrounded and outgunned by her team. "How about we give your troops a lift out of here and you and I have a chat?"

Ranford's eyes moved from the raging fires to his troops as well. He nodded.

As they took off, an alarm screeched in the back of the transport. Lori rushed to the medic whose gloved hands moved with haste and precision over Chastain. Her blood-stained gloves gave away that she was losing the battle. "I can't stop the internal bleeding." She wiped her brow. "She won't survive another landing and takeoff. We need to go to Marin. Now."

Lori grabbed four parachutes and approached Sierra who was in the cockpit. "Take Chastain straight to Marin. Keep Chipps overnight. After that, drop her off to wherever she wants. Leave a small detail to protect her."

"A small detail?"

Lori dug deep for patience. "Yes, they're all incompetent down there, and when I need New Cal, I'd like to find someone alive."

"I mean, should it not be a large detail? 'Cause they're all incompetent down there." There was no hint of a smile.

"Do whatever you think is necessary."

Lori put on her parachute and walked back into the loading bay. "Here." She tossed three parachutes to Ranford and his officers. They didn't move. "Unless you want to spend the rest of your days inside a Marin cell, I suggest you follow me." She opened the door.

"I've never jumped," said one who had put on the chute like the other two.

Lori grabbed the pull cord and put it in his hand. "Count to three and pull this, and when you land, stay put. Those sharpshooters can pick you out from miles away. I wouldn't give them an excuse to use you for target practice. Remember to pull on three."

She pushed the officer out the door. She pointed down. Ranford jumped as did the second officer. Lori followed them. The cold air rushing against her cheeks let her unwind for a few seconds. The broken land hurtling up toward her was flat and dry, a reminder that any victory against nature was short-lived. Traces of the long-dead, geometric farms that had carpeted the valley were barely discernible from ten thousand feet. At a thousand feet, they disappeared altogether.

As she landed, Lori turned around to face her chute. She released one toggle, and her chute dumped its power and collapsed. She walked downwind to gather it. Ranford had done the same, but the rookie was fighting his chute, tugging and pulling against the wind, which dragged him farther downwind. The second officer rushed to help, yelling to be heard over the swishing of Kevlar. She approached Ranford.

"Here is the deal. There is a base a hundred miles southeast of here. Neither Kern nor Marin or perhaps both Kern and Marin."

Ranford did not reply, but he didn't show surprise.

"You noticed?"

Ranford nodded.

"That base was my target, but you diverted me by holding Chipps and Chastain."

He remained motionless, eyes fixed on her. The transports had landed about two hundred feet from where they stood. They marched his men out and into four rows of about twenty.

"My medic told me Chipps and Chastain have bruises consistent with—"

"No one laid a hand on—"

"—being tossed during the explosion. Believe me, that's the only reason we're having this conversation." She lowered her voice. "Chipps will be fine. As I said earlier, they walked out, you walked away. But Chastain's odds of making it are fifty-fifty."

"Now wait a minu—"

"I'm not done. We can't wait and see how it all works out. I only got three quarters of what I came for." She waited to make sure he followed her accounting. "That means the lives of a quarter of your men are forfeit."

Blood drained from Ranford's face.

"You can pick one of those rows." She pointed to the men standing by the transports. "They stay here. You can take the other three rows and leave."

Ranford's neck stiffened. "No."

She nodded. "Or you can join me on a mission and provide the ground offensive. Odds are better in that option. If we do it right, you'll lose a lot fewer men."

"You're crazy."

Not today. "Perhaps, but those are the options."

"You're going to rearm my men and walk into a battle with us? What makes you think we won't shoot you?"

"You could try, but we'll shoot back, and we have air support. If you want to sacrifice eighty men to take out a few of us, go ahead. I'm betting you're smarter than that."

"Who is at that base?"

"I'm glad you asked. It's the people who've manipulated Kern and Marin into a war. They're the reason you and I are shooting at each other. The reason Marin decided to take your base out when I showed up. I assure you that isn't a Kern base."

"I suspected that for a long time."

"There you have it. Do we have a deal?"

"I'd like a word with my officers."

"Fine, but we don't have all day."

She walked away, but it took only a few moments for Ranford to call back. "General Rose." He walked toward her. "I don't appreciate the threat to execute my men, but whoever is on that base is no friendlier to us than they are to you."

"Good to hear. Also, we'll need to perform a simple procedure on your arm."

"Procedure? What for?"

"I'll explain on the way. We're taking off in two minutes."

"May I ask what happened to the insurgents?"

"No, you may not." Two of the six Puries had decided to cooperate. They were now providing information on the Purie base. There was no need for Ranford to know how she had gotten that cooperation. That not everyone pushed out of the transports had received a parachute.

When Colonel Eze's forces joined her in the afternoon, Lori had an army again. The good colonel didn't blink at having to work with Ranford. Lori felt less comfortable with the state of Marin. Now that Kern was no longer a threat, Lester had again issued a warrant for Lori's arrest, quoting a long list of charges that made her proud of her accomplishments except for the accusation that she was responsible for Ross. No one should have believed that nonsense, but the longer that charge stayed unchallenged, the more doubt crept into everyone's mind.

For now, Herrera was in charge of the armed forces. Lester had pardoned Generals Kuipers and Gardner, most likely to isolate her. The generals were spending their energies mediating, using their newfound neutrality to prevent hostility on Marin soil. That was what they were good for. Lori was good for other things.

"General." Eze stood in front of her with a frozen expression. Something had rattled the unflappable colonel.

"What is it?"

Eze's eyes moved from Lori to her dark screen. "It's the chancellor."

Lori's jaw tightened. "Yes?"

"There was a break-in at her compound. She fell from her office window."

We can't be that lucky. Fell? That was such an awkward word that there had to be more to the story. Eze's wince screamed that Lori wasn't going to like it.

"What the hell happened?"

"We're short on details, just have reports of corrupt security and lock sniffers. Tran was at the compound, roughing up the security detail. There was a struggle in Lester's office that ended with an intruder named Bayley and the chancellor flying out of her window. The chancellor's cond—"

"Fuck Tran, and fuck the chancellor," she snapped. "How's Mika?"

Eze's eyebrows shot toward each other, confusion painted on her face.

"How's Bayley?"

Eze glanced at her tida. "No report."

Lori closed her eyes. The chancellor's office was on the fifth floor. She didn't need a report to know the outcome. Her initial shock was replaced with despair. She had seen the intensity burning in Mika's eyes. She had known he would do something rash, something stupid. But she hadn't seen this one coming.

"Get me Sierra. Now."

In the twenty seconds it took to connect to Sierra, Lori's fury had shifted. Mika must not have given her a choice. He was going in with or without her help, so Sierra had probably ensured he didn't get shot outside the building. Sierra's face appeared on the screen. Lori recognized the military hospital north of the city in the background. "General."

"Is Jane there?"

"Dr. Canales is by the chancellor."

"Get her to Mika, now."

Sierra nodded. "General Herrera's troops are on their way. Executive Yim ordered the hospital sealed till we know what happened."

"I don't give a fuck what Yim wants or what Herrera wants. Secure the hospital, and do not back down. Herrera's troops are not getting in there."

"Yes, General."

"I'm on my way." She cut the connection and turned to Eze. "Colonel, you're on your own." They had overpowered the first Purie base with Ranford's ground force. They now had the Puries backed up to their last stronghold. The one with the scrammies and the AHtX. They were at a stalemate with the threat contained but not neutralized.

Just when she saw the light, it was snatched away again. Lester had been her problem. A simple one she knew how to handle. Just like Chipps' situation had been. But no matter what she said or did, the root cause of all her problems was always the same.

No one ever listened.

CHAPTER 31

TRUTH

"Three may keep a secret if two of them are dead."

—BENJAMIN FRANKLIN

Rendon coming to pick her up puzzled Amy. They'd dropped her off in Cal City barely twelve hours earlier. Then again, there was a lot she didn't understand. Her rescue and Marin's newfound interest in her raised more questions than they answered, and with her headache, she couldn't concentrate long enough to figure any of it out.

"What did you say this is about?" Amy asked, trying to focus.

"I'm not at liberty to discuss it, but General Rose was adamant you needed to be there." Rendon held the transport's door.

One of Cavana's men stepped in to inspect the transport. "One moment, ma'am."

"That's not necessary," Amy said. They had grumbled at the force Rendon had left behind but adapted. Since her abduction, Cavana didn't let her go anywhere without armed escort.

"That's fine. They can keep their guns," Rendon said and pointed them in.

As they rose above the Golden Gate, Amy recalled the same trek she'd taken barely two weeks ago. Eric had been guarded as though dragged down by the weight of capturing a long-sought treasure, but the promise of a united California had been real along with the optimism she'd felt despite the hostility of Marin officials. All of which stood in direct contrast to Marin's current goodwill, which masked a pervasive pessimism.

Amy let her thoughts spill over. "Why are you suddenly so accommodating?"

Rendon said after a long pause, "You're a good ally."

"It would be nice if you stopped giving me the mushroom treatment."

"Mushroom treatment?"

In addition to the leadership lessons she'd absorbed from Eric, she had been exposed to a healthy dose of pre-Purge idioms. Some hadn't made sense or fit their reality. Some, though, were timeless. Now that they were orphans, she felt entitled to use them. "Yes, as in keeping me in the dark and feeding me shit."

Her security detail snorted, but Rendon's expression was the real prize. She started to laugh, but when the implication reached her brain, it cut off, resulting in a distorted grin, which disintegrated, restoring the apprehensive soldier's face. In that split second before her brain had interfered, Rendon's cheeks had stretched and relaxed, allowing Amy to see a real person.

"It's not always about you," Rendon said after she recovered.

"It is when you come personally to pick me up half a day after you dropped me off."

Rendon squinted. "It's about Bayley."

What had Mika done this time? Her face must have broadcast her question.

"He'd want you there, and we owe him one," Rendon whispered, "or three."

Amy had given up predicting what Mika would do or who'd owe him.

"Governor, do you have any idea what he did?"

A stranger was defending Mika. It was endearing and infuriating. She shook her head.

"He got us a tip that saved Marin from a Kern invasion. He

rescued a man who possesses critical information about what the Purge might be about, he saved my life, and last night, he cleaned up another one of our messes."

"Where is he now?"

Rendon looked away with a pained expression. "In intensive care."

Amy hopped off the transport as they touched down. She ran across the damp lawn to the hospital door and headed straight up to the third floor. There were more soldiers than doctors, nurses, or patients put together. Not one of them attempted to stop or question her.

Three chest-high partitions separated the waiting area from the corridors. Two sofas faced each other across a two-by-four, gray laminate coffee table. A recruitment brochure was strewn on the table, the irony of a cheery soldier's image in a military hospital lost on whoever had placed it there. Aside from two guards at each of the two doors controlling access, Rose was the only person there. She sat on the sofa facing Amy, leaning forward with her chin on her fists, her elbows on her thighs.

"Any news?"

Rose lifted and shook her head. "Not for another three hours."

The room was featureless with nothing to indicate what was going on around her. Nothing linked her to Mika. Amy walked closer. "I didn't get a chance to thank you."

"You're welcome."

She sat across from Rose. "Why did you come for me?"

"What makes you think it was you I came for?"

"Because you came. You didn't send a team, and I spent five days talking to Chastain. I know you didn't come for her."

"Chastain is going to be fine, by the way."

"That's great." Relief let her face relax to a smile, but she did not let go. "Why?"

Rose gave her an amused smile.

"No one on your staff tried to talk you out of it?"

The edges of Rose's lips moved up, forming a tenth of a genuine smile. "They would have before your speech. After it, they'd have been disappointed if I hadn't come for you."

Amy had had no idea her actions were even noticed, much less discussed, in Marin. She pointed to the operating room, inquiring.

"They've been in there for two hours. I'd tell you what they're repairing, but the list of what they're not repairing is shorter," Rose said.

That they were operating was good news.

Rose reached over to a bag by the side of the sofa. She took a bottle of red wine and two glasses. She offered Amy a glass.

The brief run had amplified her dizziness. Her headache was permanent. "No thanks."

"We're going to be here a while. I need this, but I don't feel like drinking alone."

She took the glass. It wasn't like her headache could get any worse. Whoever had coined the term *mild concussion* had never had one. As Rose poured, she still didn't see a person across the table but an idea, but ideas didn't drink wine.

"What's going on with the troops out there?"

"Still working? Seems Marin is trying to decide what to do with me."

Amy allowed herself a sip. "I take it you don't see eye to eye with Lester."

"Lester is dead," Rose said as though this was common knowledge. "No, I didn't see eye to eye with her, and yes, half the army is following someone who was following Lester. You can sit tight in New Cal, and in a few days, there might not be a Marin left."

Half of what Rendon said on the way over snapped into focus. "You don't believe that."

"No, I don't. It's nothing we can't clean up."

"Not likely to be clean, is it? At some point, it might make sense to stop shooting."

"Perhaps. I'll let you know when I get there." Rose swirled her glass and took a sip. She swallowed and closed her eyes. "I don't get you. Why defend the people who wanted you dead?" She pointed behind her. "The people who put Mika in that room?"

It never ceased to amaze Amy how smart, capable people could be so blind. She didn't have a bin for Rose, but she'd have to create one for single-minded leaders whose dogged determination and tunnel vision robbed them of perspective. With the recently departed, it was likely be an undersubscribed bin. "I'm not defending them. I'm defending you."

"How do you figure?"

"Because this never ends. I hear the path from hero to tyrant is a short one."

A flash of anger flickered across Rose's face, fighting with amusement. Anger lost. "Harsh words but not likely to be my path, because I don't want this." She opened both hands, palms facing up. "I'm stuck with it, but this is my final battle. I can't do it anymore."

She could not imagine Marin without Rose. Gone? She found it hard to believe.

"It must be nice to have clean hands and a clean conscience," Rose said. The words were patronizing, but there was no bitterness in them.

"No one is clean in this world."

Rose grinned, and her eyes warmed up just enough to reveal she didn't believe this.

Amy brought the glass to her nose. The aroma of green pepper and olives greeted her. It was exactly the type of wine Mika didn't like. Thinking of how he'd have argued that vegetables had no place in wine brought down all her barriers. She took a sip and let herself open up as though she were talking to him, not to this stranger. "When I first moved to Cal City, one of Eric's staffers made my life miserable. He touched me at every turn, made crass comments, described his dirty dreams about me. The more I pushed back, the more insistent he became."

She still remembered every advance, every putdown, and how though she'd claimed it didn't affect her, she'd burned with fury. "When I told him he had to stop or I'd go to his boss, he tried to get me fired. He framed me for a screw-up at the water treatment plant, but I had an alibi. I thought he'd back off after that, but he got even more aggressive. I moved a few names, a few files, swapped assignments, and sent him to the Uregs. The fool never complained. He thought he was on track to be a field operative."

"Good for you," Rose said, not impressed.

Amy flicked a few strands of hair behind her ear. "He was dead a week later, victim of a stray bullet."

Rose didn't react.

Amy didn't know why she had an intense desire to impress Rose. Then again, she did. Rose was the only person who struck fear in her heart. Not a primal fear borne by danger or the learned fear of Kern but a deep sense of unease that undermined her lucidity.

Rose had split into two people in her mind, and she couldn't reconcile them. Rose was Marin's chief commander, the woman whose reputation scared far more powerful people than Amy, but she was also Mika's childhood friend, a connection that Mika cherished and hid deep inside. The first Rose held the military power to undo in one day what had taken Eric decades to build. The second Rose held the personal power to destroy Amy's relationship with Mika without uttering a word. That was two weapons too many.

"Like I said. Clean." Rose absolved her with four words.

Amy sipped her wine but did not reply or meet Rose's gaze.

"I got a sniffer from Kevin Jezek about your whereabouts," Rose said. She must have seen Amy's confusion. "Your earlier question. Why I came for you."

"Jezek?" Amy did not recognize the name.

"Hound." She put her hand flat with the sofa. "Here's the league of the best hounds." She moved her hand to her chest. "Here are the special ones." She raised it above her head. "Here's Kevin in a league of his own. He reconstructed the events of your abduction and the reasons."

"Where did he get the data to do that?"

"That's what he does, but he got help from Mika, who broadcast pieces of conversation from a tida embedded in his arm while flying out the window. He was consistent to the end. People always talk about sacrifice and causes worth dying for, but really, how many mean it?"

"He's not dead." Amy's anger soared. Anger at the world, anger at Kern, anger at Lester. To be fair, none of it was directed at Rose, yet she was here and the others weren't.

Rose closed her eyes. "I'm grateful for that, but it kills me to think that whatever went through his mind when he took that final leap, he must have had no expectation of surviving."

The images became too vivid. "You came for me based on that?" Amy asked. "Story fragments captured and interpreted by a hound? That's a serious leap of faith."

"I question just about everything, but Kevin's skill? No, not that, and though we've had our differences, I don't question his intentions either when Mika is concerned."

"I sense a story."

"A far simpler one."

"Than what?"

"Than the one you really want to know. Why I came for you, why you're here."

Amy avoided eye contact. She wanted to scream but didn't say anything.

Rose picked up on her discomfort. "I have to admit I'm a touch jealous."

Amy nudged the recruitment brochure and put her glass on the coffee table. It wasn't that she feared losing Mika to this woman. She didn't know how to respond, how to relate to Rose.

"Oh, it's not you I'm jealous of," Rose said. She grinned and became downright unsettling, but at least Amy saw Rose as a person and not an idea or a negotiator across the table. Was Rose negotiating again but for different spoils? No, that was too simple a view. "He has you, you see, and I...let's just say I'm fast running out of candidates."

Amy glanced at the operating room door, but there was no news, no change there to hint at a resolution. She leaned forward to pick up her glass and took the last sip. "Okay then. What's the deal between you and Mika?"

Rose ran her finger along the rim of her glass. "I'm going to pretend we're not strangers, though we are. Do you know how many of Mika's girlfriends I've met?"

Amy stiffened, bracing for the "you girls come and go, but I'm special" cliché.

"Zero," Rose said and refilled their glasses. "I met Mika when he was eight. What a scrawny little thing he was. He walked up to me near the market and asked me if I wanted an orange. I was skeptical, but I hadn't eaten an orange in forever. I didn't see how he had one, but I said yes. He launched into a solid scheme to net us oranges and more, but I told him to get lost, because I didn't see how an eight-year-old could have hatched that plan. I followed him to see who had put him up to it. He never went to anyone. I was surprised he wasn't running with the older boys, who usually took in the little ones, forming gangs that got pretty dangerous, especially for a thirteen-year-old girl. When I caught up to him later, I asked him why he was alone. You know what he told me? That he didn't like the big boy running the gang. Sound familiar?"

Amy smiled in agreement. The more they talked about a precocious Mika, the less she thought about the broken husk lying in the next room.

"After that, we spent a lot of time together. A year later, a drifter kicked the door to my cabin open." Rose stood and put her hand flat between her upper lip and her nose. "I was about this tall, which isn't much." She sat down. "She knocked me down and sat on me, pinning my arms with her knees. Her hands crushed my throat. I couldn't free my arms, and as hard as I kicked and bucked, I couldn't dislodge her. I couldn't breathe. She was choking me to death, and I was powerless to stop it. It's a strange feeling. I wasn't giving up, but I also didn't see how I'd get out. My body kept struggling, but my mind was fading away.

"Then she screamed and shuddered, and her hold on me weakened. I scrambled away, grabbed the baseball bat I kept under my bed, and swung. She was slapping back so didn't see it coming. I connected with her jaw. She had a dazed expression, so I hopped up and swung again, putting my whole body into it. I got her in the back of her head. There was no loud crack or anything, just a muffled thump. Her neck folded at a funny angle, and she fell over. She didn't move again. Mika stood a few feet away with fiery eyes and a bloody mouth. I thought he was bleeding from the woman's slap. But it wasn't his blood. He'd bit her, not like a petulant child but like an angry dog. He'd torn flesh right off of her arm and neck. That's why she couldn't keep her hold on me or fight back." She took a sip of her wine. "We stuck together for good after that. No more shelters, and no more careless trips to town. Years later, we lived at the edges of what became Cal City. I worked in the hospital."

Amy cocked her head in surprise.

"It was long before the first Kern war. I hadn't yet moved to Marin. Late one night, Mika, my boyfriend Tom, and I were walking home. Mika and Tom had been good friends. Anyway, halfway to my place, we were accosted by three Kern thugs. Cal City was neutral in name only. The local security had long ago given up any illusion of control."

Amy brought her right hand up to her head, pressing her open palm to her forehead with the fingers massaging her scalp. It did not help her headache.

"We had nowhere to go. They laughed at their own jokes. They told us they were hunting degenerates and traitors." Rose downed her drink in one gulp. Her grip implied she wished it had been something stronger. "This was a long time ago, before Mika dragged me to those dojos, before I joined the Marin army, and before we became who we are. I knew Mika knew some sort of self-defense, but I didn't see how it could help. All three were armed, and one kept his distance, rifle aimed in our direction. I knew none of us would walk away if we played their game. I looked at the big one— Caldwell, his badge said—and told him I'd make it worth his while if he let them go."

Rose played with her empty glass, alternately holding it tight and tracing its curves gently. "I saw that if you give a jackass a uniform, you end up with a jackass in uniform, nothing more. I should have had more immediate concerns, but at that instant, all I could think of was that we would never get out of the mess we were in. That as a species, we didn't deserve to get out of the mess. Behind me, one of the soldiers yelled 'Down on your knees!' and 'Which one first?' The lust in Caldwell's eyes brought me to my own reality.

"I made a choice. I wasn't going out a victim. I leaned back, and as Caldwell moved toward me, I smashed my forehead into his face. I was too short to hit his nose, but his mouth exploded. He stumbled but grabbed my arm before I could get away. He slammed me to the wall and then to the ground, tightening his hands around my throat. I felt the same helpless feeling from those years ago. From the ground, I saw Mika move a few steps closer to the soldier. Caldwell yanked my head up and slammed my cheek on the pavement. I kept clawing at him to keep his attention on me and to keep the other two looking in our direction. That's when I heard a shot." Rose closed her eyes. "A three-second gap, then two more shots, and a fourth."

Amy reached over the coffee table for Rose's hand.

"I'll have some more of that wine," Rose said, opening her eyes at Amy's touch.

Amy refilled their glasses.

Rose took a quick sip, making it plain that she needed the wine more than she wanted it. "Mika was still a kid, barely seventeen, and Tom was a goofball. When I heard the shots, I thought they were both gone. Caldwell let go of me and looked up, one knee on the ground. I took quick breaths and saw the butt of a rifle land on his face. His weight fell on me, but Mika kicked him aside and helped me up. The soldier who'd been closest to Mika had been shot in the chest. His head hung at a weird angle. I later learned that Mika had broken his neck and used him as a shield. The soldier who had kept his distance was sprawled on the floor a few yards away. He had no face. Mika standing up next to me was so comforting that it took me a while to look for Tom. Mika tried to pull me away, but my eyes wandered. I memorized every stone in that brick building. I can still see it all—the façade with the chipped fourth brick, the rusted lamppost sticking out of the orange-hued bricks, and Tom, lying there, cheek down, with a small, red hole in the back of his head and a much bigger one where his right eye should have been.

"I walked back to Caldwell, kicked him as hard as I could in his ribs. I kicked him again, and this time he grunted and opened his eyes. As I stood over him, he protected his face with his arms. This big brute was cowering, helpless on the ground. It should have been enough, but it wasn't. I grabbed him by the hair and slammed his head to the stone. He screamed, part pain, part fear. Mika was whispering that he wasn't worth it, that we had to leave. My throat was on fire. I could barely breathe, and the back of my head throbbed, but I wasn't ready to run. I kept pounding his head to the pavement until the back of it caved. I grabbed the rifle from Mika and smashed the butt against his face."

Amy flinched as though she had heard the crack.

"We ran and hid with Mika disappearing for hours, doing what I had no idea. He later said he didn't know whether I could handle his seeing me so vulnerable. He was giving me space to heal, while each hour we delayed put us at risk. Such a precious soul, your Mika."

Rose gave a slight chuckle. "It took me two days to move my head without thinking it was going to explode. By then, Mika had gotten us new identities from Kevin. Anyway, that turned into almost a full year on the run. When I was ready to give up, he kept me going. When he was beat, I picked him up. We survived because we wouldn't let the other one down. Yes, he's a childhood friend, but those nights are what bind us. In two nights we went from children to survivors to killers to fugitives. There is no denying it. We both changed after those nights. Seeing Tom's body. Killing—I can't even remember what I felt when I killed that intruder with the baseball bat. That's because I didn't have time to feel anything. One moment I was choking, and the next she was on the floor and I had a bat in my hand, but when I kicked Caldwell, I woke him so he'd see that I was going to kill him. Mika tried to say it was all the same, but it wasn't. Mika had done what he had to like I had those years ago. What I'd done was revenge, fueled by the rage I'd let take over."

Rose took a gulp of wine. "I came for you because Mika needs you. And there is nothing I won't do for him. Nothing."

Amy absorbed the words. Rose didn't seem to need sympathy or forgiveness, so Amy gave her the only thing she could: silence.

In that silence, Amy cataloged how she felt. It was a combination of empathy, relief, and respect, but most of all, it was a feeling that Rose belonged to a different world, one where the rules were different. Her thoughts returned to Mika. The Mika that Rose had described was not that different from the Mika she knew. He was the same person at eight, seventeen, or thirty with the same worldview: do what needs to be done, and don't look back.

The *click* of an opening door startled Amy awake. She had dozed off, succumbing to the wine and tiredness. They both stood as a nurse walked out of the operating room. "Dr. Canales will be out shortly," the nurse said and disappeared down the stairs.

"One last thing," Rose said. Amy tensed. "You're the first person I told this story to, and you're the last person I will ever tell this story to. I know Mika won't ever speak of that night. I promised myself a long time ago that one person in his life would have to know, and if I want anything, it's to see Mika happy." She tried to smile, but her lips barely twitched. "I saw in his eyes that you were the one."

Amy flashed a fleeting smile. They'd been running for their lives, fighting strange new enemies. The future of their state, their world, was at stake, and Mika had found the time to talk to Rose about her?

"Though no one, least of all me, has a right to offer blessing, I want you to know. Take good care of him. For what it's worth, he's all the family I have." Rose pushed the bag by her chair toward Amy. "Here, a gift for you two."

Amy glanced at the bottle of wine and narrowed her eyes.

"We didn't part on good terms," Rose said. "Let's say this is as close as I'll get to an apology."

"You don't have anything to apologize for."

Rose leaned over the low table and grabbed her half-full glass of wine. She raised it and downed it. "How I wish that were true." She walked toward the stairs.

"Aren't you going to wait for the doctor?" Amy called.

Rose shook her head. "I need to go find new ones."

Amy kept her eyes on Rose, who stopped and turned around when she reached the stairs.

"I've had enough soldiers in operating rooms to know the staff's secret dance," Rose said. "If nurses and doctors come out one after the other, the patient is fine. They all want to give you the good news, to share their relief. If Jane comes out first, alone, the patient is dead. No one wants to be seen before the good doctor does her duty."

Neither had happened, but that didn't make Amy feel better.

"If nurses slither away before you can talk to them but there is no sign of Jane, it means the patient is alive but isn't expected to make it. They're all trying to get out from underfoot while Jane figures out what to tell the family." A sad smile crossed Rose's face. "That's us, I guess. We're family now." She turned around and walked away.

Family. Rose? She couldn't picture it. Maybe someday if she could think of her as *just* Lori.

Dr. Jane Canales came out thirty seconds later. Her eyes scanned the room, probably looking for Rose. She was a professional, so her eyes settled on Amy. She spoke softly as though her tone would blunt the impact. It didn't. The avalanche of words overwhelmed Amy. Broken. Long list of bones. Torn. Tendons and ligaments. Lacerated. Pancreas. Liver. Ruptured. Spleen. Punctured. Collapsed. Lungs. Fractured vertebrae. Plural. Cervical. Thoracic.

Amy didn't grasp it all, but she didn't need to. These were not words in any combination to describe a living person. The long list of injuries would have healed in time, but the conclusion was inescapable.

There was no repairing the spinal cord.

CHAPTER 32

NEW ENEMIES

"You can waste your lives drawing lines. Or you can live your life crossing them."

–SHONDA RHIMES

Lori had always valued her ability to compartmentalize her attention, to let go of problems that didn't have an imminent solution and focus on those that did. She suspected that was at the root of her reputation as a cold and heartless commander. She had made sure Mika had the best minds in the land by his side. Beyond that, she was powerless. Yet she could put him out of her thoughts for only a few minutes at a time. Perhaps she had been cold and heartless all these years.

But in those minutes in between, she had decided to not attend the executive council meeting that afternoon. Yim was the de facto chancellor as the last survivor of the permanent council, but Lester had appointed Herrera to the executive council to replace Dey. They had a dysfunctional council of three: two generals, each controlling half their forces, with Yim as referee. It had all the makings of a civil war.

The arrest warrant still hovered over her, a powder keg waiting to ignite. The last thing she wanted was to light the match by showing up for the council meeting.

She'd arrived in Nancy Yim's office before anyone else did and sat in full view to not startle Yim. "Good morning, Nancy," she said as Yim walked in.

To her credit, Yim didn't react. She glanced outside. There'd be no clues there, nothing but her staff and two security guards. She closed the door and took short steps to her desk.

"How did you get in here?"

Lori smiled.

Yim strained to act normal. "Have you had coffee?"

"No."

"Can I call?"

"You can do whatever you want, Nancy. I'm here to talk."

Yim touched her screen. "Lise, please bring a pot of coffee and a pot of tea. Two cups." Yim bolstered up her resolve and faced Lori. "What do you want?"

"I don't want anything. Now, I know you've been exposed to Lester's narrative, so let me provide an alternative one."

"Will that explain why the person who murdered our chancellor is under Marin military protection receiving the best medical care Marin can provide?"

"Mostly."

Yim's expression froze. "Well then, I'm all ears."

"First, had I followed Lester's orders, Kern would have won. She was a threat to Marin."

"Funny. That's what she said about you."

Lori forced a smile she hoped wasn't threatening. "Except I'm right."

An aide knocked on the door, walked in with a tray, and put it on the coffee table.

"Thank you, Lise. I'll take it from here," Yim said. The aide gave Lori a furtive look and disappeared. Yim walked around her desk and poured a cup of coffee. "Sugar?"

Lori sized up the porcelain cup, thin and narrow. "Two please."

Yim paused for a moment and took the lid off the sugar bowl. She spooned the sugar, added a stirrer, and extended the cup to

Lori. Yim poured a splash of milk into her own cup and filled it with tea. She came around the coffee table and sat in the chair next to Lori.

"I don't care what Herrera claims," Lori said as she stirred. "You are the new leader of Marin. You need to form a new executive council to unite Marin, and you need to find a way to get New Cal on board. But the first thing you need to understand is that Lester was working for forces outside Marin. No one she appointed should be allowed in a position of power."

"That's a serious accusation, but let me ask you one thing. What happens if I call security? After all, there is a warrant for your arrest."

Lori gentled her voice. "The troops on this floor are mine. If you make that call, nothing will happen. Your security team will recognize an indefensible position, but if their loyalty to you trumps their common sense, a few of them will get hurt."

"You say my security is neutralized," Yim said. "You walk in here unannounced and ambush me. You tell me I should fire Herrera. It's hard to look at your actions and not conclude that you run Marin, that you're in fact the military dictator of Marin right now."

"I have no such ambition. Now, there were two wars being waged. Marin against Kern? We won that one, but there was another one, with a group that infiltrated both Marin and Kern. That one is still raging."

"Group? Like a political faction?"

"Yes."

"What does this faction want?"

"To weaken us both and rule a unified California for their own ends."

"A little hard to believe."

"Yet true." Lori put her cup down and walked to the door. "I know this doesn't prove my claims, but it should show my goodwill." She opened the door wide, and Asher walked in.

The skeptical leader melted away, and Yim's lower lip quivered.

"Oh my God." She dropped her tea on the floor and rushed to cup Asher's face, tears forming in her eyes. "Oh my God."

"Hi, Ma." Asher smiled and bit her lip.

Yim hugged Asher, her hands cradling the back of Asher's head. She turned to Lori. "Thank you."

"Don't thank me. Thank the one whose access to Marin hospitals you were questioning minutes ago. He found her. He rescued her. I just drove her here."

Yim's expression hardened. "Not much I can do for him."

Lori walked to her chair, reached for her coffee cup, and took a sip to take the sting out of that truth. "Lester's every move was part of a coordinated plan: the kidnappings, the attacks in the Uregs, and hitting Ross. She knew the attack was coming. That's how she survived it. We need to go after them before they come for us."

Yim kissed Asher's forehead. "Can you give us a moment, dear?" She pulled her in and hugged her again. "Don't go anywhere. I'll be out in a few minutes, and call your mother." Yim's eyes were stuck on the door as Asher walked out. It would have been hard for anyone to conclude she wasn't Asher's biological mother, but why should that have mattered? Genetics couldn't have strengthened her bond to Mika.

"Did you have Lester killed?" Yim asked as the door closed.

Lori's fingers tightened around the cup handle. "Of course not."

"You're saying you're beyond such actions? Beyond assassinations?"

"No, that's not it, but if I had wanted her dead, I'd have shot her." Her voice shook and rose. "I sure as hell wouldn't have sent Mika to fly out the fucking window with her."

Yim picked up her chipped cup from the carpet and put it on the tray. "What now?"

"I need you to reinstate me officially. I need a free rein to tackle this problem. This would be a lot easier if I didn't have to look over my shoulder the whole time."

"You're vague about the extent of the threat. Who are they? Where are they?"

"We have their stronghold in the Uregs surrounded, but they have biological weapons."

Yim's eyes grew wide. "Biological weapons?"

"AHtX."

"What kind of damage?"

Damage was a poor word, but she knew what Yim wanted. "Enough to threaten thousands. They have two scrammies, which are hard to shoot once in the air."

"Let's not let them get in the air then. Do not engage. I want them contained but no hostilities while they have bioweapons aimed at us."

Lori didn't have the troops to mount an offensive anyway. "We'll keep them contained for now. We also have to worry about Kern forces in the Uregs. Their command is fractured, but they could coalesce any moment."

"I can think of only one enemy at a time." Yim looked pensive, uncomfortable. "If you're not part of Lester's circle, why did she put you in charge of the army?"

"She knew there'd push back had she put Herrera in directly. She assumed I'd go after Kern. We'd burn LA, they'd burn Marin, weakening us both. After she got what she wanted, she could frame me for Ross. Who'd defend the crazy general who couldn't save Marin? Appointing Herrera at that point handed her Marin on a silver platter."

Yim stared into the tea-stained carpet for ten seconds. "Very well. I'll clear up the charges, but I want the tension ratcheted down, not up. Do not go after Kern or these people and certainly not after Herrera. I don't want fighting in the streets of Marin."

Lori nodded.

"Anything else?"

"Yes, a suggestion." She waited for Yim to nod. "Figure out how to work with Chipps. Having her on our side might prove helpful."

Yim smiled, more mischief than levity. "New Cal? Since when are they a real entity?"

"Since Czernak invited them to the table and since Chipps' stunt in the capitol. Not only does she have New Cal behind her, but half my soldiers see her as a hero. She's what they want us to be: a strong woman taking charge of an integrated state."

Yim was somber as though she had a new burden. No, it was as though an earlier burden had gotten heavier. "Don't you wonder why I bought your conspiracy theory so easily?"

Lori did, but she didn't reply.

Yim took a tida out from her desk and placed it on the coffee table. "A letter from the chancellor."

"Why would Lester write to you?"

"Not Lester. Czernak, chancellor to chancellor. The security sniffers considered the wording to refer to me now. It's double encoded to the office and the position."

That was a lot of trouble to go through for delivering a message. "And?"

"Apparently, we're not the last survivors in North America."

Lori blinked, trying to process the information. "What?"

"Czernak was obsessed with finding survivors. She sent scouts in all directions. Most came back empty handed. A few never came back, but none ever came back from one particular area, so she sent more. Early this year, two scouts came back with reports of settlements."

Thoughts raced in Lori's mind. On one level, finding survivors was great news, but she also saw a new potential enemy who wanted to keep their presence secret.

"Where?"

Yim touched the tida, and a map floated up. A shaded area appeared to their north, extending from Northern Nevada to Oregon and Western Idaho.

"How is this possible?"

"How should I know? But that was the reason Czernak reached

out to Fontaine. She needed a strong, unified state that could stand up to a new player."

"Who else knows?"

"You, me, and whomever Lester may have told."

Lori tried to work through the implications. There were too many. Before her mind settled on a particular one, Yim gave her one more point to consider. "Czernak had told Fontaine. It turns out that's why he was so agreeable during the negotiations."

"What happened to the scouts?"

"Dead. One on a follow-up scouting mission, one in a Uregs skirmish."

"Let me guess. Both happened after Lester took over."

"Correct. What are you thinking?"

Some news she could have done without. She'd been so close to wrapping up the Kern war, but the introduction of the Puries had turned her analysis upside down. She couldn't figure out their motives or their strategy. Why keep Kern and Marin fighting without anyone winning? Why not infiltrate a side and make it win? What was the point of years of stalemate? It all made sense now. They'd wasted their resources and been so focused on each other that they couldn't see the world beyond their narrow borders. "They're not going to be friendly."

Yim's expression showed more concern than disagreement. "Let's not jump to conclusions. We know nothing about them."

"We know quite a bit." The attack on Ross finally made sense. It had removed two heads of state who knew the existence of a new player, eliminated witnesses, and kept that player's presence secret. She'd called them a faction for Yim's benefit, but she had no doubt they'd found Lester's home.

"Shit."

"What?" Yim eyed her as though she wasn't in on the joke.

"Lester was the beachhead."

CHAPTER 33

DEAD END

"If you obey all the rules, you miss all the fun."

—KATHERINE HEPBURN

Mika's condition had not changed in three days. Lori didn't stop in his room twice a day because she had anything to contribute, but she'd witnessed too many doctors give up on patients. The difference in outcomes between treating a living patient and one already left for dead was real. Her presence was a reminder that Mika was a living patient. Even if they didn't quite believe it, they at least disbelieved it less intensely.

Today, her presence wasn't necessary. To Phillips, Mika was a living patient. Phillips had Mika's body covered with gray patches and tidas, some reflecting light through his skin. A few connected to thin, dark computational wires, increasing their processing power. She almost believed Mika was ensnared in a black web, held at the center of an alien spider's lair. But the cold air and plastic smell broke the illusion, reminding her they were in a sterile hospital room.

A nurse walked in with a tray and stopped at the door. Her eyes moved from Mika to Phillips. "Who authorized this?"

Phillips ignored her.

"I did," Lori said from her corner.

The nurse walked out without replying.

As Lori had expected, Canales was in the room less than ten minutes later, accompanied by two junior doctors and the nurse. "General, I know what you want. I indulged your requests for second and third opinions, hoping you'd see there is nothing we can do, but I won't let you make a mockery of science in this hospital. Voodoo will not save him."

Lori respected Canales. Other than a few old timers, every doctor at this hospital had been directly trained by her or someone trained by her. But Canales' science had failed her. Voodoo or not, Phillips was Mika's last chance.

"I'd like you to meet Dr. Phillips."

Phillips glanced their way at the sound of his name but did not move.

Canales approached him. "What's your specialty?"

Phillips eyed Lori. When she nodded, he waved. "Dr. Canales. My specialty is molecular genetics." He had the tone of someone who had done this a thousand times. "More specifically, the evolutionary pathways of small population viral pathogens with short DNA sequences."

Canales' eyes moved from Phillips to Lori and back to Phillips. "Assuming I buy that, it still doesn't answer my question. Not that you're old enough to have been anything before the Purge." A touch of melancholy tainted her next words. "I used to be a heart surgeon. Now I'm not. In light of the shrinking need for your specialty, Dr. Phillips, what have you been doing for two decades that qualifies you to treat Bayley?"

He ignored the jibe. "That's complicated."

"Uncomplicate it for me. Otherwise, I'm going to have to ask you to leave."

"Would you like the short answer or the long one?"

"Short will do for now."

"Basically, I'm stimulating his immune system to repair the nerve cells in his spinal cord."

Canales laughed. She stopped long enough to ask, "With tidas and computational wire?"

"Among other things."

Canales turned to Lori. "I want him out of here. Now."

"Jane, walk with me."

They walked out and down the corridor until they were out of earshot. "You need to give me some leeway here. I know this is your hospital, but there is nothing you can do for him. Let me try another path," Lori said.

"Like growing him a digital spinal column with tidas?"

"Some things are hard to simplify, but it's a fascinating story. You should hear all of it."

"I don't have time for stories. This is a hospital, and I'd like to stick to real science."

"You can order us to leave, but you can't physically make me do so. And if you order that, we'll both lose. I'll look like a bully."

"That's exactly what you'll be."

"You'll look weak, like you don't have control of this hospital. Let this one go."

"How do I explain this nonsense to my staff?" Canales said.

"Let's seal this floor. You have, what, a dozen patients below? Say Bayley was infected with an unknown virus. Neither your doctors nor the nurses have any reason to suspect it's anything more than Phillips studying this new pathogen. That really is his specialty."

"That might work."

"It will."

Canales nodded. "Don't ever do this to me again. When the dust clears, you'll have to tell me who Bayley is, because you're acting so far out of character I don't recognize you."

"Don't you want to know what Phillips is trying to do?"

"No." She was firm. "Here's some friendly advice. Don't buy into it just because you want to. Miracle purveyors are good at selling hope, but they never deliver."

———————————

LORI BARELY HEARD THE OFFICIAL SOUNDING NONSENSE CANA-les spouted to get her team to seal the floor. Once they were gone, she found Phillips and pointed to the gray sheet covering half of Mika's body. "What are these?"

Phillips ran his fingers through the patch covering Mika's ribs. "Time-released chemicals and tiny pins. They stimulate virus activity and blood flow to speed up repairs."

They clearly weren't doing that. The screens monitoring Mika displayed each organ's function. The lungs were at zero. The only thing keeping Mika alive was the humming pumps that pushed air into his lungs. The screens also displayed viral activity in each organ, bone, and tissue. The knee and collarbone showed the most activity. "Why these?"

"Previous injuries of broken bones and bruised ligaments. He's had enough of them that the Purge knows what to do with them," Phillips said.

"And these?" She pointed to his liver and kidneys, which were above the baseline.

"Recent injuries and the ricin treatment I gave him last week."

The spinal cord had no viral activity. "Isn't there a ricin equivalent for the spine?"

"Neurotoxins, but I've tried three already. They're not working."

"What do you mean?"

"Look, you need to train PRG progressively. You can give a little toxin to repair a small injury, but you can't give a lot of toxin to repair a big injury. You need newer, nastier toxins spread over months. I'm running out of toxins, and he's running out of time."

"How did it work last week?"

"Last week, he only had a problem with his kidneys, so ricin was enough. I escalated the dose a little at a time until it balanced the physical damage, but this isn't partial damage. It's complete shutdown of half his organs."

"This is bullshit. You never mentioned this. You can't rely on hurting everything once."

Phillips smiled as though she were a good student. He may not have meant it, but his condescending attitude made her want to deck him. She took a deep breath to resist the urge.

"Not in the long run, but early on you do. That's why we follow a schedule of injuries and poison. In a controlled setting, you can activate the virus without damaging the host, but unfortunately, too many things are failing at the same time here."

"The answer is more varied neurotoxins? Like botulinum toxins?"

"He's too weak for anything that radical. I'm at a loss on how to treat him."

"My good old doctors tell me that regularly. I don't need you to tell me the same thing."

"I can tell you it'll all be fine then."

"I'm not in the mood for games."

He pointed at a number next to the schematic of the spinal cord. "See this? It's at zero. No activity. Botulinum toxins are neurotoxins, yes, but they can't repair a severed spine."

"You saved him before. Just do it again."

"Look, that was busted kidneys. This is a spinal cord severed in two places. Surely even a general can tell the difference."

"Don't push me."

"Railing against me isn't going to help. I'm not the one responsible for his condition."

"I'm responsible. Kern is responsible. Puries are responsible. Even Marin, by allowing Lester to take over, is responsible. But you, with your big mouth and half-formed accusations, you were the one who pushed him over the edge, so you're responsible too."

"There's no need to get angry."

"Angry? I haven't even begun to get angry. If he doesn't make it, I'll show you angry, and it won't be pretty, because there is enough anger here," she tapped her chest with two fingers, "to burn it all."

Phillips had a smug expression as though she'd said something he liked. She had intended it as a threat. "Perhaps I picked the right man for the wrong reasons."

"What?" The word came out like the snap of a whip.

"If his death will make you dismantle Kern and the Puries, perhaps it was meant to be. Perhaps he can still save the world."

Some thoughts, when expressed in words, caused her physical pain. They unleashed a primal cry for violence. She had learned to fight and, to some extent, to control that urge through the years. With deep breathing, she could ease the pain and regain control.

This time, she chose not to try.

She closed her eyes as her hand reached for her gun. She steadied herself and fired four shots in succession as she opened her eyes. They connected with Phillips' chest, and he staggered back against the wall, a confused look stretched across his face.

"Bloody hell," he breathed as he slid down, leaving a dark-red mess on the wall.

She moved to the door, but it flew open before she reached it. Sierra stood with an ashen expression, gun drawn. Her eyes moved from Lori to Phillips.

"Clean up this shit," Lori said and ducked out, though she didn't go far. She'd left Phillips slumped on the floor, head listing sideways. She waited to overhear Sierra's reaction.

"Are you going to be okay?" Sierra asked.

He grunted.

"Can you speak?"

Phillips took a breath. Words came out one a time. "Easier if bullets are out." A few seconds of silence followed. Lori guessed Sierra had called a doctor. His words got more connected. "There must be a doctor around here...somewhere."

If he could joke, he'd be fine.

"What happened?" Sierra asked him.

He spoke slowly. "Told her I couldn't do anything for Mika." He wheezed through a breath. "She got angry, threatening everyone." Another breath, and he started speaking normally. "I told her his death would mean something if it'd make her take out the Puries."

"She doesn't like that joke."

"It wasn't a joke."

"Lucky for you she didn't realize that. Otherwise, she'd have aimed higher," Sierra said.

Good. At least someone is paying attention. Lori left Sierra to deal with Phillips and walked away but was accosted by Canales. "What is going on here?"

Lori kept walking, so Canales followed. "I agreed to this charade, but I assumed you'd keep quiet. This is a hospital, not a shooting range."

"It won't happen again."

"Make sure of that."

Lori nodded and walked into the office she'd appropriated. The knock was quick, arriving before she had finished opening the wine bottle. It was a hard knock. She may have missed the first one. "Yes," she said as the cork came out with a *pop*. She poured a glass.

Sierra walked in and closed the door behind her without speaking. Lori wasn't eager to discuss what had happened, but that probably meant she needed to. There were too many triggers, all conspiring to boil over, and Phillips had provided the release.

"Wine?"

Sierra hesitated but nodded. Lori poured Sierra a glass. Sierra took it before speaking. "How did you know he'd survive?"

Lori took a sip of her wine. Sierra was learning. "I didn't."

"You must have suspected."

"I did, but I didn't know. I owed him one," she said as though her reaction had been normal. She had never been good at the measured response concept.

"With all due respect, General, he gave you a nick. You emptied your gun into his chest."

"You're here to inform me that he'll be fine."

Sierra played with her glass.

"I appreciate your concern, but I'm fine. So is Phillips."

"About Phillips—"

"I overreacted. I'll apologize next time I see him." She smiled.

"I promise I won't shoot anyone else tonight."

Sierra stopped playing with her glass and put it on the side table. She had not had a sip. Lori let her eyes stay on it a second too long. Any illusion that this was a social call disappeared. Lori took a big gulp and put her glass down as well.

She needed to get out of here, even just for an hour. "Find me some toxicologists and some toxins. I'm going home for a shower."

CHAPTER 34

NEW MISTAKES

"Knowing what must be done does away with fear."

−ROSA PARKS

Lori folded forward and hugged her knees, letting her calves stretch. The hot shower beat on her flesh, attempting the impossible task of melting away her tension. After eight breaths, she let go of her knees and put her hands on the rough, warm slate, leaning forward. She took another eight breaths before putting her hands on her shins and straightening, letting the water massage her lower back. She stood and let the water beat on her neck. When she brought her face toward the shower's nozzle, her lips and cheeks stretched and pulled with the water's force, as though she could be cleansed.

But no amount of hot water would absolve her of her sins.

As she reached to shut off the water, she heard a *thump* like a padded door slamming upstairs or a sack of rice hitting the ground. She did not have an upstairs, and she did not have sacks of rice. Thompson, the armed escort Sierra had insisted she take, was the only person in the house, and she was far too cowed to slam anything.

Lori let the water run and slid out of the shower. The stall spanned the full width of her narrow bathroom and faced the door. The toilet was to her left followed by an above-the-counter sink that sat atop four rows of drawers. The towel rack and closet were to her right, running all the way to the door. She'd left the bathroom door ajar to let the steam escape, but after a ten-minute hot shower, the mirror should have had more fog.

She reached for the top of the towel rack, but her gun wasn't there, because she'd left it on the coffee table while convincing Thompson to accept a mug of coffee.

She toweled off her arms, hands, and feet before running the towel over her face. The heavier the towel got, the better. She stepped behind the door, disappearing into the closet.

The footsteps of someone who wore military boots and shuffled in quick, small steps approached. A gun extended behind the door, aiming for the still-steaming shower.

Lori rolled the towel and held both ends in her hand.

Two quick shots shattered the fogged-up shower door. Lori didn't wait for the shards to land and expose an empty stall. She brought the towel hard on the attacker's wrist, sending the gun sprawling on the tile floor. She let one end of the towel go and whipped it around the shooter's neck. She grabbed the loose end of the towel and pulled. The shooter clawed at Lori's hands and elbowed back but didn't have enough purchase to make her let go. Lori slammed the attacker's head into the door jamb twice. She let the towel fall and broke the dazed shooter's neck in one swiping motion.

She stepped over the body and scrambled after the gun that had bounced into the hallway. She grabbed the gun, but before she stood up, the cold tip of a barrel was pushed against the back of her head.

"Uh uh."

Lori let go of the gun and turned slowly. Tran stood in her long, black leather trench coat, collar up, holding a gun in her leather gloves. Every second Tran did not fire was a victory.

"I was not expecting you this soon."

Tran smiled, but her face did not warm up. "I find that hard to believe."

"I knew you'd want to clean up that cock-up in the Uregs, but I thought you and Herrera had too much brains to do it this way."

"I don't expect you to understand."

"Understand what? That you're helping Herrera complete Marin's takeover? That you're dumb enough to think my officers will accept Herrera's orders?"

"They will when you're not around to tell them otherwise."

"I wouldn't count on that."

Tran took a few steps back, gun still pointing at her. Lori stood slowly. The hallway was five feet wide with a doorless opening to the living room. A round, wooden coffee table dominated her living room. A swivel leather chair sat to the right of the coffee table; a light gray, microfiber, three-seater sofa was straight ahead of her. The sofa separated the living space from the kitchen island to her left. Three stools were scattered around the island, facing the sink and fridge at the back wall.

Lori pointed down the hallway. "How about I put some clothes on?"

Tran tilted her head and furrowed her brow. "No." Five seconds later, she waved toward Lori. "They should find you like this."

Lori ran her hands down her chest and sides, then down her thighs, shucking off excess water. "What are you waiting for?"

Tran pointed to the gun. It was Lori's. "Poetic justice, don't you think?"

Lori put both hands on her forehead and pressed her hair back, forcing water down her back. The chill of cool water hitting her skin gave her goose bumps.

"You were distraught, guilt stricken, and couldn't bear it anymore."

"No one will buy that."

"Your actions led us to the brink of civil war. Stress gets to all of us, doesn't it? In the end, you chose to go out alone rather than face arrest and a court martial." Her lips curled up ever so slightly. "Or maybe some redemption? You decided to prevent a civil war by ending it all."

"No one will buy that either."

"No one will question it. You think Rendon will?" Tran gave three quick nods. "She probably would if I let her, but I won't."

"I'm a little disappointed."

Tran's jaw pulsated. "Why? Because I didn't revere you like everyone else did? Is that it?"

Lori smiled. "No, that you're this sloppy. Seems you didn't learn a thing."

Tran narrowed her eyes.

"There were two of you, you were armed, and you had the element of surprise." Lori pointed to the body on the floor of her bathroom. "This is where we are."

Tran took a step toward her. The gun was two feet from her nose, but all she smelled was Tran's leather glove. "Where is that, huh?"

Lori kept her eyes on Tran's but didn't reply.

"If you're stalling, waiting for help, you can forget it. No one is coming. Your bodyguard wasn't much of one. I have two more agents curbside, waiting, so how do you think this ends?"

Lori sighed. "With a lot more bodies than I'd have liked."

Tran chuckled. "Gotta hand it to you. You play the persona to the end, don't you?"

Tran's attention went to her ear. She spoke to her tida. "All good. It's under control. I'll be done in ten." She put the tida in her pocket. She turned to Lori and pointed to the swivel leather chair. "Sit."

"That's not where I'd do it."

"No?"

"No. Perhaps if I had a glass of wine, if I wore my uniform, I'd consider ending it on that chair." She looked Tran in the eye. "Do we open a bottle of wine?"

Tran shook her head.

"Well then, if I'm naked and distraught, as you say, it'd have to be the bathroom. Sitting on the toilet."

Tran's eyes moved from Lori to the bathroom and back. "What are you playing at?"

"You're the one about to start a civil war. I'm still trying to prevent it."

Tran didn't respond.

"If they find my naked body in the living room with execution-style bullet holes, you can't avoid bloodshed. No matter what you want to believe, I have a lot of fans, and no matter what you say, they will find the truth and expose you. But a single shot to the head with my own gun? If I'm sitting on the toilet? After the last few days I've had, you just might get away with it."

Tran looked puzzled, but she gestured to the bathroom before pointing to the dead shooter's body with her gun. "Move her out of the way."

Lori pulled the body from the ankles, clearing the path. The bathroom was hot and muggy with the water still running.

"Shut it off and sit."

Lori reached through the broken glass and turned off the water. The sudden silence made the humid air feel muggier. The tea tree oil from her shampoo still perfumed the heavy mist. She sat on the toilet and wiped the steam and sweat from her forehead with the back of her hand.

Tran followed her in and pointed the gun on Lori's left temple. "I'm right handed."

"What?"

Lori raised her right hand, ring and little fingers folded, middle and index fingers extended, and thumb cocked to form a gun. She touched her middle finger to her right temple. "I'm right handed."

"Right." Tran moved in closer into the narrow space. The shards sticking out of the shower door frame prevented her from getting the correct angle on Lori's head. She moved the gun to her left hand, and as she brought it back up, Lori launched herself at her.

Lori's right hand caught Tran's gun-toting left arm below the elbow and pushed it up. Tran fired at the ceiling. They slammed into the broken shower door. Tran's back caught the shards, and her face distorted from the agony of multiple puncture wounds.

Lori kneed Tran in the abdomen, and as Tran buckled forward, she slammed her forehead into Tran's nose.

Lori bought both her hands around Tran's left arm and swept them up toward the hand. She twisted Tran's wrist and grabbed the gun in one motion. She took a step back and fired into Tran's chest. Tran fell backward into the shower.

"Did not learn a fucking thing," Lori breathed and fired into Tran's head.

She exhaled and took a step back. A red mark on the fogged-up mirror caught her attention, and she glanced down. A four-inch shard of tempered glass stuck out of her right oblique. She grabbed it with a towel, pulled it out, and wiped away the blood with the other end of the towel. She opened the top drawer underneath the sink and fumbled for the skin stapler. She held her flesh between index finger and thumb of her left hand and drove the staples in with her right hand. Seven staples later, she stopped and wiped off more blood. It wouldn't hold for long, but it didn't need to.

She plodded to the living room, tapped her tida, and called Sierra. "I need a transport to pick me up. Oh, and send a nurse."

"Is everything all right?"

"Just get me the transport, now."

"We'll be there in eight minutes."

She tapped the tida shut and headed to her closet. She put on pants, undershirt, turtleneck, socks, and finally boots. She returned to the bathroom, lifted Tran, and took off her trench coat. She wiped the blood from the collar and back with a wet towel. The garment's back was shredded, but that wouldn't matter. In this light, it would do just fine.

She walked to the kitchen. Thompson lay between the sink and island, throat slit, hair coated in her own blood. Lori sidestepped the body and reached the coffee pot. It was still warm. She put the trench coat on the island counter and poured coffee into her mug. She twisted the lid off the brown sugar jar and tapped it over her cup. A large clump fell in. She stirred and sat on the middle stool, eyes fixed on the door. Whatever Tran's team thought was going on inside, they did not budge.

Three sips of too-sweet-even-for-her coffee later, she tapped her tida. "ETA?"

"Two minutes, General," Sierra said.

Lori took a final sip of coffee and put the mug down. Her damp, slicked-back hair was dark enough in this light to not give her away from afar. She put on Tran's trench coat and lifted the collar up. She walked out, hands in pocket, head pointing down. As she reached the car, the passenger door opened. "We have incoming—"

Lori shot the soldier in the face and leaned in to fire two shots into the driver. She took off Tran's coat and tossed it in the car. She slammed the door shut and went to sit on her porch steps. She'd just sat down when two eye slits appeared to the left of her orange tree.

"I'm afraid I don't have anything for you tonight," she said.

The tabby took that as invitation and strutted forward. She stopped by the steps, nudging her nose to Lori's boot. Lori extended her hand, and to her surprise, the tabby didn't retreat. She licked the scratches on the back of Lori's left hand where the first attacker's nails had dug in. Lori patted the tabby's neck with her right hand.

"You keep this up, and we'll have to renegotiate our agreement," she said.

The tabby's head jerked up, and after a quick look at Lori, she bolted, disappearing behind the bushes. Lori heard the transport before she spotted it. The searchlights came on, and it was impossible to see anything but the dust storm the landing transport was creating.

She ignored Sierra's incessant questioning and the nurse's prodding as they took off. She had bigger concerns than a flesh wound. By letting herself be preoccupied with Mika's condition, she'd let Herrera think they were in a stalemate.

They weren't.

CHAPTER 35

NEW INSIGHTS

"Sometimes accidents happen in life from which we have need of a little madness to extricate ourselves successfully."

—FRANCOIS DE LA ROCHEFOUCAULD

As Phillips came into her view, Lori realized that until this moment, she had not fully grasped the new reality. After the nurse had restitched her oblique, the painkillers had dulled the ache, and the soreness hadn't yet kicked in. Her healing thigh had been an abstract experiment. She'd not had any real indication that she'd healed faster. Asher's multiple recoveries ranged from implausible to magic tricks. But she'd shot Phillips two hours ago, and here he was walking and talking. He didn't even seem upset.

She'd always struggled with apologies. She despised the insincerity of fake contrition. Still, she had an assortment of half apologies in her arsenal, those she used when she bumped someone in the corridor, or stepped on their toes, or forgot their birthdays, or offended with her words, but she had nothing for Phillips. Ironically, her remorse was real this time. She'd shot him in the chest four times. What exactly were the words for that apology?

The toxicologist Sierra had brought was already in the room as she walked in, but though she'd only been here minutes, she was putting her coat back on. "Dr. Hathaway," Lori said.

"General." The voice was cold. "As I explained to your team, I don't do weapons."

"I'm not asking you for weapons."

"Of course not, and yet the questions focus on biological agents, their availability, toxicity, and communicability."

"There is a simple explanation."

"I'm sure there is." Hathaway's smile wasn't sincere.

"Actually, there isn't." She'd reached another dead end. "I'm sorry we wasted your time." Her frustration rose as she watched Hathaway leave. Every attempt had failed. There was no improvement in Mika's condition. She tossed the tida she had been playing with at the screen. It bounced off and landed on the floor.

"Immortal, huh?" Her jaw was clenched.

Phillips took two steps toward her. He hesitated and put a hand on her shoulder. It was a very human gesture, one that Lori had thought him incapable of. "It's a repair mechanism, not magic. Some things it can repair, some things it can't."

"Why?" Her voice was rising. "His head is still attached. His brain is still intact. It's just a few nerve cells. What is the damn Purge doing?"

"You need to rest."

She moved away. Of course she needed to rest, but she wasn't going to until she resolved this. She tilted her head back and exhaled.

"Where is a stash of smallpox when you need it?" he said.

She barely knew what smallpox was, a nasty disease eradicated long before her time, but the flippant way Phillips spoke triggered a thought. They'd been going at this based on what they had access to, but what about going after the nastiest agent out there?

"What about AHtX?" she blurted. They had mentioned it at the safe house and dismissed it. But why had they done that?

Phillips whipped around as though yanked by a chain. She felt the first sign of hope. In the six seconds since she'd spoken, he had not said no yet, which had been his stock response to any biological agent up to now.

"Do you have any?"

"Forget that. Would it work?"

Phillips thought a little longer. "Most likely, it'll kill him, but what do we have to lose?"

A lot. But it was a good enough start. Her mind raced. "You figure out the timing and doses." She headed for the door.

"Where are you going?"

She'd assumed that was obvious. "To get you AHtX."

Lori went over the tactical analysis on her screen again. Ranford and Eze had executed her plan to perfection. The Puries were down from three bases to one. However, isolating them and cutting off their supplies was one thing. Getting them desperate enough to give up their AHtX was another. She hadn't found the pressure point for that yet.

"Hello."

She looked up at Chipps knocking inside her open office door. She'd dozed off on the mess that was her desk. It reflected the mess that had become her mind. "I wasn't expecting you."

"We need to talk."

Lori sat up and ran her hand through her hair, trying to get it into a manageable tangle. "This isn't a good time."

Chipps took a step in and closed the door. "There is never a good time."

That was true. She hadn't seen Chipps since Mika's surgery. How long had that been? Four, five days? Lori couldn't tell anymore.

"What can I do for you?"

"Dr. Canales says Mika can't recover, that you're extending his suffering."

Chipps' expression screamed that she wanted to believe there was still hope. It was a difficult argument to make. For the medical staff, Mika wasn't even on borrowed time anymore. He had already defaulted. Lori wasn't ready to let go, but she had nothing that would reassure Chipps. "That's why she's no longer treating him." She fought to control her quivering voice.

"Sometimes," Chipps sniffled, "Sometimes, no matter how much we want to and no matter how much we try, we can't change the way things turn out."

"I don't accept that."

"You don't get to decide what reality you accept. We all play the cards we're dealt."

That made Lori crack an eighth of a smile. "A wise boy once told me I draw my own cards. I don't intend to disappoint him, so I'm going to keep drawing until I get the one I want."

She wasn't trying to spread the thin sliver of hope she still had, but her words brought the spark back to Chipps' eyes. "Okay, then tell me what you're doing, so I can help."

"I can't, and you can't."

The spark was gone again. "It would be a lot easier if we didn't work at cross-purposes."

"You can help by not getting in my way. I don't need your militia running around. What I need is more leeway, not more obstacles."

"I'll see what I can do," Chipps said. "Maybe I can convince the chancellor to give you the leeway you're after."

"So you two are pals now?"

"We're not, but we're renegotiating the treaty, so there's a lot of give and take."

"Renegotiating? What part?"

"Many parts. For one thing, the vice chancellorship is now non-negotiable."

"What makes you think she'll give you that?"

"We live in a different world from the one we did a few days ago."

"Marin is in a stronger position. How is that cause for you to push for better terms?"

"Militarily, you're stronger. Morally, not so much."

Lori chose not to get offended, and though she'd spent only a few days in the executive council, she had many years in military strategy sessions. In her experience, moral strength didn't enter the equation. "Good luck with that line of reasoning."

"I just wish I knew what you were doing here or out there in the Uregs with the troops."

"I can't talk about it."

Chipps tried to smile, but her face froze halfway as though she couldn't allow herself a smile. "It's just that I don't want to hand matches to a pyromaniac."

When a conversation reached a dead end, it sounded a lot like this. "Don't worry. I have more than enough matches."

Chipps' half smile turned into a frown. "I don't care what you do. Just fix him."

In the hour after Chipps left, Lori focused on the tactical problems associated with the assault on the Purie base. She could not find a single option that prevented the Puries from destroying or deploying the AHtX. Her screen buzzed, shelving her dilemma for the time being. She stood up to receive her next guest who was here for another problem.

"I got nothing to say to you." Kevin plopped down on the wingback chair across from her desk. He put his feet on her desk, displaying defiance and indifference in equal amounts.

"Thanks for coming," she said, though she'd not given him a choice.

He played with a tida, flipping it up and down his fingers with his thumb as though it climbed an unending ladder. It reminded her of the drawings in Czernak's office with the stairs that climbed indefinitely. That drawing always reminded her to be careful of how you interpreted what you saw.

"There is always trouble when you call. What is it this time?"

She sat back down and stretched her neck to her right. She massaged the knots, and one tight module crumbled under pressure. She zeroed in on a small lump until it dissolved. She breathed out, enjoying her small victory, no matter how fleeting. "I need to unlock a secure package," she said.

Locks to Kevin were like yarn to a cat. As she'd expected, his curiosity overcame his sulking. "How secure?"

"Secure enough to contain AHtX and definitely booby trapped against tampering."

"Fuck me. How many thousands of corpses are we leaving in our wake this time?"

"Here's something you don't want to acknowledge. The body count of the Hollister battle had long been determined. You made it mean something."

"It didn't mean shit."

"You can tell that to yourself if it feeds your cynical worldview." She softened. "Now I know you think in terms of input-output mappings, so I'll make this simple for you. The output of two armies that come together is corpses—young ones at that. I don't have the luxury of treating war as an abstract evil. I see the reality up close and personal. All those corpses you sometimes get a glimpse of, the bloodied faces that make you want to turn away and pretend you didn't see them? I know their first names, so you don't get to tell me their deaths don't mean shit." She stopped, giving him time to catch up to her. "I'll tell you one other thing. You may wash your hands of the whole thing, but you did save hundreds of my troops."

"I don't need spin doctoring. I know what happened."

"What happened, Kevin?"

"You used me. Not as a ruse but as a weapon."

She picked up the wooden box that had contained her gold stars. It was the box that had let her believe the fantasy that all of Marin was on the same side. They all created fantasies, because it made it easier to live with themselves. Just like Kevin had created the fantasy that his distraction would have scared Kern away, avoiding a confrontation. Now she had to shatter his fantasy and run over his ego or his guilt. His ego was by far the less fragile of the two.

"C'mon, Kevin. You were only one part of the subterfuge. You're not responsible for the war or for our victory."

He smirked. In reality, his ruse had been critical in freezing the Kern force, not only making them think they were under a larger attack but disrupting their sensors long enough for panic to set in. She had pounced while they'd been disoriented, laying waste to their barracks and frontlines alike.

"Besides," she said, "the early morning fog was as disruptive as your sniffers."

"Seems fog is more pissed at you that I am. Won't show up this time. You only got me."

"I'll take it."

"Why should I help you? You know I promised I'd never do that again, right?"

"Don't help me. Help Mika."

"Wow." He pushed his chair back, rotating it to face away from her. "Use the one person I didn't think even you would use."

"Use him? You self-righteous fuck, I'm trying to save him."

He frowned. "Save him?"

"What did you think I need the AHtX for?" At his blank look, she filled him in.

"How is AHtX gonna help?"

"How do you think? You heard Phillips describe what the virus does, what it needs."

Kevin shook his head. "Jeez. I didn't take that to mean this."

"What did you think it meant?"

"I don't know, that it'd work like a vaccine, somewhere between preventive medicine and body building."

"And?"

"Just because something has preventive value in small doses doesn't mean it'll cure you in large doses."

"Never mind all that. Can you break the codes if we get the AHtX?"

"Not likely."

She opened and closed the lid on the box again and again. "Are you sure?"

"Given a day or two, I can break any code. But there ain't no way that shit won't be sterilized in the process."

"Can't you override those safeguards?"

"Maybe, but that'd take weeks in a specially created lab, and that's assuming you can create a safe enough lab to try."

"We don't have weeks."

"I figured as much, but I don't get one thing." He scratched his head. "Why exactly are you trying to steal the scrammies and pick the locks again?"

"I need the fucking AHtX!"

Kevin stopped scratching his head. "I got that part," he said as though speaking to a slow-witted child. "Ain't that shit sitting on a missile right now?"

"What's that got to do with breaking the codes?"

Kevin ignored the question. His attention was elsewhere as though he needed a minimal amount of energy for this conversation. "Don't missiles fly to come find you?"

The box became weightless in her hand. As always, she had squinted so hard to see what she needed that her peripheral vision had failed her.

"Fuck!"

Kevin smirked. "Just saying."

CHAPTER 36

MADNESS

*"I'd rather regret the things I've done than regret
the things I haven't done."*

–LUCILLE BALL

L ori opened her eyes at the chiming emergency sniffer. She had
dozed off in her office. The time stamp was blinking 5:24. Why
did everything always go wrong at the crack of dawn?

She had no idea what had caused Yim's change of heart, but
the reinforcements she'd authorized wouldn't reach Eze and
Ranford until midday, which meant this was a more immediate
problem. She glanced at the tactical display on her tida. Herrera's
troops had started moving. She grabbed her jacket and headed
out the door.

Sierra stood in the antechamber between their offices, listening
to her earpiece. "Two battalions have cut off the hospital from the
city center. They're blocking the streets and moving toward us."

Lori could still order surgical strikes to Herrera's headquarters.
But that meant dozens if not hundreds of civilian casualties. Door-
to-door fighting would lead to a heavier toll. "Get the transports
in the air. I want the blockades gone before noon."

"Yes, General. What about—"

Both their tidas chimed again. "It's the doctor on duty." Sierra
listened to her earpiece and spoke in fragments. "The night nurse

revived Mika. Thirty minutes ago. They revived him once more since then. He's not going to last."

"How long?"

Sierra waited for a reply. "Couple of hours. Give or take."

Take, Lori thought, but it wasn't a choice she'd been offered. She had half a solution to two problems she could not solve without raining death and destruction all around.

Two half solutions. The simple math hit her.

There was only one path now, and she cataloged the players involved. "Wake Kevin up, and tell Ranford I need to talk to him." She hesitated before stepping out. "Get Phillips up and running in the hospital. Tell him I have what he needs. I'll meet him there in thirty."

Sierra froze but only for a second. They both knew she didn't have a thing. "Copy."

The sun wasn't up yet. Lori tried to pinpoint the spot where it would start its daily ascent. She gave up after ten seconds. By the end of the day, her entire existence would be altered. She didn't think in terms of good or bad anymore. Those concepts didn't capture the possibilities. She had a few hours to discover which of her mistakes would haunt the rest of her days.

She walked into the secure room in the basement Kevin had appropriated while he worked on the scrammies. The same room they'd conducted witness interviews an eternity ago. She set the lights to full brightness, ignoring his squinting. "Assuming they fire one of the scrammies, can you make sure it lands in the courtyard?"

"What courtyard?" Kevin's eyes were closed, but he sat up on the sofa he'd slept in.

"The hospital's."

He opened his eyes and blinked twice. "Fuck me! You *are* insane."

"This was your idea."

His eyes widened in horror. "My idea was to shoot it down far away from here, then get some biohazard suits and vacuum the shit you need. Out there. Waaay the fuck out there."

She couldn't figure out whether Kevin was that naïve or he played at it to absolve himself of his sins. Then again, she didn't care.

"Can you?"

"I always thought you were crazy. Now I know."

She didn't reply.

"You'll regret this."

"I'll regret it more if I don't try. Yes or no?"

"Doesn't work that way." Kevin went to the screen and tapped. "But the one aimed downtown is close enough. Hey, what do you have two hundred miles north of here?"

He was like a six-year-old with the emotional maturity and attention span to match. "Focus." He swiped at the screen. "Can you steer them?" she asked when he didn't speak.

He scratched his head. "Steer?"

"Make it go where you want."

He shook his head. "No. No steering. The target is hardcoded, so we can't make it do anything other than hit what it's aimed at. Even if I confuse it, it'll correct in milliseconds."

This had been exactly what she'd feared.

"Can't steer. Maybe nudge it though," he said.

"How much can you nudge it?"

"A few miles." He tapped again. "Five. Eight, tops."

"Why so little?"

He grimaced. "Because I can't nudge the scrammy. It'll go where it's aimed."

"What the fuck are we talking about then?"

"I might nudge the targets."

"Please start making sense."

"With the gaps in the satellite coverage, all scrammies have correction codes for when the signal gets interrupted. When it's real close, it will seek a final update on the target. That gives us a tiny window, but you can't just put in a new target. It'll ignore anything that blatant. But we can slip in ghost satellite signals to shift its reference frame. When it uses the new reference frame to verify the target position, the target will shift just a tad in the real world. The trick is to do this without making it recompute its own position in that new reference frame, which means it has to happen in the last three to four seconds, which means we can nudge only a few miles."

"Have you done this before?"

"On cruisers, yeah, sure. On a scrammy? Of course not. Jeez. It should work though. Yeah, should work."

"Okay, get on with it."

"Now?"

"Yes, now."

He frowned again. "Not good."

She closed her eyes. "What now?"

"This is a biological weapon. It's going to release the payload and crash. Sure, the kinetic energy will cause a blast, but there is no explosive to vaporize the guidance system."

"Why is that a problem?"

"There is no way I can erase the tampering. If I had time, I could set up a ricocheting signal to hide the origin, but I don't. I'll need to use a direct link to the scrammy."

She frowned, still not grasping the problem.

"I mean, I'll wipe these screens, but it won't take long for any competent analyst to trace it all back to this room."

She laughed, unclenched her jaw, and undid her fist. Her knuckles were white, and she flexed her fingers back and forth.

"If it works, I don't give a fuck, and if it doesn't, I don't give a fuck."

"So long as we're clear."

"Crystal-fucking-clear."

WITH ONE BALL IN THE AIR AND TWO READY TO BE TOSSED, LORI headed back to her office.

Sierra was waiting in the antechamber, tapping on her tida. "What next, General?" she asked as Lori walked in.

"I have three final orders for you."

Sierra straightened, and her grip on her tida tightened. "Final orders?"

Lori forced a half smile. "Nothing you can't handle."

"Anything, General."

"This will all make sense tomorrow. But today, I need you to trust me. One, call Kuipers."

"I spoke with the general yesterday. She is not getting involved in a civil war."

"I don't need her to fight. I need her to coordinate the evacuation of a three-mile radius around this hospital. Once you explain the threat, she will do it."

"Three miles?" Sierra tapped her screen and waited. "That's over two thousand civilians."

"She needs to start now."

"Yes, General."

"Two, for the next six hours, I don't give a fuck who controls the capital, but Herrera's troops are not crossing this line." She drew a line on the map her tida projected and flicked it to Sierra. "Engage them if you have to, and if you do, don't pull your punches."

Sierra frowned and nodded. "Very well, General. May I ask a question?"

Lori nodded.

"Is this a cover story, or is the threat real?"

"Very real."

Sierra didn't reply.

"We're facing a biological attack."

Sierra snapped to attention. "I'll pass that on to General Kuipers. We will hold the line and have everyone out of here by noon."

Lori glanced at the wall clock. It was 5:50. "I need them out in the next hour."

Sierra swallowed. "Very well. The third order?"

"You need to take care of Herrera. Now. Join Kuipers only when that's done."

"Take care?"

Lori narrowed her eyes and locked them onto Sierra. "Is something unclear, Colonel?"

"No, General."

"Good. We can't have our forces staring each other down in the streets of Marin. Someone is going to blink and soon."

Sierra seemed to run through her options. "Getting to her isn't going to be easy."

"If you can get Mika into Lester's office, I'm sure you can find a way to get to Herrera."

Sierra's cheeks turned beet red as though she'd been slapped. As an olive branch, Lori swiped her tida and pointed to Sierra's. "Time stamped for tomorrow."

Sierra accepted it, saluted, and walked out, a formalism she'd stopped doing long ago.

"Thanks," Lori whispered, but Sierra had long closed the door behind her.

Lori boarded the transport as Ranford returned her call. She swiped her tida, ready to toss the last ball and reach the point of no return. She skipped the pleasantries. "Change of plans. We need to move up the assault."

"Move up? When do the reinforcements arrive?"

"Not in time."

He did not look amused. "We can't contain the scrammies without reinforcements."

"I am aware of the tradeoffs."

"Please make me see the value in what you're asking. If we can't contain the scrammies, why are we moving now?"

"We don't have time for this."

"General, I've followed orders all my life. Many of them teetered on the line separating logic from nonsense, but I had the excuse—" He stopped. "No, the justification there was a chain of command.

I don't have that luxury anymore or that curse, and your orders aren't teetering anywhere. They're so far over the line you can't even see logic from where they stand."

She didn't have anything to offer.

"I recently made a promise to myself that I would no longer blindly follow orders, a promise triggered by your revelation, I might add. I've lived up to my end of the bargain, but for what you're asking me now, I need to understand what you are after."

She couldn't lie, not because she didn't want to but because he would see through it, but she couldn't tell him the full truth either, mostly because the risk analysis was not justifiable at any level. "Herrera's troops are moving. If we wait until you receive reinforcement, Marin will turn into a war zone. The AHtX menace will at least keep Herrera's troops off the streets for a while. Besides, we need to crush the Purie machine, remove their claws from our councils, from our military. We can't let them blackmail us with this forever. That threat has to be contained."

"Contained?"

"We are evacuating the landing site."

"General." Ranford struggled for words. "This is not a good idea." He shook his head in resignation when she didn't respond. "How much time do we have?"

"I need you to hit them now."

"I need forty-five minutes to coordinate with Colonel Eze and another seventy-five to get the troops and weapons ready. The earliest we can hit them is two hours from now."

"You have one."

"Very well. Full-on assault with limited resources." He snickered. "The scrammies?"

"Scrammy 2 cannot be launched. You need to focus all your fire on that one."

"Copy. We'll concentrate on Scrammy 2. I'll leave a few hand-helds to the north in case we catch Scrammy 1 before it goes supersonic."

"No!" She softened. "You can't split your resources. Make sure Scrammy 2 is destroyed. Let me deal with the other one."

Ranford swallowed.

"Can I trust you to do exactly what I'm asking?"

"That's an odd word to use considering what you're asking."

"Yet I'm asking."

His head tilted. "Are you certain?"

"Yes."

"Very well. We will concentrate on Scrammy 2."

"Good day, Colonel."

The connection didn't cut off, and Ranford's eyes remained on her. His statement about the chain of command applied to her as well. Until last week, she'd followed orders and kept Marin's interests above all else. Because those two masters had agreed, she'd not needed any soul searching. Last week, she'd disobeyed a direct order from the chancellor but still held the conviction she'd been protecting Marin. Now she was disobeying another direct order from another chancellor who had been clear about not engaging the Puries, and this time she did not have the consolation that she was protecting Marin.

In one week, she'd gone from loyal servant to reckless renegade with a pit stop at loyal renegade. It wasn't the career path she'd envisioned, but it was what it was.

"General, I really hope you know what you're doing," he said.

So do I.

The hospital's courtyard grew below them, and as the transport initiated their final approach, she shook her uncertainty. "Absolutely."

CHAPTER 37

MONSTERS

*"If only we did not have to die at all.
Instead, become ravens."*

—LOUISE ERDRICH

The blaring sirens reached their peak as Amy landed in the hospital's courtyard. They had flown over chaos, with troops and Humvees herding civilians away from the hospital. As they proceeded in the opposite direction of the exodus, she felt as though she were swimming upstream, unaware of the monster hiding around the next bend. But there were no monsters here.

At least not the kind with scales and sharp teeth.

She resented that Mika's last moments were taken from him, from her, by yet another drill or other nonsense. The courtyard was deserted, with no trace of even the Special Forces soldiers she'd started to recognize after nodding to and walking past them for a week. On her way up, she stopped momentarily on the floor where she had spent a long evening with Rose. With *Lori*.

Today, the waiting room was empty, unaffected by the drama unfolding in its midst. On the floor above, she found Mika resting in an ocean of machinery just like the last time she'd been there. He might not have been dead yet, but he was no longer alive.

"What are you doing here?" Lori asked, as though the reason for her presence was not self-explanatory, as though she hadn't come here every morning at the exact same time. Lori stood by a door connecting Mika's room to an adjacent one, holding a gas mask. "You shouldn't have come today. It's not safe."

The repeated warnings had been over the top. Whatever drill they were running had half of Marin participating in it. But Mika did not seem to be going anywhere, and neither did Lori. A man in the adjacent room tapped at a screen, in no apparent hurry to leave either. "What's the drill about?"

"Drill?" Lori closed her eyes and tilted her head back, exhaling. She shook her head in apparent disbelief. "We're under a biological attack. What did you think the sirens were for?"

Amy swallowed. That made no sense. Why would anyone attack this part of Marin? Her mind kicked into action. "We need to get him out of here."

Lori shook her head. "We can't. We can't move the life-support system, and he won't last two minutes without it."

"I am not leaving him here to die alone."

"He is not alone."

"None of this makes any sense."

"It doesn't," the man said as he walked into the room.

"Who are you?"

"Phillips," he said as though that would provide context.

Amy approached Mika, her eyes moving from wire to wire, tube to tube, machine to machine. Though she did not want to, she had to agree with Lori. There was no way to move him.

"Soon, even this won't help." Lori tossed her the mask. "Go while you can."

Amy snatched the mask in midair. Lori was not acting like someone concerned about an imminent attack. "The biological attack is a cover, isn't it?"

"Oh no. I assure you it's real."

"What did you do?"

"I drew my own card."

A fog of anger had engulfed Amy as she had approached the

hospital. The fog had covered a vast, diffused area without concentrating on any one target. Lori was doing her best to burn off the fog and focus the anger on one place: herself. The additional troops she'd convinced Yim to provide Lori would have given her the leeway she'd wanted. "Tell me you didn't incite a biological attack to win your battle with Herrera." Amy's eyes found Mika, propelling another scenario. "To get your hands on that shit."

Lori didn't even offer a half-hearted denial. Amy had handed her not a match but a flamethrower. "Are you insane?"

"It's more complicated than that. I can't let a power-hungry general terrorize my streets or allow a bunch of lunatics threaten us with biological weapons forever. I'm neutralizing them both. If that also helps Mika, I'll take that too. Now you have a few minutes here. What do you want from me?"

"I want a simple explanation."

"There isn't one."

Amy walked closer to Mika. She tried to put the mask on him but couldn't stretch the straps around his head. There were too many wires in the way. Amy's anger dissipated as she looked at the general.

Lori looked as concerned as Amy was. She moved closer and held Mika's head as Amy threaded the straps between the wires. "You need to get out of here," Lori said when they were done. "If not for yourself, for your crew. You're gambling their lives on this being an idle threat. I assure you it isn't, and take the western route back. Do not fly over the capital."

Amy tried to find Mika's hand but couldn't. His hands were lost in a pit of wires. She squeezed his elbow and leaned over. She nudged the mask up slightly. "I'm sorry," she whispered and kissed him on his lips. They were cold. She wasn't sure whether she was apologizing for not being able to help him or for having been angry with him.

Or for leaving him now. Despite all the evidence to the contrary, she had expected Lori to find a way to save him, but the barely human form on the bed had not stirred. Lori had failed her.

She stopped by the door. "I know you tried, but no matter what happens next, you and I, we're not done."

Lori stood motionless and did not reply.

Amy walked down the stairs to reach the waiting transport. The expression on her pilot's face was pure relief as she emerged into the landing pad. She suspected it was as much at seeing her as it was for not having to explain why he had returned without the governor. Her self-control got her into her seat and allowed her to utter a few meaningless words, but by the time they took off, her frustration turned to sorrow, and she could no longer hold the tears welling in her eyes.

CHAPTER 38

LIFTOFF

*"The most difficult thing is the decision to act,
the rest is merely tenacity."*

—AMELIA EARHART

Lori checked her watch. It was a quarter past eight. Not the impossible one-hour evacuation she had requested but close. She had no doubt that Sierra would be just as efficient executing her third order. As Lori thought about Herrera, all screens in the room turned red, shrieking like a red fox in heat.

Whatever little control she might have had was now gone.

The seven-minute countdown on the screen reminded her that her plan was nearing its unnatural conclusion. She should have felt terror but instead felt relief.

"Do you remember much about the space program?" Phillips asked.

She tried to keep her attention on her screen, but it no longer provided useful information. "What?"

"Lori. We've exchanged bullets, so I'm going to assume we're on a first-name basis." She nodded, and he continued. "How much do you remember of the space program?"

"Okay." She chuckled. "What might your first name be?"

"Phillip. Used to go by Phil."

"Phil Phillips." She paused. "You cannot be serious."

"Phil Bettencamp. Phillips is a nickname I picked up in grad school, because I could fix anything. It seemed safer after the Purge, and now I'm stuck with it."

Considering the backlash against scientists, she didn't blame him. "Okay, Phil. I don't remember a thing about the space program."

He looked disappointed. "Here's the thing. We've been space faring for essentially a century, and along the way, we improved everything. Life support, propulsion, safety, AI, you name it, and it got better to the point you took them for granted. But whatever your mission was, when you were done, you had to get back down to Earth. Reentry never became routine. When you start falling, your spacecraft heats up. For three to twelve minutes, depending on the speed and the entry angle, there is total silence as the ionization of the atmosphere around the spacecraft prevents communication. As violence rages around them, the crew sit and wait and hope that nothing goes wrong with their heat shield."

"Sounds like fun."

"Four minutes of terror, they called it in the early days. If everything was done right, you reemerged in friendly skies." He grimaced. "If not, no one ever heard from you again."

Her eyes found the timer on the screen. "Seven minutes of terror?"

"Exactly."

She glanced at the counter. Five left. "What now?"

"Relax."

She snorted. "That's a good one."

"You can put your mask on."

She had told herself she was going to take the same risk as Mika. Phillips sensed her hesitation. "Don't be thick. Mika may or may not need one, but you do. Even if this works on him, it won't work on you." He put his mask on. "There, if it makes you happier."

"You need it?"

"Sure." His words were muffled but intelligible. "These strains are tricky. I might handle it, or it might give me a terrible headache or a nasty fever. There's no need to take chances."

"That thing can kill thousands." She put her mask on, closed her eyes, and stood in front of Mika. She could almost pretend he was in a gentle sleep, but there was nothing gentle in the battle they were going to unleash in him in a few minutes.

She flinched when she felt a hand on her shoulder. She opened her eyes. Phillips stood next to her, eyes on Mika. She had to agree that posthuman or not, without Phillips, none of this would have been possible. But she had come to expect the technical help. It was the human touch she had not expected. She may have been wrong about that. "We're not the astronauts. He is," she said.

"True," he said, letting go of her shoulder. "The terror didn't apply just to the astronauts. Everyone in mission control had that same helpless feeling. They all held their breath, hoping to hear something witty from the spacecraft at the end of the silence. You're right—you're not the astronaut. You're the flight director. You put all this together. You're the one in charge. If anything goes wrong, it's on your head. Though you think you're in control, you're not. From the moment a spacecraft blasted off to the moment it touched down again, the flight directors knew they were only one step ahead of disaster, just like now."

She stood there, motionless, letting the last few seconds tick in silence. There it was, the deep rolling roar like an angry dragon belching. The speeding mass had met a stationary object. The room undulated like a boat on a swell.

"What happened?" she yelled.

"Scrammy contact a quarter mile northwest."

"No, no, no." A secondary bang followed, closer this time. "What was that?"

"Our payload." Phillips checked the readings. "Kevin came through. He couldn't have aimed any better had he controlled it with a joystick."

Of course. The payload had ejected before the scrammy crashed, released its load, and landed seconds later as it should have. She checked the magnified trail of the AHtX and couldn't believe the readings. It was floating like windswept dust over the hospital's courtyard.

Phillips disappeared, and she allowed herself to hope. He returned holding several vials. He had set up an elaborate system for collecting the AHtX with exposed vials he could manipulate, seal, and cleanse for handling. He put the first vial on the metal scaffolding attached to Mika's arm. He hit a button, and the timer activated. It would bring infinitesimal amounts of toxin in contact with Mika's skin every fifteen minutes like a snow globe attached to his arm.

"Eight percent jump in viral activity upon skin contact," he said after the second timed release. After the fourth release, the activity had dropped back down. "This is weird."

The numbers on the screen didn't mean much to her. "What?"

"He's not reacting the way I predicted."

She did not even know what to ask.

"AHtX doesn't affect him much."

She allowed her expectation to rise. "Isn't that good? He's handling it?"

He frowned. "Except that's not what's happening." He moved to the other screen. "The AHtX concentrations are lower than they should be. It's diluted, more than tenfold."

That made no sense. "Why would anyone dilute a bioweapon?"

"Terror? They can cover ten times the area with this concentration."

Then what? Another thought occurred to her. "Could they use it to differentiate us from Puries?"

"No. At these levels, everyone would have mild symptoms. Everyone except people like Eva and me." He froze. "Bloody hell!" He shook his head. "Clever bastards."

"What?"

"It'll act as the first trigger. The virus starts working even with the tiniest dose."

"And?"

"You think you have drops in birth rates now? Wait until everyone gets a sniff of this."

Lori closed her eyes. Mass sterilization with virus activation was a nightmare she had not even considered, and she'd considered quite a few. "We evacuated the area." He didn't seem convinced, but she let it drop. She pointed to Mika. "What now?"

"Now we increase the dose and go straight to the lungs."

He opened the respirator's intake filter. He put a vial in and sealed it. The same timed releases now hit his lungs. "Immediate response. Viral activity is up twenty percent."

Mika's heart rate dropped as did all vital signs. A new alarm went off, reminding Lori there was an infinite number of obnoxious sounds.

Phillips looked impressed with himself. "This is great."

"What do you mean?" Her eyes were stuck on the terrifying displays.

"I mean, diluted spores or not, with what I did, he should be dead. He's not."

Phillips' work had always been outside her grasp, black magic that she had been happy to leave in his expert hands. Not until this moment had she realized how much of it was guesswork. She decided to not ask any more questions, as the more she understood, the more the mystique evaporated. She didn't like the unforgiving reality that replaced it.

Once they had completed the sixth pulmonary release of the toxin, Phillips leaned over Mika and undid his mask's straps, pulling it out.

"We know one thing."

"What are you doing?"

"AHtX isn't going to kill him. It's in him now, and his system can handle it."

"That's good. Right?"

"Yeah, well."

"What's the problem?"

"The problem is AHtX wasn't the trouble to begin with. His brain still can't send the signal to breathe to his lungs." He chuckled. "A deep breath of this shit will kill you. In his case, it won't, but he can't take a deep breath. That's irony for you."

"That's not funny."

"Real irony rarely is."

She went back to her screen. "We'll have company in less than an hour. Bioagent cleanup teams and troops. Lots of troops."

"That's our cue to leave," he said.

"Not gonna happen."

"Lori, we're done here. His virus is in overdrive. He's resistant to AHtX. It's all turning out the way we'd hoped. What's the point of causing a confrontation?"

She had no reply.

"Seriously, how do you think finding you here will play out with the chancellor?"

She went back to her screen and smiled despite her misgivings. It seemed her inexorable XO had completed all three of her tasks. "It's Kuipers and Sierra."

"Even better. Mika will be in good hands. Let's go."

She hesitated. "Where to?"

"Does it matter? Look, this strain of AHtX is lighter. It will spread over a larger area."

She closed her eyes as the implications sank in. "How large?"

"I don't know but well beyond the radius we'd anticipated, but with luck, that far out, it won't be potent enough to kill anyone. But birth rates are going to drop. No way around that."

Yeah. It was real lucky she was sterilizing a whole swath of Marin. Would she have gone through with it had she known? She pushed that thought away. She had enough to worry about without adding hypothetical moral dilemmas to her plate.

That she didn't have a quick answer was probably damning enough.

"We need to go," Phillips said. "You've gone well beyond insurrection now." He swirled his index finger around. "This is somewhere between abuse of power and terrorism."

Yim would be furious. Though Lori had neutralized the Purie threat, she'd done so by disobeying direct orders and at a cost few would have approved. Eze, and particularly Randford, would feel betrayed, their trust stretched beyond their consent. Kuipers? Not likely to be sympathetic with the contamination she'd be inheriting. Chipps had walked out angrier than she'd walked in. Even Sierra had every reason to feel betrayed.

Had she even done all that for the right reasons? To pin Herrera's troops to prevent street fighting? To eliminate the current and future threat of biologically armed Puries dictating policy to Marin? Were those excuses to justify the risks she'd taken to save Mika? Not that the answer mattered to Yim or Ranford or Kuipers.

Phillips must have followed her mental arithmetic. "The way I see it, only two people are complicit in this with you. My reactions are not a good barometer for how others react. I'd wager neither are Kevin's."

She didn't disagree with him, but Phillips still hadn't given her a way out.

"What I'm trying to say is that no one is going to find Kevin for a while. That's the sensible thing to do. I intend to do the same. So should you."

"You think I deserve a new beginning?"

He smiled, but she saw no humor in it. She guessed it was filled with real irony. "Not relevant, but yes, I do."

She couldn't smile back. "I can't run and hide for the rest of my life."

"Who said anything about running or hiding? I'm saying we go away, preferably to someplace warm. I'm sick to my bones of cold summers. Let's get the hell out and forget about this place for a while. Marin will survive."

Will Mika? That was the wrong question. She no longer controlled Mika's fate. She focused on the possibility Phillips was suggesting. "Fugitives. Didn't see that coming." She knew it was a lie the moment the words left her lips.

"You should have. After what you did in Anderson Valley, I don't blame you for thinking they owe you a statue." He smiled. "After today, it's more likely they'll crucify you."

She allowed herself one moment of levity, squeezed to occupy the sliver of space between Mika's still unmoving form and the approaching troops. "Are those my only options?"

His smile vanished. "In time, I'm guessing you'll get both. Unfortunately, crucifixions always come first."

She walked back to Mika. His liver and pancreas showed signs of life, and there was even some action in the lungs. The viral activity in the spinal cord had skyrocketed as though his nerves were reaching from the organs to the spinal cord, seeking out instructions.

"What's the prognosis?"

Phillips shrugged. "He is not dead."

A few short days ago, those four cold words would have made her question Phillips' humanity. She now grasped the layers of insight he conveyed with them. She moved to the window. She'd unleashed a wicked killer miles from the center of the capital, and it covered the space between her and her transport.

"How do I even make it into the transport?" The AHtX might have been diluted, but they were at ground zero. She'd been wildly optimistic that morning, assuming her reality would hold until sunset. The sun hadn't even reached its midpoint yet, and she was already out of options.

Phillips moved to the room next door and opened the closet doors. He pulled out two hangers and displayed them for her. They contained military-issue biohazard suits.

"Here." He pointed to two fat bottles of green goo stored at the bottom of the closet. "This will neutralize anything that sneaks in. You strip down, rub this on every pore, and suit up."

"Are you serious?"

"Fabric traps the AHtX." He smiled. "I won't enjoy it one bit."

"Fine, but we still won't make it far in that transport."

"I figured. Let them shoot the transport down. This place will be crawling with a cleanup crew soon." He winked at her. "How about we do some cleanup?"

"Dodging missiles on autopilot? That transport won't get a mile. What happens when they find no bodies?"

"Oh, it'll get a mile or twenty." He smiled, too eager to impress her. "I had Kevin hack the autopilot."

Now she was impressed, because that would put the transport halfway to the Farallon Islands, where no one would find wreckage or bother looking for bodies. She smiled at her unexpected prospects. "Seems you've covered all the bases."

He feigned offense, but then a smirk stretched across his face. Despite all her apprehension, it was friendly.

"I always have an exit strategy."

CHAPTER 39

PHOENIX

"You only live once, but if you do it right, once is enough."

—MAE WEST

The room was dark, or his eyes did not see. He tried to blink but could not, or he could but could not feel it. He couldn't be sure whether he had opened his eyes or imagined opening them.

He tried to move his hand to his face to feel his eyelids, but nothing moved. He took a deep breath and felt pressure as though someone was sitting on his chest. He exhaled and took another one. He felt discomfort on his right side, but it wasn't pain.

He blinked again, and this time he felt his eyelids move. He discerned some shapes, and the room was dark. His head did not move, but his eyes shot side to side. The room was mostly empty, and no one was sitting on his chest.

He was on a metal-framed bed with side rails. A chair stood to his left and medical devices to his right. It was a hospital then.

His eyes cleared, and the equipment came into focus, lit by the screens around them. Top-notch stuff meant this was not the Cal City hospital and definitely not a Uregs clinic. What was he doing at a good hospital? Where was he?

He cataloged what he knew. He'd felt cold. Right before that, he'd burned. That didn't make any sense.

He closed his eyes and breathed out. *Focus.* The last thing he remembered was—

Oh.

Shock displaced his thoughts, shock that he had woken up at all. It all came rushing back: the painful burning on his back, the screaming ribs, his ears not working, flying into the night clutching Lester, and landing. When with his last conscious effort he had driven Lester's head into the ground with as much force as he had left, just in case.

He moved his fingers, wiggled his toes, and watched. He was happily surprised they obliged. IV drips and wires disappeared into his right hand and arm. He noticed the chime from the device next to him was getting louder.

Remembering the silence his ears had inflicted on him, he wondered if the sound was in his head. He tapped on the edge of the bed. *Tap, tap, tap.* He heard it loud and clear.

Before he hatched his next exploratory moves, the light reached a blinding intensity, and he shut his eyes. He heard a shout and squinted at the motion by the door. Someone reached for his arm, and a hand pushed his eyelid up and shone a bright light at him.

Great, like he really needed that.

He tried to say he was all right, but his tongue didn't cooperate. No sound, not even a grunt, came out. His eyelids felt heavy again, and as suddenly as they had coalesced, his surroundings melted into darkness.

AMY GREETED THE GUARDS WITH THE SAME DISAPPEARING SMILE she'd worn for the last two weeks. She'd found Marin officials more at ease after she smiled and then realized that also went for her own staff, but a smile was too ephemeral, so she had perfected the postsmile mask where the hint of a smile remained on her face.

The news that Lori's transport had been shot down over the Pacific had polarized Marin, and though Amy felt for the woman who had saved Mika by sheer strength of will, she couldn't spare any sympathy.

It wasn't because she was ungrateful but because she didn't believe for a second that Lori had been on that transport. They'd found no bodies, and she could not reconcile the woman she'd watched over the last month with someone who would get shot down over open water. That outcome was sloppy, a word that did not apply to Lori.

Lori had exited the stage, hiding her intentions from them, which was probably for the best, as neither she nor Yim needed to operate under Lori's long shadow right now.

Amy had not been surprised when Yim had agreed to her terms. For all her dogmatism, Yim was first and foremost a bureaucrat, and bureaucrats abhorred chaos. The order Amy promised was not the order Yim would have chosen, but in the end, any order was better than the alternative. Amy was now the governor of New California and the vice chancellor of Marin.

Along the way a fundamental truth had dawned on her. Some people embraced power. It didn't matter whether they sought it or not. What mattered was that when they wielded power, it fit. Those were the people who changed the world. Yim was not one of those people. Eric and Czernak had been. Lori was.

So was she.

Amy pushed the door open. The room was twice as deep as it was wide. The blinds were down on the window opposite the door, hiding the morning sun. Three IV pole stands and a vitals monitor stood behind the bed that jutted out from her right. The smell of antiseptic permeated the room, overpowering the untouched egg breakfast that sat on the nightstand.

Mika lay on the bed, eyes facing straight up, almost peaceful, disconnected from any sign of violence. She had no idea what was going through his mind at this moment or, for that matter, ever, but after a week on life support and two in an AHtX-induced coma, she was glad anything was going through his mind.

Mika's eyes followed her as she approached him. She took his hand in hers, careful to not bend the wrist with the IV drip. She sat next to him but did not let go of his hand.

"What?" Mika smiled.

She'd stared at his vacant face for three weeks, imagining it springing to life and saying something endearing. This hadn't been what he'd uttered in those daydreams, but it wasn't eloquent words she'd missed. It was that mischievous smile, the exuberance escaping from the gap between his teeth and filling the room. She leaned and kissed his cheek. "You scared me."

"You scared me first."

The room was devoid of human touch. She glanced at the low wooden chair to her right. It looked more ornamental than functional. "Do you need anything?"

"The coffee here sucks."

"Is that your only complaint?"

"I'm still trying to put things together. Burning a three-mile ring in Marin for a week? That's crazy."

"It contained most of the AHtX till it drifted back down. It was Rendon's idea." She still didn't understand what Lori had done. None of the doctors could come up with an explanation for how AHtX could have produced a drug useful to Mika, but it had. For all her cooperation, Rendon had been cagey about that topic.

Mika shook his head. "Casualties?"

"No one will move back there for a while. Rendon got the civilians out. A few hundred were hospitalized, but they all survived. There were four fatalities. Soldiers who got careless."

He pointed to a map on his screen. "What happened out there?"

He was pointing at the scrammy's point of origin. Rendon had been more forthcoming there, saying how it was a rebel Kern base, how they had intended to infiltrate Marin and blackmail the executive with threats of biological weapons, and how Lori had defanged them at considerable risk and without orders.

"A hidden Kern base. Some say it was hit by Kern dissidents. Others say it was Marin. Cavana says both and that not much survived," she said.

He nodded. "What's this about a near-civil war in Marin?"

"Forces loyal to Lester agitated a bit, but fighting in the streets was contained by the AHtX scare. With General Herrera's sudden death two weeks ago, it's all under control. Kuipers is in charge of the army, and she appointed Rendon as head of Special Forces."

"Seems you're on top of everything. Maybe I should sleep more often."

"You slept enough," she said, more for her own benefit than his. She knew he could go on like this endlessly, filling up the time and space with meaningless chatter that relaxed those around him.

"Executive and Vice Chancellor Chipps." He extended the *ps*, as though he was announcing her arrival at an event. "Has a ring to it, though I'm not sure where that leaves Governor Chipps. That's a lot of titles for one person."

"They're not real."

"Oh, they are. I like governor best. It's constructive. Executive sounds like it needs a noun after it, and that's never good." He gave her half a smile. "And you're not vice anything, but I suppose that one is a better stepping-stone."

First Eric, then Rendon, and now Mika. Everyone always thought of her next step. She'd have to face up to it at some point, but not today.

"I need to run, but I have three things to say to you."

Mika tried to put a pillow behind him. His left arm hung at an odd angle, not bending far enough. Amy leaned over and held the pillow. Mika sat up fully, and Amy let go of the pillow. That she even worried about his arm told her how far Mika had come. She sat down.

"One. His name is Rowan."

Mika's eyelids fluttered.

"The guy who took the letter to Garcia, the guy who did the work, didn't ask stupid questions, got the job done. That's his name, Rowan. He's the focal point of the story. Garcia is a bystander. Your father's lesson should have been called Rowan's Quest."

She saw confusion turn to understanding. He shook his head. "It doesn't work if you make it about him."

"Trust is a difficult thing for me," she said.

His glassy eyes made her wonder how together he was and whether she had rushed this conversation. She suspected it was possible the healing was still partial. Maybe it wasn't just his arm's range of motion that was limited. Her doubt evaporated when he spoke.

"We're not talking about Rowan, are we?"

All she knew was how she'd felt when he'd woken. Current worries and past scores had become irrelevant. "We're not talking about anything," she said.

The fire returned to his eyes. "Tell you one thing. Rowan is tough and reliable, but he's not a mind reader. You want something from him, you gotta spell it out. Can't give him a letter and expect him to guess who to take it to. You can't tell him you don't need him only to complain later that he's not there when you need him."

She didn't have the will or the inclination to fight him. Besides, on a fundamental level, she agreed with him. "We're not talking about Rowan, are we?"

"We're not talking about anything." He grinned back.

There was no reason to push to win an argument that didn't need a winner. She gave him one slow nod and pushed her hair behind her ear. "Two. Once you get your strength back, we're going to spar, and I'm going to kick the shit out of you."

"What for?"

She pulled the bottle of vintage port from her backpack and put it on his nightstand. "A present from Lori. To the two of us."

He studied the bottle for a second. "I see."

"Do you?"

He remained silent.

"We got to talk, and she told me about you two, your past, your bond."

His gaping jaw broadcast more disbelief than surprise.

"I'll make sure to add a few extra punches for right this moment when you're still wondering what I know and whether you should be hiding something still. She told me quite a bit, including what she did the night Tom got shot."

His lips contorted in a half smile, half wince.

"Oh, you think funny faces will get you out of this one? I don't think so. No, I get it. Your bond with her doesn't need my approval, but you could have told me something rather than let me guess." She hadn't needed the gory details that Lori had bashed the soldier's head into pulp. An accounting of the casualties would have sufficed.

"I wasn't—"

She put her hand up. "Don't I-wasn't-ready me, and we'll wait till you're stronger. I have a lot of pent-up energy."

He turned pensive. "At least you got to know her a little."

That was true. She had gotten a glimpse into Lori's mind, but she wasn't convinced that was a good thing. Watching Mika breathe and smile was enough for Amy to banish any ill will she may have harbored toward Lori, but she didn't understand Lori on any level. Her actions oscillated between brilliant and insane at a dizzying frequency. There was no one you could discuss her with, no one who wasn't in awe or terrified of her.

Except Mika.

"That woman is crazy, absolutely, batshit crazy. She does not think or act like a normal person."

"Yeah," he said. "She was pretty far gone the last time I saw her, burning with rage, but she came through. She saved both of you."

Amy's thoughts went to Chastain, but that didn't track. "Both of us?"

"To come for you, she had to let go of her obsession with Kern. I wasn't sure she was capable of it, whether she had anything but hate left. I'm glad to see she did."

"It wasn't hate I saw. It was detachment, like everyone else was a pawn she could move. She has no restraints, no brakes that stop normal people from doing insane things, no little voice to whisper right from wrong."

"She's always thought outside the box."

Amy shook her head. "I don't think she knows there is a box. She didn't just move heaven and earth. She moved hell too."

Mika winced.

"Don't get me wrong. I'm grateful, and I'm not judging her. I'm saying she scares me."

"She's not that scary over a glass of wine."

That made her laugh out loud and snort. "Not true. She terrorized me over wine."

Mika's tone softened. "I'm still glad you got to talk to her. You'll like her more once you get to know her."

I need to see her again? The thought gave her a jolt, but she let it go. She didn't see how, but she accepted that this was one of those trust things. She had to take his word that the possibility existed, no matter how remote, that she might like Lori if she got to know her.

"You think she made it?"

He nodded.

"What makes you so sure?"

"She has a garden to plant, geraniums to talk to."

Mika's every answer brought Amy three more questions, but she stood. She'd stayed far longer than she'd intended, far longer than she'd been supposed to.

"You need to rest, and I need to go."

She put her fingers on his forehead, moving them down, barely touching his face. She tapped her index finger on his lips. "I'll see you later."

He did not speak till she was at the door. "Hey."

She stopped. "Yes?"

"You said three things."

Right. He'd kept track, of course. This was not the time and place for this. Then again, that's what she had thought over dinner at Mika's place. They had been attacked. That's what she had thought that night in the capitol. He had disappeared. Doubts, ifs, and buts had gotten in her way, and the world had conspired to pry them apart. In the last weeks, the world had gone through another contortion.

For once, it seemed to have moved in the right direction. She now dared look at the future with a dash of optimism. It was a small dash in a big, tasteless soup, but it was a start. If the whole world could get a new start, so could they, and seeing Mika smile, she knew what she felt: no doubts, no ifs, no buts.

Still she was not going to let events dictate her actions, her words. She would tell him what she had to tell him on her own terms in her own way, not toss a grenade of tightly packed and overused words into the room on her way out.

"Tomorrow," she said and closed the door.

Tomorrow was a simple word, but it painted a future she had almost given up on, a future that had appeared and disappeared like a mirage over the last few weeks.

Tonight it looked solid enough that the smile she wore was no longer a mask.

ACKNOWLEDGMENTS

Runners say, "It's harder to go from zero to 5k than from 5k to a marathon." I can't speak to that statement's truth. The longest I've run is a half-marathon—about 20k. But I get it. Getting off the couch and running is hard, and the first miles are painful. But it gets easier, though not easy. In the end, running is a process. Once you drop the excuses, set realistic goals, and stick to them, the miles become manageable, even fun.

Writing is like that too. Going from thinking about writing to writing is hard, and the first pages may be painful. But once you write a few chapters, it becomes a process. A first novel is a lot like the half-marathon of writing: it looks impossible from the couch, is a satisfying enough goal to reach, but it isn't the end of the process. On my path from couch to novel, I received plenty of help and encouragement, so I'd like to thank:

The mentors and fellow writers at the Fairwood Writers Workshop in Seattle, Rhiannon Held, Frog Jones, Erin Tidwell, Suzanne Brahm, Renee Stern, Russel Ervin, and Susan Matthews. Thanks for reading the opening chapters and providing invaluable feedback. And a special thanks to Adam Rakunas, whose kind words were particularly encouraging at a time where I needed them most.

Jason Ideker, who gave me a crash course on asphalt and how different types of roads would age. Bethany Kolb, Jaime Michaelson, and Mike Broyles, who walked me through the medical procedures and the differences between the recoverable and fatal injuries I'd concocted. Needless to say, any remaining errors are mine.

Colas Gauthier, who found time in his incredibly busy schedule to sketch the cover art, and Claire Flint Last, who designed the cover. Thanks to you both, I sure hope they judge this book by its cover.

My editors, Julia Houston and Lori Stephens, who not only improved this manuscript but taught me a whole new set of skills. Kate Sullivan, who was the first purchasing editor to believe in this story. Though life happened and the project found a different home, that first offer will always have a special place for me. Patricia Marshall, Kim Harper-Kennedy, Jamie Passaro, and the entire production team who professionally and patiently moved this project along. Thank you for the crash course in publishing.

My mom, Guniz Tumer, and my mom-in-law, Imre Yildiz, who showed their enthusiasm by asking when they'd hold a physical copy of this book for years and years. Thank you, and just so we're clear, now we're even on the "are we there yet," conversation. Oh yeah, hi Mom.

My friends and beta readers, Hazem Arafa, Guillaume Brat, Bridget Tyler, Liney Arnadottir, and Willem Visser, who provided critical advice and tough love along with many glasses of wine. They've been subjected to too many drafts to count and patiently picked through embarrassing plot holes and character inconsistencies. Thank you for reading and improving this book.

Irem, who was at different times my first fan, my first critic, my first agent, and my first editor. It's safe to say without her patience and encouragement this book would never have existed. But more importantly, it would never have had a reason to exist. I'm a strong believer in finding the one reader you're writing for, and I guess I'm not spilling a huge secret here, but this book is for you. So thanks for believing in me. And I'm not talking just about the book.

KAGAN TUMER is a science fiction author and professor of robotics and AI. He attended seven schools in five cities in four countries, all before reaching high school and is steadily moving west, from Virginia to Texas to California to Oregon. Along the way, Kagan worked as a food server, registrar's office clerk, print shop copier, soccer referee, math tutor, and well logging engineer. He has a PhD in computer engineering and spent nine years at NASA working on multi-robot coordination. When not writing, he ponders AI ethics, teaches robotics, consults for TV/ movie AI projects, and mentors future scientists.

Made in the USA
Middletown, DE
24 September 2020